CAGED
WOLF

CAROLINE PECKHAM   SUSANNE VALENTI

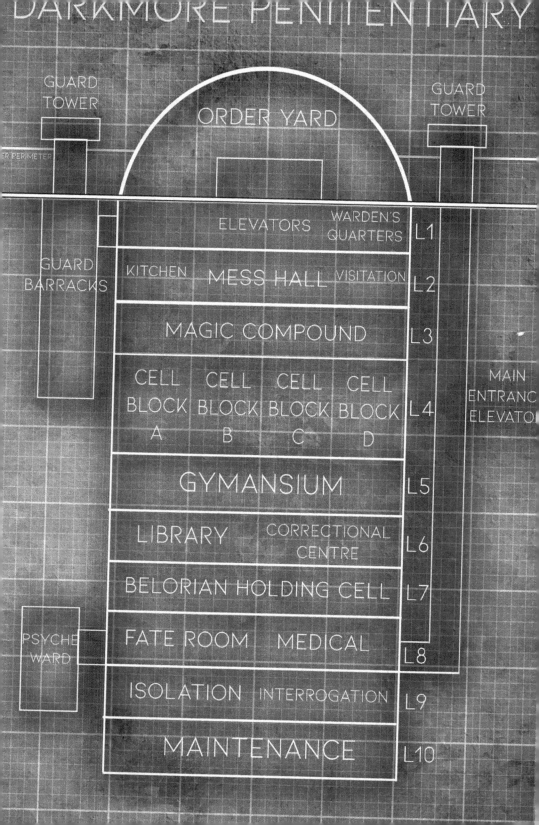

Caged Wolf
Darkmore Penitentiary #1
Copyright © 2022 Caroline Peckham & Susanne Valenti

Interior Formatting & Design by Wild Elegance Formatting

Caged Wolf/Caroline Peckham & Susanne Valenti – 1st ed.
ISBN-13 - 978-1-914425-67-7

WELCOME TO
DARKMORE PENITENTIARY

Your rights have been revoked, your punishment has been decided, your sentence is about to begin. Fight for your place like Fae, or die and be forgotten. This is your one chance for redemption. May the stars be with you.

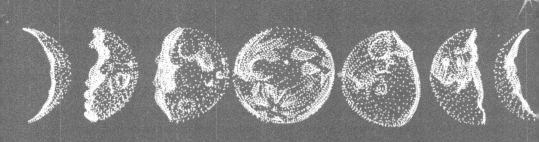

ROSALIE

PRISONER #12

CHAPTER ONE

Keep *out of trouble, Rosalie. Leading a pack is a big responsibility, Rosalie. You don't* always *have to challenge the Alphas, Rosalie.*

My Aunt Bianca's words echoed through my head a thousand times, mocking, taunting, chastising me. Because right now, in this moment, I just wished I'd goddamn listened to her.

But this job had been too fucking perfect to turn down. And they'd needed the best. Which everyone knew meant me.

Besides, I'd been waiting for an opportunity like this for a hell of a long time. There was a debt I needed to pay. A wrong I had to right. And it was long past time that I made good on my promises.

I gritted my teeth and just kept crawling, using my earth magic to force the dirt and rubble aside as I went and channelling it behind us. And yes, that meant that I was filling in the tunnel as I created it. And yes, that meant I was effectively burying us alive. And yes, that was about eighty percent terrifying. But merda santa, *holy shit,* if I pulled this off I was going to be a motherfucking legend.

Last night I ran beneath the light of the moon in my Werewolf Order form for so damn long that I thought my legs would drop off. But it had done what I'd needed it to. My magical reserves had been fully replenished by it and now in my Fae form I could wield the full extent of my sizeable power to get this job done.

And what a job it was. The vault at the Solarian Bank was said to hold over twenty million auras. If I could do this, my name would go down in history. My entire Clan would howl *Rosalie Oscura* to the moon and dance naked beneath the stars in celebration.

If I pulled it off.

The bank itself was well protected from subterranean Earth Elemental attacks, but that wasn't how we were going to get in. We were only crawling through the dirt to get close. And we only had to do that because the bank was deep into the Lunar Brotherhood's Territory. And no matter what anyone said about the state of things since everything that had happened with the rival gang's leader, Ryder Draconis, Oscuras were absolutely *not* welcome here.

My cousin Dante cursed as he crawled behind me and a smirk twitched at my lips. "Can you make the tunnel wider, Rosa?" he growled. "I'm twice the damn size of you!"

I twisted my head awkwardly so that I could look back at him, his dark features illuminated by the orange Faelight he'd conjured into existence so that we weren't lost in the dark. As an air Elemental his job was to make sure we didn't suffocate down here, which I was glad to say he was doing damn well. But as a Dragon Shifter, he was also one big motherfucker and he had a point about the width of the tunnel which was currently crushing his broad shoulders.

"Are you sure you haven't put on weight, cugino?" I teased as I wielded more earth away from him. "You know what they say about getting too comfortable when you're married. If you don't watch out, you might find your wife's attention wandering…"

"My wife's attention is always wandering," he joked as we crawled on. "But she'll never grow tired of me."

"Maybe watch the pies anyway…"

I yelped as he shot me in the ass with a spark of his Storm Dragon electricity and decided not to taunt the only Alpha I knew who was strong enough to rival me. Not that either of us had ever challenged each other. There were more than enough Oscura Clan Werewolves for us to run two packs within the family and I was happy to call him the head of the household, so long as he never actually tried to make me bow. Which he wouldn't. Because despite what everyone liked to think about our pack having two Alphas, we made it work for the good of our family. And love could overcome our natures all the time we were never faced with a situation where we *had* to challenge each other.

I clawed through dirt and muck until my GPS watch pulsed to let me know we'd reached our destination.

"Here we go," I muttered, my Wolf stirring beneath my skin, hungry for the challenge ahead of us.

I growled as I drew the earth apart above us with my magic, breaking through soil and stone with a grunt of determination as I clawed my way up towards the surface. I kept going, sweat beading along my brow until my fist burst through the concrete above me and I was able to clamber up into the alley behind the bank.

Dante cursed in Faetalian as he forced his way up after me and I quickly threw my magic out in a silencing bubble to make sure no one heard us.

I offered Dante my hand as he breached the surface and he gripped me tightly as I yanked him up to his feet.

He might have been twice my size, but I was damn strong after a lifetime of training in every kind of martial art and hand to hand combat I could perfect. I made plenty of money by participating in the underground cage fights in the rougher parts of Alestria, but I loved the rush of pulling off a real job like this. Not that I'd ever attempted anything quite as insane as this particular job before. But there was a first time for everything. And I wasn't exactly known for being level headed anyway.

Dante's mamma called me a live wire and my pack called me a free spirit. But Dante was the only one who called it like it was. When I was thirteen years old, he'd caught me diving off of the cliff out by the flooded mine in Jerrytown. My Werewolf Order had Emerged by then so I was able to shift, but as Fae didn't have their magic Awakened until we turned eighteen, I hadn't had any real chance of surviving if the water had turned out to be shallower than I'd thought.

So when Dante caught me with his air magic while I was only half way down the cliff, he'd cursed and threatened me, promised to banish me from the pack and make me into an Omega if I ever did something so foolish alone again… And then he'd jumped from the cliff right beside me. Because my cousin might have been responsible for the safety and well-being of our entire Clan, but he was also a straight up badass and the only Fae I knew who really understood me.

When he flew me back to his mamma's house out in the vineyards that night in his Storm Dragon form, he'd told me straight he knew what my problem was. *You're wild, Rosa. And you'd better make sure no one ever tames you.*

I smirked to myself at that memory as I pulled every scrap of dirt off of the two of us using my earth magic. I sent it back down into the hole in the ground before forcing the concrete to merge back over the tunnel again for good measure.

Dante pushed his dark hair back like we were about to walk into a photo op instead of a heist and I rolled my eyes at him.

"So vain, cugino," I teased. "You're worse than a girl."

"When my wife finds out where I went tonight, I'll need to win her forgiveness," he said with a shrug. "It won't hurt to look my best while I'm grovelling at her feet."

I snorted a laugh. "Will the great leader of the Oscura Clan be in the dog house tonight then?"

"Only because I didn't invite her along," he teased and knowing what I did about his wife, I had to agree with that assessment.

"Come on then, let's hurry before she notices you're missing."

"She won't for a while yet. I gave mio amico the job of keeping her thoroughly distracted for the evening."

"Oh hell," I groaned, not wanting to know any more about it.

Dante chuckled as he moved past me straight towards the fuse box on the back wall of the bank. It was warded against Elemental magic to make sure no one managed to shut off the power to the bank, but we were willing to bet they hadn't thought to guard it against the electricity of a Storm Dragon.

I moved to stand guard as Dante ripped the fuse box open, the hairs rising along the back of my neck as if my Wolf hackles tried to stand on end even in my Fae form.

The wind whipped along the alleyway as Dante summoned a storm and my long, black hair was tossed around me in the maelstrom he created.

Thunder crashed through the sky and electricity rose in the air as his immense power crackled all around us.

People all over Solaria spoke about the Dragon born of Wolves, but feeling the strength of his magic was something you could never comprehend until you were standing by his side in the centre of one of his storms.

Rain tumbled from the sky in a torrent and Dante laughed as the storm built in his veins. With a flash so bright I was half blinded, a bolt of lightning slammed from the clouds straight into the fuse box which Dante held open.

His booming laugh rang out as the bank's lights all went out at once. More lightning crashed from the sky, striking power lines all over the surrounding streets and the whole block was plunged into darkness.

"That should have knocked out the anti-stardust wards!" I said enthusiastically as the rain plastered my clothes to my body. I yanked my drenched sweater off and dropped it in a puddle, leaving me in a black tank and leggings.

"Let's find out," Dante said, pulling a little silk bag from his pocket as I moved to stand before him.

Inside the bag, I caught a glimpse of sparkling black stardust as he drew a pinch between his fingers. He tossed the glimmering substance over our heads and the world around us melted away as we were surrounded by twinkling light and transported through the stars to the destination Dante had given them.

My feet hit solid ground a moment later and an excited laugh spilled from my lips as we landed right inside the bank's vault.

Golden bars reached up behind us from floor to ceiling and the walls before us were lined with little doors for the safety deposit boxes which held all manner of dark, dangerous and wildly valuable magical treasures. This bank was well known for housing the secrets of Solaria's most wicked and ruthless Fae, and I could only guess at the wonderful contents of those boxes.

Each of them was magically locked with enough power binding them to make it impossible for us to crack them all open. But we didn't need to open all of them. We were here for the contents of one box in particular.

"Three eighteen?" Dante confirmed as he strode forward, hunting the numbers on the boxes for the one we needed. He was more than powerful enough to crack one of the magical locks and there was a nice big haul of aura notes just stacked up at the back of the vault to make up the rest of the haul.

I prowled towards the bars at the front of the vault, sharpening my hearing by calling on my inner Wolf and using my Order gifts as I listened for the guards.

Magic rippled over me as Dante threw a shield of hardened air magic up between us and the bars. If anyone came down here, they'd have to unlock the door to get to us. The adrenaline pumping through my veins ached for a fight and I was hoping I'd get one.

As a Taurus, I'd been gifted the power of Earth Magic which I also liked to think of as the *best* Elemental power. All Fae could command Cardinal Magic to use spells for things like healing, creating Faelights or any number of other useful things. But Elemental magic was different. It was linked to the stars we were born beneath. This effectively meant that your star sign determined which Element you were blessed with the power to wield, though a few lucky bastardos ended up with additional Elements too. Not that I was jealous. Earth magic was a beast to wield and I was more than happy with what I'd been gifted.

"Found it!" Dante called, barking a laugh.

I glanced over my shoulder and spotted him with his hand pressed flat to the safety deposit box we'd come here for. His brow furrowed in concentration as he worked on cracking the lock and I started pacing to expel a bit of nervous energy from my limbs.

"Shit," he cursed a split second before an alarm sounded.

"Did you trip that?" I accused with a frown.

"I told you we should have asked Leon to come," he growled.

"I don't need help from a Night to do my job," I muttered. At least not that particular Night. Their family might have been made up of the greatest thieves in the whole of Solaria, but I'd planned this job out myself and I didn't need their help. Though for the next part of this plan to go right, I *would* be needing his brother...

Footsteps thundered toward us and I strained my neck to try and see further along the empty hallway beyond the bars.

My muscles flexed with the desire to shift, but I ignored the pull of my Wolf. I wanted to give my magic a workout and use my fists. I didn't need to shift into my Order form to take out a few guards.

Dante kept working the lock and static crackled through the vault as his excitement built in the air around us.

I kept my eyes on the bars and summoned whips of long, thorny vines to grow from my palms as I waited for the guards to find us.

The sound of a door hitting a wall came half a second before eight guards rushed into the space beyond the vault.

They didn't waste a moment as they threw a combination of magic at us. Shards of ice, balls of flames, wooden arrows and blasts of air all slammed against Dante's shield as they tried to penetrate it through pure force.

Dante's booming laugh echoed around the vault as each of their strikes crashed uselessly against the strength of his magic and a savage smile pulled at my lips. Dante Oscura was the Dragon born of Wolves, the King of the Oscura Clan and one of the strongest assholes I knew. If they wanted to get through his magic they'd have to try a lot harder than that.

I stayed completely still, poised and ready to strike right before the gate as the guards continued to batter Dante's magic.

"What's the matter boys?" I taunted. "Are you afraid to fight us like Fae?"

A few of them balked at my accusation. True Fae fought one on one. In our society, power meant everything. Those with the most magic rose to the top and if you wanted to claim a higher position then you had to challenge another Fae for it. We didn't attack each other in groups. It only showed weakness. But these guards were clearly battling with the pull of their nature and the rules of their job description. No doubt they were willing to sell out their Faehood for their paycheque.

One mean looking bastard squared up to me through the bars with fury blazing in his eyes. "Open the gates," he snarled.

"But Lee, protocol-"

"Fuck protocol," Lee hissed. "I'm gonna make this bitch bleed."

My smile widened and the vines in my hands writhed like snakes as my magic trailed through them.

Dante was still working on the safety deposit box behind me and there

12

was no way in hell that I was gonna let this job fall to shit. We needed the contents of that box. Everything hinged on him getting it. So it was on me to hold these stronzos back while he worked.

The other guards hesitated and Lee shot a fireball at them. One of them damn near pissed his pants and my smile widened as I watched him sprint for the vault's locking mechanism.

My heart beat to a solid rhythm in my chest and I rolled my shoulders back as the thrill of the fight called to me. This was what I lived for. What got my blood pumping and my soul blazing.

My gaze trailed along the line of guards as they positioned themselves before the gate. I'd taken note of which magical Element each of them possessed as they'd battered Dante's shield. I was ready.

I drew in a deep breath as the gate slid open, enjoying that one pure moment which always came right before violence broke out. That second where I assessed my enemy and they assessed me before one of us chose to strike first.

This time it was me.

I whipped the vines in my arms as hard as I could and released my hold on them as I sent the full force of my magic into their movements. They shot towards the guards, growing, lengthening, sprouting new shoots with thorns as sharp as knives before they collided with them.

Three of them were taken down by the first vine and two by the second. They screamed as the vines kept growing, tightening, cutting, immobilising them despite all of their efforts to break free with their own magic. Dante may have been one of the most powerful Fae I knew, but I was his equal in that. Within minutes the vines would choke out the guards and render them unconscious, saving me the bother of having to restrain them.

That was the problem with low paid jobs like security; you just couldn't find powerful Fae who would take the positions. Which meant when a tough bitch with more than her fair share of magical brawn like me came along, the poor suckers didn't stand a chance.

Dante's laughter punctuated my footsteps as I ran straight at the three guards who were still on their feet. He tightened his air shield, pulling it back off of me to keep them away from him while letting me have free rein to play.

Lee snarled as he lunged at me, throwing a fist coated in fire at my face.

I dodged it and swung my leg around, aiming for the backs of his knees but before I could land the blow, the asshole shot away from me faster than was Faely possible. Or at least faster than was possible for any Order of Fae aside from a motherfucking Vampire.

I cursed as my missed shot left me vulnerable to the two other guards who both lunged at me from either side.

My palms hit the ground and I sent a quake through the stone floor, making it tremble and shatter at their feet.

One of them fell, but the other threw a dagger of ice straight at my heart.

I spun aside, cursing as the damn thing slammed into my bicep and agony ripped through me.

In the next heartbeat, I tore it out and threw it at Lee as he shot back to join the fray. I missed thanks to his damn Vampire speed, but he had to leap aside to avoid it, buying me half a second so that I could press healing magic into my arm and fix the damage that blade had caused.

I sprang to my feet, shaking the earth around me again as the guards ran at me once more. Vines shot from the floor at my command, grasping, reaching, hunting as the guards ducked and leapt aside.

I caught one of them and my vines instantly grew and grew, cutting into him and pinning him down with the others in the thorny cage I'd created.

He fought to free himself but I commanded the vines to find and bind his hands, effectively cutting off his magic and halting his fight. The others were already unconscious and he'd soon join them.

Six down, two to go.

I backed up as Lee shot across the room and I was forced to dive to the ground, rolling across my own vines, the thorns cut into my skin as mercilessly as they did my enemies'.

I hissed a curse and sent the ground trembling around me again, but the hollow tug in my chest was warning me that my magic reserves were finally starting to run low. Digging that tunnel had taken its toll and I needed to end this before I ran out of mojo.

The guard with the water magic threw a huge blast of it at me but instead of trying to avoid it, I ran forward, ducking my head and snarling my determination as I fought against the will of the current he was creating. His magic was weak and he'd thrown too much of it into the attack.

The moment it faltered, I leapt at him, my shoulder connecting with his chest as I knocked him clean off of his feet where he landed on top of his friends who were caught in my vines. My magic instantly snared him too, growing and growing so that he was immobilised and I was left with just one stronzo Vampire to deal with.

I turned back towards the vault and glanced at Dante just as he wrenched the safety deposit box open.

Triumph sizzled through my veins and I grinned tauntingly at the final guard.

Lee cast fire around his feet which burned my vines to a crisp and gave him a chance to shoot towards me again.

This time I couldn't jump aside fast enough and the solid weight of him collided with me.

I let out an oomph as my back slammed into the bars and his fangs snapped out as he lunged for my throat.

My heart leapt in panic as I threw a plate of stone from my palm, just managing to get it between us before his fangs could find my flesh. If he managed to bite me, I was done. Vampire venom immobilised the magic of the Fae they were feeding on and stole the strength from your limbs at the same time. The second that bastardo managed to bite me, I was doomed.

Lee tried to break through the stone shield I'd erected and I threw a solid punch straight into his gut.

He wheezed as the air was driven from his lungs and my knuckles sang with joy at finally being entered into the fight.

I hit him again and again, catching him in the jaw as he was forced to stumble back. My stone shield fell to the ground as I abandoned it and I pressed my advantage.

I clocked him straight in the nose and he bellowed with rage as blood flew.

"Give up, stronzo," I taunted, swinging at him again as he staggered back.

My next strike caught him in the centre of his chest and he fell back to the ground with a curse.

"Psycho *bitch*," Lee wheezed as my vines snared him and I laughed like a madman as the thrill of the win washed over me.

"You don't know the half of it," I taunted.

I tipped my head to the roof and howled, cupping my hands around my mouth and arching my back so that my hair swung down behind me.

Dante echoed me and our combined voices bounced off of the walls of the confined space so that it sounded like a whole Wolf pack was in here with us.

I turned my back on the guards and strode to join my cousin with a swagger in my step.

"Fuck yes! Did you get it?" I asked, my blood humming with energy as the thrill of the fight faded from my limbs.

Dante patted his pocket with a smug grin. "We could just leave now, you know?" he suggested, a soft plea in his eyes. "Forget about the rest of it?"

I barked a laugh, throwing my arms around his neck and squeezing him so tight it should have hurt. He crushed me against him in return, knowing there was no chance in hell I was changing my mind.

"You'd better come visit me, stronzo," I said seriously as I released him.

"When I get the time," he teased as the two of us headed for the stack of auras at the back of the room.

The Oscuras didn't really need any more money. Our Clan was so rich that we didn't know what to do with all of it, but it would have been a damn shame to leave all that lovely cash just sitting there.

Sirens started up out on the street and I stilled at the finality of that sound. It was all well and good planning this, but actually going through with it was something else. I was born to run free, to lead my pack, to make bad choices and make them again. I wasn't meant to be locked up. Maybe this was a terrible fucking idea. But I'd given my word now and I wasn't going to go back on that. Besides, I had a debt to pay.

"Tell Aunt Bianca I'm sorry," I said, smiling sadly as Dante hopped up on to the huge pile of aura notes and sat on it like it was a goddamn throne.

"She's gonna whip your hide until it's bloody when you break out of there," he warned, pulling the pouch of stardust from his pocket and holding a generous pinch of it ready.

"A morte e ritorno," I said fiercely, quoting our family motto. *To death and back.*

"A morte e ritorno, Rosa," Dante said fondly, hesitating one final moment before throwing the glimmering black stardust over his head and leaving me behind.

He disappeared alongside the whole stack of aura notes and I couldn't help but laugh as I turned back to await my destiny.

Instead of finding it, I found a pissed as hell Vampire with a fist full of flames charging straight at me.

"Oh fuck!" I leapt away, but with his goddamn Vampire gifts he was too fast for me.

His arms wrapped around my chest and his weight knocked me from my feet.

I cursed him as I swung my fists into his side, his back, his head, punching him as many times as I could before-

The sharp bite of his fangs cut into my shoulder and I cried out as my magic was locked away deep inside me and the strength slid from my muscles.

He groaned in pleasure as he started draining me of my blood and magic, stealing what little power I had left.

My heels scrambled against the floor uselessly as his weight pinned me down and I hissed curses at him beneath my breath.

Lee groaned again as he stole the last dregs of my magic and a horribly empty feeling echoed through my chest.

He didn't remove his fangs from my shoulder, but his hands slid between us and ice froze my veins solid as he unbuckled his belt.

"What the fuck are you doing?" I growled, trying to shove him off despite

the leaden feeling in my muscles which sapped all of my strength.

A dark laugh escaped him and panic gripped me for a moment before he snatched my wrists into his hands and yanked the belt tight around them.

He grasped a handful of my hair into his meaty fist and finally pulled his fangs from my flesh. But before I could strike at him, he shot across the room with his Vampire speed, dragging me with him by my hair and using the belt to tie me to the bars of the vault door.

He stood back with a triumphant grin as he looked down at me and the sound of sirens drew ever closer overhead.

"I'll be praised as a hero for catching you," he snarled wickedly.

A bark of laughter left my lips as I looked up at him. "Joke's on you, stronzo," I said with a grin so wide it made my cheeks ache. "I always wanted to get caught. Besides, what kind of hero will you be when they realise my accomplice got away with every penny in the vault?"

I kept laughing and Lee snarled as his palms lit with fire. "Well it's a shame the Fae Investigation Bureau got here too late," he hissed, his eyes lighting with a sadistic gleam.

"Too late for what?" I taunted.

"Too late to arrest you before you tried to kill me and I was forced to defend myself."

My eyes widened as a fireball shot straight for me. I lunged aside but with my hands tied, I couldn't avoid the flames entirely.

Pain exploded across my side and I cried out as the fire burned through my clothes and charred my flesh. It was agony unlike anything I'd ever known and it set the beast inside of me howling with the need for blood.

"Coward!" I yelled as he readied another fireball. "Fight me like Fae if you think you can!"

"Why should I?" Lee growled. "When I've already won? I'll be praised for taking down one of the thieves who dared to steal from the Solarian Bank!"

Fire flew at me again and I screamed as it blazed across my skin. The Wolf in me was howling, baying, begging to be set free and I did the only thing I could as I gave in to the call of the moon.

The shift came on me hard and fast, my clothes shredding off of me as my huge Werewolf form burst from my flesh and my skin was coated in pure silver fur.

My lips pulled back and I snarled my rage as I leapt towards the creature who hungered for my death.

Lee threw more flames at me and the scent of burning hair filled my nostrils as I charged right into it. I ignored the pain as I raced forward, jaws wide and a growl tearing from my throat.

Lee screamed in fright as my paws collided with his chest, the weight of my huge Wolf form slamming him to the ground as I bared my teeth in warning.

He threw his hands up, fire blazing from his palms and pain seared across my body in an agony so pure I couldn't think or feel or do anything at all other than follow the nature of my Wolf.

My jaws pulled wide, a snarl left my lips and I lunged forward with one powerful snap of my teeth.

The iron tang of blood coated my tongue and the scent of burning hair overwhelmed me as he pressed his hands to my chest in an attempt to fight me off.

I shook him like a rag doll, tossing him away from me before stumbling back, whimpering in pain as I rolled on the floor, trying to put out the flames.

Something metallic clattered into the vault and I twisted around as a canister rolled towards me, the top flicking open as purple gas spilled from it to fill the room.

The second I inhaled the noxious gas, my bones twisted within me and I gasped in panic as the power of my Wolf was stolen from me.

I was forced back into my Fae form without ceremony, a sob spilling from my lips as the agony of my burns flooded me. Without a drop of magic left in my reserves, I had no way to heal them and it felt like I was burning alive with the pain.

"On your feet with your hands on your head!" a strong voice barked and I blinked through the smoke to see countless FIB agents flooding into the vault, each wearing a gas mask to protect them from the Order suppressing fumes.

They held magic stunning guns and the one in front brandished a pair of power restricting cuffs which glowed blue through the smoke in the room.

"On your feet now or we shoot!" the officer demanded.

Somewhere deep inside me, I found a nugget of strength and clung to it with all I had as I pushed myself to my feet with my hands raised.

I was butt naked, bloody, bruised, looking like hell warmed up and fresh out of magic.

Not the way I'd envisioned this going...

"Step towards us, slowly," the officer said and I did as I was told.

Just before I made it to her, my bare foot slipped in a puddle of something warm and wet and I automatically looked down to see what it was.

Blood pooled across the floor, soaking my feet and making my heart skip a beat. My eyes slowly trailed across the ground, following the flow of blood back to its source and my pulse found an unsteady rhythm as my gaze fell on Lee's lifeless eyes.

18

My lips parted and horror washed through me. I hadn't meant to kill him. I'd only been trying to protect myself. I never wanted-

Manacles snapped closed around my wrists with a resounding clang and my eyes whipped up to meet the gaze of the agent who'd chained me. There was no mercy in the woman's eyes as she scowled at me darkly through the gas mask she still wore.

"Take her straight to Darkmore," she snarled. "They'll see that she faces the wrath of the law."

CAIN

COMMANDING OFFICER

CHAPTER TWO

"CMF in holding," Jack Hastings' voice sounded over the radio followed by a boyish chuckle.

CMF = Crazy Mother Fucker. He had a string of code names he thought were fucking hilarious. He also thought we were friends, so that went to show how switched on his single brain cell was. I could count how many friends I had on a closed fist.

The new kids always seemed to think I was open to casual conversation and after work drinks. Apparently the murderous look in my eyes and the two hundred and fifty pounds of pure muscle that towered over them didn't give them enough of a hint. You'd think the fact that I only smiled when I bled someone dry of magic and only laughed when the punchline was a dead body would have given them fair warning to back off. But no. Still, they tried to befriend me.

Fact: every Fae in the world would cut my throat and take my position given the chance. It was what Fae did. I was about the only one who worked here who didn't pretend like that wasn't what everyone was thinking. It was what *I* was thinking. I wanted as much power as I could get in my veins. That was why I'd wanted this job. As a prison officer at the only maximum security penitentiary in the whole of Solaria, I had access to some of the most powerful Fae in the world within the cells. And as a Vampire, I was more than happy to bend the rules and sink my teeth into them whenever I got the chance to fill my magic reserves. Plus they tasted fucking divine. They were like different brands of candy and I couldn't say I'd found a favourite yet. I was sure looking hard though. Technically, I was only allowed to bite an inmate to subdue them in an attack. But when it was my word against some lowlife criminal's, who was the Warden gonna believe anyway?

I knew where the cameras were in this place, every last one of them. I also knew when the guards who watched the security feeds changed shifts and that old Jeff always slept through from midnight to three. I organised my work hours around him, but the new boy seemed to be organising his pissing shifts around *me*.

Hastings was like a stray dog yapping at my heels. He was fresh out of Starlight Academy with his shiny-ass certificate of excellence to prove it. Unlike the little shithead, I hadn't had rich parents to pay my way through one of the prestigious magical training academies. I'd learned to fight on the streets and clawed my way up through society by brute force.

After all the shit I'd done in my life, it was a miracle I wasn't sitting behind these bars instead of looking in.

Our society might have been based on climbing the ranks through a show of power, but that didn't mean there weren't any rules. Killing outside of Council approved Fae on Fae tournaments, magical training accidents, through permitted jobs like mine and marriage pairings contests in Eastern Voldrakia, was strictly against the law. Besides murder, high level theft, bedazzlement, Order suppressing in children, and rape were amongst a few of the reasons the inmates of Darkmore had ended up here. To put it frankly, they were scum. And I was more than happy to drain them dry and make their lives as miserable as Faely possible. Nothing in my contract said I wasn't allowed to enjoy it either.

"Copy that?" Hastings asked over the radio, still laughing.

Fuckwit. "Copy," I grunted as I pressed the button, clipping the radio back onto my belt and heading out of the rec room. "I copy that you're a fucking waste of oxygen," I muttered to myself.

The newbies were always keen, but most of them didn't last more than a month. And Warden Pike just loved assigning them to me to train. I'd say she had it in for me, but she was a ruthless bitch to a hundred percent of the Fae population. Something foul and diseased must have crawled up her ass at birth and taken root in her soul if you asked me.

I headed up the stairs to the double doors that led out of the Guard Barracks into the main prison. I pressed my palm to the magical scanner to step through the first door then again to open the next one, stepping through onto the first floor corridor. The staff only elevator stood to my right and I moved toward it, scanning my palm again and moving inside.

I took the elevator down to the processing rooms on level eight, the mirrored walls reflecting me in every direction. Short dark hair, midnight eyes, teeth as straight as my uniform. I wouldn't have stood out if I wasn't over six and a half feet and built like a fucking Minotaur in its shifted form. I was the perfect weapon for this job. As a Vampire, I had super speed and super strength. There were only a few mean fuckers in this prison who really caused me any problems, but as their magic was on lockdown ninety percent of the time, I only had to worry about it the other ten. And in all fairness, I relished a good fight with a powerful opponent. It also tasted as sweet as pie to lock them up in isolation or send them down to Dr Quentin for interrogation. They didn't look so hot when they came back from a visit with him. The guy even gave *me* the creeps. Magical torture was his speciality. And I particularly relished sending the rapists to him; it wasn't hard to goad them into infractions.

The elevator door slid open smoothly and I stepped out into a long corridor with metal walls. I passed the turning that led to the Fate Room then hurried past the medical bay to the main entrance into the prison.

Another heavy steel door barred my way forward and I headed through it, spotting a guard behind a grate to my left and a set of wide elevator doors to my right. That was the single way in and out of this prison. There were only four authorised staff in the whole of Darkmore who could open those doors and, as a Commanding Officer, I was one of them. They were locked tight with magical scanners, bio scanners and a master key which was locked up tight in the guard's booth beside me when it wasn't in use. The guards could head out of here when they weren't on shift, but every exit was recorded and filed. To put it simply, once you were down in Darkmore, you didn't get out again unless the Warden said so.

"Evening." Officer Lyle scratched at his red beard, his eyes skipping to the CCTV monitor beside him. The angle it was at meant I couldn't see the inmate in their magical holding cell, but Lyle's concerned expression made me frown.

"She's a wild one, the FIB almost didn't want to risk healing her on the way in, but she was burned real bad," he commented, signing something on a form before placing a lightning taser in a tray for me to take.

"I won't need that," I tsked.

Lightning tasers were for the crazies. Ten thousand volts zapped the magic right out of them and left them completely unconscious. When they came around half a day later, they were disorientated and tended to be pretty fucking compliant, but it wasn't without risk. Those fuckers could kill and if I offloaded one, I'd be filling out paperwork for weeks to come over some dead delinquent. They were three times as powerful as the shock batons we carried around and that was saying something.

"Warden's orders," Lyle said with a shrug. "Apparently she's a biter."

I snatched the lightning taser with a sigh and moved to the security door. It slid open and I stepped into the space before the next door while the first slid closed behind me. A buzzing noise drilled into my ears then the door opened and I marched into the processing room.

The first thing I noticed was that the girl was tit-to-toe naked, standing in the centre of the room between glowing blue bars which reached from the floor to ceiling around her. The cell containing her was barely a meter wide which meant she must have been climbing the walls in here before they'd caged her. The magical cell could be set to any width and the crazies always ended up in the smallest space.

The glowing blue cuffs on her wrists kept her magic locked down, but she flexed her fingers like she hoped to fight her way past the barrier blocking her power all the same.

Her body was lithe, and lean muscle clung to every inch of her, her waist tight and her skin bronzed. A flowering rose vine tattoo curved up the left side of her body from her thigh to her neck and ebony hair fell around her like a sheet, covering her tits but her pussy was bare and I wasn't Fae enough to stop my reaction to that. My jaw tightened as my dick swelled shamelessly for the wild-looking girl in her cage. I was way above fucking inmates, but more than one had tried to seduce me for the sake of a few privileges. I never caved. Was never even tempted by a prisoner before now.

"What's your Order?" I demanded, pulling out my Atlas to fill in her intake form. The small, top of the range tablet fit in the back pocket of my pants and was just one of the perks of working here.

"Werewolf," she said, a growl leaving her throat and I didn't let her see my surprise at that. I would have guessed she was a Siren based on her allure; they were built for temptation and lust. "I'm Rosalie Oscura, Alpha of the infamous Oscura-"

"I don't care if you were the Vegas' personal bodyguard or you gave Lionel Acrux blowjobs for a living. You're nothing more than a number in here now. Twelve to be precise. And do you know why you've been assigned that number?" I strode forward, surveying her through the bars and forcing her to look up at me even more so as I drew closer.

"Because it's your favourite number?" she asked sweetly.

"I don't have a favourite anything, Twelve," I said with a sneer. "The last inmate to wear that number got shanked in the night. Forty eight puncture wounds to the lungs. Bled out in less than a minute. You can't rely on your magic in here, the physically weak and the terminally stupid end up in body bags faster than it takes to process them. So if you're going to cause me all

24

that paperwork, I suggest you be a doll and slit your throat now to save me the hassle."

Her jaw tightened but she didn't pale at my words. I liked when they squirmed, but she was holding firm.

"I hope they got me a new jumpsuit then, it sounds like the old one was ruined," she said lightly, giving me one of those apple pie grins again.

I wonder if her blood is as sweet as her smile.

"Element?" I demanded, raising my Atlas once more.

"Earth," she answered.

I filled in the box then tapped the controls on my Atlas, dissolving the cage around her and pointing to the glass shoot across the room. An orange jumpsuit slid down it, her Order and Element now magically printed on it in silver alongside her number. Plain black underwear, a white tank and black boots already waited for her beside it.

"Get dressed," I commanded.

"What's a girl got to do to get a drink around here? I'm parched." She ignored my order, walking toward me with her hips swaying and her eyelashes fluttering. She tossed her hair back to expose her pert breasts and desire rose its head in me like a deadly animal.

"Get. Dressed," I growled, taking a wider stance. "Do not test me, inmate." I coaxed flames into my hands with my fire Element but she didn't back off, still moving toward me like a seductress, all long lashes and naked perfection. I was hard as stone and furious as hell as she closed the gap between us. She was about to find out exactly what happened to people who tried to bribe me.

I waited for her to move up into my personal space, letting her grind her body on me and enjoying the feeling of those hardened nipples pressing through my black shirt.

"Just a little glass of water," she breathed, giving me the bed eyes which had probably worked on men her entire life. But she'd picked the wrong officer to try and wrap around her little finger.

I caught her by the throat, wheeling her around and threw her against the wall. She gasped as I slammed my chest to her back to hold her in place, wrenching her head sideways with a fistful of her hair. She went to retaliate and I pressed against her harder.

"Fight back and you'll earn yourself a month in isolation, is that really how you wanna start your sentence?" She fell still and a satisfied smile pulled at my mouth. "If you refuse a direct order, Twelve, you pay the price. If you try and seduce a single officer in Darkmore again, I'll have you sent to magical interrogation and perhaps Dr Quentin will stitch you right up so you can't ever spread your legs for a favour."

"I'd cut your dick off before I ever touched it!" she snapped.

A smile pulled at my mouth as I held her in place, wrapping my hand tighter in her hair. I secretly loved a rebel, especially when I got a drink out of them. But I couldn't do it here with four cameras pointed at me.

"Looks like I let the wild animal out of her cage at last. Try to bullshit me again, Twelve, I dare you," I growled in her ear.

I couldn't do much about the fact that my cock was pressed to her ass and throbbing with need. The best I could hope for was that she mistook it for my shock baton because it was kind of undermining my fucking point.

She laughed manically, throwing her head back and resting it against my shoulder to look up at me. "That's a very professional boner you're sporting, *Officer*. What will the Warden think of that?"

She looked straight up at one of the cameras in the corner, but Lyle was the only one watching and he was under my thumb. Besides, he probably didn't have the volume up, he'd be too busy listening to some romantic audiobook and taking notes on how to spice up his sex life with his boyfriend.

"Get dressed!" I roared, throwing her across the room with my Vampire strength. She stumbled into the table, before snatching her clothes and pulling them on. I watched unblinkingly, folding my arms and waiting until she had the jumpsuit in place and tugged her hair out from under the collar.

"Now what?" she asked, that fucking smile back on her face. I had a feeling that smile was going to taunt me a lot during her time here.

My breathing was heavy and I tried to drown my desire for her by sheer force of will. She probably wouldn't be a problem for long anyway. New inmates often ended up dead while trying to fight for positions of power in the prison. She wouldn't even get a cell if she didn't force someone out of their bed for it.

"You'd better learn to keep your mouth shut and your head bowed around me, inmate. You don't want to make an enemy out of me."

"No, Officer," she said in a low voice, all her girlish charm abandoned as she strolled toward me with a sinister look in her eyes. "*You* don't want to make an enemy out of *me*. I ran half of Alestria back home. I rose in the ranks faster than any of my siblings or cousins. I'm a queen where I come from, an Alpha of the most powerful Werewolf pack in Solaria."

I smirked down at her. "This is Darkmore Penitentiary, Twelve. Alestria might be the most dangerous city in the kingdom, but it's not the most dangerous *place*. You're about to be locked up with vicious murderers, Fae who take pleasure in cutting off pieces of pretty little Werewolves like you." At last, she paled and my heart swelled with victory as I wound my way under her skin. I dipped my head to get right up in her face. "And if you think I'm employed to protect you, you're wrong. I'm here to keep you inside these walls. I'm here to punish you when you break the rules. I'm here to carry your dead body out of your cell piece by piece when a monster crawls into your bed and guts you in the night."

She wet her lips, blinking hard as she lifted her chin. "Not if I gut them first though, right Officer Cain?" she read the name on my badge then turned away, rolling her neck and stretching her limbs like she was preparing for a fight.

I didn't respond but my lips were tempted into a smile. I lifted my Atlas, wondering what this girl could have done to land herself in here as I flipped back through the form the FIB had filled in. She already had a sizeable criminal record, but it looked like she'd gotten away with most of it by paying fines. *Bribes more like.* If she really was from the Oscura Clan, she and her Wolf gang would have had law enforcement paid off on a regular basis.

Tonight, she'd gone too far. She'd robbed a Solarian Bank of twenty million auras and murdered an innocent security guard in the process.

Fucking killer.

Twelve crept closer in my periphery and I caught her glancing at the screen. "Stand back, inmate," I snarled.

"I just-" she started.

"Stand back!" I commanded.

She laughed, snatching the Atlas from my hands and I saw red. There was only one way to teach a rogue Fae like her the rules. And I was done playing nice.

I snatched her arms into my grip, letting my fire magic sear out of me and scorch her skin. She yelped in pain, dropping my Atlas and I bared my fangs at her.

"You obey or you pay," I growled in her face.

"Stop!" she cried, trying to yank her wrists free as I continued to burn her, the first sign of fear flickering in her eyes. I swung her around, losing all sense of myself as determination invaded me and speared through every nerve ending in my body. I needed utter compliance, and she was going to learn how to submit the hard way.

The door flew open and Lyle raced in, throwing out a hand and knocking me off of her with a gust of air magic. I squared my shoulders at her as she stared at me in shock, rubbing the blisters on her arms.

"If you disobey me one more time within these walls, Twelve, you'll find out how much pain I can really deliver." I shot from the room with my Vampire speed, leaving Lyle to bring her down into the main prison.

If an inmate made an enemy of me, I became the devil in this underworld.

I had a blaze of hellfire living in my veins which could make a Fae's time in here insufferable. And it looked like Twelve had chosen her fate already.

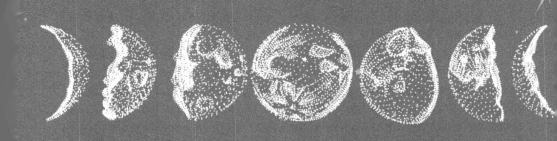

ROSALIE

PRISONER #12

CHAPTER THREE

I stood in the wake of psycho Officer Cain, my skin flaring in agony along my wrists where two huge hand prints had been burned into my flesh. I'd done my research before coming here. He'd seemed like a straight up power hungry asshole. A little into rough sex with women he met online and didn't have to hook up with twice. And a little into the underground hunting scene where he paid other Fae to let him hunt them using his Vampire skills so that he could delve into the darker urges of his Order. But nothing I'd found out about him had suggested he was a full on sadist. Sure, there were plenty of rumours about the guards in this place being rougher than necessary with the inmates, but I hadn't expected him to flip on me like that. Maybe he'd just been pissed about the fact that it had been obvious how much he wanted to fuck me and I'd pointed it out. Not that it would ever happen. I mean, sure, he was hot in that dark and unattainable kind of way with his I'm-the-big-I-am attitude, and under other circumstances I might have even been up for letting him push me about a bit. But was I going to start screwing a guy who could literally cut my food rations when I got bored of him? No.

Officer Lyle ground his teeth as he closed in on me, releasing his shock baton from his belt as he raised a radio to his lips. "Officers Nichols, Rind and Hastings to the holding cell," he said in a firm voice, eyeing me like I might just bite him.

"You having trouble with the CMF down there?" came a response which was accompanied by a dark chuckle.

Lyle didn't respond but he muttered something beneath his breath that sounded like *damn newbies.*

"So, Lyle, are you going to be healing this shit on my arms or do I need to take it up with your boss?" I asked, holding my hands out towards him to showcase my blistered wrists. They hurt like a bitch but I'd had enough experience of pain in my life to know how to lock it away. I'd been left to bleed for days from wounds worse than this before and it was really just a matter of focus. If I ignored the sensation with enough determination then I could block it out. Mostly.

The blue magic restraining cuffs which encircled my wrists slid down an inch as I presented my arms and I bit my tongue against cursing at the pain of them hitting the burns.

"If you behave for the transfer then I'll give you a medical before you go into gen-pop. And I can assure you, you really don't want to go mouthing off at the Warden on your first day. She doesn't take kindly to visits from pouting little pups," he said calmly.

"I'm no pup," I growled, my shoulders tensing at the insult.

"Every untested newbie is a pup. You wanna drop that nickname? Then I suggest you prove yourself amongst the big boys in your cell block the moment you arrive. Because if you can't assert yourself, they'll eat you alive in there. Literally. We have more than one inmate who's in for eating another Fae while in their Order form. And a few that just like the taste of Fae flesh even when they're not shifted."

Ew.

I smiled darkly at the challenge in his tone. I wasn't afraid to prove myself, I did that on a daily basis back home. I hadn't lost a fight since I was eighteen and I sure as shit on a Sunday wouldn't be doing it now.

The door buzzed loudly behind him and three burly guards crowded into the space. I recognised two of them instantly from my research. Rind and Nichols. Both Minotaurs, both fairly weak magically and as strong as an ox physically. Neither of them held any deep and dark secrets that my research had uncovered, though Rind had a thing for wearing women's underwear.

Guard number three was unknown. Which had to equal new. I cocked my head, locking my eyes on him as he assessed me with his chest puffed out and a show of bravado which I was pretty sure I could crack with a few rounds in the ring…or the right kind of manipulation…

"Well don't you just look like a choir boy dipped in idiota?" I purred, biting my lip as I dragged my eyes over him. He was a little taller than me with beach blonde hair and the kind of pretty face that would make nice girls swoon. I tended to prefer my men with a touch more utterly corrupted to them, but he didn't need to know that. And bedazzling was one of my crimes after all, so it would be a shame if I didn't implement my skill set during my incarceration. Technically, using my allure to charm other Fae into committing crimes on my behalf was illegal, but I liked to think that it was a kindness to let them do things for me if it made them happy. I couldn't help it if the strength of my magic and alpha nature drew weak little Fae to me like moths to a flame. And it would have been a total shame if I didn't make use of that from time to time.

His uniform had the name *Hastings* sewn onto the lapel and I made a mental note of it, wondering if I could mould him into the weak link I needed.

"I don't speak Faetalian," he replied, raising his chin as he kept a hand on his baton. So the idiota couldn't figure out what idiota meant? How sad.

"Ti farò diventare la mia cagna, ragazzo del coro," I purred, twisting my fingers through a lock of my ebony hair and widening my eyes seductively. *I'm going to make you my bitch, choir boy.*

His lips twitched and his gaze slid over me slowly before he glanced at the other guards. "Now what?" he asked.

"Now we take her to gen-pop and hope she doesn't flip out again on the way there," Lyle said, seemingly unimpressed by my act.

"I'll be good," I swore, painting a cross over my heart before stepping towards Hastings and holding my hands up in offering so that he could lead me away.

The rest of the guards closed in, the Minotaurs holding their shock batons ready. I'd done a little preparation for those fuckers before coming here in the form of letting Dante hit me with his lightning strikes until I built up a certain level of tolerance to the pain of it. Those things were meant to completely incapacitate the Fae they struck, but I was pretty confident that I could power through the agony of a hit from one if it was necessary now. Not that I intended to test that theory unless I was forced into it.

The experienced guards didn't seem to buy my innocent act. But my nice choir boy was giving me a look that said he almost felt bad for poor little Rosalie as he reached out to take my wrists.

I whimpered in pain, putting a little extra pathetic into the noise as his fingers brushed my burns.

"What the-"

"That other guard, Cain, attacked me for no reason," I breathed and there were damn near tears welling in my eyes. I could have been an award winning actress in another life. One that was a lot less fun and a lot more law abiding.

Hastings glanced at Lyle for confirmation on that and he gave him a shrug which didn't deny it. A moment later, healing magic swept along my skin and the burns were wiped away as if they'd never even existed in the first place.

I sighed, flexing my fingers so that they brushed along his arm as he continued to hold my wrists. "Thank you," I breathed, batting my eyelashes.

Hastings looked at me a little suspiciously and I wondered if I'd gone a bit too far, but he cleared his throat before joining my cuffs with a chain of magic and drawing me out of the room. He didn't say a word to reprimand me and I tried not to smirk.

We left the processing cell and I glanced back over my shoulder towards the one and only exit from this place. Meters of steel and several locked doors parted me from the elevator which had delivered me to this concrete hole beneath the ground and that was the only way anyone ever left too. Or at least it was at this moment in time; I planned on coming up with an alternative route pretty soon.

Hastings drew me away from the exit and we passed through another steel door which scanned the guards' magic and their faces for good measure.

Lyle stopped me as he lifted a handheld scanner from a table on the far side of the door and held it up to my face. A red light shone in my eyes for a long moment before a bleep sounded and the number twelve flashed up on the display as the machine recognised me.

"Whenever a guard comes to take the count, you look into the scanner just like that. Failure to obey this rule is an infraction and you will be punished for it. Understand?" Lyle asked, his blue eyes skimming over me like he knew I was trouble already.

You haven't got the faintest idea, stronzo.

"Yes," I replied in a sweet voice.

"Yes, *sir,"* he growled.

"Thanks, but you don't have to call me sir," I replied.

Hastings snorted a laugh and I flashed him a bright smile before he schooled his features.

"If you keep up the smart comments, I'll revoke your breakfast privileges for tomorrow," Lyle warned, his red brows lowering as he tried to force me into line.

"Sorry, sir," I said in a mocking tone, offering him a curtsey.

He exchanged a look with Hastings, growling beneath his breath before turning on his heel and continuing down the concrete corridor.

The Minotaurs muttered something behind me as they fell in at our backs and Hastings maintained his grip on my cuffs as we followed.

So Officer Lyle could be taunted without repercussions and Officer Hastings had a sense of humour. Good to know.

I faked a stumble and Hastings lurched forward to catch me before I could faceplant on the concrete.

My hands landed on his chest, and I bit down on my bottom lip as I looked up into his ocean blue eyes.

"Thank you, ragazzo del coro," I said in a low voice before stepping back quickly. He was definitely the knight in shining armour type and I could easily work with that. I guessed none of my escort spoke Faetalian because they hadn't called me out on christening him *choir boy* and the glint in his eyes said he quite liked my little nickname for him. I almost felt bad for him, but I needed every advantage I could get in here and if it came to it, I was going to eat him alive.

Lyle turned to glare at us and Hastings tugged me into a trot as we hurried to catch up with him again.

"This is Level Eight," Lyle informed me as we reached him. "Medical and Fate Room. So you'll only come down here if you're having really bad luck or really good luck."

He laughed at his own joke and I gave him crickets in response. But I did cast my gaze towards the Fate Room doors further along the corridor. I'd done my research well before coming in here and I knew about the various units which made up the prison. The Fate Room was the only place down here where we would be offered access to things like tarot cards, crystals and our horoscopes. Access was granted infrequently and at random so I couldn't expect to get in there very often, but whenever I did I'd be sure to make the most of any glimpse I could get at my fate.

"What's down there?" I asked, pointing to a corridor which led away beyond the Fate Room. A sign hung above it which read *Authorised Personnel Only.*

"Psych," Lyle grunted. "And you might want to thank the stars that we aren't leading you in that direction."

I raised my eyebrows at him and fell into step with Hastings again as we turned towards a huge stairwell. I had no real interest in what went on in the Psych Unit. That place was for the criminally insane, dangerously unstable and magically fractured souls who were too depraved to be housed within the main prison. And if they were too fucked up for Darkmore then I was more than sure I didn't want to make their acquaintance.

Lyle moved to the right and started heading up the stairs, but I hesitated as I looked at the flight leading down.

"What's that way?" I asked, turning my gaze on Hastings curiously.

"You don't want to go there either," he replied with a faint smile. "Interrogation and Isolation."

"Fondly known as the hole," Officer Rind muttered behind me and Officer Nichols guffawed appreciatively. I got the impression they were the tweedle dumb and tweedle dumber of this fine establishment, more brawn than brain.

My skin prickled as I craned my neck to get a look down the stairs towards the unit which housed the prisoners who were too dangerous to be allowed to remain in the cell blocks with the general population. My target was waiting for me down there and he didn't even know his guardian angel had arrived yet.

"Get moving," Lyle barked and we continued up the stairs.

We made it up to level seven and Lyle turned down the corridor, tossing an amused look my way as he beckoned me after him.

"Sir?" Hastings asked, his brow pinching in confusion. "Why are we taking her-"

"Little Miss Curious wants to know all about the things we keep in this place," Lyle interrupted. "So I figured she'd like to see what we keep on seven."

We headed along a dark corridor and I shivered as the temperature dropped around us.

Lyle strode ahead purposefully and we followed him towards an enormous black steel door which blocked our progress on. "You seem to be keen to prove how tough you are, Twelve," he said, his lips hooking up into a smirk. "So why don't you come and meet your new cellmate?"

Lyle beckoned me over and Hastings released his hold on me so that I could approach him.

I raised my chin as I walked closer and Lyle pointed me towards the steel door.

A prickle of warning raced down my spine as I drew closer to it, my Wolf instincts warning me to be wary.

A strange scent filled the air, growing stronger as I closed in on the door. It was like something had been left to rot behind the black steel with an underlying tinge of smoke.

"What is that?" I asked, but at the sound of my voice, a deep growl rattled from beyond the door.

I sucked in a sharp breath as something huge crashed against the metal.

"I bet you didn't read about the Belorian in the brochure," Lyle joked and the Minotaurs laughed darkly behind me. "Go on, say hi." His hand landed between my shoulder blades and he gave me a shove towards the doors.

If I'd been able to shift I'd have done it in a heartbeat. As it was, I bared my teeth anyway.

"I thought you might lose a bit of that attitude when you were faced with our resident beauty," Lyle mocked and I growled at the insinuation that I was full of shit.

I was Rosalie Oscura and darkness knew to fear me.

36

I pressed my shoulders back as I strode towards the door, ignoring my instincts which screamed at me to run and moving to within an inch of the thick steel.

"Are you satisfied now?" I asked, turning to look back at the guards.

An enormous crash sounded as something slammed into the steel door and the whole thing rattled as a terrifying roar echoed through the silence.

I leapt away from the door with a shriek of fright as whatever the fuck was inside that room fought tooth and nail to get out.

"She's hungry," Lyle said with a bark of laughter. "The Belorian is an entirely Fae made bio-weapon. The only one of its kind. Think T-Rex on steroids with a more bloodthirsty nature and a dollop of magic mixed in."

"Why the fuck would you have something like that down here?" I gasped as my heart thundered against my ribs and the desire to run the fuck away damn near consumed me.

"Don't worry, inmate. We only let her out at night. Just a little extra incentive for you to make sure you head back to your cell block before the count. Because once you're all locked up tight in your beds, the Belorian here gets let out for walkies. And she's *always* hungry."

I swallowed thickly, backing up another step as the Belorian continued to try and batter its way out of its cage.

Jerome hadn't mentioned that shit covered nugget of crap when he'd offered me this job. Breaking out of the highest security prison in Solaria with a high profile psychotic inmate? Yeah. Getting past a bio monster bred to hunt and eat runaway convicts? Nope. He hadn't uttered a word of that. I was damn tempted to ask for a bigger pay cheque.

"Pretty scary, huh?" Hastings teased as he caught hold of the magical chain linking my cuffs again and drew me back towards the stairs.

I went willingly enough. The further I was from that beast the better. And I hoped the cell block doors were ten times as thick as the one currently containing it or I doubted I'd be sleeping one wink during my incarceration here.

"She's got your scent now, Twelve," Lyle goaded. "So she'll know who she's sniffing if you ever miss curfew…"

I lifted my chin and gave him a cocky smile. "Well I guess it's a refreshing change from the stink of asshole on the air."

Hastings snorted a laugh again and Lyle still refused to be baited. I was beginning to like him and his bushy red beard.

We headed up the huge stairwell again but Lyle didn't make any more detours, instead he just pointed at the entrances to the two floors we passed and explained what they held in layman's terms.

"Level six, the Correctional Centre and Library. Level five, the Gymnasium – you can work out in there during your free time in the evenings assuming you don't have your privileges revoked for infractions. Entrance is granted via facial scanner and if you're not allowed in because you've been a prick then the doors won't open."

"Good to know," I muttered. I'd be in serious need of some stress relief in the gym and I just hoped they had a sparring ring so that I could kick some ass to vent my rage.

We made it up to the fourth floor and Lyle led me off of the stairs and we passed an enormous grey door with a blood red A painted on the front of it. "The shower unit is located centrally and you get access to it in the mornings and evenings, taking turns with the other cell blocks for who gets to wash first."

We passed Cell Block B and then the showers where a damp, mildewy scent caught in the back of my throat. Lovely.

We kept going down the long, grey, emotionless corridor, passing Cell Block C and heading to the very end of the hall.

We came to a halt by a huge metal door with a red D scrawled across it which blocked the way on.

"Cell Block D," Lyle announced as if I couldn't read.

Hastings released me, removing the chain which linked my cuffs so that I could use my hands freely and the four guards stepped back to give me some space. "Each cell is designed to hold two Fae. There's two bunks, a toilet and a nice metal door which locks up tight at night time. There are currently five hundred and fourteen Fae in this cell block and one hundred cells which means two hundred beds. However, not everyone who has claimed a cell chooses to share it. So if you want a bed, you're going to have to challenge someone for it. If you fail, you sleep in the coop on the lower deck which is basically a big old cage with no mattresses and only four toilets to share. In the open. And we provide blankets but again, there aren't enough to go around so you'll need to work hard to keep yours, particularly if you can't claim a bunk. Obviously sleeping out in the open with a bunch of psychotic assholes isn't ideal and there is a fairly high rate of overnight *incidents* for those Fae who can't secure themselves a cosy cell."

"So, just to clarify. When I claim a cell, I don't *have* to let anyone share it with me?" I asked, rolling the sleeves of my jumpsuit back.

The Minotaurs guffawed like the idea of me claiming a cell was insane and I smirked to myself. *Just watch me, boys.*

"*If* you managed to claim a cell and *if* you were able to defeat anyone who tried to claim the spare bunk in said cell then no, you wouldn't be required to share. But there are only a handful of Fae in the whole Penitentiary who have managed that, so I wouldn't go getting your hopes up."

"And is there a cell that you would think of as the *best* cell in the block?" I asked sweetly as I reached up to twist my long hair into a knot, wrapping it tightly in case any little bitches got any ideas about pulling on it.

"I believe the inmates enjoy the view from the third floor. Up there, you can't hear the screams from the lower deck so loudly in the night," Lyle said, looking amused as fuck by me like I had no idea what I was getting myself into. But that was where he was wrong.

"Alright then," I said, shaking my hands out to get the blood flowing to my fingers. "Let's go."

Lyle turned from me to a panel on the wall and I watched as he pressed his hand to it, unlocking the door with a pulse of his magic.

A deep buzz sounded and an orange light illuminated above the door as it rose from the ground and slid up to reveal the cell block beyond.

I licked my lips as I took in the huge open space that spread out ahead of me. Fae in orange jumpsuits loitered around the communal space, sitting at metal picnic benches which were bolted to the ground or boxing in a far corner where a ring of spectators placed bets on who they thought would win.

Everything was built of pale grey metal which glimmered with some internal magic which no doubt imbued it with strength. Metal staircases led up to more gangways which allowed access to the three levels of cells.

All I could see of the cells from my position on the ground were rows of dark doorways, each of which had a number painted above it in blood red.

A few of the inmates looked my way curiously, rising to their feet and circling closer like sharks who smelled blood in the water. Most of them were bulked up with muscles, tattoos scrawled across their skin and had a general murderous look in their eyes. One even blew a mocking kiss at me and grabbed his crotch. I winked at him casually, though in all honesty, half bald dudes about forty years my senior weren't my type.

A metal gangway slid into place before me, extending from the floor beneath my boots to create a bridge into the cell block and making the floor tremble slightly as it moved. I didn't wait for the guards to nudge me into action before striding out onto it, my boots echoing hollowly as I crossed it. Beneath the bridge was a magical void which appeared to be made of nothing but black smoke, but I knew what that was. Evernight vapour could knock a Fae out cold for six hours if you inhaled it and all the time you were unconscious, you would feel like you were being burned alive from the inside out. The Void extended for twenty steps, and when the cell block door was closed, the bridge would retract into the wall and none of the inmates would be able to get close to it.

I looked around at my new home curiously, spotting a guy hanging from his ankles as he swung from the second floor gangway, screaming obscenities at everyone in sight.

A prickle ran up the back of my spine and I instantly picked out several other Werewolves in the crowd, my Order form recognising them instinctively from within the confines of my Fae flesh. My gaze skipped between them, the beast in me seeking out the Alpha on instinct as I resisted the urge to growl a warning. A true Alpha didn't need to assert their dominance through petty displays like growling or the baring of teeth. The pack would fall into line beneath me soon enough without them.

I noticed symbols on the uniforms of some of the other prisoners as I drew closer, marking out their Orders and magical Elements. There were Harpies, Centaurs, Sirens, Griffins and even a herd of the meanest looking Pegasuses I'd ever seen. For an Order who usually radiated happiness and excitement, the Darkmore herd sure looked like a miserable bunch of fuckers. One of them even had a tattoo on his bicep of a Pegasus spearing a Fae to death on its horn. Nice.

I didn't offer the Fae closest to me much attention. They were the bottom dwellers, lurking close to suss me out, wondering what rank I might claim in the cell hierarchy, but not really looking to challenge me. They'd wait and see how I faired against some of the bigger fish in the tank before they'd take their chances.

The four guards escorted me over the bridge, but they stopped at the edge of it.

"These are yours," Lyle said and I turned to look at him as one of the Minotaurs held out a bundle of material. "One grade B blanket, one cot sheet, one pillow. I suggest you hold on tight to them if you expect to keep them." The look in his eyes said he didn't think I could manage that simple task and I accepted the bundle with a sweet smile.

He turned from me, cupping his hands around his mouth as he shouted out to the other convicts. "Fresh meat!"

The call was taken up by the other inmates and the walls echoed with the sound of their voices as they announced my arrival. Some of the Wolves started howling, prisoners on the gangways stamped their feet so that the metal rang to a hollow beat. There were growls and grunts, shrieks and squeals as the prisoners let their inner beasts be known to me and I walked straight into the centre of the crowd like I didn't have a care in the world.

The sound of the guards leaving came from behind me, but I didn't look back to watch them go.

"Look at you, little pup," a girl with snake tattoos lining her arms purred, the sigil on her jumpsuit marking her out as a Medusa.

"Wanna bunk with me, pup?" A Manticore with way too much nose hair grunted as I passed him.

I was going to be shedding that nickname fast.

"This place will break a pretty little pup like you," another voice promised.

"You wanna join my harem, pup?"

"Why don't you hand over those blankets before you get hurt?"

"I'm gonna watch you bleed, pup."

"Darkmore will eat you alive."

I ignored them, drowning out their pointless threats and promises as they closed in around me.

A hand reached out to grasp my arm and I caught it, dropping my bundle of blankets and twisting their fingers in my grip with a vicious wrench that broke bones.

The Fae cried out but I shoved him away from me with no more interest, my gaze falling on a Siren girl with full lips and mean eyes.

"Twenty Seven," I snapped, using her number to name her. "Pick up my shit for me."

"My name's Sandra," she growled.

"I don't give a shit if your name is Darcy Vega. I say jump, you say how high. So pick up my shit, Twenty Seven."

Her lips pursed and it seemed like she might object, but as I held her eye with my chin raised and a challenge in my gaze, she suddenly looked to her feet and hurried to grab the blankets from the floor for me.

The noise in the place stuttered as the inmates watched the exchange and more than a few of the bottom dwellers backed up, giving me space to breathe.

I ignored them. No one important would be down here, checking out the new girl like a pack of fleas looking for a mutt to bite. No. The Fae who mattered in here wouldn't lower themselves to that. They'd have sent their people down to check me out while they remained uninterested. As far as they knew I was just another nobody come to make up the numbers, but they were wrong about that.

And I was gonna make them take note.

"I'll be needing a cell," I called out, loudly enough for my voice to carry while not enough to call it an actual shout. "One on the top floor, without a cellmate. Anyone wanna volunteer to vacate?"

Slow footsteps echoed across the walkway above me and I tipped my head back to look as a few of the occupants of the top floor stepped out of their cells to take a look at me.

41

Towards the end of the right hand gangway, a huge figure stepped out of the cell marked with a big, red twelve and my lips twitched as I eyed him up. The guy was massive, built like a tank with muscles on his muscles. I pegged him for a Dragon Shifter even before he stepped into the light and I spotted the sigil marked on his chest.

"You're in my cell," I called, pointing up at him. "I'm number twelve."

The Dragon laughed darkly, resting his arms on the railing as he peered down at me. His hair was flecked with grey and receding along his temple and he had a scar that ran straight across the centre of his cheek. Which was impressive because there weren't many things that could scar Fae flesh beyond the power of healing magic. Although I knew from personal experience that there were a few weapons more than capable of causing marks that wouldn't fully heal.

I bit down on my tongue as bile filled my mouth for a moment as those memories tried to press close but I forced them away with an iron will. I refused to face them when I was awake, though they tended to find me in my sleep.

"Is that so?" the Dragon asked, his jaw tightening as he assessed me.

"Yeah. So maybe you can save us the hassle of me kicking your ass and just pack up your shit?" I suggested.

The inmates who had been circling close to me were quickly backing off. I guessed they caught a whiff of crazy on me or just didn't want to get caught up in the crossfire of what was coming next, but either way I was cut some relief from the scent of stale bodies by their departure.

The Dragon laughed in the deep throated, I'm-the-king-of-the-assholes way that big fuckers like him tended to do because they thought that their size automatically made them an Alpha. But as he walked along the gangway casual as fuck, I didn't catch the scent of Alpha on him. And I always spotted one of my own.

The Dragon headed down the stairs and a few more Fae appeared on the upper levels, emerging from their cells to watch. I didn't spare my attention for them as I waited for my opponent to approach.

Years of underground cage fighting had taught me more than enough about assessing my foes and as he moved closer to me, I noticed the way he walked with a rolling gait that favoured his right leg. When he'd adopted that douchebag way of walking, I was sure he thought it looked cool as fuck but over the years that kind of thing unbalanced the muscles in your legs. Not much. But just enough for me to take advantage of.

The Dragon made it to the bottom floor and stalked towards me. I'd thought he was huge when I'd looked up at him on the top floor but I'd been wrong.

He wasn't huge; he was a fucking giant. My cousin Dante was a Dragon and he was the biggest fucker I'd ever met, but this guy must have been seven foot tall. I wasn't exactly short but at five foot seven, he towered over me, not to mention the fact that my entire body was about the width of one of his legs.

"What's the matter, pup?" he taunted. "Changed your mind about taking me on?"

"I'm just wondering how the hell they found a jumpsuit to fit you. I bet they had to sew four together just to cover that ass."

He growled at me, flexing his muscles so that the number two hundred was stretched across his broad chest and I had to wonder just how much he must have weighed. Probably best if I didn't let him throw that weight at me to find out.

"I'm going to take that pretty little face of yours and smear it all over the floor," Two Hundred promised. "And then I'm going to make you beg for-"

I swung my fist straight at his face and my knuckles rang from the impact as I struck him square in the nose. Bone crunched, blood flew and he roared like the fires of hell had just caught light up his ass.

He swung for me with fists like battering rams and I danced between his attacks, twisting closer to him before throwing three sharp punches into his side.

The other inmates were cheering, yelling, placing bets and whooping with shock and laughter at this little Faetalian girl who had decided to take on a Dragon the moment she walked through the cell block doors. But I was used to people underestimating me and I was pretty damn fond of proving them wrong too.

Two Hundred lunged at me but I was already gone, leaping behind him and swinging my foot up in a roundhouse that collided with his ass and should have knocked him from his feet.

He only stumbled, catching himself on the stair railing and throwing himself around at me again.

He was slow, slow enough to make me think he hadn't actually been in a fight for quite some time.

"Come on, big man," I taunted. "I thought you were gonna teach me a lesson?"

He swung at me so fast that I couldn't escape it and his meaty fist collided with my jaw, splitting my lip and sending me flying. I hit the floor, rolling over the concrete and tasting blood as my body sang with the pain of his strike.

Two Hundred strode forward to finish me and I laughed as he came, spitting blood from my mouth and swinging my leg around so that I caught him hard in the side of his left knee. He fell like an oak toppling in the forest and I rolled aside before he could crush me.

Bet that cool walk doesn't seem like such a great idea now.

I was on my feet in a heartbeat, leaping on him and straddling his chest as I threw my fists into his face as many times as I could before he recovered.

My knuckles rang from the impact with his thick skull and blood splattered over both of us.

Two Hundred threw a heavy punch into my ribs and I cried out as a horrifying crack sounded in response.

His hands locked around my waist and he launched me off of him like I was nothing more than a ragdoll.

I flew into the crowd of inmates, taking three of them out so that we fell in a heap. Twenty Seven scrambled to her feet as I did, almost dropping my blankets as she righted herself.

"I'm holding you responsible for my shit, Twenty Seven," I warned. "So you'd better not let it get dirty."

Her eyes widened and she clutched the blankets tighter as I turned and ran back towards the Goliath as he pushed himself back to his feet.

Agony raced through my ribs but I ignored it, focusing all of my energy on the fight and refusing to let pain distract me from my goal.

I howled to the sky as I ran, my voice echoing off of the walls before I leapt forward and landed on his back.

I locked my arm around his throat and caught my wrist in my other hand as I exerted every inch of my strength into choking him out.

Two Hundred roared beneath me, swinging around as he tried to catch hold of me but I wouldn't let go.

I snarled, gritting my teeth as I drove my knees into his spine and leaned all of my weight back to speed up the process.

The Dragon tried to roar again but my grip was too tight to allow any air to pass his lips.

He clawed at my arm, trying to break my hold as he staggered to one side before stumbling to the other.

A smile tugged at the corner of my mouth as I squeezed harder, victory singing in my veins with a promise so sweet I could almost taste it.

Two Hundred spun about, his arms grasping at me and he managed to grab a fistful of my hair, ripping it out of the knot I'd tied in it.

I cursed beneath my breath as he almost wrenched me off of him, but he only managed to tear a lump of hair from my head instead.

I cried out but didn't loosen my grip, driving my knees in even harder as all of my weight hung from his neck.

He crashed to his knees and the force of the collision with the ground almost unseated me, but I didn't let go. I planted my feet on the concrete floor and snarled as I squeezed even tighter and the fight drained from his limbs.

I felt the moment he fell unconscious in the way his body became limp and I released him a second before he dropped to the floor face first.

I cupped my hands around my mouth and howled to the moon which was hidden far beyond the roof of the building, the sound echoing all around me in the silence that followed my victory.

A beat later, every other Wolf in the room joined in and they sang a chorus of my victory to the stars which couldn't see us. We were the forgotten Fae, buried beneath ground for our crimes as if our bodies were equal to corpses. But there was so much life in me yet, and when I was done with this place, no one would ever forget the name Rosalie Oscura.

I looked back down at Two Hundred, my lip peeling back as I spotted the thick lock of black hair twisted around his fingers. Who the fuck pulled hair in a fight? *What a little bitch. I should have kicked him in the balls.*

I reached up to touch my fingers to the sore patch of skin on my scalp and sneered at the unconscious Dragon Shifter before turning away from him like he meant nothing at all to me.

But that was bullshit. Because what he was was my ticket into this place. No one would underestimate me again now and despite the fact that there was blood coating my tongue from my swollen lip and I was fairly sure he'd cracked my ribs, I wasn't going to let anyone know that that had been anything less than easy.

"What are you staring at, Twenty Seven?" I snapped as the Siren's wide eyes caught my attention. "Go and make up my bunk and get rid of his crap while you're at it."

She turned and scurried away through the crowd without so much as the hint of a complaint and I moved after her at a leisurely pace.

Eyes followed me as I went and the Werewolves in the crowd reached out to brush their hands over my arms in a silent offering. But I didn't have any inclination to bring them with me. If someone wanted to join my pack then they could earn their place in it. I wouldn't take just any Fae.

But that was an issue for tomorrow. Tonight, I just wanted to rest in my shiny, new cell.

ROARY

PRISONER #69

CHAPTER FOUR

I rested my elbows on the railing of the highest floor, gazing down to the bottom of the cell block where Rosalie Oscura had just put a ten ton Dragon on his ass.

That's the feisty little pup I know and love.

She didn't even notice me as she headed up the stairs and walked past me with a crowd of applauding asswits behind her. Didn't even spare me a glance when I pushed my long, dark mane away from my face. She just sailed into the cell beside mine where Twenty Seven was finishing clearing out Christopher's stuff. Rosalie stepped past her and the Siren bundled up the last of the Dragon's shit in her arms, hurrying out of the space. I lifted a finger, beckoning her over.

Her eyebrows arched and she scurried toward me without a moment's hesitation.

"Toss it," I directed, pointing over the railing.

"But if Christopher sees me-" she started and I rolled my eyes.

I put two fingers in my mouth, whistling sharply and making everyone look up at me from below. Including Christopher with his wounded pride expression and pouty, bruised face as he came round. I snatched the bundle of stuff from Twenty Seven's arms and tossed it over the edge, letting it rain down like confetti.

"Have fun sleeping in the coop with the other castaways, Christopher! I won't miss the sound of your toenail clippings pinging off the walls or your wheezy snore which keeps me up at night," I laughed and he flipped me the finger, scowling as he set to work picking up his shit.

I seriously didn't mind my new neighbour moving in for a hundred reasons. I stretched my arms languidly above my head then strode toward her cell at a leisurely pace.

I rested my shoulder against the doorway, the barred door currently locked open for daylight hours. Not that we actually got any daylight in here. We were the stars only knew how many feet underground, so everything below the Order Yard was lit by artificial light. And a Nemean Lion needed the sun like a Werewolf needed the moon. So these bullshit fluorescent bulbs were no substitute.

Rosalie was bent over her bed, smoothing out the creases of her freshly changed sheets. My gaze shifted over the roundness of her ass before I remembered she was ten years younger than me and my friend's baby cousin.

"Well if it isn't little Rosalie Oscura," I purred and she stood upright suddenly, turning to me in surprise. She swiped at her bloody lip and straightened her spine as if to show me she wasn't hurt. But my insides twisted at knowing she was. I couldn't offer her any sympathy though. She was too proud to bear anyone pointing out her weaknesses.

Her cheeks pinked in that way they always had around me, then she schooled her expression and I tried not to smirk too hard. She'd had a crush on me growing up. Our families were close, the Oscura Werewolves and the Night Lions. And it looked like she still had a thing for me. The last time I'd seen her outside of visitation had been the night I was arrested. I'd done a job with her and her cousin, Dante at Lionel Acrux's manor. In hindsight, going up against a Celestial Councillor, one of the rulers of Solaria and most powerful Fae in the world, had been a terrible fucking idea. To say it had been a shitstorm was an understatement of mind-blowing proportions.

"You don't look surprised to see me," she said, her eyes narrowing as she placed a hand on her hip. She was trying to gain the upper hand, so I stepped into her cell, dominating the space and grinning down at her to make sure any thoughts she had of that were fast abandoned.

"My brother told me you were coming," I said. "But he didn't say why...I didn't peg you for a bank robber, Rosa. But even if you are, why did Leon have so little faith in you pulling off the job, hm?"

She stepped closer instead of cowering, lifting her chin and the scent of her washed over me. My little pup never wore perfume, she always smelled like mischief and strawberries. But there was a new scent to her now, something enticing and pure Alpha.

"Maybe I got sloppy." She shrugged and turned away from me, but I caught her arm, pushing her back against the wall and laying my palms either side of her head.

Her breath hitched and I smiled broadly. Maybe I secretly liked the way she looked at me. It wasn't like when I used my Lion Charisma on a girl and they turned into a mindless, doe-eyed slave. No, when Rosa looked at me I could practically see the blood pumping through her veins, feel the rush of adrenaline that clawed under her skin. She might have been way too young for me, but Rosalie had blossomed into a sinfully beautiful girl and I wasn't beyond drinking in her attention.

"The Oscura Werewolves don't get sloppy," I said in a low growl. "How about you tell me the truth? Because we're family, Rosa, I deserve more than a lie."

"We're not family," she said coolly. "And if you don't mind, I've got a life sentence awaiting me so I'd like to get started on it." She moved fast, ducking under my arm and throwing herself onto her bed. She pursed her lips against the pain in her body and I clenched my jaw, fighting the urge to call a guard to heal her. But she would have hated me for it, and as much as I cared for the little pup, I respected her too much to embarrass her in front of the block.

She shut her eyes, pretending to sleep and I arched a brow at how easily she dismissed me. I didn't like to admit how much that bothered me as a flicker of irritation ran through my chest. But I wasn't giving up yet.

"Well let me make some intelligent guesses then." I dropped down onto the end of her bed, lifting her legs to make room for me then dropping them over my lap. A growl left her throat, but she said nothing as I rested my hands on her calves. "You don't need the money to bother with a bank job, and you certainly wouldn't fuck one up if you did. So…you're in here for a reason."

I watched her expression closely, but she kept her eyes firmly shut. A smile tugged at the corner of my mouth. "Come on, put me out of my misery, little pup."

Her eyes flew open and she scowled at me, making heat burst through my chest. I'd gotten a reaction, so I'd definitely scored.

"I'm not a pup anymore, Roary," she said in a dangerous voice.

"You'll always be a pup to me," I taunted and her cheeks puffed out angrily. It felt too good winding her up.

She flipped upright, catching the collar of my jumpsuit in her fist. "I just beat down a Dragon and I've got enough energy to upend a Lion Shifter too."

My grin widened. "Please try. It would make my day."

Her upper lip peeled back and I could sense she was really about to try it so I reached out and pulled her in for a hug, aiming to totally disarm her.

"It's good to see you, Rosa. I'd tell you to stay out of trouble, but you're already in the most dangerous prison in Solaria, so I don't think you can get yourself in any deeper."

She pulled out of my arms, a smile gracing her lips and drawing my attention for far too long. When did the little pup get full, lickable lips like that?

"Trust me, Roary," she said in a husky voice that had my throat tightening. "I can get into *far* more trouble than this."

I cleared my throat, pushing her off of my lap so she hit the bed, treating her like the young Wolf I used to tussle with without a single inappropriate thought. Though I regretted that a bit as she winced again. "Well lucky you, because you've got one of the toughest guys in here watching your back."

"Really? Where is he?" she asked innocently as she moved onto her knees and her dark hair tumbled around her.

I snorted a laugh, rising to my feet and leaning down so we were nose to nose. "Still got that quick wit I see, little pup. It won't do you any favours in here. There are fucked up creatures between these walls that would gut you for less."

"I can look after myself," she said with an eye roll.

"Why not let your childhood crush live out your fantasies for you? I'll take *real* good care of you, pup."

She lunged up, shoving me in the chest with a snarl. "I'm not a pup. And I never had a crush on you."

I chuckled softly, catching hold of her wrists. "It's okay. Half of Dante's cousins had a crush on me. It's my Charisma. Although, you're definitely still blushing right now and I can't use my Order gifts while they're pumping suppressant through the vents. So what do you think that means?"

As a Nemean Lion Shifter, I had the power to sway other Fae to do my every desire. I just had to turn on the charm and people came flooding around me like I was a god. I'd used it to gather a decent sized following in here, but I had to reinforce my sway over those I'd gathered every time I went into the Order Yard. If you didn't have a gang in this prison, you were automatically at a disadvantage. Numbers meant power. And without power in Darkmore, you were gonna fall to the bottom of the food chain fast.

She huffed, yanking her wrists free of my hold. "Why would I have a crush on an old Lion fart?"

I held my heart, stumbling backwards until my back hit the wall, pretending I'd been shot. "Shit, Rosa. You hit me right where it hurts. I'm thirty four not a *hundred* and four like your old Grandpa Fernando."

She broke a laugh and the sound set off a deep purr in my chest. I moved toward the door, lingering there as I glanced back at her. "You know...you might have beat one Dragon but you're gonna have a hundred more Fae challenge you in here in the next week. You're fresh meat. And power levels mean nothing outside of magical hours. Scores are settled in blood more often than not."

"I've been fighting my own battles for as long as I can remember," she said lightly. "You really don't have to worry about me."

"I know you can hold your own in an honourable fight, but people play dirty in here. Are you sure you're prepared for that?"

She smiled in a way that set my pulse racing and she nodded easily. "I'm prepared for everything, Roary."

"Alright." I rapped my knuckles on the bars of her cell so a metallic gong rang out. "But I'll be right here when you realise you need me."

"I run half the Oscura pack these days. But I guess you wouldn't know that since you've been in here since I was a kid."

"Yeah," I grunted, an ache of sadness filling me over that fact.

I'd missed out on so much during my time in Darkmore. My brother visited weekly, keeping me filled in but it wasn't the same as being out there in the real world. I'd missed his wedding for fuck's sake. And I'd missed seeing Rosalie grow up too. She'd visited me on the odd occasion, but never alone. And never regularly enough for me to really know her anymore.

And all because of one fucking cock-up. One job gone wrong. But a part of me couldn't regret it. Because that night on the Acrux grounds, I'd been torn between a choice to run or go back for Rosa. I'd chosen her. And I'd gotten her out of there, saving her from a stretch in juvie before ending up in this hell hole. Though apparently that had been for nothing, because here she was right beside me anyway. Fuck, she better have known what she was doing by coming here. It was a place where dreams came to die a bloody death.

Any hopes I'd have of a reduced sentence had been crushed like a nut in a nutcracker a long time ago. Lionel Acrux had ensured I paid for my crimes with my youth. Since then, I'd tried to live vicariously through my brother's stories. In here, it was all about survival. And I'd been caged so long, I'd almost forgotten what it was like to live without watching your back at every second.

If Rosa thought she knew what she was in for in this place, she was going to get the shock of her life. I'd seen Fae with far more swagger than her stalk into this prison like royalty, only to be dethroned in a brutal execution days later.

"The Dragon will strike back at you," I told her. "Keep your eyes open."

"I know what I'm doing, Roary," she said casually, dropping back down onto her bed.

"I really hope so, little pup."

ROSALIE

PRISONER #12

CHAPTER FIVE

T he darkness pressed in on me as I waited in the closet, my knees curled to my chest, my thin arms wound around them. It was cold in here. And the dust always made my nose tickle. But Mamma said I mustn't ever let the man know I was here. So while he visited, I stayed hidden.

I could hear their voices in the front room, not loud enough to make out much of what they were saying but Mamma's high pitched laugh reached me over and over while the deep baritone voice of a man came in between.

This was the easy bit. Before they made it into the bedroom where I was hiding. If I had my own room then maybe I could have hidden in there instead. But Mamma said runts didn't get beds for their own so I slept on the floor in the kitchen, although sometimes I snuck onto the couch.

The bedroom was dark beyond my hiding place, but there was a thin gap along the edge of the closet door which I could use to peek out. So when they stumbled into the bedroom, I caught sight of Mamma's slight frame wrapped around the man. He was tall and wiry with dark hair and cruel eyes. Mamma said if he ever found out about me, he'd drown me in the nearest lake.

'Alphas don't want runts.'

So I hid.

Mamma started peeling off her clothes as the man watched through hooded eyes, swigging whisky straight from the bottle.

He pulled his shirt off then unbuckled his belt and I closed my eyes, clamping my hands over my ears as I waited for this part to be over.

He always left when it was done. Then I'd wait for Mamma to fall asleep and slip out of the closet. If I was lucky they'd have left some of their dinner uneaten like last time.

I could still hear Mamma as she said something to him and I wriggled further back into the closet, clamping my hands down harder to try and block out the sounds before the bed started creaking and the man started cussing.

My shoulder knocked against a jacket hanging in the back of the closet and it slid from the rack, disturbing the dust and making it billow around me.

I slapped a hand over my mouth and held my breath as the most unbearable itch started up in my nose. My bare feet scrambled against the hard floor as I fought it, but my body was betraying me and I was going to lose the battle-

The sneeze burst from me and the room beyond my closet fell utterly silent.

Heavy footsteps beat across the floor.

"Come back to bed, Felix," Mamma called, a hint of fear to her voice.

The cupboard door was wrenched open and I found myself looking up into the eyes of a monster.

"Well, well, well, what have we got here?" he growled.

I jerked awake as a roar sounded outside the cell block door and something huge slammed into it. Someone screamed a curse down in the coop and someone else replied with a string of profanities while others yelled for them to shut up.

My pulse hitched as the Belorian continued its attack on the door for another minute before it gave up and headed away with another angry shriek.

That thing was going to throw a serious spanner into the works of my plan. I was either going to have to figure out a way to trap it in its cage one night or I'd have to adjust my plans so that we escaped during the day. It was damn frustrating, but there wasn't anything I could do aside from adapt.

The nightmare tried to cling to me but I shrugged it off again, refusing to fall into the trap of its clutches. I might not have been able to escape my past in my dreams, but it would be a cold day in hell before I'd allow one single second of my waking moments to be ruled by it.

My first night in Darkmore Penitentiary had been filled with the sounds of snuffling, crying, the odd scream, a fight which I was almost certain had ended in someone dying down in the coop and the most moon awful, earth rumbling snores coming from the dude in the cell to the left of mine. Whoever the hell was sleeping in cell eleven was officially on my shit list.

And now, as I'd finally dozed off, I found myself woken again by a repetitive snip, snip, snip.

"Ooo yeah, that's the business," a low male voice sounded and I pushed myself upright with a snarl of irritation.

The snip, snip, snip was coming from somewhere outside and I shoved myself to my feet, prowling towards the bars which lined the front of my cell and were currently locked into place for the night. I shivered in my white tank and boring black panties. My great aunt Marina could have chosen more appealing underwear than the standard issue bullshit I was currently sporting and she was eighty four and about as prudish as a prune in a basket of grapes.

I made it to the front of my cell and draped my arms through the bars as I looked out over the wide open space to the gangway opposite mine.

"Merda santa," I cursed as my eyes fell on the cell directly in front of me. *Holy shit.*

A man stood butt naked with one leg on the floor and the other hooked up onto the bunk beside him as he bent forward and trimmed his pubic hair with a pair of scissors fashioned from what looked like plastic canteen cutlery. He had a wiry body and thick grey hair *everywhere* which he seemed inclined to individually trim in full view of every fucker on this side of the cell block.

"What the fuck are you doing?" I demanded, my upper lip curling back in horror.

"If you like the view, you can come on over for a closer look when the doors *slide* open, new pup," he purred, thrusting his hips so his dick flapped back and forth.

"If I come over there it'll be to do some cutting of my own," I warned, baring my teeth.

"You can come and play armies with me if you like?" he offered as he finally dropped his leg from the bunk. My relief was short lived as he moved into a squat, giving me an even more graphic view as he started trimming his ball hair. "I'll lie down and you just come and blow the fuck out of me..."

"Per l'amore della luna!" I snarled. *For the love of the moon.* "Why don't you hang a fucking sheet?"

"The more attention Plunger gets, the harder he works for it," Roary's voice came from the cell to the right of mine. "Just ignore him or he'll bend over and give you a real show with a full view of his asshole."

"Plunger?" I asked with a grimace, wondering if I even wanted to know what had earned him that nickname.

"Yeah," Plunger called. "Because I'll plunge into *anything.*"

I turned away from him in disgust as he started making kissy noises at me and I began pacing my cell, muttering to myself in Faetalian about perverts and freaks.

"You should start hanging a sheet so you don't have to look at him," Roary said from the other side of the bricks which separated us. His voice came to me clearly and I frowned as I looked at the wall which divided us, smirking when I spotted a little metal grate in the rear corner of the cell.

"I don't have a spare sheet to hang," I muttered.

I wasn't going to be sleeping on that mattress without something to cover it. I hadn't missed the old stains on it when Twenty Seven had been making up my bed. Some of them looked like blood and the others…well I didn't like to think too much about that big ass Dragon Shifter being alone in here at night when his body got *urges*.

Blugh, I might just puke if I focus on that too much.

"Well maybe you should get yourself one today. Or I could get one for you…for the right price."

"And what would you want me to do for a sheet, Roary?" I asked as I dropped onto my hands and knees and peered through the grate into his cell. My bruised ribs twinged uncomfortably at the treatment, but I gritted my teeth against the pain and forcefully ignored it. The metal was thick and strong with little holes in the shape of stars punched through it to allow the air to flow freely. I guessed they wanted to make sure the Order Suppressant they pumped into the cells could get everywhere easily, but it also meant that I could see Roary while talking to him if he got out of bed to join me.

"I'm sure I could think of something you could do to earn it," he replied in that flirtatious tone I used to daydream about when I was younger. Not that I'd ever admit that I'd had a crush on him as a teenager but if I was being totally honest with myself, I'd been borderline obsessed. Every time he'd been at my Aunt Bianca's hanging out with my cousin Dante, I'd found myself tongue tied and blushing. But I wasn't that innocent little girl anymore.

Okay, so maybe I'd *never* been innocent but I had been a teenage girl who was surrounded by dipshit boys who couldn't handle me.

Roary was all Alpha, and in the years since he'd been carted off to Darkmore, I'd come to realise that that was what I'd liked about him. I was drawn to men who were my equal. It was a Wolf thing. We craved mates who could match us and there weren't a whole lot of men who I could say that about.

Werewolves were generally polyamorous with their pack in the years before they found their true mate, but I'd stopped participating in the pack orgies years ago. For a start, three quarters of my pack were my relatives so I only had a choice between the other twenty five percent anyway. And with the options available to me, I hadn't found a single true Alpha amongst them. I just couldn't summon any enthusiasm for sex with a guy who wasn't my equal and they certainly couldn't handle me on the occasions I'd tried. Who wanted shit sex with a guy who couldn't turn you on, let alone get you off? Not me.

And since I'd started on the Alpha diet I'd realised that there was no turning back. Not that there were ever many of them around to pick between. Solaria may have been filled with powerful Fae, but for every Wolf there seemed to be a thousand sheep.

"Come down and talk to me at the vent," I said, shifting my hips to get comfortable on the floor.

"Do you want to stare into my eyes while you get all moony over me?" Roary teased, but I could hear him climbing out of his bunk all the same.

I blew out a breath of irritation. This teasing was going to get old fast. I wasn't some little girl for him to push around and mock anymore. I was Rosalie Oscura and I didn't let anyone make a fool of me.

"You need to get over yourself, Roary," I muttered. "If you seriously think I'm anything like the little pup you used to push about and make fun of then you're wrong."

Roary moved to the other side of the grate, laying down and looking through at me with a smirk on his lips. It was hard to make out much through the small holes while the lights were still out but I could see his mane of long, dark hair falling around him and that mischievous look in his eye which had once had me swooning when I was fourteen.

"Are you ready to let me in on your devious plans?" he asked in a low voice to keep our conversation private.

"They don't concern you," I replied lightly. Although that wasn't true. If I was going to successfully escape this place then I needed him on side, and I fully intended to bring him with me when I went.

Not least because it was my fault that he was in here, not that he had ever admitted it. But I knew in my heart that it was true. Dante had told me to stay behind that day but I'd refused and because of me, it had all gone to shit. Roary wouldn't have been caught if he hadn't been protecting me and as they'd hauled him away, I'd sworn on all I was that I'd get him out of this place somehow. I was pretty late on making good on my promise but there wasn't a day that had passed in the last ten years when it hadn't crossed my mind.

But there were things I needed to do before I had to recruit him to my plans and I was happy to let the Lion bastardo sweat while I worked on it. He'd earned a little torture for the years of it he'd given me. I'd spent too many nights dreaming of the day when he'd stop looking at me like I was a little kid and see that I was perfect for him. And even now, when I was well and truly over my childhood fantasies, he still looked at me that same way. Like I was some idiota child nipping at his ankles. Stronzo.

I pursed my lips as I thought about the things I needed to do to further my plans once I was released from this cell for the night. Firstly and most importantly, I needed to find Sin Wilder. He was the one I'd come to break out of here after all. According to my contact, Jerome, he'd been stuck in isolation for way too long, though he couldn't tell me what he'd done to earn himself that severity of punishment. Isolation was hard on any Fae but for an Order like his, it would practically be torture…

"I meant what I said last night, Rosa," Roary breathed, drawing my attention back to him. "This place chews up pretty little things like you and spits them back out again. I can see you've changed, that you're stronger than you used to be, tougher too, but don't underestimate this place. Even those who seem friendly will be after something. Even if it's just to ride on your coat tails and bathe in the glow of your glory. Nothing comes for free in here. Everything has a price…"

"And what price have you paid, Roary?" I asked, touching my fingers to the metal grate as I sensed there was something he wasn't saying.

He looked at me through the little holes for a long moment before lifting his hand to press it to the grate too. His fingertips brushed against mine through the tiny gaps in the metal and my damn heart leapt at his touch like it used to when I was fourteen all over again. Not that I let it show.

"I've paid in more ways than you can imagine," he breathed eventually.

A loud bell blared before I could say anything in response and I stilled as I looked around, wondering what it meant.

"Are we about to be let out of here?" I asked hopefully.

"Not yet. That sound means there are guards in the block. They'll be doing the count before we're let out, though this is a bit early for that."

Footsteps pounded up the metal stairs outside and Roary offered me a smile before shifting away from the grate and getting to his feet.

I followed suit, dropping down to sit on my bunk with my back to the wall as I waited for the guards to arrive.

My gaze caught on Plunger on the far side of the block as he started doing squats with his hairy ass pointed towards the door.

I fought the urge to vomit in my mouth and looked away again quickly.

"Where's Twelve?" a deep voice boomed from somewhere on the bottom floor and I cocked my head towards the door. That had sounded suspiciously like the asshole guard who'd burned me yesterday.

"Sounds like you're off to meet the Warden, little pup," Roary muttered.

"Oh really? Let me just put my tiara on and practice my curtsy," I replied.

He snorted a laugh as the sound of the guards' footsteps pounded up the stairs, some cowardly Fae giving up my location to them. I swivelled in my bed, flopping back on my mattress and placing my hands beneath my head as

I closed my eyes, feigning sleep.

Eventually the guards' footsteps drew closer and closer until they stopped outside my cell.

"How the hell did a little thing like her snag a top floor cell to herself?" Hastings asked in a low voice which definitely sounded impressed.

The corner of my mouth twitched with a smile. "I'm number twelve," I said without opening my eyes. "This is cell twelve, I assumed it was meant for me so I kicked the Dragon out, ragazzo del coro." *Choir boy.*

"Don't let her allure fool you, Hastings," Cain growled. "This one's a stone, cold killer. Get up, Twelve, you're coming with us."

I sighed dramatically and pushed myself up onto my feet, walking towards them with my hips swaying. Two more guards stood further down the walkway waiting to help escort me out of here and I smirked at them as I made it to the door of my cell.

"Do you really think I'm alluring, Officer Cain?" I asked, looking up at him from beneath my lashes.

He damn near snarled at me and I cut my gaze across to Hastings instead, biting my bottom lip as I looked up at him.

"I think you're damn irritating," Cain growled. "And if you're looking for time in the hole then you're going the right way about it. Get dressed, the warden wants to see you." He shoved a fresh set of clothes through the bars and I took them from him slowly.

"Are you just going to stand there and watch me change?" I asked as I moved to place the clothes on the spare bunk above mine.

"Hurry up or I'll be forced to reprimand you," Cain snarled, gripping his shock baton at his hip threateningly.

I pouted, looking at Hastings like I wanted him to help me but he just offered a shrug, seeming a little unsure and clearly not willing to challenge Cain.

I turned to face the bunk with my new clothes on it and slowly drew the white tank top up over my head before dropping it to the floor. I'd slept without a bra on and the cool air of the cells made my nipples harden as it kissed my skin.

I dropped my panties next, making no attempt to shield my body from them and smirking to myself as Hastings cleared his throat and turned his back like a proper gentleman.

Cain didn't look away though and I turned to look at him as I slowly pulled my new clothes on. There was a darkness in his gaze which said he hated me, but the heat that blazed within his eyes said he wanted me too.

I offered him a taunting smile, my gaze sliding over the way his black uniform clung to his broad frame as I took my time putting my new clothes on, finishing with the orange jumpsuit which I only buttoned half way, leaving my white tank on show beneath it.

"Open on three, cell twelve," Cain commanded, lifting a radio to his mouth.

A deep buzz sounded and my cell door slid aside, rattling open so that I stood before the two guards with their magic and their weapons and their looks of mistrust. Although as my gaze slid to Hastings, I was pleased to see my choir boy had a hint of concern in his gaze just for little old me.

"Sembri un agnello, ragazzo del coro. Dovresti temere il lupo," I said, dropping my voice an octave as I looked up at him, shifting my weight so I was angled towards him. *You look like a lamb, choir boy. You should fear the wolf.*

"I told you I don't speak Faetalian," he replied, clearing his throat as he reached out to take my arm.

"She said she's going to eat you alive," Cain snarled as he snatched my other arm. "And if you don't get that starry look out of your eyes then I might start thinking she's right."

Hastings frowned at me like he didn't know whether to believe Cain or not and I batted my eyelashes innocently as Cain wrenched me into a fast walk.

My gaze snagged on Roary's as he leaned against his cell door with his arms trailing through the bars, watching me go. For a moment it seemed like he was concerned about me, but his features shifted subtly and I couldn't see anything beyond a blank mask. I smirked at him all the same, offering him reassurance if he wanted it. I wasn't afraid of this stronzo or any of the other guards. They may have been harsh, brutal even, but they weren't going to risk killing one of us without a good reason and getting locked up with the monsters they were paid to contain. If that ever happened, their deaths would come surely enough, though not before the dark Fae who resided here made them suffer to the full extent of their power. And even without the use of our Order gifts or magic, there were a lot of creative ways that someone could be made to hurt with a bit of time and effort involved.

Cain and Hastings were quickly flanked by the two other guards who I recognised from my research, Teresa Taylor, a Manticore with a thing for eating raw turnips and Cam Martin, a Centaur whose whole life was her work. I hadn't been able to find out much about them that would make them good candidates for turning so I didn't have any intentions to attempt to win them over.

We headed down the metal stairs which ran between the gangways and I could feel the eyes of my cell mates crawling over me, assessing me, underestimating me. They'd gotten a taste of what I was made of when I'd taken down the Dragon asshole yesterday but beating Two Hundred wouldn't be enough on its own. Even now, some of them would be looking at my small stature and slim frame and thinking it had been a fluke. They'd come for me soon enough to test their theory. I had plenty of challenges left before me to prove myself in here but I wasn't afraid. If there was one place I thrived then it was in the midst of a fight.

We made it to the ground floor and the guards led me over the bridge which crossed the evermist trap and my gaze trailed down to look at the coiling smoke with interest. I'd heard all about the way that shit made you feel if you came into contact with it, but I had to wonder if it really was as bad as they claimed. My Aunt Bianca's voice rang in my head as I almost considered jumping in there to test it out. *Curiosity killed the cat, Rosa!* But I was no kitty cat and curiosity had only ever made me stronger.

The cell block doors opened as the guards unlocked them and I glanced back at the cage where the lower ranking members of my cell block had to sleep all penned in like pigs. Wide eyes and curious stares followed me and I tossed them a wink before I was dragged out into the long grey corridor and the cell block door closed behind us.

We headed past the doors for the wide staircase which led to the other levels of the prison and I was directed into a slim elevator. I watched as Hastings activated it with a flare of magic before the doors slid closed and we started ascending.

"Not to be a bother…" I said slowly.

"If you don't want to bother us then don't talk," Cain growled.

"Yeah. Totally. Shutting my mouth… But I was just wondering what I have to do to get a bit of medical attention?" I eyed Hastings hopefully, pouting with my busted lip and a grin tugged at the corner of his mouth.

"I guess kicking a Dragon Shifter out of his cell takes a bit of doing," Hastings said, offering me his hand.

Cain grumbled irritably but didn't stop me from placing my palm in Hastings' and I smiled widely as healing magic slid beneath my skin, repairing my lip, the tender patch on my scalp and the bruised ribs too.

"Thank you," I purred, keeping hold of his hand for an extra beat before drawing back.

Cain scowled at me and I gave him my most innocent look in return.

When the doors opened again on the first floor, we stepped out onto thick black carpet and warm air surrounded me. I glanced about, looking casual while I was really inhaling every single detail of my surroundings.

We passed a set of double doors which stood open, showing a huge lounge where a few off duty guards sat about, watching tv and chatting before a crackling fire. I caught sight of a well-stocked kitchen where some more guards sat eating their breakfast around a long dining table and a door which held a sign for showers on it.

We passed through another corridor and my gaze snagged on a row of blue lockers with the guards' names printed on them in silver lettering. That was where they stored their shit between shifts. Batons, uniforms, magical cuff keys...

Cain yanked on my arm with a sharp jerk as he caught my attention fixing on the lockers and he dragged me flush to his powerful body as he leaned down to snarl in my ear. "Keep your eyes down." His grip bit into my arm painfully but I didn't let it show as I looked straight into his grey eyes while we were nose to nose.

"Or what?" I breathed, a clear challenge in my tone.

His grip on me started to burn as his Elemental power slid to the surface of his skin. He was too quick to anger. He wouldn't have done well in a cage fight. Emotions equalled a battering in a brawl, but then that wasn't what he liked. He liked the hunt, the chance to unleash that rage in him and lean into the bloodlust of his kind. Vampires weren't really supposed to engage in the hunt. It was in their little code, but Cain clearly didn't like to tame the beast which lived beneath his flesh. We had that much in common at least.

Cain bared his fangs at me, but before he could reply with some dark threat against my safety, a door at the end of the corridor swung open.

"Is there a reason you're lurking?" a woman's voice came from inside the room and Cain dragged me into a fast walk again.

"We brought Twelve, as requested, ma'am," Cain announced as he dragged me into the ostentatious office and pushed my ass down into a hard seat before the Warden's mahogany desk.

I raised my chin as I looked into the beady eyes of the woman who ran this place. Audrey Pike, a Pegasus with the Element of air. She was one of those overachieving, goal orientated people who drove me to fucking tears. I'd done my research on her the most thoroughly of all. There wasn't a week that went by in this place when she didn't try out some new idea, strategy, creative path to criminal rehabilitation. She was also a hard bitch. She may have been all for pushing the prisoners here to try new things and work on their inner Fae, but I'd read between the lines of those glossy articles. Punishments were up fifteen percent since she'd taken the role as Warden. Stints in isolation were longer, time in the interrogation more common, she had implemented tighter restrictions on magic and Order exercise despite the fact that Fae could sicken and die if they were cut off from their powers for too long. She presented the face of fairness and sung the song of wanting to better the lives of the prisoners in her care, but as far as I'd been able to grasp, this prison was run to her tune. So you either listened to the beat and got your ass shaking along in time or you'd be tossed in the rejects corner with the dudes no one wanted to dance with and left to rot until you found a way back to the rhythm she set.

So overall, not someone I wanted paying me much attention.

"Rosalie Oscura…" Warden Pike said thoughtfully, her discerning gaze scraping over me from my long, black hair which was tangled around my shoulders to my half buttoned jumpsuit and landing on my standard issue boots which I hadn't bothered to tie. "Stop lingering like a bad smell, Cain. I'll call you when we're done."

Cain turned and left the room without a word, but I didn't miss the fire that flared in his gaze for half a heartbeat. He didn't like being spoken to like that. Not one bit.

"Nice to meet you, Warden," I said, sweet as pie as I offered her my cuffed hand to shake.

She had ice blonde hair and cold eyes which took in the gesture thoughtfully, cynically. I got the feeling my innocent act didn't fly with her for a single second, but she went along with it all the same.

"A shame it isn't under better circumstances," Pike replied, grasping my hand and shaking once. She didn't squeeze hard like some asshole trying to prove how big his balls were, simply shook and released, nothing to the gesture which could be taken as any kind of posturing. I guessed she didn't need to try and intimidate me anyway. We both knew my ass was hers for the duration of my stay.

"I like your blazer," I commented. She was wearing a white suit. All white without a speck of dirt on it, not even a blob of breakfast. That was its own special kind of impressive.

"And lucky for you, orange seems to be your colour," she replied easily.

I smiled at her and she raised a defined eyebrow at me. I imagined half the male inmates had fantasies about breaking her perfect poise and ruffling her feathers. She was that unattainable kind of beautiful. That painted on perfection which you usually only saw in the media and I imagined took a whole lot of work to maintain. Wildly alluring was more my bag. It took a lot less prep anyway.

"Your power levels are high, you ranked in the top ten of your class at Aurora Academy and you received a special distinction for Elemental Combat," Pike said, sounding like she was reading from a file while she was actually just speaking from memory. "So much potential…but you're an Oscura so I suppose blood will out. Your upbringing in one of the most infamous gangs in Solaria would be what led you into crime, though you don't strike me as the type to be easily led. In fact, despite the fact that you're clearly an Alpha, there's no reports of you ever having challenged your cousin Dante for his place as head of your family, care to tell me why?"

I shrugged a shoulder. "A morte e ritorno," I replied as easily as breathing. *To death and back.* "It's my family motto. Dante is the best person I know, I don't care if our natures should push us into conflict, it's never going to happen. Besides, the Oscura Clan is more than big enough to hold two lead Alphas. Dante never tried to clip my wings, he encouraged me to flourish, even offered to fight me for the top spot. But I love him. And he's a great head of our family. I have no intention of seeing him unseated."

"You speak as if you think you'd win that fight," Pike commented. "Do you really believe you could take on a Storm Dragon and win? His rap sheet is even longer than yours…"

I smirked. "Every Alpha thinks they can win all battles," I replied. "But that's a question I don't ever intend to have an answer for."

Pike's eyes stayed fixed on me like I was a puzzle she was trying to figure out and I just smiled. I might have been full of secrets but she wouldn't be getting any from my lips.

"Assault, affray, driving under the influence of the moon, minor in the possession of stardust, Alpha Wolf status abuse, hijacking a Pegasus and trespassing on private property, Coercing of law enforcement, bedazzlement and finally, bank robbery and murder…It seems like a bit of a deviation from your usual vices. And the reports claim that the great Storm Dragon abandoned you to the FIB. Seems like a strange thing for him to do if your bond is as strong as you claim."

I smiled sweetly without speaking a word. Was I about to confirm that Dante had been with me on that job? Fuck no.

Pike got the hint and dropped it. "I invited you up here so that we could have a quick face to face. You'll soon find your way around the prison and get to learn the rules. But there's only one which really counts. Don't. Cross. Me. Take out your rage and your petty issues on the members of your cell block, run off steam when you're up in the Order yard, channel your magic into whatever you feel you need to while you're in the Magic Compound. But don't break the rules I've set. Don't go up against my guards. And *don't* go thinking you're special."

"Okay," I replied easily, laying some sugar on my tone. She didn't buy it. This bitch could see people as clearly as I could and the Wolf inside me was raising her head at the challenge. *Fuck*, I loved finding a worthy opponent.

"Cain?" Pike called, raising her voice just enough to be heard from outside the room, though with Cain's Vampire senses I was going to guess he'd been listening in on that little chat anyway.

"Ma'am?" he asked politely as he pushed the door open behind me.

"I think Twelve would benefit from a firm hand, so I'm assigning you as her corrections officer. Hastings can be her second, he could learn a thing or two from how you deal with an inmate like this." She didn't bother to explain what she meant by an inmate like me but I was going to guess she had me pegged. Game on. "I want you to give her a six week assessment before she begins the correcting process. Observe her temperament, her strengths, her weaknesses, how she responds to the other inmates and how she adapts to the prison lifestyle. Make notes on anything she needs to improve upon." She spoke like I wasn't there and I fought the growl which rose in my throat. I didn't like the sound of being *corrected*. Papà had tried and failed to whip me into shape a long time ago and if his punishments hadn't altered my personality in the desired way then I doubted anything they attempted on me here would make a dent either. I imagined Pike's 'correcting' came from a need to hit targets and show progression amongst the inmates for the sake of the parole board but if she was looking for a pet project to make an example of, she'd come looking in the wrong place with me.

"Yes, ma'am," Cain replied.

"Does this mean we'll be spending more time together, Officer?" I asked Cain sweetly, looking up at him from my seat.

The look which flashed in his eyes in response was filled with hate and a little excitement too if I was reading him right. He liked me beneath him like this. And he was planning on breaking me so that I stayed down here.

We'll see, Vampiro.

"I'll leave you to decide on her work assignment, and I expect a report on how she's settling in by the end of the week," Pike said, her gaze shifting away to her computer before he'd even had a chance to reply.

"Yes, ma'am," Cain bit out before reaching for my arm and dragging me from my seat.

We marched from the room and the door clicked shut behind me as Cain led me over the plush carpet at a fast pace.

"Did you understand what just happened there, Twelve?" he asked me in a low tone as the other guards fell into step behind us.

"All of your dreams came true?" I taunted.

"Your life just became *mine*. I own you now. From your perky tits to the soles of your feet, every inch of your flesh and drop of your blood has my name stamped over it. I decide where you work and who you spend time with. I get to be in charge of your privileges and your punishments. You belong to *me* now, and I don't take good care of my pets."

I snorted a laugh as we reached the elevator doors and he shoved me inside, pushing me up against the mirrored wall at the back of it with his hands locked around my hips.

"Don't snigger at me, don't smirk or smile or *flirt*. Your charm won't work on me and it will only buy you punishments. So if you want to get on my good side, you'll learn to bow your head and keep your lips shut around me."

I looked right into his eyes and shifted in his grip so that my hips brushed against his.

"I promise," I swore, biting down on my bottom lip.

He snarled at me as the elevator started to descend again, lowering his head so that his eyes bored into mine and his breath washed over my mouth. My heart pounded as this predator locked me in his gaze and I knew he wanted me to blink, to bow, to back down, but I just looked right back at him, daring him to do his worst. Cain could try to break me if he wanted to, but I didn't like his chances of success.

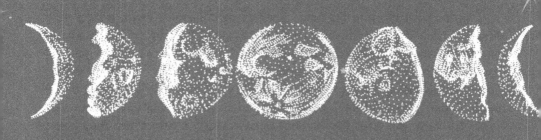

SIN

PRISONER #88

CHAPTER SIX

What can you do with a space that's six by six feet wide? Well it depended how imaginative you were. So for me, this isolation business was a walk in the endless fields of Naruvia. I was a wild animal prowling through the undergrowth one second, then a rug on the floor that was still still still. Personal record at being still? Thirteen. Fucking. Hours. A guard had to come to check if I was dead.

A rap of knuckles came at the door. Skin against metal. The closest thing to contact with another Fae I'd had for three months. And for an Incubus like me, that was one helluva fucking ache in the balls.

I moved from the corner and rolled my shoulders back, sweeping a hand through my overly long black hair which had grown out during my time here. It wasn't my usual style to sport a scruffy ass beard either, but I wasn't allowed out to the Magic Compound to use my power to shave so I guessed I had to work the hobo look for now. Going without my magic was almost as bad as going without my Order. No wait, going without my Order was worse. No, magic. Definitely magic. Fuck, I needed to get laid while casting a fireball above me, spinning it around the room with the power of air. I was a double Elemental and I was used to feeling like the most powerful son of a bitch to ever walk under the stars. In this box, I was just a tiger in a cage. My claws clipped, my teeth blunted. But beasts with hearts of steel always broke free in the end, and those that had held them captive often fell to their mercy in a shower of blood and screams.

I strode cockily up to the hatch just before it snapped open, rolling my shoulders back and cracking out a smile. It was a play I'd performed a hundred times. I was the lead role and I knew the words by heart. I could read people like books, so I knew how to improvise too. Didn't matter if they were the most guarded fuckers in the world, I'd see through it to the vulnerable little mouse underneath and take it between my giant paws. Even in Darkmore, I could still work my gifts. My Incubus powers were so robust that they bled into every fibre of my being. I may not have been able to wield the full extent of them, but my aura was always alluring. It was just how I was made.

"Officer Luscious," I said in a purr, leaning my shoulder against the door as I gazed out at her.

"It's Lucius," she corrected, rolling her eyes but a playful smile pulled at her mouth. She was five feet and seven inches of deliciousness, especially because this sweet little thing had been caught in my honey trap weeks ago. She had no idea how deep my claws were in her flesh. I could end her whenever I wanted. Because if I decided I needed someone dead, their number was up. No question about it. I'd put the Grim Reaper out of work a long time ago. But I wasn't going to kill Luscious, not so long as she was valuable.

"Do you have a present for me today?" I asked, my heart hitting a harder beat.

On Wednesdays and Fridays, Officer Luscious brought me a gift that made my time in here just about bearable. And I was tired of being rugs and trees and birds and bees. I wanted more than that today. *Needed* more than that.

There was a fine line between sanity and insanity and I danced between the two so often I didn't know which side the real Sin Wilder belonged to. I could be the most perfectly fucking normal asshole in the world if I wanted to be. In my Order form, I could be a guy called Norman who worked in accounts and had a bald patch and a pet cat called Arnold. *Or* I could be the biggest, baddest motherfucker you ever saw, with a scar down one whole side of his face and blades for fingers. It really depended on what you were into physically. Incubuses were shapeshifters of the best fucking kind. We could slip into the skin of anyone's deepest, darkest desire just by touching them and sensing it in their flesh. And the best part about that was, I held onto every skin I'd ever owned. If I had access to my Order form, I could look like any one of them. Male, female, tall, short, dark, fair, I had them all baby, and everything in between.

Of course, I couldn't shift in here, so I couldn't flex that power over my appearance. But my personality had split so many ways since my Order had Emerged that I could still hop from one to the next no bother. The real problem was knowing which parts of my personality really belonged to me and which were other people's fantasies that had gotten stuck to the inside of my head. Luckily, my real face held enough sway with girls anyway and paired with my sugary words, I could get by just fine in here. Not constant blowjobs and orgies fine, but I survived.

"Here. But only for thirty minutes. Officer Cain's on my ass today because he caught me giving a cigarette to an inmate this morning," Luscious said with a sigh.

"Seems kinda pointless," I said thoughtfully.

"Well you know Cain." She shrugged. "He likes having someone to *correct*."

"I meant smoking is pointless," I said in a gruffer tone.

"Why?" she frowned, her preened eyebrows pulling together.

"Takes a helluva lot of healing magic to cure away those cancerous cells all the time."

Luscious tutted and I shrugged innocently. The truth was the truth was the truth. I never told a lie. Not intentionally. The trouble with that was that everything about me was malleable, so it was hard to tell which things were true and which were lies. I had a few solid facts I held onto though. And they all boiled down to one special personality disorder: I was a bad, bad Fae.

Fact number one: I was a killer. The cold blooded, splatter on the walls, smile on my face type. I was a rent-a-kill hitman made perfectly for such a job considering my Order. And the reason I loved it so much? I was hired by the meanest fuckers in the kingdom to kill even meaner fuckers. I was only ever called in to slay the worst of the worst, asshole-of-Solaria types. And that suited me real good. Because I happened to be one of them too. And no one knew how to kill a monster as well as another monster. Plus, the many faces of my Incubus form meant I was near impossible to catch. *Near* being the operative word. Hence my current situation. But that was not. My. Fucking. Fault. I must have been sold out to the FIB. I just hadn't figured out which one of my endless enemies had done it yet. I had too many to count. But when I did work it out, oh holy fucking hell, I was going to rip the culprit's skin off on Christmas morning and make it into a billboard that read *This Is What Happens To Fae Who Fuck With Sin Wilder. P.S. Happy Holidays.*

Number two: I needed sex to function. My Order demanded it to restore my magical reserves, so sex was on my brain. A lot. More than your average guy with a porn addiction. If I wasn't fucking someone, I was thinking about fucking someone. I was a straight up sex junkie and happy to admit it. But as I was an Incubus, I got a free pass on the therapy for it. There was no cure for this baby. I needed sex like Pegasuses needed to fly through the clouds, like Dragons needed gold, like Vampires needed blood. It was a transaction I had

to make on a regular basis. And despite the bad rep that that gave my kind –
not that there were a whole lot of us in the world – I didn't give a fuck. See,
being me had its perks. When you were a walking talking sex doll, no one ever
really saw *you*. Which essentially made me invisible. And that was the way I
liked it.

Number three: My real name was not in fact Sin Wilder. It was Whitney
Northfield. Fucking…*Whitney*. Either my mother had a twisted sense of
humour or she'd decided to pass on her name to me a few hours before she
dumped me in a garbage can on the corner of Moonlight Street. Not *beside*
the can. Not even with the lid off. Inside, lid down, baby screaming. Or so the
newspapers had informed me years later; a witness had seen her scarpering off
into the night like a fart on the breeze. She'd left me wrapped in a blanket with
my name stitched into it, so either that crazy fuck had hoped I'd be found – *in
a dumpster, bitch!!* – or she forgot she'd left me there with a tiny clue of my
past. Had I Faegled Whitney Northfield in an attempt to hunt her down and
throw her ass in a garbage can in penance? Hell yes I had. Had I found a single
hit in the whole of fucking Solaria? Not one.

Luscious reached into her pocket and held out my gift. An iPod with a
pair of headphones wrapped around it. I wet my lips as I reached for it and
her fingers brushed mine as she passed it over. I got a hard on instantly. It was
pretty fucking low even for me. But three months in here had me humping the
walls and those abrasive bricks didn't play nice. Not even when I sweet talked
them. And for someone who liked it rough, sandpapering my dick was still a
hard limit even at this level of desperation.

"Thanks, Luscious." I turned my back on her and the hatch slammed shut
a second later.

I jammed the earbuds in and checked out her recently added songs. A
bunch of pop flashed up and I clicked on the one she'd played most. Something
called Physical by Dua Lipa burst into my ears and yes – *yes yes yes yes*. My
veins hummed with energy as the fast beat of it slammed into my soul and
made life worthwhile again.

I cranked the volume until I nearly busted an eardrum then stuffed the
iPod in my pocket and danced. And fucking danced and danced. I played it
again and again until I knew the words then belted them out and ground myself
against the wall. I needed a warm body and friction and my name tumbling
from candy red lips. I wanted to be someone's darkest desire again. I fed on
the way they looked at me when my Order shifted to give them the exact
version of perfect they fantasised about. All I had to do was touch them and
I could sense exactly what they wanted me to look like. And then they were
putty in my hands while I gave them the best night of their life and fuelled

my magic with every thrust of my hips. Being denied it was a torment unlike anything I'd ever known.

I growled as I played the song again, letting it take over everything inside me. Invade me, drown out my base needs which were ripping up my spine like sharp claws.

I need a girl with hands as soft as butter and plump lips to wrap around my cock and smear her lipstick all over it. I need one with hourglass curves and dark hair that spills down her back like nightfall.

I didn't always get the luxury of indulging in my type. Most of the time, I was just a sex toy to be pimped out. And most of the time I didn't mind that. As soon as a girl heard the word *Incubus* falling from my tongue, she stopped listening to what I had to say. Maybe that was why I talked crazy most of the time. When I was in my shifted form, no one was listening anyway. I could spout the alphabet or discuss my plans to murder the rulers of Solaria, no one would care either way. Especially once I started fucking them. I'd been called a thousand names while I screwed the life out of a girl. Baby, sweetness, king of the stars, devil boy, sex Alpha, daddy, big boy, my-husband-will-be-home-soon, Captain Big Dick, chocolate prince, honey badger – I could have gone on for days. But there was only one name that belonged to me which mattered. It was a verb, a noun and my fucking destiny. Sin. And I usually had to remind people to call me it while I was deep inside them, because screw all of those bullshit nicknames they gave me. I wanted to be called the name I'd had to wait sixteen years to be old enough to change. I'd claimed that name with every fibre of my being and I deserved to hear it pour from someone's lips while they used me for their own pleasure.

Every piece of shit I'd ever met had tried to claim me. They thought I was a commodity. Sex and killing was all I was good for. But every single one of them missed the fact that *I* was the one who was winning. I needed sex to restore my magic. *Win.* I needed to kill because every asshole I sent to hell could have been my mother who threw me in that garbage can, or my father who took zero responsibility for his sperm. *Win.* And I needed money to live. Money which they threw at me, so much of it in fact, that I'd had over two million auras in cash buried in my backyard before I came to Darkmore. *W. I. N.*

No one owned Sin Wilder. Sin Wilder owned the world. And when I found a way out of here, I was going to drive off into the sunset with a duffel bag full of cash and the only person who'd ever mattered to me in my entire life. *Me.*

ROSALIE

PRISONER #12

CHAPTER SEVEN

After Cain dumped me back in my cell, I sat waiting for the doors to unlock for the day while looking out between my bars at the other new neighbours I'd acquired.

Roary's heavy breathing kept me company as he slept and I smirked to myself as I remembered the time me and Dante had drawn cocks all over his and Leon's faces when they'd spent the night at ours. Nemean Lions were infamous for their lazy ways and sleeping habits and we'd shamelessly taken advantage of what deep sleepers they were.

Aside from Plunger, who I was vehemently *not* looking at as he performed a naked yoga routine which involved way too much time with his ass in the air and his junk flopping about, there were a few other inmates who had claimed a solo cell, but not many. Most of the cells were occupied by two residents and most of those were still asleep so it was hard to get a read on their occupants. There were several sheets hanging as makeshift doors like Roary had suggested and I had to admit that that looked like a good idea. Especially as my gaze fell back on Plunger as he pulled his toothbrush from his wash bag and dipped it into his toilet before starting to brush.

"For the love of the moon," I snarled, baring my teeth in disgust as he grinned at me.

"I like to brush four times a day, but we can only go to the shower blocks twice," he explained, the toothbrush wagging in his mouth as he spoke.

Probably because you've got the taste of shit in your mouth from doing that!

My stomach turned but I forced myself not to utter another word, heeding Roary's warning not to rile him up. But that was pretty damn hard when it came to that kind of behaviour.

The sound of the bell ringing to signal the guards' arrival saved me from the horror of his shit show and I sighed in pleasure as I got to my feet.

I rolled my shoulders back and started hopping up and down on the spot to loosen up my limbs just in case anyone decided to test me before breakfast. I couldn't afford to let my guard drop for a second around here.

The sound of the guards beginning the count downstairs rang up to me and I moved back to the bars. I leaned against them to get a look over the railing to the coop below where all the low ranking prisoners were lining up and approaching the guards to get their faces scanned as they took the count.

I sighed impatiently as I waited for them to get through the prisoners in the coop, leaning my forehead against the cold bars.

"If you don't like predictable and boring routines, you've come to the wrong place," Roary said through a yawn and I tilted my head to try and get a look at him in the cell beside mine. It was impossible but as he draped his bare arms through the bars I focused on them, my gaze lingering on the strength of his muscles for a moment before I looked away again.

"Good thing I don't plan on hanging around for long then," I muttered.

Officer Cain marched up the stairs in his black uniform with his dark hair swept away from his face harshly and a scowl in place that said he wasn't in any better of a mood than he'd been earlier. Hastings followed him, looking less like death warmed up and more like a kid on his way to a theme park. His gaze slipped to me and I gave my little choir boy the kind of smile that was really too sweet for me, though the sparkle in his eyes said he didn't know it.

They walked along the opposite gangway first, Cain scanning the prisoners on Plunger's side of the block before turning and stalking along our side.

His gaze was hard as he reached me, but he didn't utter a word as he held the device up to scan my face. A green twelve appeared a moment later and he strode on to check that my other neighbour was still in his cell.

When he reached the end of the line, he lifted his radio to confirm we were all accounted for and a long buzz sounded as all of the cell doors slid open.

I stepped out to join the masses heading for the Mess Hall and was almost trampled by the beast who occupied cell eleven as he stomped past me.

"Hey to you, too," I muttered as he didn't so much as acknowledge me. He was at least seven foot tall and almost as broad, his huge frame damn near bursting the seams of the orange jumpsuit he'd squeezed himself into. Inmates scattered as he barrelled through them and I couldn't help but stare a little as he lumbered away.

"I see you met Pudding," Roary commented lightly, moving to walk at my side as we followed the behemoth towards the exit.

"Pudding? Has he got a sweet tooth or something?"

"You could say that. Suffice to say that you should *never* try and take anything from his cell without asking. But if you want a friend for life then just hand over your puddings. Hell, he's even pleased to accept the empty pots if you wanna eat it first."

"Seriously?" I asked in confusion.

"Yeah, he's a Monolrian Bear Shifter. They replenish their magic by stocking their home with supplies and hibernating, which means his cell is basically a trash heap."

I snorted a laugh and reached out to brush my hand against Roary's on instinct. Werewolves were pack animals and we were tactile by nature, though I was nowhere near as full on as some of my cousins could be. For example, I was perfectly content in my own bed and didn't feel the need to sleep in a pack huddle. But it was in me to touch and hug more than other Fae and sometimes it was hard to stop myself from giving into those urges, even when they put me in the firing line for looking like an obsessed idiota.

Roary cut me a glance but he didn't comment, hooking his pinky finger through mine for a moment before releasing me again. It was innocent enough but my stomach flipped over and my heart leapt like he'd just kissed me, not brushed his fingers over mine.

Grow the fuck up, Rosalie. He's never been the one for you!

I opened my mouth to ask something else about Pudding as I fought off a mother fucking blush, but I was saved as Cain barked my name. Or rather, my number.

"I won't call you again, Twelve!" he snarled as I drew closer to him in the crowd and I slipped away from Roary to join Officer Bastardo.

"Yes?" I asked sweetly, offering my choir boy a smile too.

"When was the last time you ate?" Cain demanded.

"Before I was caught. Yesterday lunch time," I replied with a shrug which was punctuated by my stomach growling.

Cain's eyes lit cruelly and I fought against the urge to curse him as I got the distinct impression he was about to ruin my meal.

"Let's start your work detail now then. Instead of eating breakfast, you can help prepare it. Kitchens seems like a good fit for you," Cain growled.

"But ah- is that the best idea?" Hastings asked hesitantly. "Putting an Oscura in the kitchens? It's all Lunars in there. Shadowbrook will kill her if-"

"Are you afraid of the Lunar Brotherhood or their leader, Twelve?" Cain

77

demanded, his eyes hard.

"The Brotherhood are the ones who should fear *me*," I replied easily. I wasn't going to balk at the idea of being thrown to the Wolves. Which was an accurate description if I was about to come face to face with Ethan Shadowbrook. He was the leader of the Lunar Brotherhood inside the prison and the Alpha of their Wolf pack. He had a reputation for acting first and asking questions later, not least with the women he screwed. Rumour had it he'd had more than half the women in this prison in his bed within the first year of his sentence. Aside from his manwhore tendencies, he was brutal and bloodthirsty and if the photographs I'd seen of him were anything to go by, he was hot as all hell too.

The Lunar Brotherhood and the Oscura Clan had been enemies for as long as anyone in our generation could remember, but if my cousin Dante could bend the rules as far as they were concerned then so could I. And I already had a plan in mind for the Lunar Alpha. I needed him on side if I wanted my idea to work. I needed to have the entire prison under my sway, which meant uniting a few of the biggest gangs in here to give us unquestionable numbers.

I was already strengthening my ties with Roary which meant I was making an ally of him too. He ran one of the most notorious gangs in here, though the Shades weren't as flashy about their power as the rest of the gangs. But his followers were loyal to their bones and there was nothing wrong with subtlety. It was impossible to count the members of his gang. I hadn't even seen one yet myself, but I knew we were surrounded by them all the same. They'd make themselves known if they were needed.

So I was making progress towards merging the gangs already. And though the idea of blending the Lunars and Oscuras sounded insane, I'd done my research on the other gang leaders in here and I didn't trust them one bit. They were devious killers who would just as easily cut your throat as stick to any bargain they'd struck. Ethan was a Wolf like me. If I could win him over on an animal level then our bond would be unbreakable. I just had to hope I could surpass the major problem of us being sworn rivals.

Cain caught my arm and drew me through the crowd, shouting warnings to make everyone move and let us through. Hastings fought to keep up and we finally made it to the bridge which led out of the cell block.

Cain drew me over it before anyone else was allowed to leave and he made a beeline for a small elevator which stood in the centre of the grey corridor outside. He hit the call button, activating it with magic and pushing me inside as it arrived.

I turned back towards the doors just in time to see the prisoners disappear into a huge stairwell across from us and start climbing.

The elevator ascended quickly and I waited to find out what new game my C.O. had in store for me.

The doors slid open on level two and we arrived in the Mess Hall before anyone else. For a moment, I looked around at the unfamiliar space, trying to get my bearings. Cain marched me between rows of metal benches with plastic seats as the scent of bleach assaulted my nose without giving me much chance to take it all in.

He headed all the way to the far end of the enormous space and pushed through a set of double doors where the scent of oatmeal filled the air and around twenty men and women were working to prepare the food.

"Fresh meat!" Cain called, drawing the attention of the room full of Lunars. I hadn't spotted Ethan yet, but he must have been somewhere nearby. "Look after her for me, Shadowbrook. I've got my own breakfast to eat."

I glanced around at Cain as he backed out of the room, his eyes sparkling with malice. Hastings seemed inclined to protest about leaving me here and I offered him a sweet smile. *Poor little choir boy, worried about me already?*

He clearly didn't have the balls to talk out against Cain twice on this though so he backed away with an apologetic smile and the doors swung shut again behind them, leaving me to the mercy of my mortal enemies. Not that they knew that of course.

In his excitement to leave me here, Cain had forgotten to tell them I was an Oscura. And what they didn't know couldn't hurt me.

I glanced between the closest Fae dismissively then strode into the kitchen with a swagger in my step and my hair swinging down my spine.

"You can start chopping onions for the lunch," a girl commanded, pointing me toward a bucket full of onions.

I swept my gaze over the symbols stitched to her breast pocket. Centaur, water Element, irrelevant.

"No," I replied, waving a hand at her dismissively.

She bristled angrily but I just kept walking.

The kitchen was huge, long metal work surfaces taking up the centre of the space with ovens and stoves dominating one wall and a door which led through to the pantry in the back corner.

I checked the room one more time, studying the Fae in it again as I ignored the curious looks I was getting. My aura was powerful enough to make them hesitate instead of coming at me and I could probably count on having another minute or so before one of them grabbed a hold of their balls and tried to rein me in for a second time.

Ethan wasn't in sight so I headed towards the only place he could hide.

The pantry door opened easily enough and I stepped into the dimly lit space without bothering to knock.

A deep growl sounded and a huge girl stepped in front of me, barring my way on. "Get out of here, pup," she snarled. "Before I have to break something."

I sized up Ethan's Beta with interest, her dreadlocks pulled back into a bun and her dark features set in a wall of don't-fuck-with-me. She certainly had a dominating presence and I could tell she was a Werewolf without having to look at the symbol on her chest, but I doubted she'd pose me too much of an issue if I had to force her aside. But like Aunt Bianca always said, you won more friends with honey than lemon.

"I was just hoping I could grab an apple or something," I said innocently. "I haven't eaten since before I was arrested and I'm *ravenous.*"

The Beta opened her lips to chew me out, but another voice spoke before she could.

"I've got something you can wrap your lips around here, love," a guy called. "Give us some privacy, Harper."

Harper eyed me irritably for another moment before stepping out into the kitchen and closing the pantry door behind her.

I took another few steps into the room until I rounded the enormous freezer and I took in the large pantry with interest as I finally found what I'd been looking for.

Ethan Shadowbrook was perched on what looked like a heap of potatoes at the back of the wide space and I moved towards him as my eyes adjusted to the dim light.

I could feel his gaze scraping over me as I moved and my inner Wolf lifted her head like she'd caught the scent of something truly worthy of her attention.

My heart beat faster as I came to stand before him, my eyes scraping over the white tank top he wore, his jumpsuit tied at his waist to reveal the sleeves of intricate tattoos which lined his powerful arms.

He leaned forward with his elbows on his knees as he assessed me just as keenly as I was him, causing a little cascade of potatoes to roll to the floor by my feet. His dark blonde hair was swept away from his face, accentuating the strong lines of his jaw and cheekbones and his piercingly blue eyes caught me in their snare and reeled me in.

I could feel the power of our inner Wolves rising to the surface of our skin to assess each other, and I released a slow breath as adrenaline trickled through my limbs. This wasn't just some top dog built for posturing, he was a true Alpha, someone who could pose me an actual challenge, someone I could get into trouble over.

"My, my, what big eyes you have," he teased as he continued to keep me captive in his gaze.

"I thought you had something for me to eat?" I asked, fighting against the desire to move closer to him. That was what he wanted, to reel me in like every other girl he'd fucked and ditched. But that wasn't me. I didn't chase anyone.

"Get on your knees and I'll give it to you."

I laughed, tossing my hair over my shoulder and turning my back on him. It was damn hard to do, but I wasn't going to bow to this Alpha. And I was willing to bet no one usually turned their back on him; I certainly couldn't remember the last time it had happened to me. It was one of the most insulting things a Fae could do to another Fae, it said that you didn't see them as a threat and I was pretty damn sure he'd hate that idea.

I headed away from him, setting my gaze on a crate of apples as the sound of a potato avalanche filled the room and announced Ethan getting to his feet.

I kept walking as I felt him closing in on me, snatching an apple from the crate just before he caught me and whirled me around. His hands landed on either side of me, gripping the edge of the crate and boxing me in.

A growl escaped him as he leaned in close to me and a shiver ran down my spine. "What's your name?" he demanded.

"A name can hold a lot of power," I replied. "Maybe you should just call me Twelve."

"And maybe you should be bowing to the ruler of this place," he said icily.

"Oh? Who's that then?"

"Me. I'm number one around here," he replied cockily, like someone who really believed that and I couldn't really deny that his arrogant bravado was turning me on.

"I don't bow to anyone," I replied evenly, refusing to show him my cards as he hounded into my personal space, his hips pressing flush to mine.

"I don't think you understand," Ethan said darkly, lifting his jumpsuit where it hung from his hip and unfolding it so that I could see the number one standing proudly beside his Werewolf symbol and the Elemental sign for water.

"Oh wow," I breathed and his lips twitched. "I didn't realise you were a water Elemental. Do you like getting wet then?"

A dark laugh escaped him and I had to bite my lip to stop myself from leaning into him as my muscles tightened at that sound. I had thought getting close to the Lunar Alpha would be difficult but it wasn't. It was harder to keep away.

"That smart mouth will get you into trouble around here," Ethan growled.

"Is that a promise?" I took a bite from my apple and he inhaled deeply as he leaned in to me, his nose pushing into my hair.

"Do you want it to be?"

My inner Wolf howled *yes*, she was already panting with need in a way that made my fingers tremble where I gripped the apple, but I forced myself to hold back. If he wanted me, he could do the chasing.

"I haven't decided yet." I took another bite from my apple and Ethan shifted forward, biting into it too. I inhaled sharply as his hands moved from the crate behind me to grip my waist and he pinned me firmly in his gaze.

"I beg to disagree." He plucked the apple from my hand and tossed it away. "Give me your name," he demanded, like he just *had* to know it.

The Wolf inside me was scratching at the confines of my skin, aching to get out and prove herself to him. She wanted to challenge him, fight him, make him bend to her desire and I was having trouble holding her in check. There was something about this stranger which called to me like the song of the stars themselves. I wasn't sure if it was fate or pheromones, but my body was aching to find out.

"Earn it," I dared him and his piercing blue eyes glimmered with the challenge.

He caught my chin in his grip and tugged me close, his lips brushing mine for a fleeting second before I turned my cheek and he kissed that instead. Ethan growled as he ran his mouth down my neck and I gasped as pleasure raced beneath my skin from the rake of his lips against my flesh.

His hands found my jumpsuit and he pushed it off of my shoulders in a move so casual, he had to have had *way* too much practice doing it. I growled at the thought of that, my Wolf not wanting him near any other women despite the fact that I'd literally just met him.

I let him push the jumpsuit off of me, the material falling from my shoulders and cascading down my thighs to pool around my feet.

Ethan growled as his hands brushed along my bare thighs before he shifted them up beneath my tank top, his calloused fingers moving over the firm muscles of my stomach.

Pleasure chased the movements of his hands on my skin and it took me a moment to realise I was touching him too, my hands griping his firm biceps as I explored every curve of his huge arms.

I could have tried to keep playing him, but we both knew where this was heading now and it seemed pointless to dance around it. I caught his chin in my grip as his mouth made it to my collar bone and yanked him back up so that I could kiss him like I ached to.

Ethan growled hungrily as he kissed me, his tongue pushing between my lips in a firm demand which I gave in to without any protest. He tasted like honey and sin. I shouldn't have been kissing him like this. I certainly shouldn't have been about to do anything else with him. He was born to be my enemy but he was my equal too. I could feel it in the pit of my soul. Wolves spent their lives hunting for a mate who could equal them and I'd all but given up on finding another of my kind who could rise to the challenge, but now here he was. A man with a tattoo on his arm branding him as someone who I could never be with. Someone who had sworn to fight against my family to the bitter end. And yet he was also someone who was making me feel things I'd begun to believe I never would with another of my kind.

When I'd come in here I'd been hoping to trick him, charm him, maybe bedazzle him a little whenever I had access to my magic…or a lot… until he was pliable enough to bend to my will. To unite the packs. I'd planned to make him chase me around with half promises, making him ache for me with no chance of me actually fulfilling them. But I hadn't counted on this. I hadn't even entertained the idea that he might have been a Wolf strong enough to match me, to challenge me and to make me work to bind him to me rather than just falling at my feet like a lower ranking pack member would.

I kicked my boots and socks off as I stepped out of my jumpsuit and his grip on me tightened.

I hadn't meant for this, but now that it had begun it felt like I'd have a better chance persuading the wind not to blow than I would in trying to stop us from coming together.

Ethan pulled away from me and yanked his tank off, revealing more of his body to me and making me growl with need as I moved towards him again, kissing him as I ran my hands down his chest. He gripped my ass beneath the moon awful panties, dragging me against him so that I could feel just how hard he was.

He hooked his thumbs into my panties and bent low to drag them off of me, his fingers running down the full length of my legs as he helped me out of them and ended up kneeling before me.

He looked up into my eyes with a heat in his gaze that had me aching for him and I had to fight not to pant with desire.

"What's your name?" he demanded like he *needed* to know and I laughed, dragging my white tank top off to complete the job he'd started and pulling the shapeless bra with it so that I stood entirely naked before him.

"I thought you were meant to be earning it?" I teased, pushing my hands into his perfectly styled hair and messing it up without giving one shit.

Ethan smirked at me, standing suddenly and gripping the backs of my thighs as he lifted me onto a closed crate beside the apples.

He dropped to his knees again, pushing my thighs apart as he caught my ankle in his grip and placed his mouth against it. He eyed me greedily as he slowly started moving up my leg, licking and kissing his way towards the centre of me and driving me insane with need.

I arched my back, gripping the edge of the crate as the anticipation drove me wild and he took his sweet fucking time about getting to the point.

When his mouth landed on me, I cried out, begging him to give me anything and everything as he began moving his tongue over the perfect spot at the apex of my thighs.

I moaned again, shifting my hips in a rhythm against his mouth that had me breathless as I could feel myself tightening already.

Ethan growled in satisfaction as I moaned for him and he brought his hand up my thigh too, pushing two fingers inside me as he felt me moving closer to oblivion.

My inner Wolf was still aching, begging for more, for me to dominate him and control him and I fisted my hands in his hair as I tried to give her what she wanted. I ground my hips into his movements and my toes curled as I felt my muscles tightening in anticipation.

He growled hungrily, dragging his tongue over me again as his fingers moved in the perfect rhythm.

I damn near howled as my climax ripped through me and I fell back against the lid of the crate panting as I released my grip on Ethan's hair and he drew his fingers back out of me with a satisfied smirk on his face.

My head was spinning as the sound of his jumpsuit and boxers hitting the floor found me and suddenly he was looming over me, his dick driving into my thigh with need as he looked into my eyes.

"Tell me," he snarled, knowing full well he'd earned his answer.

"Rosalie," I breathed, not offering a last name.

Ethan's mouth hooked into a smile as he reached out to paint his fingers along the lines of my tattoo. A huge rose vine crawled up the left side of my body, starting on my thigh and finishing on my neck, each of its buds and flowers representing a member of my family. My skin tingled as he continued to toy with the tattoo and he eyed the ink on my skin with a feral kind of hunger.

"Rosalie," Ethan groaned and I had to admit my name sounded damn good on his lips. "Now you're about to find out what it's like to be owned by the top dog."

Ethan gripped my hips and flipped me over, bending me over the wooden crate before him and fisting a hand in my hair as he prepared to take.

A growl escaped my lips. That was how Alphas fucked their bitches, but I sure as hell wasn't one of them. I was an Alpha in my own right and no Wolf was going to bend me over a crate and claim me like some common pack whore.

I shifted back suddenly, forcing him back a step as I pushed myself upright and I turned in the cage of his arms. His blue eyes widened in surprise like he'd never had a girl call the shots on him before. But if he wanted to fuck a pack whore then I was sure he had plenty of them sniffing about. And I was an entirely different breed of beast.

I kissed him hard, tasting my lust and the lingering sweetness of apple on his lips as I pressed my hands against his chest to make him back up.

He resisted for a moment then gave in as our kiss deepened.

I wasn't sure where I was pushing him to, only that I was going to take charge of this if it was going to happen. His hands were all over me as he backed up, exploring every curve of my body as his flesh lit a fire beneath my skin.

Ethan gasped in surprise as his foot caught on one of the potatoes which had fallen across the floor and he fell backwards, his tight grip on me meaning I went down with him. We landed on the mountain of potatoes with laughter tearing from our lips and his hand moved to cup my cheek as he looked into my eyes.

"What are you doing, little she-wolf?" Ethan demanded as I pushed him further back onto the mound and shifted so that I was straddling his hips.

"Haven't you ever let the girl take charge, Ethan?" I purred, my hands sliding down his chest until I was gripping the hard length of his dick.

He began to shake his head and I smiled darkly as I slid my body onto his, gasping as he filled every space inside me.

I gripped his shoulders, kissing him again as I started to ride him and he growled with a deep satisfaction as he watched the movements of my body on his, his hands roaming my flesh.

I started moving faster and potatoes tumbled all over the floor as Ethan shifted upright to steal another kiss from me.

His hands fisted in my hair as I upped my pace and his hips matched mine thrust for thrust.

We were both panting, sweating, each of us pushing the other as hard as we could like this was more than just sex, it was a test. I couldn't remember the last time I'd been with a man who could keep up with me and I moaned loudly as Ethan managed it with ease.

He gripped my hips as he tried to take control of my movements and I snarled at him, knocking his hands off of me as I regained control again.

He growled right back but moved his hands so that his thumb started circling against my clit and his other hand toyed with my nipple. I gasped as

I felt myself coming undone, gripping the back of his neck so tightly that my nails cut into his flesh as pleasure cascaded through my body again.

I cried out, tipping my head back as my body fell apart and was remade in his arms. Ethan growled my name as he poured himself inside me, finding his release with mine.

He fell back onto the potatoes, panting as he dragged me down with him and I lay on top of him, listening to the thundering of his heartbeat as I pressed my ear to his chest and we tried to catch our breath.

"Fucking hell, Rosalie, where did you come from?" Ethan breathed, his fingers sliding through my hair and sending tingles dancing across my scalp.

I laughed as I forced myself to sit up, looking down at him as he laid beneath me and really liking the view of him submitting like that.

A smirk toyed around his lips, letting me know that there was no way in hell he was actually rolling over for me, but a girl could dream.

I pushed myself to my feet and headed back to pull my clothes on. Ethan followed me at a slower pace, moving to wrap his arms around my waist as I finished dressing.

"You need to join a pack in here, love," he breathed in my ear, nuzzling into my hair.

"I do," I agreed, not mentioning the fact that it wouldn't be his.

"Where's Twelve? If she's still alive, I need to take her back to her cell block now!" Cain's voice boomed from somewhere in the kitchen and I sighed as I realised he wasn't done with me yet. That guy seriously needed a new hobby. I didn't want to be his latest pet project, but it seemed like I wasn't going to have a choice in the matter.

"What cell block are you in?" Ethan asked, not seeming inclined to let me leave.

I turned in his arms, tiptoeing up to press a kiss to his lips and lingering in the afterglow of what we'd just done for a moment.

"I'll see you around," I said, slipping out of his arms and grabbing a fresh apple from the crate.

"That's it?" he asked as I walked away from him and I paused by the pantry door to look back at him, drinking in the sight of his naked flesh.

"Were you hoping for a thank you?" I teased. "Or just a pat on the head for being a good boy?"

Ethan growled as he pulled his clothes back on, but the light which was dancing in his eyes told me he didn't hate me mocking him as much as he should have.

"Catch you later." I smirked at him as I took a bite from my apple then headed out into the kitchen.

Cain was still hunting for me with a scowl on his face and I took my time walking over to join him as I continued on my apple.

His lips twitched with irritation as he took in my appearance and the lack of flesh wounds and I had to bite my tongue on laughing at the spectacular failure of his plan.

His gaze slid over me, taking in my just fucked hair and flushed cheeks as I finished my apple but if he had any idea of what I'd been doing, he didn't react to it. More likely he thought I'd been pushed about a bit or engaged in a Wolf tussle.

The Lunar kitchen workers were all cleaning up after the breakfast rush and I could see some guards lingering in the Mess Hall, clearly waiting to take them back to their cell block while Cain waited to return me to mine.

I spotted a Wolf near the door as I closed in on my C.O. and caught the whiff of a low ranking member of the pack.

I tossed my apple core at the Wolf and it bounced off of his arm before falling to the floor.

"Pick that up," I commanded, letting the Alpha tone ring in my voice. The Wolf did as I commanded before he even got the chance to consider it and I smirked to myself. The Lunar pack would fall into line like dominoes. All I had to do was secure my alliance with Ethan. Which really wouldn't be all that bad if we continued in the way we'd begun...

I moved to Cain's side with a sweet smile and he instantly snatched my arm, pulling me out of the kitchens and half forcing me to jog as he dragged me back towards my cell block.

"I see that you're not suited to kitchen work after all, Twelve," he said in a low voice as we walked. "But I'm sure I can come up with something even better for you."

ETHAN

PRISONER #1

CHAPTER EIGHT

I couldn't get Rosalie's big brown eyes out of my head, especially the little flecks of silver which ran across them like brush strokes. I had a thing for eyes and hers were something special. But I didn't usually fixate on a girl after I'd claimed her. So why wouldn't she get out of my damn head?

I sat on my throne at the top of my cell block. It was made from a bunk that someone had ripped out of cell six and the guards hadn't bothered to do anything about it. Pillows lined it, given to me as gifts by my pack and the rest of the block. Of all the prisoners in here, ninety percent of them were in my gang, the Lunar Brotherhood, and ten percent were unallied. That was no coincidence. If the guards put Oscura Clan scum in here, they knew they'd end up dead before the day was out. So they tended to keep us separate as often as they could.

I wondered if Rosalie would be open to transferring to this block and joining my pack. I could probably pull some strings with the warden. She liked me – like most women did. Rosalie needed her own kind around her and I didn't want her enrolling in the Oscura pack before I could get my hands on her. She had the signs of an Alpha about her. And if that was true, I'd have to force her to bow to me. But once she was beneath my heel, she'd be more than happy to please me. And I wouldn't have to give up my usual playthings either. My kind were polyamorous by nature and I liked my fair share of the Wolves in my pack, but I had more than Werewolves aligned to me. There were pretty Sirens and sexy ass Harpies, sweet little Pegasuses and hot as fuck

Sphinxes. I had my pick of the lot. And I picked them. A lot.

One of the Pegasuses in question headed toward me, moving through the sea of my pack who were lounging around at my feet. I was running my fingers over Harper's shoulders while she hummed softly. She was my Beta and always had such a soothing presence, but the Pegasus suddenly had all of my attention.

A sideways smile hooked up my lips and I rose from my seat, my Wolves parting for me as I walked toward her. She was blonde with the kind of pouty mouth I loved to silence. She was a talker and she'd definitely told me her name a bunch of times, but I couldn't say for sure what it was. *Lilly?*

"Hey, love," I said, looping an arm around her petite waist and steering her back away from my pack and toward my cell.

She started telling me about her morning, droning on and I nodded, smiling as I pretended to listen. Her pouty lips didn't look quite as tempting as I remembered. My mind snagged on Rosalie's mouth instead and I forced the memory away as I guided – *Emily??* – into my cell.

"-and then Abigale was like, oh my stars did you just tell Kimmi to go stuff that cookie up her kooch? And I was like, she's got enough room in that kooch for a whole packet of cookies, Abigale."

I forced a laugh, nodding again as we made it into my cell and I lifted the sheet to cover the bars and give us some privacy.

I frowned as – *Jackie??* - started unbuttoning her jumpsuit, getting a flashback of yesterday with Rosalie riding my dick like we were the last Fae on earth and we were trying to repopulate the shit out of it. Fuck me, that girl was hot. I wanted her body wrapped around me again and again. I needed to lick every inch of her, drive her wild with my tongue until she moaned my name-

"Ethan?"

I snapped out of my reverie, pushing a hand into my blonde hair. "Sorry, love. I've got some stuff on my mind actually. Rain check?"

She sighed, standing up and pressing her hand to my chest as if she could tempt me in. "Are you sure you don't have a little time to spare?"

"No," I sighed, reaching out to brush my thumb across her cheek, doing a good impression of a guy who really gave a shit. "I'll catch you later though. You know you're my one and only."

A smile split across her face and she ducked beneath the sheet covering the door. I drew in a long breath, leaning back against the wall and trying not to get hard over the new Werewolf chick. Again. But shit, she was one helluva fuck. And those eyes…gah they got me all tingly inside. I was all about those Bambi hazels.

I headed out of my cell and found a sad-looking Harpy girl staring at me like I'd just broken her heart. This one was called Elizabeth, I was like eighty percent sure of that.

"Ethan," she said with her lower lip quivering. "Did Shante just come out of your cell?"

Shante, that *was the Pegasus girl's name.*

"We were just talking, love." I moved forward, pulling her close and running my nose up her neck towards her ear. She didn't smell as good as Rosalie. *Dammit, stop thinking about the hot new Wolf.* "You know you're my one and only." She giggled softly as I pulled away and I winked. "I'll catch you later."

I headed back to my pack, throwing myself down onto my throne and letting them climb up around me to soothe me with gentle touches and soft caresses. But there was only one Werewolf I wanted to touch me right then. The one who had made me so hard, I'd had to work not to spill my load the second I was inside her. She'd almost turned me into a bad lay. Which was pretty damn fucking impossible. But I'd held on, drawing more pleasure out of her body than she could probably handle. She was no doubt thinking about me right now too, touching herself while she lay in her bunk. Yeah, I had that effect on girls. They just didn't normally have it on me too.

"Everyone up! You're heading to the Magic Compound!" a guard called and a bell sounded as they lowered the bridge at the bottom of the block.

I leapt off of my throne with a howl of excitement because I was going to see Rosalie in the Compound. And maybe I could plan a little hook up the next time we went to the Order Yard, because I wanted to see her naked again pronto. Scrap that. I *needed* to.

My Wolves fell in to step behind me in the order of their rank as I led the way down the metal stairs to the bottom of the block. Not a single prisoner crossed that bridge before me. They knew the rules. I wasn't just the Alpha of my pack. In this cell block, I was their emperor. And if they didn't like it, they could take it up with my fists and teeth. No one had ever come out looking pretty from a fight with me. Except myself of course.

I made it to the bridge, striding across it past the guards on the other side and into the stairwell. I headed up, up, up, the sound of footfalls ringing around us as every cell block spilled into the stairway on all sides.

We were corralled down the corridor on level three, heading past the pale stone walls toward the huge metal door at the other end.

I got into the queue, impatient as I hunted for Rosalie in the crowd but I couldn't spot her. I grabbed hold of Harper, swivelling her toward me and leaning in close to check my reflection in her eyes. "How do I look?" I demanded.

"Perfect, Alpha," she replied with a grin. But she always said that. I mean sure, it was most-likely true. But she wouldn't tell me if it wasn't.

I smoothed my hair down as I reached the front of the line. The door slid aside to admit me, closing smoothly behind me a second later. I placed my hands into the holes through the glass screen to my right and the officer behind it took hold of my wrists, switching off my power-blocking shackles with the twist of a key. Not enough to unlock them though. Half way turned them off, another turn would set me free entirely.

Officer Lyle eyed me closely, a smile tugging up one corner of his mouth before he swept his hand over his dark red hair. "Morning, Shadowbrook. You're looking well today."

Dude had a boner for me the size of a meteor trail and I was more than happy to play into it. Keeping guards on side was a speciality of mine. That was why I'd never ended up in the hole in all my time here. I could sweet talk my way out of anything. And I wasn't beyond flirting with any guard I had to to keep them from paying too much attention to me beyond my exterior.

"Not as good you, Officer." I leaned towards the glance with a wink. "That boyfriend of yours is a lucky man."

He waved a hand at me with a chuckle then pressed a button and I practically bounded out into the Magic Compound. The fence and ceiling pulsed with blue light. It was a cage of mesh surrounded by guards beyond it, watching us from the outside. There were sets of bleachers around the edges and groups of picnic tables in the middle. They hadn't exactly gotten an interior designer in to make the place look nice, but it was functionable. The entire level contained the Compound and the space was so big that they could never man us too closely. Not unless they wanted to step in here and face the wrath of a thousand psycho inmates' magic. *Unlikely.*

The ground beneath my feet was concrete, the yard intersected by one wall at the centre of it where we could play wall ball. The Lunar Brotherhood gathered on this side of the wall and the Oscura Clan gathered on the other. The rest of the cliques and gangs split between the two sides. A lot of Fae gravitated towards their Orders while others banded together in various alliances. Gustard and his unFae crew of fuckers he called The Watchers were beating the living shit out of a guy already while he was held down with magical vines. The guards shouted out to them in warning, preparing their stun guns and Gustard called off his dogs before they offloaded them. The fact that tattoo-faced fucker had his people attack as a unit instead of Fae on Fae made me sick. He had no pride, he'd sell his soul for power. And there were plenty of people in here willing to follow him because of it. Next to me, the

Alpha of the Oscura Clan and Roary Night and his Shades, he was the other top power in here. And his cutthroat ways had quickly made him an enemy of mine for more reasons than one.

I headed to the long row of benches beside the wall where I always held court, casting shards of ice in my palms and sighing at the release of my magic. If Fae didn't use their power regularly, it could drive them to insanity, and it wasn't worth a prison full of violent nutters to keep us from using it. So this was their solution. Allowing us out here every afternoon to keep us sane. Even the hours I had to wait in between always made me desperate to let my power out. I couldn't imagine what any longer than that would be like. Hence why I worked so hard to keep myself out of isolation. It wasn't that I didn't get up to bad shit in here on a daily basis, I was just clever about it. I made sure nothing led back to me, and if it did, I always had an exit strategy.

I sat down at the centre of the front bench, eyeing the wall as several Fae snatched up the worn red ball which lay beside it and started kicking it. The best thing about that wall, was that it wasn't just a bunch of bricks. It held magic within it which had been put there by an infamous prisoner called Regan Novak who'd gotten himself executed in here a long time ago. He'd been a genius because he'd subtly set up this wall without the guards ever knowing. And so long as you knew the secrets it hid and how to access them, you had a serious advantage in Darkmore.

We called it the Veiled Wall. Anything you needed, you could post it on the wall in secret then other Fae could place offers to take the job, naming their price until you found one you were willing to pay.

I nodded to Harper and she whistled to the Fae playing wall ball. One of them tossed it to her and she passed it to me in turn, her gaze falling to her hands to check the jobs. I spun the smooth ball between my fingers then tossed it back to the players. I only needed to touch it once and the latest jobs revealed themselves to me on the back of my hand. Only I could see them. It was an illusion that fucking genius Novak had come up with and it made it impossible for the guards to detect.

I always got a high breaking the rules. I just didn't know when to quit. Maybe I was addicted to adrenaline. Who really knew? That need lived in me as physically as my damn organs. I just couldn't resist a rush when it came calling.

I scanned my eyes over the jobs on my hand, the words appearing in inky lettering that almost looked the same as the tattoos of my sleeves. There was always the usual thing, inmates wanting food, money, drugs. Then there were the more interesting jobs. Someone wanted a shank made while another wanted a Kripclaw bone. I got my pack to take on jobs if I needed anything. I was getting pretty low on hair product and I knew a guy who knew a guy who could get me a Kripclaw bone in here fairly easily. There was a drop point in commissary where items could be delivered anonymously, packaged up with a number on it that related to the job they'd done.

The ball bounced my way again and I caught it, rubbing my thumb over the plastic and using magic to reply to the Kripclaw job before tossing the ball against the wall to send the message. My offer would appear on the hand of whoever had posted the job. It could even be some Oscura scum for all I knew. But that was how the Veiled Wall worked. Keeping the jobs anonymous meant no one could snitch. And I was willing to accept I was probably doing a job or two for the Oscuras on occasion for the sake of keeping the wall intact. It was valuable beyond belief.

The last of the Fae were filing into the yard and my eyes hooked on Rosalie as if a magnet had drawn me to her. A flash of yesterday flared in my mind, her body bending and bowing to mine then pushing me down, trying to dominate me. She was a wild creature I needed to tame. It had been so long since I'd been challenged, I was itching to make her fall at my feet and howl to the moon just for me. *Soon, love. Soon.*

I growled as I spotted the Oscura pack swarming around her and rage sliced at my gut. Had they claimed her already? Had I really lost her to my enemies so soon?

I pushed to my feet as an Oscura bitch directed Rosalie beyond the wall, but there was no chance in hell I was letting her pass into their territory. She was going to be *mine*.

I strode forward, hunting for the Oscura Alpha in the group. I'd challenge her for Rosalie and claim her as mine right here, right now. *Where the fuck is she?*

I spotted her stepping to the front of the group with her head held high. Amira Kumari was an empty hearted witch who always looked at me like I was a piece of dirt. And she gave me that same look now as she noticed me approaching.

Rosalie moved to the front of the group as she spotted me. "Hi," she said lightly, her brows lifting and amusement dancing in her big eyes. I got captured in them for a moment, offering her a smirk.

"Hey, love. I need a word with your Alpha. No one steals you away from me without a fight." I looked to Amira and she bared her teeth.

"I'm challenging you, Alpha. I want this Wolf as my own," I growled, rolling my shoulders back.

"Oh really?" Amira laughed like I was missing something. "You sure you want this pup in particular?"

"Yeah I'm sure," I said in a snarl.

Rosalie stepped forward, raising her chin, getting right up in my personal space, a twisted sort of smile gracing her lips. She rested her hand to my chest as that psycho smile grew and my heart thudded unevenly under her palm.

What the fuck is happening right now?

"I've already chosen the Oscuras," she said simply. "In fact, it was never really a choice."

I barked a laugh, fucking howled it. Because bull. Shit. She was mine.

"Don't worry, love, I can undo that choice for you real fast." I looked over her shoulder at Amira who looked like she was about to laugh her head off, but Rosalie caught my chin, yanking my head around and setting her jaw.

"I'm Rosalie Oscura of the Oscura Clan. I was raised by Bianca Oscura, mother of the Storm Dragon who I've ridden with in the clouds countless times."

I fell back a step, horror sinking into my bones. My skin crawled with ants as I felt her hands everywhere on me, remembering her touch like a burning flame.

"No." I shook my head, denying it. "No!" I snapped, lurching back into her face and baring my teeth. "Do you know who I am?!" I bellowed and silence rang out in the yard as every single head turned in our direction.

That smile of hers danced, lighting a fucking furnace in my chest as she nodded.

"I knew," she whispered, her breath fluttering over me and tasting too fucking familiar.

"Bitch!" I grabbed her shoulders, throwing her to the ground with a blast of water.

She rolled fast, baring her teeth as she lunged upright again and vines twisted around her palms a second before she shot them at me. Two snapped around my throat and she force me to the ground with a sharp whip of her hands. I coughed against the tightening vines, casting a blade of ice in my palm and slashing right through them.

I leapt back to my feet as adrenaline crashed through my veins and I threw the blade at her with a yell of fury. She dodged aside and one of the Oscura Wolves melted it with a flash of fire as it sailed toward their ranks.

"Hey!" Officer Cain's voice carried to me from the fence behind her, but I was in too much of a rage to stop fighting.

I sent a tsunami of water towards Rosalie and she bent the concrete beneath her feet, ripping it up and building a wall between the wave and her pack. I snarled, racing forward as the wave broke against her magic and casting steps of ice up the broken concrete before leaping over it.

Just as I fell on top of her, Cain offloaded a stun gun and the shot slammed into my chest. I hit the ground as what felt like a thousand volts of electricity raced through my limbs. I bit my tongue as I jerked on the ground, losing sight of everything around me. When the pain finally stopped, I pushed myself up onto all fours, panting heavily as I lifted a hand to my chest to heal myself.

Rosalie was still under the influence of another shot, a scream ripping from her as she writhed on the ground beside me.

"Fix the mess you've made or you'll both lose Compound privileges for a week!" Cain roared and I pushed myself to my feet, my head spinning, but I still managed to laugh at Rosalie on the ground. That whore deserved to hurt for what she'd dared do to me.

She was freed from the electricity at last and her pack rushed forward to help her up. She pushed them back, getting to her feet herself and eyeing me with her upper lip peeled back.

I siphoned the water away around us while she put the concrete back into place. Earth Elementals could only dig so far down in the ground in here before they hit another magical fence, and from the sparking blue light that was shining up from the holes in the concrete, I guessed she'd hit it.

The urge to shift ripped through to my core, but I couldn't do it here. It wasn't possible. And even if it was, I couldn't fight her properly with the guards watching. But I was sure as shit not gonna let this lie.

As she finished fixing the ground, I strode towards her and cast a circular wall of ice around us along with a silencing bubble. I knew we only had a few moments before Cain melted it away; I could already feel the heat of his magic pushing at mine. But I was powerful enough to keep it intact long enough to have this conversation.

"Why would you do this?" I demanded and she batted her lashes like she was entirely innocent of anything.

"Do what Ethan?"

"You know what!" I fought the urge to attack her again, starting to pace as I clawed a hand through my hair. "I'm your enemy, why would you even want to fuck me? You knew who I was!"

She approached me with her head cocked to one side and something about her expression almost disarmed me. I could taste her magic in the air and feel the feather-light brush of it against my skin. My anger started to soften and I turned to her with a need in me so desperate it almost broke me. She was a stranger and yet she felt so familiar. Like I knew her from some other life.

She reached for me, stroking her fingers across my arm and her magic tingled gently against my skin. "Honestly? I was drawn to you...don't you feel this connection between us? We're perfectly matched."

A lump rose in my throat and the kiss of her magic slid further up my skin. It took me a second longer to realise she was trying to bedazzle me and I roared in anger, shoving her back a step. I let Cain's magic burn through my ice and water cascaded down around us, splashing over the ground.

I pointed in her face as a dangerous growl rumbled through my chest.

My pack had gathered close and hers were eyeing us up as if this might break into an all out war. But that wasn't what I wanted even if we could have gotten away with it here. I wanted it to be *me* on *her* in Wolf form. I was going to tear her throat out and show her who the true Alpha of this prison was.

"I'll see you in the Order Yard," I hissed, painting on a smirk despite the fact that everything inside me felt hollow, dead.

"I'll be waiting," she said easily.

I stood my ground, watching as she moved into the Oscura pack with her head held high and they headed beyond the wall. She threw me a glance over her shoulder before she stepped beyond it and those large brown eyes cut deep into my soul. She'd made a fool of me. Fucked me like a whore and for what? To see me shatter now before her?

I clenched my fists as I returned to the benches, my pack swarming around me as they growled and chatted about the new Oscura bitch. She was beautiful, dark and utterly psychotic. And if she wanted to play dirty then she'd picked the wrong guy to fuck with. Because no one played dirtier than me.

ROSALIE

PRISONER #12

CHAPTER NINE

At the end of my second day of living at the pleasure of the Celestial Throne in the sanctuary for deeply darkened Fae which they called Darkmore Penitentiary, we were finally called out for a session in the Order exercise yard.

I couldn't remember the last time I'd gone a day without shifting into my Werewolf form and it felt a lot like having someone cut off one of my limbs. I wasn't whole without my Wolf to call on. I wasn't *me*. But now we were finally on our way up to the top floor of this underground prison and even better than that – I was about to see the *sky!*

Each Order of Fae needed something different to replenish their magic supplies and as I'd burned mine low fighting with Ethan in the Magic Compound, I was extra excited that this session was being held at night. As a Werewolf, I needed to run beneath the light of the moon to replenish my magic. Any moon would do, though of course I loved the extra rush of power I got from a full moon on a clear night, but even a total eclipse during a thunder storm would boost my power reserves. It was all about running in my Wolf form while the moon was overhead, and to say I loved it would be selling my own feelings short.

Other Orders required their own methods to replenish: a Dragon needed to be in contact with gold for a prolonged period of time, a Medusa needed to look into a mirror and gaze upon their reflection, a Pegasus needed to fly through the clouds. And of course the parasitic Orders just stole magic from other Fae; Sirens fed on your emotions to drain you of your magic, their gifts allowing them control over how you felt and Vampires just sucked it right out of your veins, assuming they could overpower you to do so. Not that many Vampires had managed that with me.

We got five Order Yard sessions a week, each held at slightly different times of day as there were Orders who required different things from the heavens to boost their magic. As a Nemean Lion, Roary needed to sunbathe to replenish his so this night time session wouldn't do much for his magic, but he'd chosen to join me all the same with the promise of showing me where the Oscura Wolf pack met for their runs and giving me a tour of the Order Yard for good measure.

"Are you ready to run with the big boys, pup?" Roary breathed in my ear, sneaking up on me as I crossed the gangway towards the exit.

"You should be more worried about whether or not the big boys are ready to run with me," I purred, turning to look at him. *Gah,* he was even more attractive than I remembered from my teenage fantasies. Honestly, how was it fair that someone could have such perfectly chiselled features and eyes like molten gold? It was no wonder I was always blushing around him. He looked like some kind of Demigod, especially with that dark hair spilling around his face and the light catching in his eyes...

"Rosa? I asked you a question." Roary frowned at me and I cursed internally.

"Sorry, I was thinking about...pudding..."

"What do you want?" a deep voice asked.

I damn near flinched out of my skin as the enormous Bear Shifter loomed over me, appearing like a damn ghost out of nowhere. Roary Night's pretty face had me so moon addled that even my instincts were going to shit. *Dammit.*

"Want?" I asked in confusion as the Bear Shifter waited for a reply. Roary barely concealed a laugh and I cut him a glare.

"You said you were thinking about me," the Bear growled impatiently, looking at me like I was being purposefully dumb.

"No I didn't. I said-"

"That you were thinking about Pudding. *I'm* Pudding. So what do you want?" he demanded and it took my brain a full five seconds to figure out what the fuck he was on about.

"Oh...no, sorry. Not Pudding like *you,* Pudding. I meant pudding like the little pots of-"

Pudding turned and walked away from me without another word and my eyebrows rose as I watched him go. Fae didn't turn their back on me. Like, *ever.* They knew better than to toss that kind of insult my way and expect to get away with it, but the Bear Shifter who lived in the cell beside mine clearly gave no shits. And I kinda wanted to be his best friend because of it.

"I should kick your ass for that!" I called after him. I could have sworn he snorted derisively as he just kept walking away from me and I took a step to follow.

Roary's hand caught mine before I could finish that thought and my damn pulse leapt as he kept hold of it.

"Pudding is a good friend to have," he murmured. "But you'll have to learn to put up with his shit if you're going to win him over."

"Why would I care about winning him over?" I asked. "He snores really loud and has a cell full of trash. What kind of friend is that?"

"Just trust me, little pup. I know a bit more about this place than you do."

I pursed my lips and stared after Pudding again as he carved a path through the rest of the Fae heading out of the cell block for time in the Order Yard.

"Fine," I agreed. And it had nothing to do with the fact that Roary was still holding my hand and it felt seven shades of sinful.

"Give him your pudding cups," he urged.

"You want me to work for his friendship?" I asked as we started walking again.

"It's worth having friends in this place," Roary said with a nod before retrieving his hand. Not that I'd been trying to keep it. But I should have let go myself.

I ignored the damn blush which was creeping onto my cheeks yet again and shrugged. "Okay then, he can have my puddings. That guy will be following me around with starry eyes before you know it."

"Good luck with that." Roary snorted like he didn't think I could manage it and my blood lit with the dare.

Challenge accepted, stronzo.

We headed downstairs and made our way onto the bridge which led out of the cell block, but I frowned as I noticed at least half of the Fae in our block hanging back.

"Aren't they coming too?" I asked and Roary followed my gaze.

"Exercise up in the Order Yard is optional," he said with a shrug.

"Why? Who wouldn't want to have the freedom to shift into their Order form?"

"Weaklings who might get eaten," he joked.

"Seriously?"

"Well... yeah, we might get set loose up on the top level, allowed to release our inner beasts and flex our Order muscles, but you're also putting yourself at risk. It's where most of the deaths occur in Darkmore. The Guards don't come up to the top floor with us and the dome is only partially monitored via CCTV. Besides, even if they saw something happening, they wouldn't intervene, they just like to know who killed who for their records and so they know who to send to the hole."

"It almost sounds like real freedom. Is it fucked up that I'm ecstatic about that?" I asked with a grin.

"I wouldn't expect any less from you, little pup," he teased. "All of that freedom comes with a catch of course; you enter at your own risk."

All of the members of our cell block started marching up the huge stone stairwell which carved its way through the centre of the prison and we followed eagerly. We passed the floors for the Magic Compound and Mess Hall and more inmates moved to join us as they abandoned their evening free time in favour of real free time up on the top floor.

When we reached the top of the stairs, we spilled out into a wide space where six huge elevators stood waiting on either side of us, their doors closed and alluring.

"Keep an eye on the timer!" a guard bellowed over the crowd, drawing my attention to her. "This session will last four hours and if you don't make it back to the elevators before they descend then you will be left up there when the air is sucked from the dome and you *will* die. No one will come out there to rescue you, no one gives a shit. You're Fae. If you choose to head out into the yard then you do it at your own risk, so if you're changing your mind or having doubts then head on back down to your cell blocks now!"

A trickle of adrenaline tingled through my skin at the thought of that. We were going to be alone up there. Free. Or as close to it as we could get while locked in this place. And I couldn't fucking wait.

I bounced on my heels, grinning up at Roary as the doors to the elevators slid open and the two of us strode straight into the closest one.

"No turning back now, little pup," he purred in my ear.

"Do you think you can keep up with me out there?" I teased as we waited for the elevator to fill.

"A Lion is a lot bigger than a Wolf pup," he replied cockily, pushing a hand through his mane of dark hair.

"Not as fast though," I reminded him.

"We'll see."

The doors closed and the elevator started rising as I damn near peed myself with excitement. A fine mist poured from vents at the top of the elevator as it climbed and I groaned aloud as I felt the chains being lifted from my inner Wolf as the Order Suppressant in my veins was neutralised, setting me free.

I shoved my way between the crowd of prisoners who surrounded me, snarling at any who considered objecting until me and Roary were stood before the doors.

The elevator bounced to a halt and the doors finally slid open. I howled in excitement, snatching his hand and dragging him out before the doors had even fully parted.

Roary laughed darkly, letting me pull him along as we found ourselves in a huge brick building which was open to the elements on both ends. Rows of lockers stood along the walls before the exit and Roary directed me towards them as I tried to tug him outside.

I looked around at him questioningly as he released my hand and found him unbuttoning his orange jumpsuit.

My lips parted and I could feel that damn blush trying to claw at my cheeks again, but I battered my teenage infatuation away with cold hard bravado and quickly slid my arms out of my jumpsuit too. I was more than comfortable in my own skin and I wasn't going to balk at the idea of shedding my clothes so that I could shift. Even if that did mean getting naked in front of the guy I'd spent years fantasising about.

Besides, Roary kept on insisting that I was still some little pup and I was gonna bet that was a lot harder for him to do if I was standing before him in my birthday suit.

I kicked my black boots off and stepped out of my jumpsuit, folding it in a locker before tossing my white Darkmore tank top over it and shedding my underwear too.

I flicked my long hair back over my shoulder as I turned back to look at Roary and my damn mouth dried up as I found him watching me in nothing but his black boxers, almost every inch of his golden skin on show as he leaned against the wall and waited for me.

His eyes moved down my body as I stood before him and I bit my lip as goddamn butterflies warred in my stomach. He was just, *so*...urgh. I'd really thought that after all of this time I wouldn't still feel this way about him, but it was like he'd taken a piece of me hostage and no matter how long I'd been free of him, that piece would always be his.

It took me a moment to realise that he hadn't said anything. His jaw was tight and his features controlled and I couldn't for the life of me work out what he was thinking. I lifted my chin and took a step closer to him, owning my flesh and everything I was. Because I was more than some star struck pup, aching for a moment of his attention. I was Rosalie goddamn Oscura and I didn't bow to anyone, let alone fall apart over pretty boys with gorgeous hair. And fuck me, Roary was better than pretty, he was like a damn Viking warrior with a slice of utterly irresistible smothered on top. Everything from the cut of his strong jaw and the stubble which lined it to his mane of long, dark hair which hung around his broad shoulders to his perfectly defined muscles and, hell even his thighs were enough to make my heart pound. The worst part of all was that he knew it, he knew exactly how good he looked and what effect that had on me. It was infuriating on so many levels but in that moment, his golden eyes were fixed on *me.* And I was going to make use of his attention while I had it.

"What's the matter, Roary?" I purred. "Did you really think I was still some little pup? Or are you just aching to ask me about my tattoo?"

I ran my fingers down the left side of my body where the black rose vine decorated my flesh. It coiled from my collar bone down my side, twisting over my ribs and reaching out to kiss my stomach before curving over my hip and extending down my thigh. I'd gotten it for a number of reasons, one of which I didn't like to think about, though it was mainly in honour of my family.

Roary watched me tracing the lines of my ink until my fingertips touched on my leg and he stepped forward suddenly, grasping my waist and pressing me back against the wall.

"Be careful what you wish for, Rosa," he warned in a low tone which just about had me undone.

His body surrounded me and the feeling of his skin on mine had my heart pounding. Why was it that as soon as Roary Night set me in his sights, I was transported back to being that teenage girl who'd ached for him all over again? All of my confidence and swagger just crumbled to dust and I was left blushing and flustered, fighting for the words I needed to prove to him that I was so much more than a pup while managing to prove myself wrong at every turn.

"What is it I'm wishing for?" I breathed as the rest of the inmates all finished shifting, racing out into the Order Yard without a backwards glance at us.

Roary inched closer to me. So close that his body was almost pressed to mine, but not quite. A low growl sounded in the back of his throat and he dipped his head towards mine. My heart pounded and I tipped my chin up, my lips parting in hopes of a kiss I'd dreamed about way too many times.

"Something you're never going to get," he growled, pushing away from me again suddenly and dropping his boxers as he stalked towards the door.

Blood rushed to my face and for an awful moment tears actually prickled the backs of my fucking eyes. But I wouldn't break over something so small. I refused to even crack.

I snarled at his back and leapt forward as I shifted, my silver Wolf springing free of my flesh so that I landed on four huge paws with soft fur covering my body and a mouth full of fangs which could rip a cocky bastardo apart.

The magic restricting cuffs which were locked around my wrists shifted to encompass my Wolf size with ease, staying in place just as firmly as they'd been before, meaning there was no chance of me escaping them.

Fuck him. I didn't need someone taunting and teasing me like that. I might not have been able to help my body's reaction to him, but that didn't mean shit. So what if I'd never fulfilled my teenage fantasies about him? I'd had more than my fair share of conquests. I'd bedded two of the Celestial Heirs for the moon's sake! And they were the most powerful Fae in the whole kingdom. I didn't need my confidence bolstered or shattered by some stuck up Lion who'd spent the last ten years rotting in here believing the world had stayed still for him beyond these walls. I'd grown up. I'd loved and lost and *lived*. What the fuck had he been doing in that time?

"Do you still want me to show you around?" Roary asked, looking over his shoulder at me.

His eyes widened as he took in my Wolf and I was pleased with the moment of awe that passed over his gaze before he hid it away. I was the biggest Wolf in the entire Oscura pack. Bigger than a shire horse with fur that sparkled like starlight. Because I wasn't just an ordinary Werewolf, I was a Moon Wolf which meant all kinds of untold things. I was the first of my kind in generations and my fur wasn't just pale grey, it was honest to the stars *silver* and I looked fucking awesome even if I did say so myself.

I bared my teeth at Roary in answer to his question. Did I want to spend the next few hours running around with a stuck up Lion Shifter who went out of his way to torture and humiliate me? Fuck no.

I turned my back on him and raced away without waiting for him to shift. I wasn't some little pup for him to keep mocking and teasing and I wasn't going to keep hanging around him, hoping he'd figure that out.

I didn't need his help to find my way around out here, I'd done my research before coming and I knew the layout well enough to find my own way.

I leapt out of the building and howled as my paws hit soft soil. I'd emerged on the south side of the dome where the yard was filled with thick pine trees and a pool of ice cold water waited at the heart of it. This was the section of the yard that the Lunar Brotherhood had laid claim to and once the prisoners from Cell Block A arrived, it would be swarming with Ethan Shadowbrook's pack. I needed to face him up here in our Wolf forms soon, but not today. I had more work to do on him before I'd give him the satisfaction of challenging me Wolf on Wolf.

Tonight my mission was simple: I needed to make the Oscura Wolves fall in line. I'd already joined them in the Magic Compound to get a feel for the pack, but I hadn't shown my hand yet. I knew a few of my cousins, aunts, uncles and other distant relations, but there weren't a lot of Wolves from my generation of Oscura locked up here so I didn't know any of them that well. Their current Alpha, Amira, led the pack with an iron fist but her style seemed too brittle for my tastes. I liked to let my Wolves flourish as individuals, not enforce a regime they *had* to stick by. So long as they fell into line and followed orders when it counted, I was happier for them to let their inner Wolf guide them the rest of the time. The strongest pack was one who followed their instincts, not one who were bound to so many rules that their individuality was stamped out.

A Lion roared behind me and I paused for a moment to look back at Roary in his enormous golden Lion form with his mane of dark hair surrounding his face. He jerked his chin to summon me back to him and I bared my teeth for a moment before turning and racing away into the trees. He was just lucky that I had more important things to do tonight than put a Lion Shifter on his ass, because no one summoned me like a house pet.

I heard him taking chase behind me and upped my pace. I hadn't been lying before, there was no way he could keep up with me if I didn't want him to and before long I was charging down a steep hill between the pines and skirting a shimmering lake where Sirens dove in and out of the water and a herd of Pegasus grazed on the grassy bank.

I kept running, delighting in the power of my Wolf form as my paws ate up the dirt and the world whipped by. I tipped my head to the moon and howled as I tried to get a view of it between the trees before racing on to the east of the dome.

The forest ended abruptly and my paws met with a rocky surface as I found myself at the edge of the dome. A shimmering blue wall rose up from the ground ahead of me, curving up over my head and climbing to its peak way above me where a glimmering golden timer counted down the two hours until our time out here was up.

The dome was semi-transparent so I could make out an empty landscape beyond it and the faint pinpricks of the stars shining in the black sky overhead. There was a wall in the distance and guard towers all around it plus all kinds of magical traps and defences between here and there to make sure the prisoners stayed inside Darkmore until their time was served. Or more likely, until death came to claim them first.

Lines of shimmering blue magic created a pattern something like a honeycomb across the surface of the shield which caged us and I couldn't help my curiosity as I walked closer to it.

I could feel the magic humming in the air, making my fur stand on end and a buzz of power resounded right through my core. I cocked my head at it, wondering what it would feel like to touch it. There were rumours it could knock a Fae out for three days and if they were true then I'd die out here when they sucked the air from the place at the end of the session unless some kind soul carried me back. And as I was surrounded by killers and cutthroats, I somehow doubted that would happen.

A distant howl made my ears prick up and I turned my head to look back the way I'd come as a shiver ran down my spine. I wasn't sure how I could tell, but something deep in the pit of my gut told me that was Ethan leading his pack out into the trees and for the longest moment, all I wanted to do was run to meet him.

But I couldn't do that. He wasn't ready yet. His rage over my identity would force him to challenge me and that could ruin everything if it happened too soon.

So instead of following the desires of my Wolf, I turned my head to the north and started running again, using the clear patch of land beside the dome as a path as I raced towards the Oscura territory.

As I left the pine forest behind, I found myself running alongside a frozen landscape filled with snow and icy rivers, the cold air stinging my wet nose. Beyond that, I found a barren, rocky area with deep ravines and caves carved into the land where Bear Shifters rambled around and Griffins swooped overhead.

The magic that must have been wielded to create this place was staggering and it was damn hard to force myself to run on and ignore my natural curiosity. I intended to explore every inch of this unnatural landscape soon but first, I needed to claim my pack.

Huge trees rose up ahead of me and I upped my pace as the temperature began to soar and the humidity climbed. I inhaled deeply, savouring the scent of fresh soil and thick fauna just before I dove into the tropical jungle and released a howl to announce my arrival.

A chorus of howls called back to me from somewhere up ahead and I upped my pace, my tail held high as I charged through the thick undergrowth to claim my pack.

I burst through the trees with a yip of excitement and found myself surrounded by a pack of around a hundred Wolves in a clearing beside a huge rock face.

I lifted my chin as I stalked into the space and the Wolves all turned to look at me. The lowest members of the pack dropped their heads and a few even rolled over to show me their bellies as they submitted, the sight of me enough to let them know they were outmatched.

A rugged brown Wolf raised his head and approached me head on, holding my eye for a long moment as he drew closer. I fell still, watching him as he approached and waiting to see if he'd challenge me.

He stopped a few feet away, tipping his head back to look up at me in my huge form and taking in the power that exuded from me before finally bowing his head in submission and moving forward to nuzzle me.

I allowed him that brief contact, though I didn't return the gesture, baring my teeth when he lingered too long. I didn't have time to waste on making friends just yet. I was here to challenge an Alpha.

As if she'd read my thoughts, Amira stepped out of the crowd of Wolves in her Fae form, eyeing me with a sense of acceptance as she came to stand before me.

"I take it you're making a challenge for my spot then?" she asked like she'd already known this was coming.

Most of the Oscura pack were in Cell Block B so I hadn't had a lot of opportunity to spend time with them yet, but in the Magic Compound and the mess hall, I'd let myself be known and it wasn't exactly hard to spot an Alpha for a Wolf.

I didn't bother shifting back, just bared my teeth in a challenge and Amira nodded, pushing her short, brown hair out of her eyes.

"I accept your challenge," she said before shifting. Her Wolf was big and grey with black flecks in her fur, though I still stood taller than her by a good foot.

The other Wolves backed up, circling us from a distance while yipping and barking with excitement as they waited to see how this would play out.

Amira started circling but I didn't join her. I fell forward, bracing my paws on the dirt as I readied myself to pounce

Her eyes widened as I failed to follow the usual practice and the moment she hesitated, I leapt at her.

My paws collided with her side and she yelped as she was knocked from her feet, swinging her jaws around to latch onto my leg.

I growled with anger, tearing my leg out of her mouth as blood spilled and lunging for her neck.

She rolled and leapt away from me before I could pin her, circling behind me before jumping at my back as I failed to turn and meet her.

I leapt aside and she landed hard, giving me a moment to clamp my teeth on her hind leg.

I yanked her back with a snarl and she howled in pain as I ripped her off of her feet and knocked her to the ground beneath me.

The rest of the pack were barking their encouragement and I pressed my advantage, pouncing so that my paws slammed into her chest and she was pinned beneath my weight.

Amira snarled, snapping at my face and lunging for my throat, but I was faster, diving forward and locking my immense jaws around her neck.

She fell still, a whimper of defeat escaping her lips as I growled in warning.

My heart pounded with adrenaline but this was the bit that counted. She had to submit. Shift back and put herself entirely at my mercy. If not then I was within my rights to rip her throat out here and now or banish her from the pack for failing to fall in line. That was the Way of the Wolf and all recognised packs in Solaria abided by its laws.

After another beat of resistance, she shifted suddenly and my paws slammed down on the chest of a woman instead of a beast.

"I submit," she panted as I slowly withdrew my teeth from her neck.

I glared down at her for a long moment, making sure I'd squashed any hint of rebellion from her eyes before shifting back too.

"A morte e ritorno," I breathed with a grin, quoting our Clan motto. *To death and back.*

I got to my feet suddenly, leaving her in the dirt and turning to find the entire pack shifting back into Fae form around me.

They poured forward to greet their new Alpha, reaching out to brush their hands across my bare skin or nuzzle into my neck.

The caress of their acceptance washed over me and I smiled as I bathed in the feeling of belonging. Even here, in this damn hell hole they called Darkmore Penitentiary, they couldn't stamp out the loyalty of a Wolf pack or the love we shared for one another.

"I offer myself as your Beta, Alpha," Amira said as she made it to me through the throng of naked bodies. "As is tradition."

She was right. When a new Wolf claimed a pack, traditionally, they selected the previous Alpha as their Beta if they were willing to put their disappointment at being dethroned aside. But I wasn't your standard Alpha, and I liked to make my own rules.

"Thank you for your offer, but I like to select my pack hierarchy based on things more important than tradition."

Amira balked at that and I didn't miss the flame of anger that rose in her gaze.

"Let's run together!" I called, turning to look around at every Wolf I now had under my command. "And I'll assign new pack positions once I've gotten a feel for how we'll work best together."

My pack started howling, cupping their hands around their mouths and shifting back into their Wolf forms at my command. They were excitable, bouncing and yapping at the change which had just occurred and I couldn't help but grin as I turned away from Amira's scandalised expression and shifted back myself.

A distant howl caught my attention and my ears twitched as I recognised Ethan again. It sounded like he was heading our way, but I still had no intention of dancing with him in my Wolf form yet.

With a howl of my own, I turned and thundered away from the clearing, charging into the jungle with my pack at my back.

The ruddy brown Wolf came to run at my flank and I turned to him with a bark of excitement as he matched my pace, his eyes blazing. My spirit called out to him in a way which reminded me of home. Of my family. And I was pretty sure I already knew who I'd be selecting for my Beta.

But before I got into the politics of pack hierarchy, I intended to run through every single landscape which was housed within the dome.

I tipped my head to the sky as we burst from the trees onto a swathe of sandy dunes and I caught sight of the moon beyond the roof of the dome, high, high above us.

I released a howl which echoed from my lips and made my soul ache as I thought of home. But I couldn't let myself dwell on that. This was my home for now. And before long, I'd be back where I belonged anyway.

We ran and ran for as long as we could until the final fifteen minutes were ticking down on the golden clock which was projected on the dome roof. I finally led my pack back to the main building where we would descend back down into the safety of the prison and the Order Suppressant would lock my Wolf away from me again until the next time I could come out here.

I paused as my pack flooded past me into the building to get changed and gave myself one final moment beneath the moon.

I could feel my magic reserves brimming with power deep within me after my run, but thanks to the magic restricting cuffs which were still locked around my front legs, I couldn't use a drop of it.

With a sigh and only a few minutes to spare, I trotted into the huge building which housed the elevators and moved towards the locker where I'd left my clothes.

Roary was leaning against the wall waiting for me as I entered the room and he offered me a teasing smirk, letting me know he didn't hold a grudge over me ditching him. I rolled my eyes in response to say that I didn't either and he headed off to take an elevator down without waiting for me to get dressed.

Most of the other inmates had already gone down but as I shifted back into my Fae form, Ethan staked towards me between the small crowd which still remained. He'd gotten dressed already and had tied his jumpsuit around his waist again, leaving his tattooed arms bare for me to appreciate.

"I've been looking for you," he snarled as he stalked closer.

I gave him an innocent look as around ten of my pack closed ranks behind me.

"Am I supposed to be flattered?" I teased as I pulled my clothes back on and his gaze roamed over me.

"You owe me a fight," he growled. All of my Wolves growled in response, glaring at him and moving forward like they were preparing to leap in at my defences.

"And you'll get it," I agreed casually as I untucked my hair from the collar of my jumpsuit. "When I'm ready."

I turned to walk away from him and he lunged at me, snatching my arm into his grip.

My Wolves leapt forward to defend me, but I waved them off as I turned to look up into Ethan's blue eyes.

"I'm the Oscura pack leader now," I said in a low voice as he refused to let go. "And if you challenge me it means war. Is that what you want with one minute of oxygen left in the room?"

Ethan bared his teeth, sparing a glance for the timer on the wall which was down to forty seconds. Two elevators stood open to take the last of the inmates out of here and we were the only ones left lingering as my Wolves backed up into one at a gesture from me.

"This isn't over," Ethan promised, his eyes burning with rage.

I reached out to move his hand off of my arm but instead of trying to force him to release me, I brushed my fingers over the back of his hand and onto his forearm. I shifted forward so that our lips were barely an inch apart and his gaze flickered with uncertainty as he tried to figure out what I was doing.

"No, it isn't," I breathed before stepping back and joining my Wolves in the elevator.

He watched me go for a moment before turning and heading into the other elevator with a growl of frustration.

Ethan's gaze stayed fixed on me as the doors began to close and I offered him a smile just before my view of him was stolen.

It was only my second day in this place and already my plans were coming together.

The Order Suppressant slid from the vents and I sighed in disappointment as my Wolf was chained down once more.

Not long now, Jerome, I'll finish this job in record time and be back for my paycheque before you even miss me.

CAIN

COMMANDING OFFICER

CHAPTER TEN

I watched Twelve from the corner of the Mess Hall, drinking in every detail of her behaviour. When I engaged in the hunt, I liked to know my prey well to make the chase all the sweeter. I'd give them room to breathe, to run, to hope. And just when they thought they'd made it away from me, I pounced.

I'd been watching Rosalie Oscura like a hawk since she'd arrived. Not that she knew it. I didn't usually pay much attention to the inmates assigned to me beyond keeping them in check, but with her I was happy to follow orders from Warden Pike. So I was going to bide my time, get to know my enemy until I saw the chinks in her armour and figured out where to strike. She obviously hadn't realised how much power I held over her. I decided her fate in here. Once she was entered into the correctional process, she'd soon realise her mistake. The more she let me see, the more I could exploit when it came to building her programme.

For now, I wanted her lulled into a false sense of security, to fall into the habits of the prison, find her natural place in the hierarchy. My interference would only slow the process down and this was the best way to figure out what I was dealing with.

Contrary to my initial assessment of the feisty little Werewolf, she was proving to be a serious contender for dominance in her cell block. If it weren't for her neighbour, Sixty Nine, the arrogant fuck of a Lion Shifter Roary Night, she probably would have seized the Alpha position in the block already.

Instead, it looked like they were making *friends*. Although, that word was bullshit in here. Allies was about as strong a tie as it went. I'd seen *friends* sell each other out for less than a pack of cigarettes when it came down to it. Just like in the rest of the world, Fae were all selfish creatures hunting for power. But it got amplified tenfold in Darkmore, turning Fae into sneaks and snitches. And if the new pups didn't figure out fast that the 'honourable way of the Fae' meant shit in here, they were going to find themselves with the sharpened end of a toothbrush jammed between their ribs before they could even spit and rinse.

I'd spent my childhood witnessing the darkest parts of Fae nature. I'd lived under the roof of a man who'd known how to feed sugary lies to the unwanted kids he so *kindly* took in. A man who'd pretended to be a father. Who'd faked it so well, I'd been under his spell for years. It had taken me far too long to realise he was just like every other Fae in the world; bloodthirsty and power hungry. But he'd taught me one invaluable lesson which I'd carried with me throughout my life: you couldn't trust anyone in this world, least of all those closest to you.

Twelve was laughing at something Sixty Nine was saying, her expression playful and carefree. The Oscura Werewolves banded around her, but whenever they got too near, she sent them away again. She was giving Roary her undivided attention and he was playing into her hands, puffing out his chest and acting like the big man. I knew her game. I'd seen it a thousand times in Darkmore, though perhaps not so cleverly played as this. Instead of making an opponent out of her biggest competition in her cell block, she was winding him around her little finger instead. She'd probably hold off on fucking him until he was down begging on his knees for it, and by then it would be too late for him to figure out she'd played him like a fool.

If you can't defeat your enemy physically, then invade them mentally and pick apart their defences brick by brick.

Life had taught me that. And it had clearly taught Twelve the same thing. So she might have been able to flirt and charm her way into the minds of her biggest competition, but she was forgetting one vital thing in her little plan. Me.

I had the power to throw her in the hole until she was so desperate to be let out, that she did anything and everything I said. I could chip away at each layer of security she built around herself until she was questioning her sanity. Yes, Rosalie Oscura was clever. But she wasn't smart enough to figure out that every subtle move she made was being watched, noted and deliberated. And after a few days of giving her room to breathe and feel secure in her new position, it was time for my first move. A reminder of who was really the boss in here.

I waited until breakfast hour was over and the inmates were corralled out of the Mess Hall. Most of them were split up by groups of guards as they left, taken to their jobs for the day. Not everyone in here was so lucky as to have a job. Only the new pups and the well-behaved were given the opportunity. If you behaved like an insolent fuck then you got downgraded to the shittiest jobs. Literally. Cleaning the cell block toilets by hand was one of the most menial tasks on offer. But if you were a completely useless prick then you'd be refused work entirely. And that meant you didn't earn one token an hour like the rest of your cellblock did. And as the commissary only took tokens and ignored what you were worth outside of these walls, the result was that you had to endure having the barest cell, the emptiest stomach and a lack of all privileges.

I moved after the crowd as Twelve walked with Sixty Nine toward the exit.

"Hey, I can see if I can get you a job?" Sixty Nine murmured to her. "We're fixing up an old cell block. Construction and decorating are pretty sweet jobs."

"That would be-" Twelve started and I snatched her arm, yanking her back a step.

She turned to me in surprise and a cruel smile tugged at my lips. The Lion lingered there like a bad smell and I bared my fangs at him.

"Is there a problem, Sixty Nine?" I snarled dangerously.

He eyed Rosalie with a frown then shook his head and kept walking.

"You're on level nine today," I told her, my heart thudding harder in anticipation.

"That's isolation," she breathed and I narrowed my gaze on her.

"Who told you that?" I growled.

"Officer Lyle," she said with a shrug then caught my sleeve, tugging me forward. "Come on then, what are we waiting for?"

A snarl ripped from my throat and I snatched the back of her collar, ripping her hands off of my sleeve. "Touch an officer like that again and I'll leave bruises on you as a reminder of the rules."

I laid my free hand on my baton and her eyes slid down to it, a stubborn flare in her gaze that said she was tempted to touch me again out of sheer exhilaration. It was going to take a lot to break this one. But I knew how to be patient. I'd laid in wait for prey before, hiding in the dark, and just like all those before her, she wasn't going to see me coming.

I shoved her ahead of me and she stumbled as she almost lost her footing, a growl leaving her throat. I pushed her along through the crowd, leading her out into the stairwell and heading down. The prisoners filed off into corridors around us with groups of guards as we continued to descend. No one else was working lower than level seven so when we got that far we were left alone.

Twelve looked around, absorbing every detail of the grey walls while I observed every detail of her.

I took the lead as we reached the heavy red metal door which led into isolation, flashing my ID pass at the scanner before placing my palm against it and letting it register my magical signature. A heavy buzz sounded and the door clunked as it opened.

I pulled it wide for Twelve, eyeing her with a smirk as she stepped past me into the low-lit corridor full of doors as heavy-duty as this one.

I followed her into it, spotting the janitor's trolley at the far end where I'd told him to leave it in preparation for this.

"You're going to wash every inch of this floor," I commanded, directing her toward the trolley where a mop and bucket sat waiting for her.

She walked toward it, sashaying her hips without a word in response and grabbed the mop.

I stalked after her with darkness flickering in my soul as I snatched the mop from her grip and snapped the wooden handle over my knee.

"You'll do it by hand," I snarled, pointing to a scrubbing brush on top of the trolley with the sharp end of the broken mop.

Twelve clenched her jaw, that stubborn flare rising in her again.

"NOW!" I bellowed directly in her ear and she snatched it up with a growl, grabbing the bucket and dropping to her knees before me.

A sweet satisfaction twisted through me as she started scrubbing, her jaw locked in fury.

I dropped down to a crouch, placing the sharp end of the handle under her chin and forcing her to look at me. "Do you have something to say, Twelve?"

"No," she replied simply.

I smashed the handle down on the ground, making her flinch. "No what?!"

She stared at me for a long moment, resilience burning in her gaze. Then she snorted derisively, dropping her head. "No, Officer Cain."

"Good." I rose to my feet, striding past the row of doors on my right as Twelve set to work cleaning. I paused outside cell six and reached up to the hatch, twisting the lock and sliding it open. I frowned into the dark space, my Vampire sight heightening as I hunted for the piece of shit Incubus who resided in there.

My heart ticked a little harder as I didn't spot him and I rammed the mop handle against the metal door so it banged loudly.

"Prisoner Eighty Eight!" I roared.

116

I was just about to send out an alert when he leapt up from behind the door, grinning from ear to ear like the fucking Cheshire Cat. He was a big bastard with dark skin and the kind of eyes that promised murder from a mile away. Those eyes contradicted the crazy-ass fucking smile on his face. Every other guard in this place either fell for his sugary words or thought he was cuckoo. I knew better. This guy was the most dangerous fucker in the whole of Darkmore Penitentiary. And the trail of blood he'd left in his wake told me three things: he was intelligent, calculating and not to be underestimated.

"Did you think I was goner?" he laughed in a deep tone, getting his face as close to the slot as possible. "Where would I go, Officer? To the moon?"

I sneered. "Fucking crazy asshole," I muttered, reaching for the hatch to shut it again.

"No, wait!" he demanded and I paused as his gaze fell on Twelve. She had a sheet of hair covering her face, but something told me she was looking through it. I let Eighty Eight see her because I knew it was a form of torture in itself. Incubuses needed sex to recharge their magic and this sad fucker had been in the hole so long, his Order was no doubt craving it on a base level that was driving him crazier than he already was.

"Who's the girl?" Eighty Eight made kissing noises to try and get her attention as if she was a cat and I smirked when she didn't even raise her head. "Hey kitten, come here."

"She's new," I told him. "Just processed her this week. She came in naked and wild," I taunted him and he groaned.

"Hey – look at me!" he barked at her, slamming his palm against the door in frustration.

I laughed coldly, reaching for the hatch. "In your dreams, inmate. This one's got a will of steel." I slammed the hatch shut and a sense of power ran through me, feeding my most fundamental Fae instincts.

"So you've noticed I can't be broken?" Twelve asked lightly, tossing her head so her hair fell back over her shoulders.

I moved forward so she was in my shadow, folding my arms as I glared down my nose at her. "Do you know what can break steel, Twelve?" I raised one hand, letting flames flicker between my fingers. "*Fire.*"

Her eyes narrowed and she opened her lips to retort and most likely earn her a baton to the backs of her legs, when the door flew open at the end of the corridor.

Jack Hastings ran in, his keycard falling out of his hand and skittering across the floor in his haste. I slammed my boot down on it, picking it up with a growl.

"What is it?" I hissed.

"There's a fight up on six," he gasped. "I can't get them under control."

I rolled my eyes, striding closer to him at a casual pace and steering him back toward the door. "You're Fae aren't you?" I snapped. "Use the magic your preppy academy taught you how to wield. Or was Mommy and Daddy's money poorly spent?" I shoved him through the door and glanced back at Rosalie on her knees. "I'm locking you in here, Twelve. This floor better be sparkling by the time I get back."

"Aye aye, Captain Dickwad," she said lightly.

I froze in the doorway as Jack tried to tug me out after him in his desperation to get back to the fight.

"What was that?" I asked Twelve in a deadly tone, taking my baton from my hip and whipping it sideways so it extended.

She raised her chin, saying nothing.

"Wait – sir!" Jack called as I stormed back towards Rosalie with a snarl of fury.

She waited for the attack and I took pleasure in every second as I caught her hair, dragging her upright before whacking the baton across the backs of her thighs.

She hissed in pain, pressing against me and I caught a scent of her blood beneath her skin as her throat came too close to my mouth. My canines grew to sharpened points and hunger filled me so fast, it was almost impossible to resist. A growl rumbled through my chest as I lost my train of thought, a flame of need licking at the base of my throat. But I didn't have any cause to bite her and the security cameras were pointed my way. The Warden would pull me up on it at the very least, if not suspend me from duty. I had to keep my head, but holy fuck, I couldn't believe how tempting she was.

I shoved her to the ground and her hair tumbled around her as she braced her palms on the ground. I kicked the bucket of water up and it sloshed over her lap, washing everywhere around her. I pointed the baton at her in warning, my fangs bared.

"Disrespect me again and it'll be more than bruises you have to worry about." My eyes slid to the overturned bucket as suds floated around on the ground. "Clean this shit up."

I turned and strode after Jack with adrenaline bursting through my veins.

Fuck, I'd never wanted to bite a girl so hard in my life. And I would get my teeth in her eventually. I just had to bide my time. Then she'd have a real reason to fear me.

ROSALIE

PRISONER #12

CHAPTER ELEVEN

My heart thrummed wildly as I continued scrubbing the floor, my movements slowing as I listened to Officer Cain and Hastings' footsteps as they moved away from me.

My jaw was clenched tight and I was gripping the scrubbing brush so hard that it was hurting my hand. Officer Cain was damn lucky he'd left before I'd rammed it up his ass.

I released a slow breath, calming my Wolf which was screaming at me to fight back against him. But I wouldn't do it. Not head on. That was a fight I couldn't win in my situation. But I'd learned a long time ago how to defeat an enemy who held power over me. I knew how to keep my head down and work the unexpected angle. By the time I ripped the rug out from under him, he'd really believe that I was broken. And in the end that would be his downfall. My papà had taught me that much if nothing else.

I was sopping wet from the waist down and the cold water chilled me right down to my bones in the freezing corridor. I cursed Cain in Faetalian as I sat back onto my heels. He was so sure he would beat me into submission, but he was an idiota. I didn't know how to submit. If my mamma and papà couldn't force me to when I was a pup, then one power hungry asshole didn't stand a snowball's chance up the ass of a Dragon. I'd survived in the hands of monsters until my Aunt Bianca had saved me from them and they were far more determined than Cain could ever be to see me break. I had the scars to prove it. Which was damn near impossible for a Fae. I could heal from almost anything with the right magic. But not from what papà had done. That had left its mark on me inside and out.

I ground my teeth as I thought about the way Cain was coming at me. This wasn't going to stand. Rosalie Oscura was no one's bitch. But I already had a plan for how I was going to turn the tables on him and my little trick had worked.

As he'd grabbed me, I'd made sure to tip my chin back, exposing my throat and his true desire in the same moment. I'd seen the look in his eyes, the hunger, the *need*. He craved my blood. I was one of the most powerful Fae I knew and blood filled with magic like mine sang to a Vampire like a Siren's song. And that was all I needed to know. Because there was a simple equation involved in claiming a hold over someone.

First, you exposed their deepest desire. Second, you made sure you held it in your fist and used it to lure them closer, promising it, maybe even giving it up from time to time, while never relinquishing control of it. Because all the time you maintained your hold over it, you maintained your hold over *them*.

So now I knew two things about Officer Cain which I could use to gain the upper hand. He ached for my blood, and he was addicted to the hunt.

I can easily work with that.

He was so caught up in making me his that he wouldn't even realise that he'd become mine until it was too late for him to escape me.

Once enough time had passed for me to feel confident that Cain had definitely gone, I dropped the scrubbing brush and looked around at the empty corridor, wondering if my luck really was this good.

I'd been trying to figure out how I was going to get down here and take a look at the isolation unit for myself and I'd begun to think I'd have to get myself sent down here to make it happen. This was so much better than that option.

A bang sounded behind me and I flinched as I spun around, my eyes widening as they fell on the open hatch on the front of Sin's door. Cain must not have secured it properly when he'd closed it and I suddenly found myself looking into the eyes of the man I'd come here to set free.

"If I begged the stars to paint me a portrait of the woman I've been fantasising over while I've been stuck down here, then she'd be you," Sin growled in a low voice which had the hairs on the back of my neck standing on end. "Bigger tits maybe...but I'd need to see them to be sure..."

I snorted a laugh dismissively. "You've been without tits for so long that you'd probably get excited to see Cain's if he offered."

"Mmmm, say that again," he begged in a voice as rich as velvet.

I couldn't make out much of him through the small hole in the door, but

122

his dark gaze was pinned on me and made my skin tingle. I got to my feet and turned to face him as I shook my hair back out of my face.

"Which part?" I asked.

"*Tits,*" he replied in a tone so damn sexual that my toes almost curled.

This was a creature whose nature matched his name. Sin. That was what he was, what he could be. And every sugar coated word which spilled out of his mouth was both a promise and a threat. Because a creature like that would chew you up and spit you out if you weren't careful with him.

"What will you give me if I do?" I asked slowly, playing into his game in hopes of winning him over. I needed him on side if I wanted to get him out of here and as of yet, he seemed to be engaging with me well enough.

"I can make a girl come just by saying her name in the right way," Sin purred. "If I ever get out of here then I'll give you that and a whole lot more besides…"

"That's not much of an offer though, is it?" I taunted, drawing my long hair back over one shoulder while he watched the movement hungrily. "You're stuck in there and I'm out here…"

I glanced up at the CCTV camera which sat at the furthest end of the corridor watching my every move. But it wasn't like I was doing anything wrong. I'd been left down here alone and talking to Sin wouldn't give any of my plans away. Besides, I'd broken enough laws in my time to recognise pretty much every kind of security device there was and the cameras they were using to monitor us were basic. They didn't even have an audio feed on those things, so they wouldn't be able to tell what I said to him.

"I'm a man of my word," he replied roughly.

"A man with as many faces as you could give as many words as he likes and keep whichever ones he chose to," I pointed out. Jerome had warned me about Sin's loose relationship with the truth. He never lied, but his words were always coloured by whichever part of his psyche happened to be front and centre in that moment. Meaning he could paint pictures with his words and lead you down any number of false trails before bringing you back to the point at hand. But I wasn't going to fall into his traps.

The corner of Sin's eyes crinkled and I was almost certain that had made him smile.

"Do you want me to beg?" he asked.

"I don't hate the idea," I admitted.

"*Please.*" His tone was rough with more than desire. This was need. Pure and simple. And I was pretty sure I could make good on that transaction.

"I have a confession to make," I told him, walking forward slowly and unhooking a few of my jumpsuit buttons to reveal more of my white tank top to him.

Sin groaned like I was performing a top rate sex show, not just loosening a few buttons and I ceased my movements as I came to stand just out of reach of his cell.

"I came here for you," I said slowly, watching what I could see of his face for some reaction.

"I can come for you too, if you'd like?" he offered suggestively.

I snorted a laugh. "I don't think you jerking off over me while I scrub the floors is the healthiest way for us to start off a business relationship," I joked and Sin stilled.

"I beg to disagree. Are you always this wet or is it the effect I'm having on you?" Sin asked, his gaze dripping over my soaked jumpsuit.

"Why don't I feel like you're taking me seriously?" I asked, narrowing my eyes at him.

"Because they've had me locked up in here for weeks, or months... hell, sometimes it feels like years. I don't know *how* to take you seriously or even how to be sure if you're real or not..." His eyes scrutinised me like he really was trying to figure out whether or not I even existed and I sighed. I'd known that being down in the hole for a long time wouldn't have been particularly good for him, but I was starting to wonder if he'd come unhinged. And that wouldn't be good. Not good at all. I needed him if I was ever going to execute my plan to get out of here. Worse than that; my outside help relied on me keeping up my end of the bargain. Namely, getting Sin Wilder out of Darkmore Penitentiary and into the hands of the person who'd contracted me to help him escape. Jerome would cut me off without a moment's hesitation if I failed in my part of the deal.

Before I could talk myself out of it, I crossed the hallway and walked straight up to Sin's door. His eyes widened hungrily as I approached but he didn't move, like he thought I'd vanish if he so much as blinked.

"I'm real," I growled fiercely, reaching out to touch his cheek to prove it to him.

Sin gasped as my palm pressed to his face and his hand instantly landed over it as he half dragged my arm through the hatch.

I stumbled forward a step, my chest banging into the door as my heart leapt with surprise. I cursed him, meaning to wrench my hand back, but as I looked through the hatch and eyed the rectangle of space he'd been stuck in for months, I couldn't force myself to do it. He was all alone in there. And I knew how that felt, even if I tried my hardest not to remember.

Sin groaned in a way that went beyond sexual desire, he needed this. Needed real contact with someone in the same way that I needed to run beneath the moon. It was a part of him, a part which had been starved while he was left to rot in this cage.

I flexed my fingers, grazing them along the beard which lined his jaw and a shiver raced through his skin at the simple touch like it was the most loving caress in the world.

"I was sent to get you out of here," I breathed, eyeing him as his other hand moved to grasp my wrist, his fingers sliding beneath the sleeve of my jumpsuit and dancing against my skin like he just couldn't get enough of it.

I swallowed a lump in my throat as I watched him. He was huge, easily big enough to be a Dragon Shifter, his body thick with muscle and his dark skin inked with tattoos. His black hair was scruffy like the beard which grew on his skin and I guessed that it was pretty hard to cut your hair when you were left alone in the hole. But the unkempt state of his hair only drew my gaze to the strength of his features and the light in his eyes. As a resident of the isolation block, he'd been given a pair of grey pants and a black tank top instead of the orange jumpsuits I was growing too used to and the difference it made was staggering. He seemed like this alien creature, so separate from the rest of us that he didn't even know what he was anymore.

"A friend of yours hired me," I pressed, keeping my voice low just in case any of the other residents of the isolation block could hear us, though I doubted it through those heavy doors.

Sin eyed me for a long moment but I couldn't figure out if that meant anything to him or not. Jerome had told me they were close, like brothers, but Sin's poker face was top class. Not so much as a twitch of recognition flashed in his eyes. I might as well have been talking about the weather instead of telling him about the guy who was willing to part with a small fortune to bust his ass out of here.

"I'll never be free, little bird," he murmured eventually in that deep tone which nearly had me undone.

There was something undeniably captivating about Sin Wilder which could have been his Order shining through or could have just been *him*.

"I beg to disagree," I replied, tossing his own words back at him. "I'm known for getting what I want."

Sin's eyes flared hungrily and he shifted towards me, still running his fingers back and forth over the skin of my arm while looking at me intently.

"And what *do* you want?" he asked. "I can give it to you...*could* give it to you if I wasn't stuck in my Fae form. I could be everything you desire embodied."

"How does that work?" I asked in a low voice because a large chunk of my plan hinged on a hope I had about his Order gifts, but Incubuses were rare enough that it had been hard to research a definite answer to my questions.

"With a single touch, I can get a read on your deepest desires, your darkest fantasies, and become them for you-"

"Yeah, that's great and all," I said dismissively and he raised an eyebrow at me in surprise. "But what I'm more interested in is whether or not *you* can choose what form you take on?"

"Why?"

"Curiosity," I replied innocently, shifting my fingers against his cheek again and eliciting a groan from his lips. "Could you become me for example?"

"You're my dirtiest fantasy so I'm sure I could manage it," he teased and I bit my lip against an amused smile. "Although there are a few anatomical areas which don't exactly shift…"

"So you'd look like me but you'd still have a cock?" I asked, snorting a laugh.

"A big one," he replied with a wicked smile.

I really laughed that time and he shifted forward suddenly, releasing his grip on my hand as he moved to press his face to the gap in the door.

I stepped back in surprise, folding my arm against my chest as it continued to tingle with the memory of his flesh against mine.

"*Fuck*, it's been so long since I heard a girl laugh like that," he groaned.

"I'm going to get you out of there," I repeated firmly to drive the message home because it didn't seem like he was taking in the important parts of this conversation at all.

"Kiss me," Sin demanded, his eyes alight with need.

"Aren't you going to buy me dinner first?" I teased.

Sin growled, pushing himself away from the hatch suddenly so that I couldn't see him anymore. His footsteps pounded across the hard floor of his cell and I tilted my head to try and get a look at what he was doing.

He strode back and forth a few times, clawing his fingers over his messy hair then dropped to the floor right beneath the hatch with his back pressed to the door.

I bit down on my lip as I lost sight of him, but the sound of his low voice drew me closer again as I tried to make out what he was saying. But he wasn't talking; he was singing.

"*Tick tock, tick tock, tick tock, the mouse ran up the clock-*"

"What are you doing?" I asked, inching nearer to the hatch as I tried to catch sight of him.

"*The mouse fell down-*" Sin slammed his hands against the metal door and it banged loudly, making me flinch in surprise.

"Sin?" I pressed, stepping right up to the door and wrapping my fingers around the edge of the hatch as I angled my head to try and see him.

He just kept singing, ignoring me entirely and a low growl sounded in the base of my throat.

"Sin?"

He finished his song then fell silent. My heart fluttered nervously as I tried to figure out what the hell he was doing. I'd done my research on him before getting myself locked up in here, but it was hard to get much concrete information on someone who hid in the shadows, slipping from skin to skin and wearing so many masks that it was impossible to say who the real Sin was.

But my employer had given me a file with a bit of background information on him. Not much. But maybe enough to force a response from him. Because if he didn't want to answer to his chosen name then I knew another one which belonged to him.

"Whitney?" I asked, hoping to get a rise out of him.

A low snarl sounded from his cell and Sin appeared so suddenly that I didn't have time to leap back before his hand shot out of the hatch and he snatched my throat into his grip.

I tried to gasp but his hold was tight enough to cut off my air supply and as he glared out at me from within his cage, the only thing I could see in his eyes was the monster who had earned his place in this cell.

His gaze was cold, hard and full of rage. He had me completely at his mercy and in that moment, I felt certain he was going to kill me.

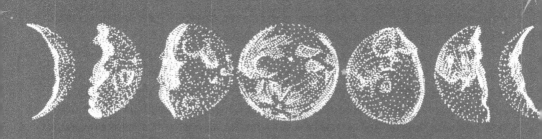

SIN

PRISONER #88

CHAPTER TWELVE

"**C**all me that name again and I'll crush you into sawdust, kitten. Now tell me who sent you," I snarled, clutching her delicate throat tighter in my grasp as she clawed at my hand.

Beautiful as she was, it didn't matter to me whether I snapped the neck of a swan or a crow. If she was my enemy, her death was already written.

"Was it Thanos?" I demanded. That fucker had it in for me, but so did a thousand other assholes. "Higgs? Amelie Falls? *Godfrey?*" *Fucking Godfrey. I bet it was him.*

She tried to rasp out something in answer and I was forced to release her. Her eyes flared furiously and that only made her look more tempting to me. *Damn, why does she look so hot when she's dying?*

"Jerome sent me," she panted. "And he doesn't want you dead, he wants you free, idiota. Just like I said before you tried to fucking kill me."

"Oh get over yourself, kitten. If I'd been trying to kill you, you wouldn't still be breathing." I turned my back on her, starting to pace.

Her words sank into my brain like seeds, sprouting little shoots that set off a bunch of emotions. Excitement, hope, concern, distrust.

If Jerome had really sent her, then maybe I could believe her. He was the only person in the entire world who I had ever called a friend. A guy who'd gone through the system with me when we were teens. He was like a brother to me. We'd been the unwanted kids of Hollow Rise foster home. Upstanding members of society didn't take in troublesome boys who were on first name terms with the local cops. They took in the sweet, innocent girls and the gentle boys who offered hugs and smiles in exchange for love.

I'd never bribed anyone to love me. I had too much pride and too little shits to give. But from those dark years had come one good thing. Jerome and me had formed an unbreakable bond. He'd always been the more likable one of us. The sort of guy who could sell water to a fish. I'd always known he'd go into business, but he just so happened to end up as one of the most powerful mob bosses in our hometown, Iperia. He'd given me work for years, using my particular, ruthless talents to take out his enemies. It suited me perfectly. I could live the lone life I wanted whilst getting paid for being the murderous bastard I was always destined to be.

So if Jerome was trying to get me out of here, I had to trust his judgement on the calvary he'd sent. But was this girl really capable of breaking me out of the most secure facility in the whole of Solaria? She probably weighed a hundred pounds and looked exactly like my last wet dream. But as much as my dick wanted to get to know her better, that didn't mean I could trust her. For all I knew, she could actually have been working for one of my enemies. But who would go to that much of a fucking bother to break me out of here just to slit my throat? It was a pretty pointless exercise considering the magnitude of the task at hand.

I twisted around again, looking through the hatch and she stared in at me evenly. The red finger marks on her neck brought on an ounce of longing in me to lick them away.

"What makes you good enough to get me out of here? Don't get me wrong, I've seen monsters in smaller packages than you, though maybe not prettier ones. I'm guessing there's an inferno of cunning living in those perky tits of yours, so how about you let me in on it?"

Her fist slammed through the hatch and connected with my nose. I stumbled backwards with a stream of curses pouring from my lips as pain flared up the bone. It wasn't broken, but a punch like that said she knew how to break a nose. So I guess I'd gotten off lightly.

"*That's* what you get for throttling me," she hissed and a manic laugh tumbled from my throat.

Wild, that was what she was. But I was wilder. By name and by nature.

I rubbed the bridge of my nose, swaggering back toward her as a crooked smile pulled up my lips.

"Tell me you fuck as rough as you fight," I purred and her gaze darkened. *Oh please stars, let it be true.*

She tip-toed up to stare straight through the hatch; if she had any fear of me she didn't show it. Which made her an idiot or an equal and my bet was on the latter.

"I've been hired to get you out of here. Any part of my plans that concern you, I'll tell you about when I'm good and ready. It's just a courtesy that I'm telling you about them at all right now. So you can either embrace the good fate the stars are delivering you or you can ignore it and I'll still get you out of here and collect my pay."

"Hmmm," the noise rumbled through my chest. "No, it's more than money you're looking for."

I could see something in her eyes that mirrored my own soul. A need to be *seen*. She didn't just wanna do this for the money, she was doing it for the glory. And oh baby did I know the feeling. I'd killed like an artist, left walls painted red like Picasso, strung my victims up and cut off pieces of them like Van Gogh, drowned a man in a bathtub of coca cola – alright that last one was *all* me. But the point was, I liked to leave my mark, I wanted people talking about the greatest killer alive. Sin Wilder was a villain who reminded bad Fae to lock their windows and doors before they went to bed. And this pretty little thing wanted her name in flashing lights too.

"Don't presume to know what I'm looking for," she said darkly.

"I'll reserve judgement then," I replied thoughtfully, but I was pretty certain I had her pegged.

"I've got something that can sweeten this for you. We don't have to be enemies." She reached down her jumpsuit and my brows lifted in hope as I wondered if I was going to get a boob flash in exchange for my time. She produced something from the stars-knew-where that was arguably better. And I didn't say that lightly. A sealed white pot with a plastic lid.

"What's in that?" I demanded in a low voice, suddenly as serious as a fucking heart attack.

"Pudding," she said simply like it didn't mean anything. But it meant everything. *Eveeeeerything*.

"What. Kind. Of. Pudding?" I ground out between my teeth, losing my mind. I lived on dry bread and no butter – not even a lick of it, not even a taste. That pudding was an orgasm in a pot. But only if it was chocolate. *By the moon, let it be chocolate.*

"Chocolate," she supplied and I lunged for it, jamming my whole arm through the hatch.

She stepped out of reach and I retracted my arm with a noise like a kicked dog.

"*Tease*," I hissed.

"I'll give it to you after you tell me one thing," she said lightly, waving the pot to taunt me.

131

"What?" I snarled, wondering if I could Hulk down this door and go after that pudding. But in all honesty, if I got out there, the pudding was going to be second on the list of things I wanted to devour.

"Why did you get put into isolation? I need a way to get you out of here."

I barked a laugh. "Good luck with that, kitten. I gutted a guy good to earn my place in here then some little fucker of a snitch sold me out to the guards." I turned and spat on the ground behind me, because if I ever found out who that snitch was, their innards were gonna become their outtards faster than a Vampire could take a piss.

"Hmm." She tapped the pot against her mouth and my dick twitched longingly. Did she have any idea what she was doing to me right now? "So none of the guards actually saw you do it? No CCTV?"

"I'm not a fucking idiot, kitten. I don't kill on camera. I mean, I *would* if I didn't get the jail time for it. I could have my own show actually-"

"You're getting distracted," she cut me off and my grin widened.

"Trust me, my attention is entirely undivided." I let my gaze roam down her curves and by the time I got back to her face, she was rolling her eyes. *Fuck my useless body. If I had access to my Order gifts, she'd be falling at my feet by now.*

"So there was no other evidence that you did it apart from the snitch giving you up?" she asked.

"Nothing. I hid the weapon like a pro. It's probably still in my old cell inside the back leg of the bottom bunk. I hollowed it out with nothing but a coin and my own fingernails. By the way, which fucker took my cell? Was it Randal? Fucking Randall…"

"Well I don't know what room you had," she said with an amused smile.

"It's easy to remember. Number one," I said in a purr. "Cell Block A. Top floor, obviously."

"So if I can just get the murder weapon and plant it on someone else…" She shrugged innocently but something told me this dandelion wasn't innocent at all. It was the kind of dandelion which fucked thistles and partied hard with poison ivy.

"Are you in that cell block?" I asked.

"No." She shrugged again and I released a gravelly laugh.

"Good luck with that mission then, honey pie. You only get in other cell blocks if you transfer. And you only transfer if you appeal to the Warden and the Warden will only-"

"You've got to think outside the box, Sin," she cut me off again, shifting closer. "But I guess that must be hard for you when you're locked *in* the box." She tapped on the door and I cocked my head, my eyes falling to the pudding.

"I gave you what you want. Now give me my reward." I lunged for the pudding again and she gave it up willingly this time.

I snatched it away, hugging it to my chest, going full Golem on its ass. *Mine.*

A sexy smile took hold of Miss Answer-To-All-My-Dreams' lips and I started to like her a whole lot more. Holy shit, there was one thing I needed more than this pudding. One thing I'd cut off a limb for. But my snatchy pudding hands hadn't bought me much leverage. So I was just going to be a full-on dick about it.

She moved closer to the hatch to peer in and I straightened, schooling my expression as I tucked the pudding into the pocket of my sweatpants and folded my arms, tensing them up real good. "I'll agree to cooperate and make this whole thing much easier on you, but only if you give me one thing in return."

"What else? I just gave you a pudding!" She frowned and I tapped my mouth.

"Kiss me, kitten. Set me free for a few seconds with those apple red lips of yours." My throat thickened as her gaze fell to my mouth and I wished I could use my Order form more than anything right then. What did this pussy cat desire? I'd give her the brand of catnip she needed. But right here I could only be one thing. Myself. And that wasn't good enough.

"Promise you'll cooperate?" she arched a brow, slinking even closer.

Jupiter must have been in my chart today, because I was one lucky son of a bitch.

I nodded keenly, pressing my body flat to the door, raising my hands above my head and clawing at the freezing cold iron. I needed body heat and lust and passion. I was going to die if I didn't get it soon.

She leaned forward, her eyelashes casting a shadow across her cheeks, her gaze hooded, her breath fluttering over my mouth. She tasted like sugar and hope and her mouth wasn't even on mine yet. I bet she tasted sinful on the inside. And if she didn't, I knew one good way to put *sin* in her.

I groaned needily, my cock swelling to press against the door and fucking ache when I gave it no room at all, refusing to budge a single inch. I *had* to have this kiss. To be refused her lips now would be my damnation. I couldn't think of one thing in that moment I desired more than just my tongue against hers, my stubble grazing her skin raw, the heat of her flesh on mine.

"Twelve!" Officer Cain's voice split the air apart and she was yanked away from me by the hair with a yelp.

"No!" I cried, throwing my arm through the hatch as I tried to reach for her.

Cain's baton smashed down across my forearm and I yanked it back with a roar of rage. His snarling face came into view as he reached for the hatch and I lost sight of her.

"Wait!" I dove forward just as the hatch snapped shut. I slammed my palm on the door again and again, pure fury coursing through my body and seizing me in its grasp. "GIVE HER BACK!"

Footsteps pounded away from me and panic lit my heart on fire. "Wait – what's your name?! Tell me your name!"

"Rosalie Os- *ah!"* She was cut off as Cain punished her and the sound of the door slamming down the corridor rang through the whole of the isolation block and reverberated through my skull.

Rosalie Rosalie Rosalie. Os…Osmund? Ostrich? O-Sin-you-make-me-so-wet? Didn't matter. The first name was all I needed as I rolled it across my tongue, saying it over and over. Then I dropped down to kneel on the floor, taking the pudding from my pocket and placing it in front of me.

"You little temptation you," I purred, slowly drawing the lid off of it. And there she stood, in all her glory. Brown chocolate goo coating her fluffy middle all the way down to her milky sweet depths. I dug my teeth into my lower lip as I slid a finger into the pot, dipping it into the chocolate and groaning as the scent of it carried up to me.

"Will you taste as good as this pudding, Rosalie?" I mused aloud, lifting my finger to my lips. I sucked off the chocolate and moaned lustfully, dropping forward so I peered down into its soul.

"You were a goner the second you walked in here, pud. Come to daddy." I dropped over the pot and drove my tongue inside it, devouring it all at once like the greedy bastard I was. Every bite was a miracle, every lick a fucking Divine Moment. I would happily be mated to this pudding for all of time. Except I ate her good. She was gone before she knew what had happened.

I rolled onto my back, lifting the pot to my mouth and licking it clean. "Sorry baby, I don't play nice. R.I.P." I tossed the pot aside and it clattered against the wall.

Cain was going to come down on Rosalie like a ton of bricks when he watched the CCTV and realised she'd given me that pudding. I was going to be due a beat down in the morning too because of it. He'd probably get the newbie, Hastings, to shove his finger up my ass to check that nothing had been hidden in that pot.

Worth.

It.

And frankly I needed the Fae on Fae contact. So if Officer Hastings needed to go to town on my ass, then I'd spread 'em and bend over like a hooker with a pocketful of cash. It wasn't always pretty being an Incubus, but when you were the most notorious assassin in Solaria, people tended not to judge.

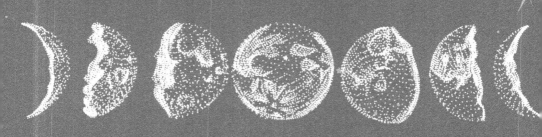

ROSALIE

PRISONER #12

CHAPTER THIRTEEN

I stood outside a locked door with Officer Hastings watching me from the opposite side of the corridor with suspicion in his eyes and a frown furrowing his brow.

Cain was currently reviewing the security footage of my interaction with Sin while I waited to find out my punishment. Although, being dragged from the isolation block by my hair seemed like punishment enough to me, especially with how raw my scalp felt.

The corridor we were waiting in was cold. In fact this whole damn prison was cold. All the damn time. And with my jumpsuit still soaking wet from the waist down thanks to Officer Dipshit, I was damn near to shivering.

I cut a glance at Hastings and wondered if my little choir boy might be ready to progress to the next level.

Only one way to find out…

I wrapped my arms around my chest and looked down at my feet as my hair fell forward to curtain my face.

After a few more moments, I let myself shiver. Hell, for authenticity's sake, I even decided to throw in the hint of a teeth chatter.

And for the cherry on top of the cake, I raised my fingers to my cheek and swiped at it while inhaling on a sniff that could have most definitely signalled the start of tears.

It only took another moment before a warm hand landed on my shoulder and I looked up as I felt magic sweeping over my skin. The water in my clothes was drawn out until it hung suspended in a bubble before us which he dispersed along the corridor in a cloud of fine mist.

I turned towards Hastings suddenly, wrapping my arms around his waist as I nuzzled into his shoulder.

"Thank you," I breathed, before releasing him just as quickly.

I looked up at him from beneath my lashes, biting on my bottom lip as I gave him an awkward smile.

His hand had shifted to his baton at the contact but he hadn't drawn it and after a moment, his posture relaxed and he gave me a firm nod.

"It's my job to look after the inmates under my supervision," he replied tersely, like he was trying to reaffirm some boundaries between us and I nodded seriously as I shifted back. "Do you...ah...want to tell me what happened with the Incubus?" he asked, glancing at the door behind us where Cain was still scrutinising the security tapes. No doubt with his Vampire ears he'd be listening in on us, but I was happy enough to give him a show too.

"I'm a little embarrassed," I replied, dropping my gaze to my feet.

"It's okay, you can tell me," Hastings said, sounding so damn noble that for a moment I felt a little bad about manipulating him. But life's a bitch and all that and it wasn't like I was going to be making him do anything against the law...yet.

"When Officer Cain left me there, he didn't shut the hatch properly on Sin's door," I said in a low voice. "And when it fell open, I...well, I *think* I must have fallen under his spell when I looked into his eyes..."

"Eighty Eight can't use his Order gifts any more than you can while he's down in the main prison," Hastings replied with a frown.

"I know that. But his aura is so strong..." I shrugged and he nodded.

"I have heard a few of the staff saying they felt a pull towards him, so perhaps you're right," he conceded.

I nodded eagerly. "Then I was just talking to him about nothing in particular, and he mentioned how hungry he was and I'd saved my pudding from lunch to have later so I gave that to him."

"And what happened to your neck?" Hastings asked, eyeing the marks Sin's fingers had put on my flesh.

I bit my lip and shrugged, not saying a word. Snitches got stitches and all that, but it was pretty obvious what had happened, not to mention the fact that Cain would see it on the CCTV tape anyway. I glanced along the empty corridor nervously and shifted an inch closer to Hastings, hoping that this part of my plan would work and that Cain really was the nosey asshole I imagined him to be. Because I needed him to hear what I was going to say next. I needed him to think I was terrified of going back down into the isolation block, because I was sure that he wouldn't be able to resist putting me back down there as soon and as often as possible if he did.

"Please don't send me back down there," I breathed, looking up into Hastings' eyes and trying to convey as much fear as I could muster.

Hastings swallowed thickly and reached out to place two fingers on my throat, sending healing magic into my flesh to remove the signs of Sin's hands being on me. "I'll have a word with Officer Cain about your work detail," he promised.

"Grazie, ragazzo del coro," I murmured with half a smile. *Thank you, choir boy.*

The door burst open behind us and Hastings cleared his throat as he took a step away from me.

Cain's narrowed eyes fell on me and he damn near bared his teeth at me as he strode out of the CCTV surveillance room.

"Giving a pudding to an inmate in the hole is a crime in itself," he snarled, focusing on the part of my interaction with Sin that he could most easily punish me for. "But as I'm the one who failed to secure Eighty Eight's hatch, I've decided to go easy on you."

"Thank you, Officer," I said with a sweet smile even though I could tell he wasn't done there at all.

Cain's eyes glimmered darkly as he went on. "So I'm going to let you choose your own punishment. You can have a night in the hole yourself, or you can take a hit from my shock baton." He loosened the baton as he said that, his muscles tensing with the desire to use it, though I could tell he thought I'd pick option A.

But a night in the hole didn't sound like much fun to me and I'd been wondering whether or not my practice with Dante's lightning strikes had paid off. This could be the perfect time to test my resistance to the guards' batons.

"I'll take the strike," I said casually and Hastings shifted uncomfortably beside me.

"Sir, are you sure she can withstand a hit from that thing?" he asked in an undertone, his eyes on Cain. "She's barely a hundred pounds and they're designed to put down a Dragon Shifter-"

"She can take it," Cain growled darkly, pulling his baton from his hip and flicking the magical gauge on the end of it to activate the electrical current. Sparks of white energy zipped and crackled across its surface and I moved to stand before him in the centre of the corridor, rolling my shoulders back.

"Last chance to change your mind," Cain growled, his eyes alight with a primal hunger.

"A morte e ritorno," I replied simply, quoting my family motto and half smirking at him. *To death and back.*

Cain's dark eyes flared with excitement, his beautifully deadly features coming alive for a moment before he thrust the baton straight towards me.

I refused to even flinch and it slammed into my stomach with the force of a tsunami. Electricity crashed through my body in a wave so intense I was blinded by it. And holy mother of fuck did it *hurt!*

I barely even registered my back colliding with the stone floor as I was knocked from my feet by the blast and a scream tore from my lips as agony raced through my body.

But I didn't pass out. In fact, I was already able to move my limbs and I rolled over with a gasp of pain, dragging down a lungful of air before pushing myself up onto my hands and knees.

I held myself back at that point, but I knew I could have done more than that. I could have gotten to my feet. I could have run. I even could have turned to fight back. And that was all I'd been wanting to know.

I was broken and reborn in pain and suffering as a pup at the hands of my mamma and then my papà in turn. Nothing could break my resolve. Not even a weapon designed to be debilitating.

A crazed laugh spilled from my lips just as strong hands wrapped around my arms and I was hauled to my feet.

Cain shoved me back against the wall of the corridor, looking into my eyes with a wild kind of longing written across his features.

I'd been knocked several meters down the corridor by the blast and Hastings hung back by the CCTV surveillance room with a startled look on his innocent face.

"Good girl," Cain said in a low voice which failed to hide how much he was getting off on what he'd just done. "Maybe you and me will find a way to get along after all."

I panted in his arms, my limbs still twitching a little from the assault of electricity as I tipped my head back against the wall and his eyes trailed down to my throat with a surge of longing in them.

I hid my smirk away for later and held my tongue, letting him think he was bringing me to heel.

A dark smile broke across Cain's face, lighting up his features in a way I'd never seen before and making my heart leap in the process. He may have been a psychotic asshole, but I had to admit that there was something about the darkness in him which called to me, challenged me, begged me to rise up and meet it with some shadows of my own.

He leaned a little closer, reaching out to grasp my jaw before pressing healing magic beneath my skin at the point of contact.

A soft moan escaped my lips as the pain in my body washed away and Cain released me as suddenly as he'd grabbed me.

"Take her up to join the rest of the prisoners in the Magic Compound," Cain directed Hastings. "I need to go and deal with Eighty Eight."

"Yes sir." Hastings hurried forward to comply and Cain gave me one last, assessing look before shooting away from us with his Vampire speed.

Hastings looked half tempted to ask if I was okay and I flashed him a sweet smile as we started walking for the elevator. My stomach growled pathetically at the fact that I'd missed lunch and I guessed that was precisely why Cain had taken so damn long to assess the CCTV footage so I refused to mention it.

I could feel Hastings watching me as we waited for the elevator to arrive and as the doors slid open, we stepped inside.

"I've never seen a Fae take a hit like that and try to get up right after it," he muttered as the doors closed again. "Hell, most Fae are knocked clean out by it."

"Well, I'm not *most* Fae," I replied, looking up at him with a shrug.

He pushed a hand through his beach blonde hair and looked away from me with a frown. But if he was trying to figure me out then I was willing to bet he'd be at it for a while.

We reached the Magic Compound on level three and the doors slid open smoothly to admit us.

Hastings escorted me to the security doors which led out to the Compound and I approached the glass containment cubicle with excitement.

The guard inside looked up as I approached, her gaze sliding past me and landing on Hastings as a faint blush lined her cheeks.

"Afternoon, Jack," she said brightly, paying me little attention as the first door slid closed behind me and I placed my manacled wrists through the hole in the screen dividing us so that she could free my magic from its confinement.

My gaze dropped to take in her name. Officer Lucius. She was blonde, pretty and had a helluva big smile for Hastings.

"How are you, Jess?" he asked as she placed her cuff key into my restraints one after the other and gave the key a half turn in each.

A sigh of ecstasy escaped my lips as I felt my magic rushing to my fingertips and I pulled my hands back, moving closer to the door which led out to the yard.

Officer Lucius took her sweet time buzzing me through, but I finally strode out into the yard as they continued to flirt and I filed away that little nugget of information on them in case I ever needed it.

The first person I noticed in the yard was Ethan Shadowbrook. He was playing with his Wolf pack, throwing a spray of water up around them as the female members of his pack ran through it in nothing but their white tank tops and black panties. Their shirts were turning transparent as they were soaked and a growl rumbled in the back of my throat as I watched them bounding about, trying to catch his eye. Though as my attention fixed on him, I realised he wasn't even bothering to watch the show, he was more interested in a conversation he was having with his Beta, Harper. He continued to toss jets of water from his palms at the giggling girls as he spoke with her, but his gaze never strayed to them.

I smirked to myself as I walked straight past his pack, aiming for the furthest end of the yard beyond the wall which divided it.

My pack yipped and howled excitedly as they spotted me and they swarmed closer, nuzzling against me and brushing their fingers over my arms and back in greeting. I smiled at them and returned their affection, seeking out Amira in the group as she hung back.

"Have you decided on pack positions yet?" she demanded as I finally found her. She held her chin high and the defiance in her gaze brought a growl to my lips.

I flexed my fingers, exerting my power so that my earth magic rumbled through the concrete beneath her feet, knocking her back onto her ass. Vines whipped up and tangled around her arms as she raised a hand to fight back and I snarled as I stalked closer to stand over her.

"I don't take kindly to people questioning the way I run *my* pack," I snarled and the rest of the Wolves circled close behind me as I felt eyes on me from all over the yard. This was a test just as much as going up against the Dragon asshole, Two Hundred, had been on my first day. I had to make sure my rule over my pack was iron clad. No gaps could ever show through. "And I *was* going to hold off on allocating the role of Beta until we had a chance to run as a pack again. But if you insist on hearing it from my lips now, then fine. You dug your own grave."

I turned away from Amira dismissively, letting the vines fall from her body as if she was no threat to me at all. Which she wasn't. I didn't need to beat her down again to gain the loyalty of my pack. I could see it shining in their eyes already. Alphas like her were ten a penny; Fae who were strong and determined enough to stake a claim on their power. And that was all well and good. But I was of another breed. People did what I wanted because they could sense the strength in my veins and the force of my will before I even parted my lips. They *wanted* to follow me. They didn't just have to because I'd beaten them into submission. And you couldn't buy loyalty like that. But I could sure as hell prove I deserved it.

My gaze scoured the crowd until it settled on a guy who stood a head taller than most of the Fae around him. He had deep brown skin and eyes that sparkled knowingly as he waited for my answer.

I pointed at him, beckoning him closer. I hadn't seen the ruddy brown Wolf in his Fae form when we'd met in the Order Yard, but my inner animal had recognised him easily as soon as I'd seen him at breakfast the next morning. I'd been watching him surreptitiously ever since, assessing whether or not my gut instincts about him could be trusted and I was pretty darn sure they could. The bond between an Alpha and Beta ran soul deep and the connection we'd formed together as we ran beneath the moon had been nothing short of true harmony.

"What's your name?" I asked as I tilted my head back to look up at him.

"Sonny Tribera," he said with a smirk.

The Triberas were a sister branch of the Oscura family; three brothers had married some of my grandpa's sisters a few generations back and their name was pretty damn common in my family. We were probably third or fourth cousins or something like that, but it was hard to keep track in a family as big as the Oscuras. Aunt Maribella would know. I might even write her a letter with the names of all of my new pack mates in it and find out just how many of them were relations of mine in one way or another. She had a family tree the size of a bus painted on the wall of her dining hall and she loved tracking down all the tiny connections between our kin.

She'd even had the great joy of turning up at my cousin Marcella's wedding and leaping up in front of the congregation to announce that the bride and groom were already related. But as they turned out to be fifth cousins once removed, they'd decided to go ahead with the union anyway. I still found it funny as fuck to tease them about being siblings whenever I was invited to their house though...not that they'd asked me over for a few years now... *Maybe they didn't find that funny after all.*

I pushed aside all thoughts of Marcella and her inbred children and fixed my attention on Sonny.

He was probably in his mid thirties and a big fucker, but the strength I could see in him shone out from the inside. It ran soul deep. I'd always had a gift for seeing the truth in people and I could tell I wouldn't regret this decision.

"You're my Beta," I said, holding his eye. It wasn't a request, it was an order and he dipped his head with a cocky smile which said he'd already known he would be. I had to admit that made me like him even more.

"Thank you, Alpha," Sonny said, stepping forward to wrap his arms around me.

The rest of the pack started barking and howling with excitement and I spent a little while bathing in their attention before extricating myself from the group. As much as I loved my pack leader role, I couldn't afford to be too distracted by it. That was why I had no intention of switching cell blocks to join them in B either. Sonny could lead them well enough when I wasn't around and it also meant I had more time to concentrate on what I was really here for.

I crossed the yard with a swagger in my step and my head high as I made a beeline for Roary Night. He was leaning back against the wall at the far end of the yard, talking to a group of huge guys who I guessed were some of his Shades. I could never tell exactly how many followers he had due to the fact that they never hung out all at once like most of the gangs did. It was a clever tactic though, because it meant most of his Shades could go undetected, no doubt gathering him intel on the other gangs as easily as ghosts. Plus you never knew when one of them might be sitting right beside you, ready to slip a shank between your ribs if you acted out against him.

One of them noticed me coming and nudged Roary to let him know.

He turned his golden eyes on me and I fought against the prickle of excitement that I got whenever I managed to snare his attention.

With a word from Roary, the Fae surrounding him slipped away and he smiled mockingly as he waited for me to join him.

"What have I done to earn myself a visit from the great Moon Alpha?" he teased as I came to stand before him.

"Moon Alpha?" I asked, raising a brow.

"You're causing enough of a stir around here to be earning yourself nicknames," he replied. "And I've got eyes and ears everywhere reporting back to me."

"That must be handy," I replied, twisting my fingers through my hair as I moved to lean against the wall beside him and we looked out across the Magic Compound at the rest of the inmates.

"You have no idea."

A wild shriek sounded across the Compound and I glanced up, spotting a convict pulling her tank off and scratching at her skin.

"Ants! Oh my stars – can you see those ants?!" She grabbed hold of another inmate by the collar, rubbing her tank into his face. I wrinkled my nose, wondering what the hell was up with the weirdo.

"What's her problem?" I murmured to Roary.

He looked at me with a frown. "Sometimes people lose their shit in here."

"Can't say I'm surprised." I glanced around at the fences and the guards glaring in at us. There wasn't a pop of colour in the place to make it remotely interesting, and I imagined days after days stuck in these walls was plenty of reason to go insane.

"I mean, they really lose their shit, pup. I've seen normal-ass people turn crazy overnight." He shook his head like he couldn't make sense of it and my brows pulled together as I watched the girl scratching at her skin, leaving reddened lines all over her flesh. A friend of hers soon arrived to help, looking concerned as she used her water magic to wash her and after a while, she seemed to snap out of it, pulling on her clothes with an embarrassed expression.

Roary and I fell into silence and I eyed the way the prisoners moved about the wide space with interest. The four factions which had claimed control of the prison weren't that easy to spot. Roary's followers could be anyone at all. I was fairly sure he even had people who were loyal to him within the opposing factions too. No doubt a Wolf or two of mine were handing over information on anything he might like to know about the Oscuras. Not that it really mattered. So long as he wasn't outwardly against me, there was nothing about my pack which needed to be kept secret. So he was free to spy as much as he liked.

"Although I clearly enjoy the attention you shower me with, I'm guessing you might have had more of a reason for joining me than just wanting to stand by this wall," Roary said as the silence stretched. "Or did you just come because you can't keep away?"

"You wish," I snorted dismissively. I might have been crushing on Roary like a fourteen year old all over again, but I would never admit it. And I sure as shit wouldn't be wandering around after him like some little lost pup either.

"Come on then, the suspense is killing me."

I cast a silencing bubble around us to make sure that we couldn't be overheard and turned to lean my shoulder against the wall, looking up at him as he angled himself towards me too. Roary raised an eyebrow as that caught his attention and I leaned towards him conspiratorially.

"I'm going to break us out of here, Roary," I said in a low voice.

He tipped his head back and laughed, the sound of it a deep rumble that poured right up from his soul. "I knew you were a little crazy, Rosa, but I didn't realise you'd actually gone insane."

I rolled my eyes at him, knowing he wouldn't really dismiss me that easily.

"Come on, Roary, you didn't really think I'd just let myself get banged up in here, did you? I don't intend on living my life in a cage."

"Neither did I, but that's what happens when you live the kinds of lives we do, Rosa," he said darkly. "And we don't get a lot of say in it if the Fae Investigation Bureau catch up to us."

"Well now I'm giving you a say in it," I purred. "Don't you trust me, Roar? What have you got to lose by trying?"

The corner of his mouth twitched with amusement and he looked down at me with interest lighting his gaze. "You seriously believe you can break out of here?"

"With a little bit of help from the right people."

"Why do I feel like you're about to get me into trouble?"

"Why do I feel like that's what you like about me?" I teased.

The corner of Roary's mouth hooked up and he turned his golden eyes on me, trailing his gaze over me slowly like he was drinking in every detail he could find.

"It's on the list," he said finally. "Come on then, let's hear your master plan."

I smirked like the cat who had the cream and leaned a little closer to him, drawing my hair over my shoulder to hide my expression from any nosey assholes who might be watching us.

"Well I'm not going to give you the whole thing just yet," I said.

"Are you trying to get me hooked with the foreplay, little pup?" he asked in a low voice.

My pulse stumbled at his words and I swallowed thickly as I looked away from him before shifting a little closer again as I looked back.

"My foreplay is so good that I could have you begging at my feet within two minutes, Lion boy," I mocked and Roary's smile changed into something that had my blood heating.

"Well don't keep me in suspense…"

"I need you to help me get around these cuffs," I said slowly, raising my hand and letting a flower bloom in my palm. "So that I can use my magic outside of this yard."

"Yeah, that sounds great. I wish I'd thought of that before," Roary said, scoffing dismissively like he thought I was kidding.

"I'm serious, Roary. I need to steal a key from one of the guards and get it back to my cell without them figuring out I'm the one who has it. And as talented as I am, I don't have the skills I need to pickpocket a guard and get away with it…"

Roary raised his eyebrows at me and ran a hand over the rough stubble lining his jaw. "You don't ask for much, do you, Rosa?"

"I'd ask for the moon if you could steal it for me. But a cuff key is a good start."

He snorted a laugh. "There's CCTV to consider."

"So let's disable it," I suggested easily.

"We can post a job for that, I guess. We could get someone to break the cameras in the Mess Hall at breakfast tomorrow. But it won't be enough. The guards work in pairs, they'll see me coming."

"My pack can start a riot," I suggested. "An all out brawl in the Mess Hall. The guards will be running around trying to break it all up, you spot a weak link and, *presto* – one cuff key for us to use as we like."

"You make it sound so easy," Roary teased. "You know those keys are on a chain? And that chain only releases at the magical signature of the guard who carries it?"

"Are you saying you're not up to it?" I asked. "Has the great Roary Night lost his touch in prison?"

"Never," he scoffed.

I moved right into his personal space, tiptoeing up to whisper in his ear and he leaned closer to me to hear it. "So prove it."

ROARY

PRISONER #69

CHAPTER FOURTEEN

My eyes kept trailing to the cameras in the corners of the Mess Hall as I ate my porridge. The single pot of honey it came with wasn't nearly enough to satisfy my sweet tooth and I glanced down the long table to where Claud was sitting, arching a brow at him. He was a stout man with a Lion tattoo on his neck that looked suspiciously like me, and dark hair which he'd been growing out since I'd met him.

I didn't normally have to wait this long to get what I wanted.

Claud nodded subtly, slipping out of his seat and within a minute, two girls arrived, placing their little honey pots beside me.

I tossed them a smile before picking up the pots and pouring them into my porridge. Rosa dropped down opposite me with her tray, glancing at the girls as they walked away and the now empty pots sitting beside me.

"Morning," she said lightly, a sense of anticipation about her.

"Are you sure you know what you're getting yourself into today, little pup?" I asked, skipping the formalities. I'd known Rosa long enough not to bother with them.

"I know exactly what I'm doing," she said airily, turning her gaze to the cameras. "But if it all goes to hell, don't go sacrificing yourself for me again, will you?"

A grin pulled at my mouth as she avoided my gaze, thinking she'd won a point against me. She'd might have been there the night I was arrested, but I wasn't going to let her think I'd gone to prison for her. Whether it was true or not. "I think you're remembering it wrong. You got your moon eyes over me and thought you'd tried and save *my* ass. That's how I got caught."

Her expression contorted in complete denial. "I didn't have *moon* eyes over you. You showed up trying to be the hero and-"

"Can't have. I'm no one's hero. And there lies the fault in your story. It's okay Rosa, it's my Charisma." When my Order gifts were unleashed, I could make Fae bow at my feet. The weak of will were the most susceptible and I knew Rosa wasn't that, but my Charisma was one of the most powerful in existence.

A snarl ripped from her lips, but I was saved her fury as a sharp *crack* caught my attention. I swivelled in my seat as another crack sounded and my eyes snagged on one of the cameras as a rock flew through the metal mesh around it and smashed the screen into a spiderweb of cracks. I hunted the room for the culprit as another rock whistled through the air, then another and another, taking out every camera with incredible precision. Movement down the end of the hall drew my attention and I spotted a pink-haired girl pocketing a slingshot just before all hell broke loose as the guards rushed around trying to figure out who had done it.

"It's time," I muttered and Rosa's spine straightened.

She lifted her chin, releasing a low howl and within seconds, her pack rose from their seats all around the room. Her Beta, Sonny, stalked across the hall and smashed his breakfast tray straight over Ethan Shadowbrook's head. The Lunar pack dove from their seats, rushing at the Oscura pack as Ethan caught the culprit by the throat and started beating the life out of him.

Excitement rushed through me and a smile hooked up my lips as the fight escalated.

Rosa slipped out of her seat as the guards rushed in to try and break up the brawling packs as chaos ensued.

I caught Claud's eye and he nodded to me, stuffing two fingers in his mouth and every one of my Shades in the room started upturning chairs and tables, causing utter chaos and pissing off every gang in the entire prison. My heart hit a harder beat and my smile grew even further.

Rosa jumped over the table, joining me and shoving me forward. "That one," she hissed, directing me toward the new guard, Hastings.

One of Ethan's pack lunged for Rosa and I slammed my palm into his face, breaking his nose and making him hit the ground before he realised what had happened. I threw my foot into his gut for good measure and Rosa caught my arm.

"Come on," she demanded and I jumped over the asshole, heading across the room toward Hastings as he tried to get between two Werewolves, hitting

150

them with his baton with powerful strikes. He was cut off from the rest of the guards and the throng of the crowd around him would give me good cover. So he was my target.

I focused as I circled around him, approaching from behind and checking none of the guards were looking in my direction. Officer Cain was using the full force of his baton, whacking Fae over the head so they dropped to the ground at his feet like dead flies. Luckily, his attention was well away from us for now.

Hastings was thrown back into me by the warring Wolves and I plucked the shock baton from his grip with a simple twist of my wrist which I'd used to steal countless things when I was a free man. Adrenaline poured through my veins and exhilaration tumbled through me. He half turned his head with a gasp of alarm, but I flicked the power on and drove it into his spine before he had the chance to see who had taken it. Hastings bellowed in pain and his eyes rolled as electricity poured into him and he collapsed to the ground at my feet. Satisfaction sprawled through me as I tossed the baton aside.

I dropped down to my knees just as a Lunar Wolf collided with Rosa, trying to rip and tear at her with nothing but her hands. Rosa floored the bitch in half a second with a solid punch to her temple and moved to hide me from view as she waited for the next asshole to try their luck against her.

I turned back to Hastings, grabbing hold of his hand and reaching into his pocket. My heart ticked faster and the thrill of thieving brought another wave of adrenaline crashing through my veins. This was what I lived for. And it had been far too long since I'd had a real challenge.

I reached into his pocket, finding the cylindrical key which could undo the magical cuffs. Excitement thumped through my gut, but I wasn't done yet. The key was on a magical chain and the only way to free it was to get Hastings' magical signature to release it. I took hold of the guy's hand, curling it around the chain then pinching the crook of his arm. There was a sensitive spot there on Fae which could force magic to their fingertips. But this fucker wasn't responding.

"Come on, come on," I growled under my breath, knowing time was running out.

Rosa was piling up more and more bodies around me as the Lunars came for her and one glance into the crowd told me Ethan was heading this way. His eyes blazed with rage as they locked on Rosa. But if he came over here and noticed what I was doing, I was fucked. He'd have his whole pack try to get the key from me and cause too much of a scene for us to hold onto it for long. And the punishment for stealing a key was more than just a few months in the hole, I'd get sent to interrogation where I'd be tortured for days, and when it was done the Warden would add years onto my sentence to make sure I never tried it again.

"*Motherfucker*," I snarled, giving up on his arm and ramming my elbow into his gut.

Magic sparked at his fingertips as he coughed and the key came free. I clutched it in my hand, a manic laugh escaping me as I rose to my feet and caught Rosa's arm.

"Shadowbrook's coming," I said in her ear as she kicked a Wolf at her feet.

She glanced over her shoulder as Ethan forced Oscura pack members out of the way to get closer, a roar of rage spilling from his lips.

"Get hold of that bitch!" he commanded his pack and several eyes turned our way.

"Not today asshole!" She flipped him the finger then caught my hand and we ran away into the crowd.

Laughter tumbled from my throat as we raced through the room together. My Shades were still causing chaos and victory swelled in my chest as we slipped between their ranks.

I glanced behind us and saw Ethan on a war path, hunting for us across the room, but he hadn't spotted us yet. I grabbed hold of Rosa, tugging her to the ground and pulling her under a table with me at the back of the hall.

"Did you get it?" she asked, her eyes sparkling. She looked wild and so fucking beautiful, it knocked the breath out of me for a moment.

I quickly painted on a taunting grin, producing the key and holding it under her nose. She reached for it but I closed my fist around it, hiding it behind my back.

"What's this for exactly?" I asked, narrowing my gaze.

"I told you, I have a plan."

"That's not an explanation," I pointed out. "I need details, Rosa."

"Everyone stop fighting right *now* or I will authorise every guard in here to shoot to kill!" Cain's voice blared through the room and I poked my head out from under the table, my heart beating out of rhythm. He stood up on a table with fire blazing in his hands and lighting the space in ominous red tones. The rest of the guards were climbing onto tables too, magic flaring in their palms and the fights in the hall abruptly stopped.

My breathing quickened as I ducked back under the table and shared a look with Rosa. Quiet fell and it pressed against my ears, making anxiety knot up my gut.

"Sir!" Hastings' voice sounded from the crowd and he stumbled through the inmates, appearing at the base of the table in Cain's shadow. Panic gripped his features and his eyes widened in horror. Someone must have healed the bastard. "My key is gone."

Rosa shared a look with me, not saying a word in case Cain picked it up with his Vampire ears, but I knew what that look meant. I had to hide the key. Fast.

"Everyone line up against the wall – *now!*" Cain roared and I glanced up at the table above me, hunting for anywhere I could put the key where it wouldn't be found. "Wait – where's Twelve? She's not with her pack."

"*Fuck*," I hissed, turning to Rosa and a plan came together in my mind. I'd once been the best thief in Solaria. I could work my way out of any problem. I hunted for cracks of light and found a way out. Always. And I had a solution which was the only option right then.

Pounding footfalls filled the air as everyone gathered at the back of the hall and Rosa looked to me in alarm.

I lunged toward her, throwing her backwards and pressing my body flush to hers, driving her into the ground. I hooked her legs up around my waist as she gasped then I dropped my mouth to her neck, biting into her flesh hard enough to make her cry out. Between the rush of the heist and the taste of her achingly sweet body on my tongue, desire burst through me and I got hard for her in an instant. *Oh shit.*

The table flipped over and I drew my head back to look up at Cain above us, his eyes full of pure rage.

He was on me in seconds, heaving me off of her and locking his hand around my throat. I clutched onto his waist, my fingers slipping into his pocket as I released the key and let it fall inside.

"Do you know what Dr Quentin does to rapists down in interrogation, Sixty Nine?" he snarled in my face, venom spewing from his eyes.

"He wasn't assaulting me!" Rosa got to her feet, tugging at Cain's arm as his grip tightened on my throat, fire blazing beneath his skin and coming close to burning me.

His cold grey eyes slid to her, his upper lip peeling back.

"I wanted him to," she said fiercely and I couldn't help but smirk.

Cain growled low in his throat then shoved me away.

"Line up with the others," he snapped and we hurried away toward the back wall where the inmates were crammed together shoulder to shoulder.

We found a spot and wedged ourselves into it, my hand falling to my side and resting against Rosa's. Heat seemed to pour from her skin and I had to work really fucking hard to sink my boner while the guards moved to stand in front of us.

"STRIP!" Cain barked.

Oh fuck fuck fuck.

My hard-on needed to die a thousand deaths right now.

I tried to think about anything except the way Rosa had felt beneath me. Her breath on my mouth, her curves moulding to mine.

I set my gaze on a female guard with a hairy upper lip and that was going to have to be good enough. I pulled off my jumpsuit, forcefully not looking at Rosa beside me as she got completely naked.

Several guards ran forward to start searching our clothes and I tried not to smirk too hard at the genius of my plan.

Cain was watching us all with his jaw ticking, rage simmering in his eyes that looked desperate to be unleashed.

When our clothes had been searched, Cain's lips twitched in irritation. "Turn around, hands on the wall and spread your legs."

Oh fuck my life.

I turned, pressing my palms to the wall and glancing at Rosa. She gave me a look of fear, mouthing, *where is it?*

I offered her a cocky smile in response, though she didn't look any more reassured by that. But she should have known I was too good at this to fail her.

It wasn't long before hands soon groped my whole body and I tried not to think about whether they belonged to Hairy Lip. If my boner had had any dreams of coming back, they were a distant memory now.

"It's not here, sir," an officer informed Cain at last.

A beat of silence passed that was wrought with tension.

"Get dressed!" Cain barked and I chuckled, turning around and pulling on my clothes.

Rosa was trying to catch my eye, probably confused as fuck right now. Maybe she thought I'd swallowed it. But I was beyond rooting around in my own shit for the sake of this key. I had too much class for that.

"You'd better check your locker right now," Cain snarled at Hastings.

"I had it with me, I swear," he tried but Cain directed him out of the room, refusing to look at him.

Cain surveyed us all through narrowed eyes then pointed to the door. "Back to your cell blocks! You're all on lockdown for the rest of the day."

We marched forward and I broke away from Rosa, moving through the crowd until I was behind Cain as he strode along with us. I threw an elbow into the gut of a Lunar Wolf beside him and the fucker shoved me hard enough to knock me into Cain. I used my momentum to twist around and half catch myself on Cain's waist, my hand slipping into his pocket and hooking the key out.

His fist connected with my face half a second later and I hit the ground.

"Touch me again and I'll break your legs," he snarled at me, striding away as the sea of bodies split around me like the tide around a rock. I held a hand to my face with a groan, pushing the key under my tongue.

Rosa appeared, hurrying forward and taking my hand to help me up. I gave her a slanted smile as we headed along with the crowd and she gave me a confused look right back.

We headed down to level four and the prisoners divided off into groups as they were directed towards their cell blocks. Cain led our group to Cell Block D and extended the bridge for us over the void, eyeing everyone closely as we walked across it.

"Everyone in your cells. Inspection in five minutes," he growled threateningly.

When he found out that Hastings had truly lost his key, he wasn't ever going to give up looking for it. So Rosa needed to hide it somewhere he'd never find it. Or she was beyond screwed. I was almost tempted not to give it to her for fear of what would happen if she was ever discovered. But I had to have faith in my little pup. She was the strongest Wolf I knew, not that I'd ever admit it to her.

I hurried upstairs with Rosa and she clung to my side, waiting for me to speak as we finally made it outside our cells.

"Where-" she started and I snatched her waist, dragging her against me and pushing my tongue into her mouth.

I groaned deeply before I could stop myself, pushing the key between her lips and lingering there far longer than was necessary as her mouth moved against mine. She was the sweetest thing I'd ever tasted. A mouth I had vowed never to claim. She was all the things I couldn't have wrapped up into a cocktail of forbidden fruits. Her tongue met mine with hungry strokes and a fire burned at the base of my spine as I fought the urge to drag her into my cell.

I broke the kiss with a tug in my gut, her eyes burning into mine for an endless moment.

"Don't think into that too much, little pup." I winked, walking away into my cell as a buzzing noise warned the doors were about to close. She scowled at me before heading into her own cell, unable to say a word to me with the key in her mouth. And thank the stars for that, because there was no way in hell she hadn't felt how much I enjoyed that kiss.

My hard-on was back in full force. And it was a traitor that was going to meet a swift death. Because Rosalie Oscura was not for me. And she was definitely not for my dick.

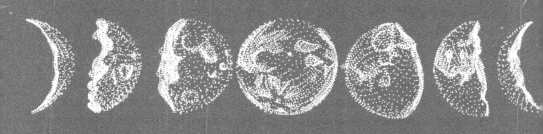

ROSALIE

PRISONER #12

CHAPTER FIFTEEN

Roary headed into his cell without a backwards glance at me and I turned and walked into my own cell too.

My heart was pounding and my lips were tingling with the memory of that kiss. A kiss I'd dreamed of, wished for, *ached* for more times than I could count. And holy Pegasus shit on a merry go round had it been worth the wait. Every inch of my flesh had come alive with desire for him and I was damn near panting with need.

His teasing rejection had knocked the wind out of me for a moment. But only a moment. Because Roary Night could claim not to want me, but there was no way I was the only one of us who had felt the chemistry in that kiss. By the stars, I could still feel his mouth on mine now and the only thing it left me wanting was *more*.

Any hopes I may have had that Roary was just an itch I ached to scratch were blasted apart by that kiss. Because now that I'd had a taste of him, I was even more certain than ever that I wanted more. And there wasn't much in this life that I'd ever desired and failed to get my hands on.

He may have been trying to dash my hopes with that little comment, but I wasn't buying what he was selling. Because maybe he'd had to kiss me to give me the key, but no way did he have to keep it going for so long. His tongue stayed in my mouth long after that key had passed my lips. Not that I had any complaints about that.

A deep buzz sounded followed by the rattle of the cell door closing behind me, forcing me to focus on what was actually important at the moment.

I quickly grabbed the spare sheet Roary had gifted me and strung it up over my door, making sure that there were no gaps for nosey bastardos to peek through before hurrying across the room to my sink.

I dropped down onto my knees and drew the key from my mouth, putting it in the lock on my left manacle and turning it half way to unleash my magic.

I sighed as power rushed to my fingertips and quickly unlocked my right manacle too.

I could hear the guards searching through the cells on the first floor, hunting every nook and cranny and conducting a repeat of the strip searches already.

My heart was pounding as I hurried to press my fingers against the mortar between the bricks and I exerted my will over it, making it crumble into sand and creating a space.

Footsteps pounded up the metal stairs outside and I stilled for a moment as I heard them coming my way.

"Oh *Officer!*" Plunger called out in a sing song voice. "I have a confession to make!"

"What?" Cain demanded and I sucked in a breath as his voice sounded from right outside my cell.

"I *may* have something I shouldn't have...*in a secret hiding place...*" Plunger said suggestively.

"For the love of the stars," Cain growled. "Hastings! Bring gloves and meet me up on three! You can conduct a thorough search of Twenty Four's cavities while I supervise."

I almost laughed in relief as Plunger's perversions bought me another few moments, but with Cain so close I was afraid he might be listening in on what I was doing.

"Roary?" I called breathily.

"Yeah?"

"Tell me what you were going to do to me before we were interrupted in the Mess Hall."

I waited, hoping he'd catch on and provide the covering noise I needed to finish my work.

"Are you so hot for me you're touching yourself already, little pup?" Roary's mocking voice came back after a beat.

"Yes," I breathed, moaning a little. "Help me finish what you started."

A moment of silence passed and he cleared his throat.

"Please," I begged like I would if I was pinned beneath him.

Roary laughed darkly and movement in the corner of my eye made me glance at the grate between our cells as he laid down and looked in at me. I waved my hand at him to encourage him to start talking and he smirked as he gave in to my demands.

"First, I'd unbutton your jumpsuit, real slow," he said in a low voice which had my toes curling.

"Yes," I breathed, panting a little as I focused my magic on creating a concealment spell. I'd been practicing damn hard at these and I could make one with such subtle magic that it was practically undetectable. But it took concentration and giving half of my attention to dirty talk with Roary Night was not the ideal level of focus.

"Then I'd run my hands over your body, feeling every inch of you, tasting your lips as I pulled your clothes off, making you beg for more," Roary said in a dark tone.

"I need more," I sighed, closing my eyes as I felt out the magic, crafting it perfectly. "Are you hard for me, Roary? Don't you want to feel what it's like to be inside me?"

I couldn't help but peek at him from beneath my lashes to gauge his reaction to my words.

A growl of longing came from Roary in response and his lips twitched as he fought to keep up his part in our game.

"Is that what you want, Rosa?" he purred. "To make me hard?"

"I think you are hard for me, Roary," I breathed. "I think you dream about me wrapping my lips around your cock just as often as I do."

"*Fuck,*" he snarled and I could see him shifting beside the grate from the corner of my eye.

"Try a little higher, Officer!" Plunger called from outside. "It's *right* up there!"

I snorted a laugh as I quickly gathered the crumbled mortar into my hands and exerted my earth magic over it, forming it into a lump of clay which would dry quickly. It would feel as hard as the mortar it was replacing if no one looked too hard, but I'd be able to pick it back out again with my fingernails when I needed to.

"Come on, Roary, don't leave me hanging. Tell me how much you want me," I begged as I shoved the key back into my manacle and cut off my magic supply again.

He growled and I threw him a look, raising my eyebrows meaningfully until he responded.

"So fucking much. When I get my hands on you properly, I'm going to make you scream my name so loud that you lose your voice," he swore.

I locked my other manacle and shoved the key into the gap in the wall.

"You'll be the one screaming my name, Lion," I promised.

"Don't try and pretend you aren't wet for me, Rosa, tell me just how much," he replied, turning the game back on me.

"I'm so wet for you, Roary," I agreed breathily, covering the key with the clay I'd made and shaping it to fill the gap between the bricks with my fingertips.

The moment I was done, I dropped down on the floor beside the grate, looking through at Roary with a triumphant grin.

"Are you touching yourself, for me?" he purred.

"Oh yeah," I agreed with an exaggerated moan as I pushed my hands through my hair and winked at him.

"I want those sheets down!" Cain's voice came from somewhere outside and I bit down on my bottom lip to stop myself from laughing.

"Come for me, Rosa," Roary dared, his golden eyes glimmering with heat between the holes in the grate.

I rolled my eyes at him and quickly pushed my hands inside my jumpsuit, driving my fingers down between my thighs and arching my back as I put on a show of moaning for him.

"Open on three, cell twelve!" Cain barked from right outside as I continued to moan for Roary.

Cain ripped my sheet down and I yanked my hands back out of my jumpsuit as he glared in at me, acting like he'd just caught me out.

Hell, I was such a good actress that a blush even came to my cheeks.

The buzzer sounded and my door rattled open as I pushed myself up onto my elbows, biting my lip in an act of innocence. Cain shot into my cell before I could move and hauled me up onto my feet, flipping me around and slamming me against the rear wall face first.

"Hastings! I want you searching cell eleven. And if Sixty Nine still has his dick in his hand then you have permission to use your shock baton on it!" Cain bellowed in my ear.

Roary snorted a laugh from the cell next door as Hastings hurried to comply with his command.

"What's wrong, Cain?" I breathed. "Are you jealous?"

He snarled in my ear, driving me up against the wall more forcefully, his whole body pressing to mine. The touch of his magic kissed my skin as he threw a silencing bubble over us and he leaned down to speak in my ear.

"If I want a piece of trashy Wolf pussy I can get it easily enough on any street corner in your old neighbourhood. I hear Oscura girls give it up for five auras and beg for more when you're done with them."

"Sounds like you have a lot of experience of that, *Officer.*"

"I don't need to pay for a piece of ass," he growled.

"No. That would be too easy for you, wouldn't it?" I taunted, grinding my ass back against his crotch.

"What's that supposed to mean?" he demanded.

"That you don't want it handed to you. You want the chase, the *hunt*. You want to go after the kinds of women you shouldn't and make them beg for you before you take them."

"Is that so?" Cain grabbed my wrists and slammed them against the wall on either side of my head a moment before running his hands down my arms, feeling for any sign of the stolen key.

"I think so. That's why you want me. Because you can't have me."

He growled and the sound of it rumbled down my spine where his broad chest was pressed against me and ran all the way to my core. I was playing with fire when it came to him, but sometimes I wanted to know what it would feel like to get burned.

"You're forgetting something, Twelve," he said, speaking right into my ear as his hands slid over my body and he continued to search me. "I already have you. The Warden assigned you to me. Your ass is *mine*." His hands gripped my ass as he said that and he squeezed firmly enough to make me gasp.

"You don't own me, Cain," I scoffed, though my pulse was racing at his words.

"Maybe not," he conceded, dropping to his knees behind me and running his hands down my legs. As he ran them back up the inside of my thighs, my pulse pounded even faster and he stood behind me again, looking into my eyes as I turned my head towards him with a challenge lighting his gaze. "*Yet.*"

He shot away from me in a blur of Vampire speed, upending everything on my bunk and the spare one above it and tossing everything I owned all over my cell in a whirlwind of movement.

"Cell twelve clear!" Cain barked as he shot back out onto the walkway and a buzz sounded before my door closed again. He flicked his fingers in my general direction, disbanding the silencing bubble before moving on to search the next cell.

I released a breath and fought hard against the shit eating grin which was battling for control of my features.

Part one of my plan was complete. Now I just had to wait until I could make use of my new toy.

We spent the rest of the day in our cells. The guards didn't bother giving us lunch and the dinner they provided consisted of a stale roll and a hunk of raw broccoli which was shoved through our cell doors about ten minutes before lights out.

I'd eaten it anyway. Food was food after all and though my taste buds didn't think much of the offering, the ache in my stomach was satisfied by it. Well, not satisfied, but quietened for a while at least.

I sat waiting in my cell for hours after darkness had fallen and the rest of the inmates fell asleep. When the sounds of fights and crying faded out and all that was left was the soft rise and fall of heavy breathing, I slid out of my bed and headed to the front of my cell. I twitched the sheet aside which I'd rehung there and looked out at the darkened cell block.

The place was near silent, though I could hear some Fae having sex on the level below mine. There weren't any guards in the block which was the main thing.

A distant shriek came suddenly from beyond the cell block doors and I stilled as I looked at the thick steel which kept us safe from the Belorian, wondering just how much I trusted the strength of it. When the creature failed to make itself known again, I released a slow breath and forced myself to turn my attention away from the monster which roamed the halls.

I slipped across my cell on bare feet, bending down and digging into the false mortar beneath my sink until I managed to dig the cuff key back out.

My heart pounded as I quickly freed my magic before hurrying back to the front of my cell. First, I threw a silencing bubble up around me to hide all sounds of what I was about to do, though I made sure it only worked one way so that I'd still be able to hear anything outside.

I twitched aside the sheet covering my door again and carefully cast a series of detection spells along the walkways and by the cell block door in case any guards appeared. The magic was subtle and near undetectable, but it would alert me if anyone passed through it.

Once I was satisfied that I'd be warned if anyone came my way, I headed back to the sink and started exerting my earth magic on the bricks beneath it, loosening the mortar until I could pull them from the wall.

I worked as quickly as I could, tugging bricks aside until I'd formed a hole which was large enough to admit me. The wall was nearly a meter thick and I kept working until I made it through to the other side.

Adrenaline shot through my veins as I found myself in a cold, dark space beyond the wall and I threw a Faelight up above my head, bathing the area in an orange glow.

My heart pounded as I looked back and forth along the maintenance shaft which ringed all of the cell blocks. A series of thick, black pipes ran along the

162

gap at head height, pumping the Order Suppressant gas into every cell block twenty four hours a day.

The gap was just big enough for me to stand up and the walls pressed close on either side, but I was small, so I could move around easily enough. I couldn't help but laugh as I imagined Cain's face if he saw me now. He was so caught up in trying to dominate me that he hadn't been paying enough attention to what truly counted. And now my plans were really coming together.

I ached to go on, explore more, find my way around in this network of tunnels…but my magic was burning low after forging my way through that wall and the guards would still be hunting for whoever had stolen the key.

I couldn't risk getting caught and I needed to use the last of my power to hide what I'd done in case they came and checked my cell again.

With a sigh of frustration, I extinguished my light and headed back through the tunnel. I used my magic to disintegrate all the bricks that had made up the central part of the wall, leaving a thin layer to rebuild the outer edges and cover my tracks.

Once I was back in my cell, I drew all scraps of dust and dirt from my clothes with my magic and deposited them in the sink before washing them away. Then I disbanded my silencing bubble and detection spells and quickly cut off my connection to my magic before hiding the key again.

I crawled into bed at last with my heart pounding and my smile growing. Everything was coming together. And I was pretty sure I'd be back out of here by Christmas.

ETHAN

PRISONER #1

CHAPTER SIXTEEN

I sat on the bleachers in the Magic Compound, my gaze fixed on the fence opposite me across the concrete as it pulsed with magical energy. Right then, I felt the current in that fence as keenly as if it lived in my own blood. I was fixated on one thing and one thing only: someone in this prison had a cuff key. A motherfucking *key*. Outside of this pig pen, they could use magic. Which made them the most dangerous asshole in the complex and my number one target. Because if anyone in this prison was going to have a cuff key in their possession, it was me. Numero uno. The top fucking dog. So who the hell had it?

I searched the faces of everyone on this side of the Veiled Wall, wondering who it could be. Half of the inmates weren't clever enough to pull off something like that. So the gang leaders were my prime suspects. But there were plenty of skeevy, low-lying molluscs who could have been sneaky enough to pull it off too.

Most of my pack were off searching for leads and the rest of them sat around me, pawing at my arms and nuzzling into me as they sensed my unease. Harper brushed her mouth over my neck in a clear offer and I elbowed her away with a low growl in my throat. I wasn't in the mood for fooling around. And even if I had been, there was only one Wolf on my mind these days. She haunted me in my dreams and in the fucking daytime too. She was everywhere. On the scent in the air, in every swish of every raven haired girl, in every pair of hazel eyes that turned my way. But none were as heart-wrenchingly, breathstealingly beautiful as hers. And I hated them. I despised how they lured me in and tugged on a cord in my heart that begged me to go to her.

I'd never met an equal Wolf before, but my sister, Eisha, had warned me of what it was like. She'd coupled up with her perfect match years ago. She'd only been sixteen and my mother had nearly busted a lung when she found out, but once she realised they were true equals. Mates. That was it. Mom fell in line and helped them organise the wedding.

Eisha was the reason I was in here, but I didn't blame her for what had happened. Every day that passed, I would pay diligently because of the decision I'd made the day the cops had arrested me. I knew I'd be stuck in here when she and her mate had their first pup, but that was on me. They'd had a bunch since and I'd missed every one of them. Eisha wasn't allowed to bring them to visitation until they were sixteen. But I could accept that. Because when I met them, I wanted to be a free Wolf, ready to earn my place as their Alpha again.

I signalled to the Fae playing wall ball in front of me and they tossed me the ball. I ran my thumb across it and a series of jobs started to appear on the back of my hand, but I wasn't interested in taking on a job today. I was going to post one.

I pushed my magic into the ball, visualising the words then I stood up, jumping down from the bleachers and dropping the ball. I kicked it at the wall and the second it hit, the job was posted. I played a few rounds for the sake of the guards watching then left the players to it and turned back to the bleachers.

A howl caught my ear before I made it there and I glanced over my shoulder, spotting two of my pack guiding a girl toward me. She was barely over five feet tall and her bubblegum pink hair was pulled up into two pigtails. She was only twenty two, but she'd earned her name in this prison. Everyone called her Bullseye. Despite the fact every Fae in here was practically mortal without their magic, we retained the inclinations of our Orders. And Bullseye was a Vampire with the keenest eyes I'd ever known. Even out of her Order form, she was a dead shot. So if you pissed her off, you could expect a stone between your eyes from the slingshot she carried about. And that shit could kill if she wanted it to.

"Hello, love," I purred as my Wolves shoved her in front of me and I lifted a hand to cast a silencing bubble around us.

"I figured she was a likely candidate for taking out the cameras in the Mess Hall yesterday," Ramsey said and I nodded at him, turning to Bullseye.

"Is that true? Did you do it?"

Her eyes flitted from me to the Wolves who I could hear gathering at my back, but there was no sign of nerves in her. Not yet.

"Yeah." She shrugged. "So what? I took a wall job."

166

I clenched my jaw. I should've guessed whoever took that key had been clever about it. There had probably been multiple moving parts in their plan. There was no way you'd get a cuff key unless your plan was meticulous. And outsourcing through the wall meant there were no leads back to the culprit.

I lifted my hand, releasing my magic to make a cloud form above Bullseye's head. She winced as it started to rain on her and I made sure it was cold as shit.

I moved a step closer, taking a threatening stance. "What did you take in payment for the job, love?" I growled.

"Hair d-dye," she said through chattering teeth, gesturing to her bright hair. "Is that a c-crime?"

I intensified the rain, folding my arms as I surveyed her. "I want you to work for me. You need hair dye in future, you come to my pack. You take jobs from the wall, you tell me about them before they're executed."

"I don't align with anyone, Shadowbrook," she said, hissing at me as she raised her palms in an almost threat. *Holy fuck, the balls on this girl.*

I smiled darkly and she shifted under my gaze. "You align with me or you fight against me."

She pressed her lips together, glancing at my Wolves then back to me. Apart from being over twice her size, I was also carrying a tsunami of power in my veins. She couldn't win. And she'd only been in Darkmore a few months, so it was time someone as valuable as her got claimed.

"So what will it be, Bullseye?" I rolled my shoulders back, letting the rain fall away and casting blades of ice in my palms instead. My Werewolves tightened the circle around us, howling and yapping excitedly. "Be forced to bow or do it willingly?"

Bullseye swallowed thickly then nodded, her pissed off expression not bothering me one bit.

"Good choice." I wrapped my arm around her, dragging her in for a tight hug as I let the ice melt away in my palms. I dropped my mouth to her ear as my muscles tightened around her in an almost threat. "If any more jobs get posted on the wall to take out cameras, I want you to accept them, got it?"

She nodded against my chest, half suffocated as I held her too firmly. I scrubbed my knuckles in her hair then shoved her away from me and my Wolves parted to let her go. They immediately rushed back toward me, running their hands over my arms and chest and I soaked in their company as determination crashed through my veins. Whoever had that key could hide it in the recesses of hell for all I cared, I'd still walk through the nine circles to get it. It was only a matter of time until it was mine.

I hadn't slept well in my cell since I'd hooked up with Rosalie. Sleeping alone wasn't natural for a Wolf, but somehow I couldn't find it in me to invite my pack into my cell since her. It was hard to get any rest at all without the brush of hands across my skin or soft breathing against my flesh. But tonight, like every night since I'd fucked that Oscura bitch, I was only longing for the weight of one body on top of mine. *Hers.*

When I closed my eyes, she was all I could see. And whenever I *did* get to sleep, I was plagued by dreams of her naked body riding mine until I woke hard as stone and pissed off as fuck.

A buzz sounded out in the cell block and my ears pricked up as the cell doors unlocked. *Fuck yes.*

Order time. The guards never gave us a heads up of when exactly we were going to get it. It was just another way to make us go crazy in here I guessed. But when it did happen, it was like waking up on Christmas morning.

I bounded out of my cell, cupping my hands around my mouth and howling to call my pack to me. Excitement tumbled through my veins as I charged downstairs and flexed my arms and rolled my neck, ready to shift and run and be free. Well, as free as was possible within these walls. The Order Yard might have been an illusion, but it was one I was willing to buy into as often as possible.

My pack caught up with me as I reached the bridge and I jogged across it with another howl, feeling like a pup again as a smile pulled at my cheeks. I couldn't wait to see the beautiful eye of the moon. That silvery vixen was always calling to me. She sang songs in my heart that made me miss her like an old friend. And it was time to reunite.

The guards directed us up the stairs as if I didn't know exactly where to go. I was already racing up past the second floor and rounding into the corridor where the elevators stood to take us to the surface. Sometimes I forgot we were half a mile underground. But these shiny doors were a reminder of how far up we needed to go to get out of the main prison.

As the first set opened, I piled into it with the entirety of my pack, taking up the whole space. It soon started climbing and energy made my pulse pound to a feral beat. There was something in the air tonight, something stirring and shifting beneath my skin.

The elevator doors opened and we poured out. I was half out of my clothes already and I tossed them to my Omega so he could put them in a locker for me, shifting instantly so my four black paws hit the ground hard. I was a beast, a creature of the night that could slip through shadows like I was made of them. My family lived up to their name. The Shadowbrooks were all dark like this and the only thing that marked me as different was the silver star that adorned my forehead. Mom had always called me her guiding star. And I called her my sun. Sometimes it felt like she was still in this world when I looked to the sky and saw her hanging there. The fact that she'd died while I'd been inside these walls had torn me apart, eaten away a part of my soul which would never recover. My brother, Tyson, had taken on the Alpha role in the pack in her absence. He was only a year my junior and I'd seen the way he'd grown since my incarceration here when he'd visited. He was a true Alpha and would be my rival for control of the pack when I got out of here in a few months. I couldn't wait to be free, the day was drawing ever closer. I could taste it on the wind.

Crackling energy spilled along my spine as I raced out toward the exit and lifted my head to the sky beyond the dome high above. A yap of excitement escaped me as I realised why I was feeling so frisky tonight. It was a full moon. She winked down at me, flirting like she always did. If the moon was a girl, she'd be one hell of a fuck.

I raced into the forest, tearing up the earth with my huge claws as my pack pounded after me. Running under the moon fuelled my magic reserves even though I couldn't use any of that power. The cuffs expanded and moulded to fit any Order, their magic infallible even out here. It didn't matter though, because tonight the only muscles I wanted to flex were the ones of my Order form. I was going to hunt down Rosalie Oscura and make her pay for tricking me. She was going to be crushed beneath my paws and begging for mercy. And the thrill of that image finally gave me some relief from the hold she'd had over me since the moment we'd met. All I needed to do was defeat her and she'd no longer be my equal. I'd stop pining after her and would be able to focus on taking pleasure from my pack again. From anyone I damn well liked in fact. She was in my head like an electrode that was cock-blocking me from having anyone else. And tonight, that ended.

I ran with the pack, listening for Rosalie's howls in the distance. I was sure she'd be out tonight. She might have been my enemy, but she was still of my kind. And her nature was to run under the moon at any chance she got just like mine was.

I strained my ears as I raced into the rocky region to the south of the dome, climbing out of the forest to an outcrop which looked back over it. I lifted my head and howled to the sky then fell quiet as I listened for her. There was a still pool of glistening water to my right and my pack shifted back out of their

Wolf forms, climbing into it. They were soon starting on an orgy and the word *Alpha* kept falling from their mouths in breathy moans as they begged me to join them. Without me amongst them, Harper was getting most of the attention and I was kind of pissed at myself for not joining in when she sat on the edge of the pool and two guys moved between her legs to pleasure her.

I growled in refusal, keeping my eyes set on the trees down below as I listened for Rosalie. She had to be out here somewhere. I refused to believe she'd given up the chance to see the moon tonight.

Eventually, a low howl drew my attention down in the trees. Not far at all.

My pulse quickened as I answered it, lacing my tone with a challenge that cut the night apart. I waited one second, two, three. Anticipation crawled through my veins like a drug. And then she answered. A challenge filled her tone too. She was accepting it at last. And I was finally going to force her beneath me.

I took off with a bark that told my pack to stay where they were, racing down the hill into the trees and howling again to let her know I was coming. Her reply told me she was waiting close by and I upped my pace, my heart thumping wildly as I searched for her.

I soon broke through into a clearing and dug my claws into the ground as I came to a halt in a circle of moonlight. I sensed her moving through the trees, the soft thud of her paws drawing closer.

I peeled my lip back, lowering as I readied to pounce the second she showed herself.

A glimmer of silver caught my eye and I twisted around as Rosalie lunged from the trees to my right, her coat catching the light as she collided with me. I was prepared for it, slamming a huge paw into her muzzle, knocking her off balance and forcing her back a step.

She was incredible to behold, a beast as large as me. I'd never seen another Wolf so powerful and it set my instincts alight with need. But no. Fuck *no*. I would not accept an Oscura as my equal. She was going to bow.

She darted around me, her tail flicking out like molten silver behind her. She dove at me once more, the full force of her blow nearly knocking me from my feet and making my heart pound harder. Her teeth sank into my shoulder and I snarled furiously as pain ripped through my flesh. I slashed at her with razor sharp claws, tearing a mark down her glorious fur and blood spilled, dripping to the ground.

Satisfaction pooled in my gut as she fell back with a yelp and I rose up to my fullest height, springing at her again before she could regain her feet. She darted away from me before I could catch her, tearing around the clearing and coming at me from behind. I swung around, but her huge paws slammed into my spine as she tried to uproot me and I barked a laugh, throwing my hind feet at her and leaping away.

I turned again with a dangerous growl, locking her in my sights as she lowered her head too, ready to strike.

We jumped forward at the same time, colliding in the air in a clash of claws and teeth. The adrenaline in my blood was too keen to feel any pain as we crashed to the ground and it was only by sheer luck that I landed on top.

I didn't waste a second, spreading my paws in the dirt and widening my jaws to grab her throat. Her head slammed into mine as she thrashed, but I managed to get my teeth into her neck and hold her still. Her paws smacked into my gut and I was almost thrown off from the blow, but I held on by sheer force of will.

She didn't yield, continuing to fight and I knew it was only seconds until I lost my grip on her.

In a flash, she shifted, slipping out of my jaws with ease as she fell naked beneath me in her Fae form. I shifted fast before she could scramble away, grabbing hold of her throat with one hand and snatching one of her wrists with the other as I pressed her down into the dirt.

She gazed up at me through those kerosene eyes which could have lit the world on fire. I tried not to blink, but energy was spilling down my spine as the moon called to me, begging me to take her. It was the most natural thing in the world and my cock betrayed me as it swelled against her thigh.

"*Submit,*" I snarled, squeezing her throat tighter.

She grinned at me, a wildness in her eyes that made me almost groan with how much I wanted to claim that taunting mouth. To teach it a lesson it wouldn't forget.

"Submit!" I roared at her, slamming her head down against the soft earth.

I squeezed her throat tighter and her eyes sparkled with some dark secret I wasn't privy to. She pushed back against me, clawing her free hand up into my hair and drawing me toward her.

"You're beat, love," I snarled, my grip easing on her throat as I fell into those eyes. The second I did, she lifted upwards and pressed her mouth to mine, her tongue pushing between my lips.

I moaned as the sweet taste of her drowned all of my senses, but the second I gave in to that kiss, she drew back and punched me right in the face.

"Fuck!" I snapped as my head wheeled sideways.

She shoved me away, wriggling out from beneath me and I was too stunned to move for a long second as she darted away into the trees. Her laughter called back to me and I growled as I rose to my feet.

"You're beat, love!" she called to me, her voice sing-song and mocking.

A snarl tore from my lips as I took chase, running into the thick woodland where rays of moonlight cut through the dense foliage above.

"What kind of Alpha hides in the shadows!?" I roared, hunting her with the desperation of a madman. I cursed myself for being so easily tamed by her and cursed my dick even more for wanting her again. I twisted my head to the moon and cursed her too, because that bitch was horny tonight and I could feel her trying to force me to claim Rosalie Oscura once more. But that wasn't what I came here for. I came here to defeat her.

Rosalie slammed into me from above as she launched herself out of a tree. I hit the ground and rolled, trying to get up, but she pushed me back onto the ground and caught my wrists, holding them down in the dirt. I yanked my arms free with a snarl. She was strong, but in our Fae forms I had the upper hand. I dropped my hands to her waist, trying to ignore the sight of her tits in the light of the moon, looking so suckable I had to bite my tongue to stop myself from claiming them.

"One of us has to submit," I hissed. "And it needs to be you."

"You're so dramatic, Ethan," Rosalie purred and I threw her off of me into the mud, rolling fast and crushing my chest to hers to keep her down.

"*Submit*," I demanded again and she laughed that musical laugh of hers that lit me up from the inside. My hard-on ground into her leg, throbbing and undermining me so fucking hard. She sucked in a breath and her eyes glittered with mirth, cutting me to ribbons.

"You're giving me mixed signals," she teased and her breath fluttered over my mouth, calling to me stronger than the moon ever had.

"Stop it," I growled. "Get out of my head."

She lifted her legs and locked them around my hips. I was half a second from losing my mind when she shoved her weight forward and forced us to roll over once more so she was on top again. We were covered in mud and blood from our fight and the dirtier she got, the better she fucking looked.

Why is she so damn tempting?

I gritted my teeth, trying to ignore the desperate need pulling at the base of my spine and lunged forward to grab her throat again. She knocked my hand aside and sprang off of me, running away into the woods once more.

"Enough!" I bellowed, pushing myself up and running after her, my body trembling with need. I had to be strong, I had to finish her. I definitely, *definitely* had to ignore my other instincts.

She circled back toward the clearing and I ran to catch her with a snarl. I was about to shift once more when she turned and dropped down to kneel before me.

My heart leapt with joy. She was submitting, right on her knees like the most obedient Beta I'd ever seen. She kept her eyes on mine, not bowing as I slowed to a walk, approaching her and swallowing hard. I just needed her to say it. The two words that would unleash me from this hell. Unbind me from this temptress.

I cupped her jaw in my hand with the cockiest smirk I'd ever worn. "That's it, love. Say it."

She rolled her eyes at me and my brows tugged together in confusion. I opened my mouth to push her harder for the words when she leaned forward and took my cock between her lips.

"Sweet *fuck*," I gasped as she took me all the way in – which was a fucking feat in itself – and I tipped my head back with a groan of pure bliss.

No...no no no. Not good.

But so good. Oh so fucking good.

Maybe she was just building up to submitting, but right then it felt like she held me in her fist and could crush me at any moment. I was hers to do whatever the fuck she wanted with. I was completely deluded if I really thought this was going to end in her bowing to me. But oh shit, maybe I'd just buy into that belief a little longer...

I cracked my eyes open to gaze at the moon, begging for it to give me the strength I needed to fight Rosalie into the ground, but if anything the moon just urged her on.

You bulbous glowy slut, I hate you.

Rosalie released me from her mouth and jumped to her feet. She grinned victoriously then turned her back on me. The biggest fucking insult you could offer a Fae and she did it right after sucking my cock. *What the hell has she done to me??*

A growl rumbled through my chest and I snapped. Fucking lost it.

I snatched a fistful of her hair and forced her around to face me. She was still smiling like she knew something I didn't, but I had no resolve to pause and question what. I leaned down and snatched hold of her thighs, hoisting her up and slamming her back against the nearest tree. Her eyes blazed as she clutched my neck with sharp nails, the need in her eyes clear. For a moment this wasn't just some game or some fight, we both gave in to each other, to this screaming desire that filled the space between us.

Her forehead dropped to mine, her eyes burning with a silent plea and a fundamental part of me needed to answer it.

I positioned my aching length at her entrance and squeezed her hips as I claimed her with one hard thrust. She cried out as I took her mercilessly, driving her back into the hard bark as every rock of my hips had me almost coming already.

Her body tightened around me as her mouth found mine in the dark. We kissed hungrily like it was our last meal and I didn't come up for air until I absolutely fucking had to. I was lost to her spell, forcing myself into her body with powerful thrusts. It felt like we were driving towards a cliff together, like she was my ride or die and the cops were after us with flashing lights. We were gonna end this together, united, and I didn't give a fuck if that was wrong.

I was on the verge of breaking apart when I remembered the moon. Remembered that this was how Wolves became mated. Screwing under a full moon with your equal was almost guaranteed to make you bond.

"No – *wait*," I gasped, but her nails dug into my shoulders and her mouth fell to my ear, her hot tongue running circles around the shell until I lost my damn mind.

"Rosalie – moon – *no*," I choked out.

"I need you Ethan, please don't stop," she panted, her body clutching me again as she started to quiver on the edge of oblivion.

That primal part of me reawakened and I simply had to give her this. I quickened my pace, my fingers digging into her skin and smearing the muck that lined her flesh.

She came apart, screaming my name with her whole body shaking and I felt every second of her pleasure like it was my own. A howl fell from my lungs as I finished, filling her with every inch of myself. I collapsed to the ground, taking her with me so she lay over me.

We panted heavily and the weight of her felt so right, I immediately wrapped my arms around her and held her close. She was what I'd been missing in my cell night after night. And now I had her, I didn't want to let go.

She lifted her head and the moon haloed her as she gazed down at me. She looked like a fallen angel, a perfect being made just for me. I tucked a lock of inky hair behind her ear, knowing this was wrong but unable to deny how right it felt. The moon seemed to shine even brighter and the glow of it felt like it was spilling into my soul until it filled up every space inside me.

A gasp fell from Rosalie's lips and she braced herself on the ground either side of my head as the moonlight surrounded her, seeming to shine from within her flesh. It took me a moment longer to realise my skin was shimmering too and I inhaled as something shifted inside my chest. All of my pack instincts, every Wolf need and desire I had suddenly angled toward her. She was the answer to everything. My equal in every way. My *mate*.

"Fuck," I exhaled, dropping my head back onto the ground and turning away from her. Because this was the worst thing I'd ever done. I'd betrayed my pack. I'd mated with an *Oscura*. Our mortal enemies. If they ever found out, they'd drive me from the pack, they'd banish me for good.

"Ethan," Rosalie breathed, reaching out to trace something behind my ear. "You're marked."

I pushed her hand away, sitting upright and a tug in my chest made me hate myself for being so cold with her. But how could I accept this?

I gripped her chin, pushing her head sideways and forcing her hair behind her right ear. There was a crescent shaped mark there like a silvery tattoo. The mark of the moon. The mark of my mate.

I pushed her off of me, rising to my feet with fear clawing at my insides. "Tell anyone about this and you're dead," I said in a low tone and her lips pursed as she rose to her feet.

"Good luck killing me, Ethan. You can't hurt me now, your instincts won't let you."

"I can have someone else do it," I spat, but even as I said it my heart shattered at the mere idea. I needed to protect her, hold her, stand at her side in all things. *Fuck no no no.*

She laughed coldly. "Well make sure they do it quick, because you'll feel my pain now too. Goodbye *mate*." She turned and shifted into her Wolf form, charging off into the trees and I was left with the most desperate feeling that I needed to follow.

ROSALIE

PRISONER #12

CHAPTER SEVENTEEN

The door rattled and I gasped as I looked over the heap of furniture I'd managed to pile against it with fear clawing at my insides.

"What's the matter, baby girl?" Papà's voice cooed as he gave up on trying to force it and laced his words with sugar. "You don't think I'm still mad at you, do you?"

There were no windows in this room. Not since the last time when I'd smashed right through them and dropped three floors to escape.

He'd caught me easily enough anyway. I could still taste the reward I'd gotten for that stunt in the swelling of my tongue. No one here ever helped me or healed me when he was done with one of his lessons. The only person to offer me healing magic was Papà himself and he only ever did it if my injuries were severe enough or if I miraculously managed to pass one of his tests.

"If you open up like a good girl, you won't have to go in the den," he promised. "Just come on out and show your papà how sorry you are and we can forget everything…"

I licked my cracked lips, wondering if there was any truth to his words or if I was a fool to hope for that.

"Last chance, poppet," Papà's voice dropped an octave as his temper began to thin and I lurched forward, yanking the creaky bed and broken chest of drawers away from the door.

I pulled it open, whimpering as I looked into his eyes and finding nothing but cold, hard fury there.

"I thought you were going to show some backbone then, runt," he taunted. "But it looks like you're just a disappointment once more."

I gasped as he lunged for me and I tried to duck around him but he was too fast, grasping a fistful of my hair and almost lifting me off of my feet so that he could glare into my eyes.

"Don't you have a kiss for your papà, runt?" he growled.

I whimpered again, scrambling forward so that I could place my lips against the rough whiskers which lined his jaw. He stank of cheap whiskey and old cigars and the mean look in his eye said he'd had too much of both tonight.

"Maybe a night in the den will help your spine to strengthen?" he hissed.

"No, Papà!" I yelped as I tried to scrabble out of his hold but he only laughed as he hauled me along, using my hair like a leash.

He dragged me out of the house and my heart thundered as I spotted the pit he'd dug at the far end of the lawn. It was five meters deep and two across. If he threw me in there again I wouldn't be getting out until he got a member of his pack with Earth magic to help me.

"I'll do better!" I cried, my fingers digging into his wrist as I tried to pry him off of me.

Several of his Wolves lounged in the yard, sitting around a bonfire set away from the pit as they swigged from beer bottles and got high on briarweed. Their eyes followed our progress across the lawn but I found no pity in their gaze. And I'd long since stopped hoping for help from any of them. Most of the time they acted like I didn't exist at all. And if any of them did pay me attention, it was only ever a bad thing.

"If you do manage to be better then maybe you won't have to come out here again," Papà muttered like this was nothing more than a minor irritation to him.

We reached the muddy hole in the ground which he liked to call the den and he snatched my arm into his other hand as he prepared to toss me in.

Fear bled through me like a building storm and a ferocious growl tore from my lips.

I lunged at him with a snarl of defiance, sinking my teeth into his forearm and biting down so hard that I tasted blood.

Papà yelped in surprise and pain, his grip tightening in my hair as he fought to yank me off of him again.

I snarled as I fought to cling on, my teeth ripping into his flesh and spilling more blood as my heart pounded a heady rhythm.

His fist connected with my gut and my jaw unlocked as I coughed out a breath, pain splintering through my frail body.

"Better," he growled, his cold gaze meeting mine as a smile almost *graced his lips. "A little more of that next time and you might avoid the den altogether."*

His hand slammed into my chest and I screamed as I fell backwards, toppling over the edge and colliding with the cold mud at the bottom of the pit.

Papà looked down at me for a long moment, the moon lighting his cruel features as he surveyed his youngest and least wanted child.

"Sweet dreams, runt. I'll see you in the morning for your next trial."

My bottom lip trembled as he left me alone and my vision blurred as tears blocked my view of the moon. I counted down from thirty until I heard the back door bang closed again and I let myself howl.

The mournful sound poured from my lips and my skin began to shiver as the shift came over me.

I'd always been more comfortable in my Wolf form anyway so I didn't resist the change as it swept through my body but once I had, I couldn't help but howl again.

I curled myself up tight in an attempt to keep warm down in the den but I was already shivering.

My mind focused on the promise Papà had made before he left me here. I'd have to attempt the trial again tomorrow. And this time I needed to pass. Because if I failed for a second time then I'd be begging for a night in the den as punishment and the alternative didn't bear thinking about...

My pulse leapt and pounded like it had back in that fucking hole in the ground when I was eight as I jerked awake. Fifteen years wasn't long enough to entirely block out those memories but I absolutely refused to acknowledge them in the cold light of day.

I growled as I fought to recover my composure. I couldn't afford to let my armour slip for a single second in this place, so I stuffed the nightmares of my past as deep down behind my walls as I could manage and forced my mind away from them.

I frowned as I spotted the open door to my cell. I'd almost slept right through our cell block's allotted time in the showers and after the night I'd had, I was most definitely in need of a shower. I was filthy in all the right ways and all the wrong ways too and I really needed to wash the mud off of my flesh after spending so much time rolling about in it.

Not that I was complaining.

Luckily, my little choir boy had been on duty when I'd returned from the Order Yard and he'd healed me of my wounds without me even having to ask.

I stepped out of my cell and walked straight into Pudding's gigantic belly. It was like hitting a fucking wall and I cursed as I fell back onto my ass, staring up at him with a growl.

"Watch it," he muttered and I fought against the desire to bite back at him, remembering Roary's suggestion that I make friends with my neighbour.

"Oh hey, Pudding," I said sweetly, despite my irritation. He just looked at me like he was wondering what I was doing on the floor so I barrelled on. "I actually got something for you yesterday, but I didn't see you before lockdown."

"What did you get?" he asked, offering me a hairy hand.

I took it and he heaved me upright so fast that my head damn near spun. I ducked back into my cell and grabbed the pot of pudding from my shelf before holding it out to him.

"I heard you like-"

He snatched it without a word and lumbered back into his cell.

My lips parted and I stalked after him, frowning as I looked at the heap of shit that filled his cell. He didn't glance back my way, but the look on his face as he added the new pudding pot to the mountain was almost serene. A smile tugged at his lips and his hairy brows raised. He took real care, lining it up just right and a satisfied groan escaped him as he stepped back to appreciate his masterpiece.

It still looked like one big old pile of shit to me, but I could tell just how much it mattered to him.

Which meant that me giving him the pot meant a lot to him too. We were practically besties already.

I turned away with a grin, leaving him to bathe in the glory of his mess as I went in search of that shower.

I bit my lip as I hurried down the metal staircases with my wash stuff in hand. I tucked a lock of my hair behind my ear, tracing the slightly raised mark which the moon had gifted me and Ethan when we were mated.

I definitely hadn't been expecting that to happen but I wasn't exactly upset about it, either. I'd been meaning to win him over to my side and now he would only want to help me more. It was perfect really. Assuming we ignored the whole the-stars-have-picked-us-for-each-other-forever side of things. I still wasn't entirely convinced on that part. He was Lunar Brotherhood after all and even if he wasn't, was I really ready to just close the door on the idea of me ever being with any guy apart from him ever again? He might have been fucking exceptional in the sack, but that was pretty much all I knew about him. So no. I wasn't jumping up and down in the hopes of saying I do any time soon. But I was all for using this bond between us to further my plans. And of course at the moment he was off pouting about the whole thing anyway, swearing me to secrecy like we were thirteen year old girls at a sleepover. But that was fine. He could take his time to lick his wounded pride and when he couldn't resist the pull he felt toward me anymore, he'd come scurrying back to my side.

The showers were quiet as I jogged into them, passing the guards who stood in the corridor to check that we didn't get any ideas about trying to go anywhere other than the showers. Not that we had any options with the steel doors lowered over the stairwells. They'd only raise them when we were permitted to head on up to the second floor for breakfast and there was absolutely no way through them without an ID pass and a magical signature scan until then.

And I had no intention of trying to go about any of my plans in such an obvious way anyway.

I moved into the emptying space which was lined with grubby beige tiles and pulled my clothes off, tossing them on a hook haphazardly before hurrying to the showers. A row of them ran along the back wall and we had the joy of washing alongside each other. Which had been particularly grim the morning I'd ended up next to Plunger.

The guards didn't bother to chase us out of here when the next cell block were allowed out for their turn, but I didn't really want to be left here when they started flooding in. It was bad enough washing in plain sight of everyone else without rubbing shoulders with them too.

I dove straight beneath the flow of lukewarm water and started scrubbing at my long hair with the bar of scratchy soap which I'd been given when I arrived here. Decent wash products were top of my list for when my commissary tokens came through, but until we were allowed to spend it at the end of the week, I had to make do with the soap.

I hurried to wash myself as quickly as I could as the pathetic temperature of the water failed to banish any of the cold from my limbs and I began to shiver.

As soon as the suds were rinsed from my hair, I shut the shower off and grabbed my towel, roughly drying myself before wrapping it around me.

I turned back to go and get my clothes and paused as I found the room had filled with a group of mean looking Fae who all had their eyes locked on me.

I took the sudden arrivals in my stride and stepped towards them confidently, searching for the leader amongst them and locking my gaze on a guy in the centre of the group. He was tall and slim in the way that suggested his clothes hid wiry muscles and something about his aura felt... *off*. Tattoos peeked out beneath his cuffs and covered his neck. There was a small Capricorn symbol inked beneath his left eye like a teardrop and more tattoos curved over his brows and right cheekbone. This wasn't the kind of guy I should have been taking lightly, but that also meant I wasn't going to back down for a single second.

"Don't tell me; you've dropped the soap? Well I'm sorry, stronzo, but you're not my type so you'll have to pick it up yourself," I said with a smirk as I continued to close in on him.

"Well, well, well. If it isn't our new *pup,*" he said in a dark voice, popping the p.

I fell still, glancing behind me as ten of his biggest, meanest looking assholes closed in around me. The Fae way was to claim your own power, fights were *always* one on one, never a gang against a single opponent. But the way they were penning me in made me wonder if they stuck to that rule.

"Gustard, I assume?" I asked casually, recognising him from my research before coming in here. I eyed his pristine jumpsuit with surprise. Honestly, the guy made an orange boiler suit look like designer chic. He'd folded the sleeves and ankles back to sit in the perfect position and he'd had creases ironed into the front of the pant legs. His lapels were so sharp I wondered if I might be able to cut myself on them and the angles of his facial hair looked like they'd been sculpted with a protractor. His black hair was swept back perfectly, as in not-one-wispy-hair-dared-to-move-is-he-made-of-Lego?? *perfect.*

I, on the other hand was wrapped in a threadbare towel with water dripping over my flesh and strands of wet hair clinging to my face and neck. I was not chic, hell, I wasn't even decent, but I wasn't about to let that phase me.

"Rosalie Oscura," Gustard replied, his gaze sliding over me like he could see everything about me emblazoned on my skin. "I hear you've been causing *quite* the stir for such a little thing."

"Just call me a ladle and this place can be the soup," I deadpanned. "Is there a reason we're having this chat while I'm standing in a puddle?"

Now that the showers were off, the wet floor was beginning to feel icy against my bare feet and goosebumps were rising over my skin. There should have been more Fae coming in to use the showers by now but as I glanced over Gustard's shoulder, I spotted members of his gang blocking the entrance. Our friendly chat seemed to be a lot less friendly after all.

"I wanted to have this conversation *alone,*" Gustard replied, brushing a non-existent piece of lint from his lapel where his prisoner identification symbols were shimmering in silver. The number Four Hundred and Six stood out beside the Elemental sign for fire and a little Cyclops eye. For one of the first times since I'd come here, I was actually glad that they suppressed our Orders because I abso-fucking-lutely didn't want to have a Cyclops using their psychic gifts to root around in my head for my secrets.

"It doesn't seem like we're alone to me," I replied, gesturing to the twenty or so men and women who surrounded me.

"In my operation, I like to think of my followers as extensions of myself. Claud here is my foot, Brianne is my eyes and Christopher here-" He gestured for the crowd to part to allow a huge man to lumber through the centre of them. I raised my chin as I recognised the Dragon Shifter I'd turned out of his cell on my first day here. "-is my *fist.*"

"Is that so?" I asked casually, looking away from Two Hundred as he glowered at me. "And where's your backbone?"

Growls and snarls of rage sounded all around me and I could feel the group of underdogs shifting closer but Gustard held his composure, lifting a single finger to warn them all back.

"This is just a courtesy, pup," he said, his pale blue eyes fixing on me. "I will give you the benefit of the doubt and say that when you joined us here in Darkmore, you didn't realise that Christopher was someone of importance. I assume that now you've been informed, you'll relinquish what was his without any need for petty violence. No doubt someone as tenacious as you can claim yourself another cell without any bother and we can return to the harmony and balance that we've held in here for years."

"You want me to give him back his cell?" I asked, raising an eyebrow and turning to look at Two Hundred with undisguised disgust lining my features. "What's the matter, *Christopher?*" I purred. "Are you too afraid of the big bad wolf to try and claim it back for yourself?"

The Dragon snarled, baring his teeth at me as he took a step forward and I bared my teeth right back. But at a slight shake of Gustard's head, he fell still again, reining in his rage.

I pouted at him mockingly then turned my eyes to the man in charge. "Well, you certainly have your bitches whipped," I said to him. "But I'm afraid that's a hard no to your request. Old lizard dick will just have to fight a weaker Fae for a cell if he wants one, I'm quite happy where I am."

A chorus of growls sounded around me again but I ignored them. There wasn't a Fae here with the balls to come at me without their boss's say so.

Gustard sighed dramatically. "Are you sure it has to be this way, pup?" he asked, sounding disappointed with me.

"As sure as I am that the moon will rise again no matter what any of us do. So you can either move aside and let me go dry my ass or get to the point of this meeting, because I have shit to be doing."

Gustard eyed me for a long moment before his gaze slid beyond me and he gave a single nod.

And here comes the shit storm...

Hands grabbed me and I snarled as I whipped around, my fist flying out and smashing into one stronzo's nose before he could tighten his hold on me. A loud crack rang out and blood flew as I twisted away from him, yanking on my other arm and unbalancing the woman who held it.

I kicked her right in the vag then slammed my forehead down on her face as she crumpled from the attack.

I snarled like a wild animal and ducked low as more hands snatched and gripped at me. I kicked, punched, bit, threw elbows and stamped on feet, dropping several more of them as I fought but the sheer number of them quickly overwhelmed me. I lost my towel somewhere in the attack, but nudity was the least of my problems as strong hands locked around my arms, legs, some piece of shit even grabbed a fistful of my hair.

I screamed and thrashed as around eight of them grasped my limbs in tight holds and I was forced to the floor on my front, spread eagle on the ground as a massive motherfucker sat on my back to keep me there.

"A morte e ritorno," I snarled, twisting my head so that I could glare up at Gustard as he approached me. "I'll kill you for this. I swear it on the stars and the earth, and the moon which owns my soul. I'll see you dead and buried at my feet and piss on your grave!"

Gustard's upper lip curled back and he bent forward to talk to me as more assholes grabbed my wrists and stretched my arms out wide either side of me, splaying my hands flat against the wet tiles.

"Werewolf is really just another term for *dog,* new pup," Gustard said in a low tone. "And there's a few lessons that a dog needs to learn before they can be brought to heel. But the most important thing is who your master is. So I'm going to hurt you and then I'm going to let Christopher here and some of his friends have fun with you for a while. And once they're done and your spirit is broken, they'll leave you for the guards to find. And they'll heal your body. But they won't be able to take away the memory of how you felt when I crushed you beneath my heel. And the next time I give you an order, you'll be that much more likely to obey like a good dog. Or if not, we can just repeat this process again. And again. Until you *learn.* "

I reared up as much as I could with a ten ton asshole crushing me and spat right in Gustard's face.

Gustard staggered back like I'd struck him, a snarl contorting his controlled features as he moved to my right.

"Hold her still," he commanded angrily and the grip on my right arm tightened.

My heart thundered with panic and I screamed in defiance even before his shoe slammed down on my hand.

Pain, white hot and blinding raced through me as he stamped on my fingers again and again and I screamed like a banshee as I fought to buck the behemoth on my back off of me.

A split second of relief found me as he stopped his assault before his footsteps sounded across the wet tiles as he moved to my left.

I shrieked again, tears spilling over my cheeks as his foot landed on that hand too and agony tore through me. I tried to fight, to thrash, to do anything at all to free myself as he crippled me, but it was no use. My ears were ringing, darkness curtained my vision and my heart was pounding to a rhythm so violent, I was afraid it would give out.

"We'll see how many times you have to learn this lesson before it sticks," Gustard's voice came to me as if from afar. "I'll leave you to enjoy Christopher's company."

The giant on my back laughed darkly at his words as Gustard's footsteps moved away and his weight shifted off of me suddenly, leaving me shivering in a puddle of my own blood on the floor.

"I'll break her in, then the rest of you can have a ride," Two Hundred's rough voice echoed off of the walls and a series of dark laughs followed as I heard his jumpsuit hit the floor.

I gritted my teeth and forced my elbows beneath me as I scrambled up onto my knees. I may have had my hands destroyed, but there was no chance in Solaria that I was going to lay there and let that fucking beast touch me. I was raised in pain and suffering, born and broken in it before I was saved by my Aunt Bianca. And the one thing I learned in the dark and through the agony was that you couldn't give up. Ever. So all the time that there was breath in my lungs and iron in my soul, I'd fight in whatever way I could.

I tried to scramble to my feet but before I could manage it, Two Hundred grabbed my hips, yanking me backwards and knocking me off balance so that my shattered hand hit the floor.

I screamed in pain and threw myself to the side, yanking my hips out of his hold and rolling onto my back as he growled in frustration.

"Hold still, pup, and I promise I'll be gentle," he growled, baring broken teeth at me in the imitation of a smile.

I snarled at him as he stalked closer, letting him close the distance between us as I lay on my back before slamming my foot out as hard as I could and kicking him right in the dick.

I cursed him as he fell back with a roar and I scrambled away, dragging myself backwards with my elbows, cradling my shattered hands to my chest and eyeing the other Fae who had remained here to hurt me further.

I growled at them and they lunged forward to grab me again.

My screams echoed off of the walls as hands locked around me and I thrashed and kicked and swore and bit, ignoring the agony in my hands as I fought for my fucking life because I would *not* let them have me like that. I'd die first.

The sound of a door banging open echoed through the space and my heart soared as I expected the sound of guards shouting to follow it. To save me. But that wasn't what came.

Instead, a deep growl echoed off of the walls and suddenly the guy pinning me down was ripped away.

I flinched as someone fell on my legs and managed to roll aside, scrambling and kicking until I got myself into a sitting position against the rear wall.

I looked up as the sounds of fighting continued and my lips parted as I found Ethan Shadowbrook and some members of his pack beating the shit out of Two Hundred and his friends.

Ethan fought like a man possessed, snarling with rage and landing punches which broke bones and caused screams to echo off of the tiled walls. His eyes were wild with fury and a deep sense of rightness flooded me as he fought to protect me. His mate.

I didn't know what the hell the moon had been thinking when it bonded us to one another, but in that moment I was more than grateful that she'd gifted me such a powerful, ferocious Fae to call my own. We may not have had any of our shit in order but there was one single, simple truth to the mate bond which neither of us could deny. We were wired to protect each other at all costs. And as Ethan sent Christopher crashing to the ground with blood pissing down his face, I couldn't help but feel pride in the man who had been chosen for me. He might have been many things, but he was most definitely my equal.

It didn't take long for the Dragon and his buddies to run for it like the cowards they were and I was left looking up at Ethan as he panted in the centre of the room. His face was lined with rage, blood coating his bare arms and knuckles, decorating the black ink on his arms in red.

"Looks like it's your lucky day, Oscura," he snarled at me. "I don't allow rapists in my prison, even when they're going after trash like you."

My heart twisted at his words even if they were more for the benefit of his pack mates than me, but I didn't let it show, growling at him instead. I was a wounded animal, backed into a corner and I wasn't willing to take much more shit today.

"Get out. And find a guard to heal her," Ethan commanded and his pack mates practically ran from the room, the door banging closed behind them as they went.

He shifted towards me instantly, dropping to his knees on the wet floor and pulling me into his arms with a soft whimper as he tried not to hurt me.

"I'll kill them for this," he snarled as he nuzzled into my hair and I let him draw me into his arms, as the relief of what I'd just escaped washed over me. I laid my ear against his chest so that I could listen to the steady beat of his heart as my own pulse started to slow and he held me tightly for a moment.

"No you won't," I growled as I gritted my teeth against the pain in my hands.

When my papà had punished me, he'd sometimes left me for days without healing me and I'd learnt every trick in the book to cope with pain. I could segment it away, lock off the part of my brain that housed it. But I hadn't often endured agony like this before either. I could force it aside in some part, but it was blinding, all consuming... *Fuck, I'm gonna kill Gustard!*

"Gustard has it coming. He doesn't fight like Fae. I won't stand for it," Ethan snarled, his grip on me tightening possessively.

"I'll handle this myself," I insisted, wriggling backwards to put some distance between us again.

He may have been my mate, but that didn't make me *his*. I wasn't some possession and I wasn't going to suddenly start letting him fight my battles for me.

"It didn't look like you were handling it when I arrived," Ethan replied darkly. "It looked like I just saved your ass."

"Yeah? Well if they come at you ten on one then I'll happily jump in at your side too, but that doesn't mean I can't hold my own."

I struggled a little more and Ethan released a growl as I tried to pull away from him, but he let me shift back so that I could look into his eyes.

"I felt your fucking pain," he said in a low voice, giving me a moment to see the distress that had caused him in his sapphire eyes. "It called me to you. So maybe fate is on your side. Though she's clearly not on mine," he added bitterly.

Ethan reached out to push his fingers into my hair, tucking it behind my ear, pausing there with his fingertips pressed to the brand the moon had given me, marking me as his. His jaw was tight with the rage he'd shown last night and I could tell he was already pulling back again, putting up walls to shut me out. Which was fine by me. I'd wanted him on side, but I hadn't asked for *this*. And I'd never needed anyone to jump in and be my knight in shining armour anyway. Though I was glad that he had on this occasion.

My gaze flicked to the side of his head where his mark was too and I noticed a new tattoo creeping up the side of his neck and behind his ear.

His gaze hardened and he turned his head to let me see the pattern of thorny roses which he'd had inked onto his skin. They covered the moon mark

187

entirely. There was no way to see it had ever even been there at all.

Something splintered in my chest as I looked at it and a soft whimper of pain escaped me which had nothing to do with my hands.

"You covered it up?" I breathed, unable to push aside the feeling of betrayal that left me with.

"Well it's not like I can just let everyone know that I'm mated to an Oscura, is it?" he asked in a low tone which was laced with disgust.

"No," I agreed. "What could be worse than that?"

My jaw hardened as I scowled at him and he parted his lips to say something else just as the door banged open and Officer Cain shot into the room.

He yanked his baton from his belt and raised it to strike Ethan as I yelled out to stop him.

"It wasn't him!" I snarled. "He saved me."

Cain looked between us for a long moment like that made no sense at all, then finally stowed his baton away. "Fuck off then, One, before I change my mind," he snapped.

Ethan got to his feet and walked from the room without another word. He glanced back at me as he reached the door and I bared my teeth at him. I didn't need his pitying looks. Especially when he was so ashamed of his bond to me that he'd hidden it. Fuck him. I didn't want that kind of bond. I'd use him for what I needed then leave his ass here when I escaped. And the stars could go take a running jump with their mate bond bullshit.

Cain stood over me for a long moment then crouched down with a grunt of frustration. "I thought you were too tough to get beaten down in the showers, Twelve," he murmured as he reached for my mangled hands.

"Well I took out six of them before they overwhelmed me," I muttered. "I'd like to see you manage that."

Cain hesitated and I shoved my hand at him, grunting in pain as he took my broken fingers in his. I gritted my teeth as I waited for him to heal me but instead of helping, he just asked me another question.

"Was that an official statement?" he growled. "Are you saying there were six of them?"

"Pfft, more like twenty," I replied. "But no, *Officer*, if you want my official statement then I just slipped and fell in the shower."

"Good girl," he grunted, his hand closing over my broken fingers and sending a sharp jolt of pain spearing down my arm. Healing magic swept from his skin into mine and a relieved whimper escaped me as the pain slowly ebbed away. "I don't imagine I need to tell you what happens to prisoners who snitch on other inmates in here, do I? And I'd rather not be clearing pieces of you off of the walls if I can avoid it."

My lips twitched in surprise at that statement and I looked up from my shattered hands and into his stormy grey eyes.

"Be careful, Officer. It almost sounded like you gave a shit about me then."

"I care about paperwork. And murders cause a bucket load of it," he replied coldly.

"There's the C.O. I know and hate," I teased and I swear to the stars he damn near smirked. Like the tiniest twitch took place at the corner of his lips, but when I looked again, it was gone.

Cain concentrated on my destroyed hands for a few more minutes then cursed and withdrew his grip on me.

"I can't heal these wounds. I've blocked off your pain receptors for now, but I'm going to have to take you to medical if you ever want to use your fingers properly again," he announced, seeming pissed off that the work was beyond his talents.

He stood, dragging me with him and I stumbled a little at the sudden movement, bumping into him and trying to catch myself on his arms. But with my hands out of action, all that happened was me falling against him tit to shirt.

Cain grabbed my upper arms and pushed me back a step, holding me at arm's length as he looked into my eyes and growled.

"Sorry," I muttered, glancing down at my bare toes as embarrassment clawed at me. I didn't like to be seen in a weakened state. I didn't like to *be* in a weakened state. Hell, I was damn near spitting about the fact that I couldn't just go and hunt those stronzos down right now and teach them all about the girl they'd just tried fucking with.

"It's fine," Cain muttered and as I looked up at him again, I found his eyes roaming over my features and his jaw locked tight.

A long moment passed and he failed to drag his eyes away from mine.

"What?" I taunted. "Haven't you ever seen a naked girl covered in blood before?"

"Do you have any other injuries?" he asked in a low voice, ignoring my jibing for once.

I raised my chin as I realised what he was really asking and defiance flared through my body. "No," I replied in a clipped tone. "Ethan walked in before… he evened the numbers. So I'm fine."

"A Lunar helping out an Oscura?" Cain scoffed.

"It wasn't about me."

Cain eyed me for another moment like he was hunting down a lie, but he finally grunted in acceptance. "Get dressed and I'll take you to medical."

He shoved me away from him and I stumbled back a step before turning

189

and heading back to where I'd left my clothes before my shower.

I reached out for the orange jumpsuit but as my gaze caught on my mangled fingers, I quickly realised that there was no way I'd be able to put anything on. Though Cain had cut the pain off, none of them would move in reaction to my commands and just looking at the bent and broken angles they all hung at made my stomach turn.

"Umm…sir?" I asked, glancing back over my shoulder at him.

"What?" he snapped.

"It's just…I can't get my clothes back on…without help…"

His eyes flared dangerously like he was about to start screaming or threatening me again but as he looked at my hands, he clenched his jaw and stalked towards me.

He snatched my clothes from the peg and yanked the horrible black, crop top bra over me before guiding my arms through the straps and then dragging it down over my chest. I could feel the heat of his skin against mine as his thumbs ran over the swell of my breasts and his jaw tightened further, like he was trying to convince himself that he didn't give a shit about touching me. But if he wasn't fooling me then he definitely wasn't fooling himself.

I stayed silent as he dropped to his knees and held my panties out for me to step into, sliding them up over my thighs and ass in a swift motion before snatching my jumpsuit down and holding that out for me too.

"I guess this is playing out in reverse to the way you've been dreaming about, isn't it?" I teased and he snarled angrily, tying the arms of my jumpsuit around my waist and cinching the knot tight in one, sharp jerk which almost made me fall into his arms.

I blinked up at him innocently as his jaw ticked with rage and what I was growing more and more sure was lust.

He dropped my white tank top over my head last and I kicked my own feet into my boots.

"Get moving," he commanded instantly, gripping my upper arm as he drew me out of the room.

I trotted along at his pace and he led me to the stairwell where we headed down four levels until we made it to medical.

The guards could heal most wounds with basic magical techniques so they only had a couple of full time healers on staff for more difficult magic.

The strong scent of pine disinfectant washed over me as we headed through a set of locked doors. Cain marched me straight inside the white space lined with beds, leading me up to the healer who was filling out paperwork at her desk before thrusting me in front of her.

"This one had a nasty fall and I can't re-set small bones like these," he announced.

The healer gave me a sweeping look but when her gaze landed on my mangled hands she cried out in alarm and jumped to her feet, catching my fingers between hers as she inspected the damage.

"Sweet baby moonlight! Whatever happened here?" she gasped, her frizzy grey hair bobbing around her face as she alternated between looking at my two hands in horror.

"I fell in the shower," I said with a shrug.

"Not by the light of a Pegasus's assbeam you didn't!" she replied, locking me in her beady gaze. "I want the truth."

"My fingers got caught in the drain as I fell," I said, offering her a hint more of a lie just to be a dick.

"If you won't give me the truth, I'll have to involve Warden Pike," she exclaimed, dropping her grip on me and reaching for a phone which was bolted to the wall behind her.

"Pike will toss her in the hole for not blabbing," Cain snapped. "Do you think she deserves that on top of her injuries?"

I glanced up at him in surprise as he weighed in on my side, but he didn't return my look.

The healer pursed her lips then sighed dramatically and reached for my hands again. "This is exactly the kind of thing that shouldn't be going on anymore. The prisoners know where all the CCTV blind spots are and they *constantly* take advantage of those holes. If I had an aura for every dramatically unbelievable *accident* that took place in this prison then I'd be a rich Fae living out my days in the Solarian sunshine!"

As she continued to prattle on about lying prisoners and incompetent guards, her grip slowly moved along my fingers one at a time as she concentrated on healing my injuries.

I watched in fascination as the bones straightened out and the damage Gustard had done was finally healed.

"And you wouldn't *believe* the amount of times someone claims to have *accidentally* stabbed themselves either! Just last week, I had a Sphinx claiming she'd fallen on a pointy carrot at dinner while I removed the sharpened end of a toothbrush from her gut," she went on as she finished healing my final finger and Cain grabbed my arm again.

"Perfect. I'll be taking her back to her work detail now," he growled, cutting off the healer's rambling.

"Absolutely not!" she cried, leaping forward like she intended to drag me out of his arms. "I recommend a thorough examination of her entire body followed by a day and night of rest and confinement here in the ward where I

191

can keep an eye on her."

"I don't need a thorough examination, thanks," I replied before Cain could. "I'm good to go." I had plans to go crawling through maintenance shafts tonight and the last thing I wanted was to spend the night here. Two Hundred might even think I'd gone into hiding and get ideas about taking my cell back and there was no fucking way I'd let that happen.

"You heard the girl," Cain said. "She wants to get back to work."

"I really must insist," the healer snapped, her jovial tone forgotten and Cain sighed irritably.

"Great. I guess I'll get started on the damn paperwork then," he grumbled, moving away from me to grab a form from the healer's desk as he dropped down into her seat to start filling it in.

"Come along, dear. My name's Brenda Grus but you can call me Mother Brenda. You'll have a nice rest here today," the healer said kindly, turning back to me as I tried to come up with another excuse to escape her.

"But-"

"If you insist on arguing, I'll have to involve the Warden. Is that what you want?" Mother Brenda demanded. I didn't know why the hell she wanted me to call her Mother but I'd take a hard pass on that. I wasn't some surrogate pup for this screw loose witch and I was beginning to think that she had been given this job for a reason. She seemed a few nuts short of a barrel full to me.

I gave in to her demands with a groan of frustration and kicked my boots off before sitting on the bed she directed me towards.

"There's a good foal," she cooed. "I'll go get you some chocolate. Sweetness always helps to take the edge off of shock."

Okay, maybe this isn't so bad after all.

Mother Brenda bustled away and I was left with Cain as he continued to fill out his forms.

"At the risk of being a total pain in the ass-" I began.

"You're always a pain in the ass, Twelve," he growled, though his tone seemed to hold less bite than usual.

"Could you maybe give another inmate a message for me?"

"No."

"It's just that, I don't want any lizard motherfuckers to think that I'm hiding out scared somewhere after…my fall. So if Roary knows that I'm here he'll make sure that my cell stays mine until I'm back tomorrow and anyone who wants it can come at me like a real Fae. One on one. Not…" I trailed off without saying anything else about the fact that Two Hundred had come at me in a group but as Cain looked up at me, I could tell he understood.

"Prisoner politics hold no interest to me," he said in a dark tone. "But I'm sure the members of your block will be aware that you'll be back tomorrow one way or another."

I gave him a wide smile as he said that. Not a taunting, teasing, mocking smile. Just a real one to convey my gratitude to him for helping me. I wouldn't ever say the words aloud, but I could let him know with that much.

Cain eyed me suspiciously for a moment then dropped his gaze back to his paperwork, turning away and ending our conversation.

I slumped back onto my pillows with a huff of frustration. It looked like my escape plans would have to go on hold tonight and I could add a few more enemies to my list too. But tomorrow was another day. And I intended to get straight back to my plans just as soon as I could.

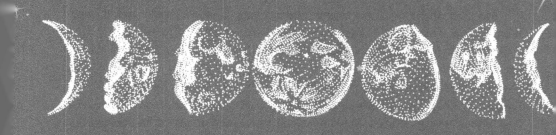

CAIN

COMMANDING OFFICER

CHAPTER EIGHTEEN

I marched toward the Mess Hall on a war path. Every muscle in my body was primed to kill and it was going to take a miracle of restraint to make sure I didn't. I had to play this right. I couldn't let anyone know what I knew. That I'd heard One fighting with The Watchers and come running. I should have been on duty outside the showers, but the Warden had swapped my shifts. If I'd come downstairs a few minutes earlier, I could have prevented this whole thing from happening. If I'd caught them in the act, I'd have had reason to punish them however I liked and send them all to the hole. Instead, I was late, which I vowed never to be again.

I stormed my way to the Mess Hall then slowed my pace, taking a breath to harness the beating of my heart. I was a hunter. An apex predator who knew how to stalk his prey. And nothing about my exterior would give away the plan I held on the inside. No crack could allow anyone to see how much I cared that Twelve had almost been raped. It was the most despicable act a Fae could commit. And I made it my personal mission to ensure anyone who fit that description in here had one miserable fucking experience.

I stepped into the Mess Hall on level three and I took in the inmates as they sat eating their dinner around the space. My gaze snagged on The Watchers sitting together at a table and I made a casual path around the hall to stand close enough to listen in on their conversation. Gustard was slicing up a cut of meat on his plate with delicate strokes of his knife and fork while he listened to the guffawing of his halfwit allies.

Most of them were swearing and cursing Shadowbrook and though number One was a fucking asshole with a girlish amount of blonde in his hair, I had to quietly admit I was glad he'd found Twelve before anything worse had happened.

"If you'd all held her down sooner, I could have broken her quicker," the Dragon asshole, Two Hundred, said and my hands tightened into fists. He had two bloody tissues stuffed up his nose and I was glad no guard had healed his injury. I especially took satisfaction in knowing no one was going to heal it anytime soon. I was going to make sure of it.

"You'll have another chance, Christopher," Forty Seven purred, her eyes bright like she actually admired the asshole for laying his filthy, worthless hands on Twelve.

"The fighters always take longer to break, but once I'm inside them they learn to bow to the power of a real Fae."

I ground my jaw so loud it was all I could hear for a few seconds. A cold darkness was descending on me. The kind that preceded a hunt. But that kind of mental state could end up in me killing someone. And I had to play this right.

Two Hundred rose from his seat, walking toward a table of Pegasuses who were sitting together and eyeing up their food. I moved after him at a slow pace as he snatched fruit pots and puddings from the Pegasus herd and they cowered beneath him. As he balanced a glass of orange juice on his tray, I stepped up behind him, close enough to smell the scent of Twelve on him. The darkness intensified until I was nothing but an animal in the body of a man. My fangs extended and pricked my tongue so my own blood washed through my mouth.

Two Hundred turned sharply with his mountain of a haul and I stood firm as the tray crashed into my chest and the juice toppled over, spilling down my uniform along with a few puddings that popped open and left chocolate smears across my shirt.

"Two Hundred!" I barked, whipping out my baton and slamming it into the backs of his knees. He toppled like a fucking mountain, his face twisted in confusion as he hit the floor. I pointed the baton down at his meaty face with a snarl, "Stealing food from other inmates, are you? And throwing food at an officer...that's an infraction."

"What – no! I didn't steal it from them, they gave it to me as a gift, ain't that right?" he called to them.

They all nodded instantly, but I ignored them, snarling down at the Dragon beneath me.

"And I didn't throw the food, it was an accident," he blurted and I was glad to see him almost pissing himself.

"Are you questioning my own fucking sanity, Two Hundred?!" I roared, gathering the attention of the whole hall.

"No, sir!" he gasped.

"I saw you steal food and if you won't admit it, maybe Dr Quentin can get it out of you," I snarled, snatching his collar in my fist and hauling him to his feet.

"Wait," he balked, turning a satisfying shade of green. "You're sending me to interrogation?"

"That's where liars go, Two Hundred. You know the rules." I shoved him along and I swear the guy actually quivered.

A smile bit into my cheeks, but I didn't let it show as I guided him from the room and led him downstairs to level nine. Gratification filled me as I dragged him past the door into isolation and along a corridor toward Quentin's room. My heart thumped solidly in my chest as I knocked on the door and Two Hundred cowered like a child instead of a Fae.

"Please, I'll do anything else," he begged of me, but I ignored him. "Whatever punishment you want."

I clenched my jaw, turning to him with a slow smile spreading across my face. "Well the way I see it, the punishment fit for such an infraction is spending an evening with Dr Quentin."

Two Hundred paled, looking at me as if I was a psycho. And maybe I was. Maybe I should have shed my uniform and stepped into an orange jumpsuit and joined the masses. But the difference between me and them was I'd never been caught.

The door wrenched open and Dr Quentin's small frame came into view. He wore a white overcoat that hung almost to his shiny black shoes. He had a slight hunch on his back, teeth that were sharpened to points and two dark red eyes. He'd altered all of his features via some twisted spells. He wasn't that ugly by nature, he chose to look this way. Which made him all the more creepy.

He ran a hand over his slicked-back brown hair and surveyed Two Hundred like he was a cut of meat.

"Evening, Officer Cain," he said, licking his lips as his eyes never strayed from Two Hundred. "What's this one here for?"

"He stole food from other inmates then lied about it," I said smoothly.

"I told you I did it," Two Hundred begged. "There's nothing to interrogate me over."

"Oh we'll see about that. Every little creature in this world has secrets hiding beneath their flesh like ants. You just need the right tools to prise them out," Dr Quentin purred and I shoved Two Hundred into the room with him. The fucker actually whimpered which made my day. No, it made my whole month worthwhile.

As the door slammed shut, I moved to stand beside the wall, resting my back against it and waiting.

Anticipation balled in my chest as I thought of Twelve being forced beneath that fucker's body. When the first scream came, the knot loosened a little.

Two Hundred and his slimy gang had officially made themselves my enemies. And my enemies didn't last very long in this world. This was the first of many more screams to come.

I watched Twelve like a hawk over the next week. I continued to bring her down to isolation to wash the floors, never letting her out of my sight for longer than I could help it. I'd taken extra shifts which meant I'd had the sum total of six hours sleep in the past three days. But I didn't give a fuck. Because if any of The Watchers decided to lay a hand on her again, I needed to be ready.

I knew I was being hypocritical by looking out for her. The girl wasn't any friend of mine. But I had my morals. And they extended to her as much as they did to anyone else in this prison. And she was under my watch, so it was only right that I kept an eye on her. *Yeah, just keep telling yourself that, asshole.*

I didn't make it my business to care whether people lived or died in here. That was up to them. I just followed the rules and punished the inmates when necessary. I knew what it was like to get attached to someone only to have them ripped away before your eyes. Unbelievable as it probably was to one hundred percent of the population, I had once been capable of forming attachments to other Fae. Vampires were solitary by nature, but when we cared, we cared hard. But that meant when we grieved, we grieved forever.

This job ensured I never allowed another soul under my skin. A solitary lifestyle was easy. I could shut down, switch off and check out without any effort. I knew I could live my life contentedly without receiving or offering love to another Fae for the rest of my days. It didn't mean I was happy. But it didn't mean I was broken either. So Darkmore suited me perfectly. Why would I care for any of these convicts? Half of them had committed crimes that made my skin crawl. And the rest were just leeches on society, thieves and lowlifes.

The problem was, watching Twelve was starting to become more than a job. It was becoming an obsession. I was currently observing the way she sat with her pack in the Magic Compound. They stroked her hands and arms for a while before she shrugged them off and they moved to sit on the ground before her. She spent more time with the Lion, Sixty Nine, than she did with her own kin. It wasn't normal Wolf behaviour even if she was screwing him. And my over analytical brain wouldn't let it lie. There was something different about her. Something that drove her actions. But I just couldn't figure out what it was.

Without taking breaks from work, I'd had no time to indulge in the hunt recently and my magic reserves were starting to dwindle. It was a requirement for my job role that I kept my power fuelled, but I hadn't had a chance to take blood from an inmate recently. Although I knew Hastings would likely offer it out no problem, I didn't like my meals given to me. It wasn't the way I operated. I needed the chase. I was addicted to it. And starving myself was only bringing on more and more of my primal urges. I'd have to feed soon or I was going to snap on some powerful inmate and get myself fired.

I wet my lips, my gaze drawn to Twelve again across the Magic Compound as I stood beyond the fence, my hands clasped behind my back. She started casting a garden of flowers over the ground and her pack laid down on the lawn she made for them. Her eyes were unfocused as she cast, seeming distracted as wildflowers bloomed around her feet. Her Beta, Nineteen, was doing walking handstands back and forth like some show monkey and a little light returned to Twelve's eyes as she watched.

The girl was an enigma to me. But I could barely even focus to try and figure out for the hundredth time what it was that tormented her mind. I was too hungry. And the more I kept my eyes on her, the more desperate I became for her blood in particular. I hadn't forgotten the scent of it, her neck under my nose was like the sweetest torture. And as I remembered how close she'd been, my throat started to ache. I didn't want just any blood. I wanted hers.

And I was going to get it.

When their time came to an end in The Magic Compound, the inmates were let out and I made my way to the stairwell as I waited for her to appear. There were a couple more hours before dinner which we opened up for those who wanted to work longer hours. I was perfectly within my rights to take charge of her and demand she do overtime. But right then, it felt like a thrill because I was about to break the rules.

She appeared leading her pack toward the stairs and I stepped into her way, letting her read nothing from my expression. Her brows arched and I snared her arm, tugging her away from the other Wolves, making her walk faster down the stairs.

"Did you miss me, Officer?" she asked sweetly, but I ignored her, hurrying down the levels as the rest of the inmates were directed back to their cell blocks or to whatever work detail they were assigned to.

I led Twelve down to isolation, but I didn't lead her through the door as usual. There was a storage room for the cleaning supplies opposite it and I dragged her toward it, unlocking it with my magical signature on a scanner. The door clicked open and I pushed her inside, following her into the space where tall shelves were filled with all kinds of chemicals and cleaning sprays.

I pulled the door shut behind us and Twelve walked ahead of me, looking around the large room. I stalked after her as she slipped between two shelves along a narrow aisle where a bunch of boxes were stacked up.

"What's in these?" she asked casually, motioning to the boxes as I followed her, my fangs extending as she moved.

"Supplies," I answered in a low growl and she glanced back over her shoulder, her eyes widening suddenly as she took in my expression.

"There are no cameras in here," she breathed, biting into her lower lip. "Are you going to hurt me, Officer?" Everything about her voice was teasing, like she wanted this. Like she was enjoying it. And that only set my pulse racing even harder.

"You don't act like a normal Werewolf, Twelve," I commented, ignoring her question as she reached the end of the aisle and turned back down another one. I stalked after her, adrenaline surging into my blood as she increased her pace.

"What does normal look like to you?" she asked, glancing back at me again. "I've never met anyone normal in my life. And if I did, I wouldn't remember them because normal is just another word for boring."

"I think you're up to something," I said in a low voice, ignoring her again as she tried to lead me into a pointless conversation. "I just can't figure out what it is yet."

"What in Solaria could I get up to in Darkmore Penitentiary?" she asked innocently.

She turned another corner and I hurried after her.

My heart lurched as I found the next aisle empty and I wheeled around as I hunted for her.

"Come out," I snarled, my heart hammering wildly with the thrill of the game.

"That's not how you play hide and seek, Officer," her voice came from somewhere behind me and I twisted around sharply. "I hide and you *seek*."

I turned back into the aisle I'd come from, falling still and training my heightened hearing on the space around me. I shut my eyes to focus, excitement rushing through me at the fact that she was playing along with this. But did she know how dangerous it was to tempt a Vampire into the hunt?

A fluttering breath caught my ear and I ran, using my full Vampire speed to rush around into the next aisle. She squealed in alarm, jumping up to climb the shelves behind her and I caught her leg, dragging her down to the floor with a grunt of excitement, pressing my chest to her back.

I caged her in with my arms, winding a hand into her hair and yanking sideways so her neck was exposed to me. Her ass ground back into me and I groaned in surprise before digging my fangs into the silky skin of her throat. She gasped, the sound driving me on and making me achingly hard for her as her blood spilled onto my tongue.

Fuck, she was a delight. She tasted like summer fruit bathed in starlight. I splayed my hand across her stomach to keep her in place and she reached behind her back, her palm sliding onto my bulging fly. I moaned as she caressed me, knowing this was fifty shades of wrong as I continued to feed on her and let her touch me like that. I was lost to the bloodlust, my inhibitions lowered as I gave in to this part of myself. I never fucked inmates, never wanted to, never even got close. This was breaking so many rules but it felt so fucking good, I never wanted it to stop.

My radio crackled on my hip and Warden Pike's voice sounded down the line. "Officer Cain, report to me in my office."

I jerked away from Twelve, my back hitting the opposite set of shelves as blood spilled over my lips. I quickly wiped it away as Twelve turned to me with a taunting grin. *Oh shit.*

I lunged toward her, shoving her back against the shelf with a snarl. "You tell anyone about this and I'll make sure you regret it."

Her lips pursed and she reached up to her mouth, licking her thumb and reaching out to wipe away whatever blood remained at the corner of my mouth. I swallowed thickly as she kept her eyes on mine, my heart beating an unknown rhythm that I liked the feel of. When was the last time I'd actually felt this awake? I'd been on autopilot for so long, I'd forgotten what it was like to really *experience* something.

"I won't tell," she swore, reaching down to hook her pinky finger with mine.

I snorted, trying to pull free of her, but she kept hold of it and shook.

"Great, now I can trust you," I said sarcastically and she nodded like I'd meant it.

I reached out and healed the bite mark on her neck, making sure the blood was gone too. I unhooked the radio from my belt, my eyes still on hers as I answered Pike's request.

"On my way up." I placed it back at my hip, taking a slow breath. "You need to go back to your block." I took her arm, guiding her out of the supply room and marching up the stairs.

She continually brushed her arm against mine and I growled in warning as she batted her lashes at me.

"Keep your distance, inmate," I said in a cold tone.

"Sorry, sir." She gave me the big eyes again and I bared my fangs at her. If she believed I'd fall for that innocent bullshit, she was more of an idiot than I thought.

My heart drummed to a war beat when I finally put her back in her cell block and made my way to the Warden's office. I knew she couldn't know what I'd done inside that store room, but some part of me started to worry that that was why she was calling me up. Maybe someone had seen us on the CCTV and mentioned it to her. Maybe I was about to get my uniform stripped from me and be turfed out on my ass.

I'd worked here since I was twenty one. I didn't know any other life than this one. I lived and breathed this place. I knew everything there was to know about it. Every position where the cameras didn't point, every chink in the armour of Darkmore. But I didn't let it be known, I used it to my advantage to feed from the inmates. And if I lost this life, I didn't know what I'd have beyond these walls. I had no family, no home. Pathetic as it was, this prison was the only home I knew. It was safer than the house I'd grown up in as a child, and that was saying something about my pitiful existence.

I took the elevator to level one and headed down the corridor past the staff room to Pike's office. I knocked on the door with my gut tightening and she called out for me to enter.

I stepped into the room, clasping my hands behind my back and trying to present a respectful officer rather than the twisted fucker who'd just been biting Twelve and getting off on it too.

"Take a seat, Mason," she encouraged and I moved forward to do so, dropping into the wooden seat opposite her wingback. She steepled her fingers together as she gazed across her immaculate desk at me, even her lips drawn in a perfectly flat line. "I'd like you to take this inmate down to the Psychiatric Ward for analysis."

I'd never seen anyone come back from their so-called *analysis*. If you were sent to Psych, your fate was already set in stone. And I had more than one question about what went on down there. Pike lifted a file from the desk and held it out for me to take. I flipped it open, frowning at the picture of Sarah Lou, number Seventy Six. She'd been acting odd lately and she'd had to be sedated twice last week. It was especially strange as the girl had seemed totally normally up until lately. But it was rumoured that the Order blocking gas in this place could send a person crazy after a while. I couldn't imagine what having that fundamental part of you suppressed would be like, but I imagined it fucking sucked. Though that was what these assholes got for being convicts. Anyone who worked here was given a daily antidote to stop the gas effecting us.

"I'll fetch her now, ma'am," I agreed, but didn't immediately stand up. The Psych Unit was off limits to Darkmore guards and whenever I handed an inmate over to them, I always felt like I was handing them to the wolves. "I could watch over her in Psych tonight, perhaps? Report on her progress?"

I didn't want to leave Twelve unattended but I'd been trying to get into Psych for years. It was the one part of the prison I wasn't allowed access to and that just drove me insane.

"That won't be necessary," Pike said, an edge to her tone.

"Why aren't the guards allowed in there, ma'am?" I asked, keeping my voice professional rather than the usual commanding tone I deferred to.

"There are specially trained guards in Psych, Mason, you don't need to go in there," Pike said, waving a hand.

"But-"

"You're dismissed," Pike said lightly, arching her two manicured brows when I didn't immediately get up.

I inclined my head respectfully then headed out of the room with frustration filling my gut.

I sighed as I headed back towards the elevators, knowing I had to drop this for now. But I wasn't going to give up. I got the feeling that something was going on in Psych. And if that was the case, I was going to find out what it was. Because no one, not even the Warden of Darkmore Penitentiary, could stop me from succeeding in a hunt if I set my mind to it. And I'd just decided to hunt down the truth.

ROSALIE

PRISONER #12

CHAPTER NINETEEN

I waited in my bed long after lights out with my heart thrumming an excited tune and adrenaline trickling into my veins. I'd been venturing out into the maintenance gap behind the walls all week after lights out and moving around the shafts as I figured out which cell block was where and how to get between them.

It had been a frustratingly slow progress, but I needed to have a clear picture in my mind of the layout before I made my move to retrieve the murder weapon from Sin's old cell. Luckily, each cell was marked with the block and number painted onto the wall in the shaft so it had been easy to locate my target.

I'd already decided who I'd be setting up to take the fall for him and it hadn't been hard at all. Two Hundred more than deserved what was coming for him and if his performance in the shower block was anything close to typical behaviour then I'd likely be protecting other Fae from his unwelcome advances too.

Once I felt confident that the majority of prisoners were asleep, I made my move, slipping from my bed and quickly retrieving the cuff key from the wall of my cell.

I unleashed my magic from its confinement with a sigh of satisfaction and hurried back to the front of my cell to set up the silencing bubble and detection spells before I could head off.

I'd already spent a bit of time dismantling the wall at the rear of cell one and all I had left to do was take down the outer bricks and then break through into the cell in question.

The main problem I had left to face was that I didn't know whose cell I'd be busting into. I could use a silencing bubble to cover up the noise I'd make by creating a hole in the wall, but once I was inside their cell, I just had to hope that I could get my hands on the murder weapon without them waking up. There wasn't exactly any way that I'd be able to explain my sudden appearance in their cell without it being obvious I'd used magic, and I really didn't want anyone else finding out that I had the cuff key. At the moment, the only people who knew were me and Roary and despite the continued checks and random searches the guards were springing on us, none of them had even come close to discovering us. Yet.

I released a long breath to help slow my pulse as exhilaration flooded my body and I quickly dismantled the wall beneath my sink where my tunnel was concealed. I put the wall back together just in case the guards came to do a random search and I couldn't get back in time for the count. I'd have to think up somewhere else to be 'found' if that happened, but it was better than them discovering the tunnel in my wall.

As soon as that was done, I crawled through the short tunnel and dismantled the thin wall at the other end, letting myself into the maintenance passage on the far side.

I created a Faelight to see by and started up a quick pace as I jogged towards the cell I needed to break into. I had to crouch in the low space and my head bumped against the pipes containing the Order Suppressant more than once, but I didn't slow down. I wanted to do this as quickly as possible. The longer I was out of my cell, the more likely it was that someone might realise I was missing.

I wound my way between the passages until I made it to my destination and I quickly took down the wall at the rear of the tunnel I'd been working on there and crawled through it.

I paused once I was pressed up against the bricks which separated me from my destination and shaped my magic into an amplifying spell so that I could listen to what was going on beyond it.

I closed my eyes as I concentrated on the sound of slow breaths coming and going for a few minutes and finally accepted that whoever occupied the cell was asleep.

I reached out to start dismantling the wall. My fingers shook and my heart pounded out of rhythm. This was by far the riskiest thing I'd done yet, but I had to do it. I needed Sin out of confinement if I wanted to get him out of Darkmore and the only way to orchestrate his release was by proving his innocence.

I wet my lips and pulled the first brick from the wall.

I held my breath despite the silencing bubble I'd cast as I moved it aside and I peered through into the dark space for a long moment, hunting the shadows for movement.

When I was satisfied that there was none, I carried on pulling the bricks aside as fast as I dared.

I kept going until the gap in the wall was just big enough for me to fit through and I moved forward to wriggle my way into the cell.

The moment I was inside, I fell still, crouching by the hole I'd created in the rear wall of the cell as I eyed the bunks to see if there were any signs of the Fae there stirring.

There was no one sleeping on the bottom bunk, but my heart lurched as I spotted the heavily tattooed arm hanging over the edge of the top.

Ethan Shadowbrook growled a little and rolled over in his sleep and I held my breath as I stared at him in fright. There weren't a whole lot of Fae in this prison who could match me, but Ethan definitely could. Although, as I thought about it, I realised this wasn't as bad as it could have been. Ethan was mated to me now, which meant that all of his instincts were geared towards protecting me. He could no sooner hurt me than take a solid gold shit.

My lips twitched at that visual and I straightened, tiptoeing closer to his bed as I eyed the leg of it where Sin told me he'd hidden the weapon.

My gaze snagged on Ethan as he shifted in his sleep again and for a moment I forgot what I was supposed to be doing here as I just stood looking at him.

Ending up mated to the Wolf who led my enemies against my gang definitely hadn't been a part of my plan, but I had to admit that if I took that irritating fact out of the equation, I could see why the moon had chosen us for each other. His strong features captivated me and there was obviously incredible chemistry between us. I still didn't really know him from Adam, but there was a base part of me which ached to find out all there was to know about him too.

I sighed as I thought about the lengths he'd been going to to avoid me since it had happened. Not only had he covered our mark with that tattoo, but he'd also been running his pack to the far south of the Order Yard when we were out there and hadn't so much as spoken a word to me whenever we'd come across each other elsewhere.

And it wasn't like I'd tried to do anything to change that. For now, I didn't need to force the issue of bringing our packs together, though I had to admit it would be handy to have the added might behind me when it came to Gustard.

I was just hoping that he was aching for me the way I did for him in the middle of the night sometimes. This bond made me crave his company even when the sensible part of my brain reminded me that he was behaving like a douche.

But I wasn't going to be the one to cave and go to him. I'd resisted far greater torture before than just aching for someone's company. He'd be the one to crack and come looking for me soon enough.

I tore my eyes from Ethan and dropped down at the foot of his bed as I hunted for Sin's hiding place.

Even knowing what I was searching for, it was damn near impossible to find and it took me a few moments to figure out how he'd lodged the weapon into the leg of the bed before I managed to pull it free.

I looked down at the jagged piece of metal as I held it in my hand. The damn thing still had bloodstains on it and my lip curled back in disgust. The guards would be able to tell whose blood it was with magic at least and when this weapon was found on Two Hundred they'd have no choice but to assume he was the one who'd murdered the Fae Sin had killed.

When I'd first started looking into Sin Wilder's reputation before agreeing to this job, I'd been more than a little concerned about freeing such a violent Fae from the confines of the prison. But as I'd looked closer at his rap sheet, I'd realised something. The Fae he killed weren't innocent. There were rapists, murderers, gangsters, dark magic practitioners, even a Fae who had been travelling to the mortal world and abducting girls to use as slaves was in his list of victims. He was ridding the world of the lowest of the low with each and every job he took on. He even had a fan club of sorts who had started up petitions to get him released. He was a vigilante. Not that the law cared about that. But I did. It was the only reason I'd agreed to the job. No matter my other motivations for coming here, I wouldn't have agreed to getting Sin out without that nugget of information.

My black hearted sinner was really a saviour in disguise.

I pushed the shank into the pocket of my jumpsuit and stood as I prepared to leave.

I turned my back on Ethan's bed but before I could take a step away from him, a strong hand wrapped around my throat and I was yanked back against his hard chest as he growled threateningly.

"Not so fast, love," Ethan snarled in my ear.

I threw my hands out, casting vines into existence and encasing him in them in an instant, wrenching him off of me and pinning him back against the end of his bunk.

"*You!*" he accused, his eyes wild. "You're the one who stole the cuff key!"

"Duh," I replied, rolling my eyes at him as I moved to stand before him with my arms folded, wondering what he'd do now. My silencing bubble and the sheet he'd hung over the door of his cell kept this interaction private for now, but I needed to be sure he wouldn't blab either.

"Let me go," Ethan demanded in a dark voice that had my toes curling.

"You'll just grab me again," I protested, making a show of massaging my neck although I didn't totally hate how it felt to have his hand wrapped around me like that.

"I won't."

I raised an eyebrow at him, wondering if I could trust him but I was the one at an advantage here. I had use of my magic and he didn't. So I wasn't really worried about what he might try and do to me.

"Be good," I warned.

Ethan growled and I smirked as I destroyed the vines with a wave of my hand, releasing him.

Ethan lunged at me instantly, a snarl escaping his lips as he caught me around the waist and drove me up against the wall.

His hands roamed over my body as he hunted for the key and I laughed as he ran his fingers all over me.

"I don't have the key on me, lupo," I teased. "But feel free to keep frisking me if you like."

"Where is it?" Ethan growled just as his hand dove into my pocket and he found Sin's shank.

He pulled it out and eyed it with a frown. "Were you going to kill me in my sleep, love?"

"No," I purred, reaching out to wrap my hand around his where he held the shank. "If I was going to kill you, I'd want you beaten and bleeding at my feet before I drove the knife in."

His gaze heated at my words and he let me draw the shank back out of his hand and slip it back into my pocket. He knew I'd no sooner be able to hurt him than he would be able to hurt me now anyway. The mate bond would never allow it.

"So why are you here?" he asked suspiciously, his gaze dipping down to take in my body before returning to my eyes.

"Why do you think?" I asked, reaching out to run my hands over his muscular chest. "The same reason you've been dreaming of me coming to you every night since we were bonded." I slid my hands lower and he groaned with need, but I stopped as I reached the top of his boxers. "Are you going to say sorry?" I taunted.

"Why?"

I reached up and trailed my fingers over the tattoo he'd gotten to cover the mark which bound him to me and pouted. "For being ashamed of me."

Ethan growled. "You're an Oscura," he spat. "It makes me sick."

"I can tell," I mocked, reaching out to caress the hard ridge of his dick through his boxers.

Ethan growled and shoved away from me as he started pacing. "I don't know why you seem to think this is funny," he snapped.

"It is a bit," I said with a shrug.

"What would your family think if you told them about us?" he demanded angrily.

"Well, I don't really think Dante would have a leg to stand on berating me about being with someone from the Brotherhood after everything that happened with him and Ryder Draconis-"

"And look how that turned out!" Ethan snarled, lurching towards me again and baring his teeth. "I don't want that to happen to me!"

I only shrugged. It wasn't really my place to comment on what had happened to Ryder and I guessed it was a pretty raw subject for his gang. Ethan might even still be grieving for all I knew.

"I didn't mean to upset you. Were you and Ryder close, or-"

"I don't want to talk about him. Especially not with an *Oscura,*" Ethan spat my family name like it was dirty and I sighed.

"We're all just Fae you know. We might be stuck in this war between our gangs, but that's just a choice we made. It's not *who* we are-"

"It's who *I* am!" Ethan snarled, storming towards me and pointing to the Lunar Brotherhood symbol of a crescent moon with a serrated edge which he had tattooed over his heart like that ink was the sum total of what he was.

"Okay," I said slowly. "Then let's just call this off. I'll keep away, you keep away and maybe the moon will let our bond fizzle out."

Ethan stared at me like he wasn't sure if that idea was genius or insanity and I turned away from him, moving towards the hole I'd carved into his wall.

His hand closed around my wrist as I made a move to drop down and he shoved me back against the wall as his mouth found mine.

I gasped in surprise and he pushed his tongue between my lips, groaning as he drove his body up against mine.

"Fuck you," he growled as he started tugging at my jumpsuit and I gave in to the demands of his flesh with a heady moan.

Ethan pressed me back, caging me in against the wall and dominating me as our kiss deepened and his hands groped at my breasts through my tank top.

"You clearly want to," I taunted and he growled again, tearing away from me and stalking to the far end of his cell as he scraped his hands through his blonde hair.

"Why do you act like this is one big joke?" he demanded as he turned back to glare at me.

I shrugged a shoulder. "It's not a joke, but I've lived through far worse than a scandal and a gang war and survived to tell the tale."

"Like what?"

I released a long breath and pulled my hair over one shoulder. I'd never told anyone about the depths of pain and suffering that lived in my past. Not even my Aunt Bianca or cousin Dante knew the truth of what I'd suffered at the hands of my mamma and papà. They knew I'd been neglected and ignored but not the rest of it. Those secrets were locked up tight in the depths of my soul and I certainly wouldn't be releasing them to a man who was too afraid to own his own feelings.

"Let's just say that there are a lot of monsters in this prison, but I doubt any of them can compare to the man who sired me. So you ask me why I act like this is a joke? Maybe it feels like one. Maybe sometimes I wonder if I'm even capable of feeling anything the way I should anymore. I got so good at hiding my emotions that I might have just lost the ability to really feel them too."

"Tell me who hurt you and I'll see them dead a thousand times over," Ethan snarled, stalking towards me with his Alpha Wolf peering out of his eyes and his instincts to protect me winning through.

"I don't need any help in fighting my battles," I replied dismissively. "Just don't go thinking that being my mate means you know me. Because I can assure you, you don't."

I dropped down to my knees and made a move to crawl back through the hole but before I could make any real progress, his hands locked around my hips and he dragged me back again before flipping me over onto my back. He fell over me, caging me in with his body while pinning me in his gaze.

"Stay," Ethan asked, his tone raw with all the things he wouldn't let himself consider for us.

"Why?" I breathed.

"You said I don't know you. Well you don't know me either. So stay and give me something real."

I looked up at him for a long moment before reaching out to trace my fingers across his jaw. He really was something to look at. I wanted to call him beautiful, though his edges were all too rough for that. But there was something achingly captivating about him. Looking at him felt like gazing upon a piece of my own soul despite how little we knew each other.

"I love my family," I said finally. "It's not about strength or loyalty to gang ideals or anything muddied in politics. It's just that. Love." My Aunt Bianca,

Dante and all of my cousins were the one thing in this world that made me feel anything I could be truly certain of. Without them, I had no idea where I'd be now or who I'd be. They'd saved me when they took me in. So much more so than they'd ever know.

Ethan considered that for a long moment before finally nodding in acceptance. He leaned down until his forehead was pressed to mine and the rich scent of oak and earth coiled around me from his skin.

"I'm innocent," he murmured in a low voice.

"What?" I asked with a frown, because that wasn't supposed to be possible. Fae were only sent to Darkmore if there was overwhelming evidence that they were guilty. Things like CCTV footage, witness statements and DNA were used to build a case and if that wasn't strong enough then the suspect had to face Cyclops interrogation where the truth would literally be torn from their head. There were a whole bunch of security guard witnesses from the bank whose testimony had sent me here and assured my conviction. But the only way that a Fae could be convicted without those things and still found guilty would be if-

"I gave a full confession. I knew all the details they required, I didn't contest a single thing, didn't even complain when they offered up the maximum sentence," he said slowly.

"Why?" I asked in confusion.

"Because I love my family too."

Ethan's lips found mine before I could ask him any more than that and I found myself giving in to him as his mouth moved against mine in a torturously slow motion which had me undone.

I wound my arms around his neck and my legs around his waist as I drew him closer to me and his right hand moved down my body inside my jumpsuit.

I could feel how hard he was as his dick strained to be set free of his boxers and I ground myself against him, moaning softly in a plea for more.

It wasn't like we'd suddenly forgotten all the reasons why we couldn't be together, more like us sharing a small portion of ourselves with each other had lowered the barrier between us. Not a lot. But just enough to let a ray of moonlight shine through.

Ethan found the hem of my tank top and his hand shifted beneath it as he began exploring the skin of my stomach with rough fingertips and firm promises.

I arched into him, pushing my hands into his blonde hair as I devoured the kiss and stole this moment with him. It wouldn't change anything about tomorrow, but it did feel like fate had conspired for us to end up in each other's arms again tonight.

His hand slid to my side where my tattoo decorated my flesh and I stilled half a second before his fingers moved over the scars I'd disguised within the ink on my skin.

Ethan pulled back with a frown and for a moment my ears were filled with the sound of screaming and the pure, raw feeling of that whip striking at my flesh. The sun steel barbs on the end of it cutting me open and burning like hell fire.

I knocked his hand off of me and shifted upright so suddenly that he was forced to sit back too.

"Rosalie, what the hell happened to you to give you *scars*?" he demanded in a rough voice as he tried to pin me down again.

My ears were ringing with the echoes of long faded screams. My own screams.

There were very few things that a Fae couldn't heal from with the aid of magic. But sun steel could cut through flesh and muscle easier than a knife sliding through warm butter. And there was no magic yet created which could heal the damage from it entirely. Hence the scars.

"I offered you one truth, not my whole life story, stronzo," I growled, shoving him in the chest and knocking him back so that I could scramble out from beneath him.

"Tell me what happened," Ethan demanded.

My breaths started coming faster as the memories of that night flooded in on me. Of being taken captive, tied up, members of my family dying and me screaming for mercy in a way that I'd vowed never to do again-

"*No*," I snarled.

Ethan growled in response and I glared at him as he got up and started pacing again. "I knew this was what I'd get with an Oscura. Lies and bullshit. How do you expect me to try and overcome the divide between us when you hoard lies like a Dragon hoards gold?"

"I don't owe you any piece of me," I replied in a low tone. "Least of all the parts that bleed so easily."

Ethan's lips parted but before another word could leave them, a loud ringing started up out in the cell block announcing the arrival of the guards.

"Inspection!" Officer Lyle's voice boomed out. "Everyone get up and get ready. We will be conducting searches so prepare to have your cells tossed!"

My eyes widened in panic and I dropped to my hands and knees, scrambling back into the hole in the wall as I started dragging bricks into place behind me.

Ethan wordlessly joined me, shoving them back where they belonged as I used my magic to create fresh mortar to bind them in place again.

As I grabbed the last two bricks, Ethan caught my wrist and looked right

213

into my eyes through the little hole which remained in his wall.

"I'm going to want access to that cuff key, love," he said in a deadly tone.

"Fine," I snapped, not having time to argue with him.

If the guards were tossing his cell block it was only a matter of time before they came to toss ours too. I had to get back through the shafts, create a hole in my wall, seal it back up and hide the key and shank before that happened.

Ethan nodded firmly and I pushed the last bricks into place so that I could seal them there.

I scrambled away from him through the tunnel that cut through the wall, casting the faintest Faelight that I could manage just in case anyone appeared in the maintenance shafts.

I crawled so quickly that I managed to cut my knee open on one of the bricks and I cursed as pain shot through my skin, but I didn't have time to even pause and heal it.

I scrambled into the maintenance passage and threw my hands at the wall of bricks there, urging them all back into place with a grunt of effort. I didn't have time to waste making sure the job was perfect and I just had to hope that no one would come through this way and look too closely at the rough job I'd done before I got the chance to come back and fix it.

I turned and ran as I fast as I could manage in the low space, my only relief being that no one had tripped my detection spells yet meaning my cell block was still clear of guards.

Sweat beaded along my spine and in my panic, I missed a turning in the network of shafts and my foot suddenly stepped out onto nothing.

I screamed as I fell, my stomach plunging as I tumbled down to the level beneath mine and I hit the floor hard, the wind driving from my lungs.

I gasped for breath as I shoved myself upright again and quickly cast vines into existence hanging from the level above so that I could climb back up.

My muscles bunched and strained as I heaved myself up the makeshift rope until I finally scrambled back up onto my level.

Concentrate Rosalie, don't fuck this up!

I started running back the way I'd come as quickly as I could, taking the turn back towards my cell and spotting the hole in the wall ahead of me with a gasp of relief.

A tingle raced along my spine as the first of my detection spells was breached and I cursed in panic as I dove into the hole.

I didn't have time to replace the bricks in the shaft so I left them, crawling as fast as I could until I reached the wall to my cell.

I placed my palms against it and the mortar crumbled away so that I could shove the bricks out of my way and I half fell back into my cell.

The sound of the guards barking orders downstairs reached me and sheer panic swept through my veins.

I yanked the murder weapon from my pocket and tossed it back into the tunnel before turning and urging the bricks to move back into place behind me.

The second detection spell was breached as a guard moved onto the stairs and the prickle it sent along my skin had my heart damn near exploding with panic.

The third spell was breached as a guard moved beyond the first floor then the fourth as they passed the second. There was only one Order of Fae who could move that quickly and one guard in particular who always made a beeline straight for me.

Shit, shit, shit, shit!

The bricks finally made it back into place and I cast mortar into the gaps between them, but I didn't have time to do a good job of it.

Terror coursed along my limbs as I scrambled for a plan.

I disbanded my silencing bubble half a second before Cain's voice came from right outside my door.

"Open on three, cell twelve."

Blind panic consumed me and I quickly dropped my jumpsuit, kicking my boots off in the same move and leaving the heap of material crumpled beside the wall in a vague attempt to cover the poor job I'd done on fixing it.

The cuff key was tucked behind my sink and I quickly shut off my magic using the key but I had no time to hide it properly again as my door began to rattle open beyond the sheet I'd hung. I placed the key into the gap behind my sink as terror coursed along my limbs.

I dropped to the floor in an instant and started doing push-ups to try and give myself a reason to be covered in sweat with my heart pounding like crazy.

Cain's silencing bubble spilled over my skin a second before his shiny black boots appeared beneath my nose and I fell still.

"Get up," he barked and I pushed myself to my feet, looking up at him as my mouth dried out. If he tossed my cell, he'd see the wall, find the key. I'd be thrown in the hole and everything would be over before it had even begun.

"Hi," I said, forcing my lips to turn up into a smile like I was pleased to see him.

He frowned for a moment, his gaze sliding over me in my tank top and panties and fixing on my knee.

"You're bleeding," he pointed out in a rough voice.

"I, um…" My brain was all out of lies. I'd used them up, run them out, told too many too often and now when I needed one most, I couldn't find one to save me.

"You should save workouts for your time in the gymnasium," Cain growled. "It's hardly ideal to rip your knees raw on the stone floor in here."

"I don't mind it rough," I replied in a teasing tone that had him growling at me while I secretly thanked him for providing the lie I needed.

"Up against the wall," he commanded, his gaze hardening like he didn't like me flirting with him. I was pretty sure he did though.

I quickly moved to do as he'd asked, choosing the wall beside my bunk so that he'd be turning his back on the sink and my tunnel to search me. I placed my hands on the wall above my head and parted my legs as I waited for him to frisk me, though I didn't know what he thought I might be hiding in my tank and panties combo.

Cain moved to stand behind me, so close that I could feel the heat of his body radiating against mine.

He reached out and ran his hands down my sides, skimming over the thin fabric I wore as my heart continued to pound with terror. I needed to distract him, to make sure he didn't search the rest of my cell too thoroughly...

As his hands made it to my hips, I spun around and leaned back against the wall, smirking up at him as he frowned.

"Disobeying an officer is an infraction," he growled. "Are you refusing to submit to a search?"

"I'm sorry, Officer," I said in a teasing voice. "Are you going to have to punish me?"

I drew my hair over one shoulder and tilted my chin to the side in offering as his gaze hooked on mine.

A deep growl left his throat as his fangs extended. "I prefer to hunt my meals than have them handed to me."

"Okay," I shrugged innocently and his gaze hardened.

Before he could say anything else, I ducked beneath his arm and darted away from him.

Cain snarled as he whirled around and he caught me in an instant, twisting me back to face him and shoving me up against the bars which lined the front of my cell. The sheet I'd hung was the only thing hiding us from the view of everyone outside and my heart leapt at the dangerous game he was playing. I gasped as he caught my jaw in his grip half a second before his fangs drove into my neck.

I'd never let a Vampire bite me in this way, not before he'd done it in the store cupboard the other day. I had to admit that I hadn't been prepared for how good it might feel. Yes it hurt for a moment, but once the sharp sting subsided and my blood and magic began to slide from my body into his, a sense of euphoria began to trail along my skin, radiating out from the point at which his mouth met my flesh.

I arched my back, pressing my body against his as he fed from me and reaching up to hold onto the back of his neck, dragging him closer as my skin tingled at his touch.

His hands moved to my hips as he pinned me against the bars and I couldn't help but moan at the feeling of his body pressing to mine.

There was something about the darkness in Cain's soul which called to me and when I was with him like this I just wanted him to draw me down into the shadows at his side.

"Mason?" Hastings called from outside the cell and Cain jerked away from me suddenly, his eyes burning with a dark promise of violence like he thought I might be about to tell someone what he'd just done. "Fifty Eight isn't cooperating."

Cain growled in frustration, reaching out to heal the bite mark on my neck and letting his magic fix my grazed knee too. He placed a finger to my lips and dropped the silencing bubble that surrounded us.

"I'm coming," he called back to Hastings with irritation lining his voice.

He held my eye for a long moment like he was trying to figure out what I was thinking and I bit my bottom lip as I gazed back steadily.

"Clean this shit up," he snarled at me before shooting away, ripping everything from my bunk and tossing it to the floor. He yanked the sheet covering my door down last and sped outside, leaving my skin burning from his touch.

"Cell twelve clear," he barked into his radio as he sped away to help Hastings and I sagged with relief as my cell door rattled shut again.

I quickly rehung my sheet and ran to fix the mess I'd made of my wall and hide the cuff key properly just in case anyone came to check on me again.

My limbs were trembling with fear and my magic was running really low after he'd drained it, but I had just enough to make a good job of the wall and hide the key away.

As soon as it was done, I remade my bed and flopped back down onto it with a smug as fuck grin biting into my cheeks.

In the morning I'd retrieve Sin's weapon from behind the wall and Roary would slip it into Two Hundred's pocket for me at breakfast. We'd already commissioned a Veiled Wall job for someone to snitch to a guard about an inmate having contraband on them while we were in the Mess Hall, and as soon as he was found with the murder weapon, he'd be dragged off to isolation and Sin would be set free.

I closed my eyes as the sound of the search continued to wash over me and my heart finally began to settle. That had been too damn close. But it had been such a rush too.

SIN

PRISONER #88

CHAPTER TWENTY

I was doing a handstand in the centre of my cell. *Isolation goal number two hundred and ten? Check.*

With all the blood in my body rushing to my head, my dick was given some reprieve from dwelling on Rosalie. I swear I'd been hard since I'd almost stolen a kiss from her. And jerking myself off in my lonely cell didn't really appeal. So I tried not to think about how much I wanted that pretty little mouth hole of hers. Didn't help knowing I was probably going to be here until I was an ancient pile of bones. I'd still have a rager for her though, right on into the afterlife.

I'd been going over in my mind the few things I knew about her. I'd seen the symbols on her jumpsuit so I knew she was a Werewolf which was fan-fucking-tastic because everyone knew that Wolves fucked like animals and were up for trying just about anything. And secondly, she was an earth Elemental which meant she could perform all things bondage related with nothing more than a flick of her wrist. And I'd imagined her doing just about all of them in the days that had passed since I'd seen her.

A voice caught my ear down the hall, a guy shouting, "I didn't do it! Someone planted that weapon on me!"

"It's been confirmed by a Chimera, fuckwit. You're going to rot in here," Cain's voice came in response. A bang sounded as the guy was dumped into a cell and a door slammed shut a second later. I remembered my first few days in isolation like a strange dream. It was easier to accept it sooner rather than later and start talking to yourself to fill the silence, because no one else was going to. It was either that or go crazy. And my twelve personalities didn't want to end up in Psych just because isolation was rough on them.

Knuckles banged against my door and I flipped over onto my feet, staggering as I readjusted to being the right way up.

"Open in isolation, cell eight," Cain's gruff voice was followed by the crackle of the radio. My heart thrashed excitedly. I got let out once a week for a shower, but I'd just had one yesterday. So this had to be something else.

A heavy clunk signalled the door releasing and it swung wide. Cain stood there with a bored expression on his face, his arms folded tightly across his wide chest.

"The stars must be shining brightly on you, Eighty Eight," he said in a low growl.

"What do you mean?" I drifted towards the edge of the cell, scraping my tongue across the roof of my mouth as I gazed out at all the free space surrounding Officer Frown.

"It means…" He stepped up into my personal space and I didn't mind that one bit. I needed the closeness, the heat of another body and I didn't care if it was his. "That the murder weapon showed up in Two Hundred's possession. So you're a free man. And I use the term free very lightly."

My heart lurched like it was about to take off right out of my chest. "No fucking way," I breathed.

"Yeah," he said, stepping closer and dropping his arms so his chest bumped against mine. So warm. So fucking good. "But I'm not an idiot, I know someone's watching your back, Eighty Eight. Do you really think Two Hundred would walk around with a murder weapon in his pocket? You should have seen how shocked he looked when we pulled it from his jumpsuit." His mouth curved up in the semblance of a smile as he recalled that and I shrugged in answer, a shit-eating grin tugging at my mouth. Rosalie had pulled through for me. She was clearly as badass as she claimed. And I planned to claim that bad ass pronto.

"I'm as innocent as a nun in a whorehouse," I said sweetly, leaning close to his face, refusing to blink.

He didn't balk like most people did when I looked at them like that. My eyes always betrayed my unpredictable nature, but I guessed Cain knew he had the upper hand.

"I'll be watching you," he said in a dark tone, then his hand closed around my wrist and he dragged me into the hall. I swear the air tasted better out here already, but nothing would compare to the daylight and sweet air up in the Order Yard. How long would it be until I got to go there? I was dying to get out in the sun, but more than that, I needed to hunt down my Wolf girl and fuel my magic reserves with her sexual energy. I was going to shift into her darkest desire and claim her body like no Fae had ever done before. They didn't call me wild just because of my name. I had a reputation of becoming pure animal when I fucked a girl.

Cain lifted his radio to his lips as he guided me out into the stairwell and I just about pissed myself with excitement. "Sin Wilder moving to general population. Backup needed at Cell Block B for reintroduction."

A dark smile pulled at my mouth as we moved upstairs. They knew what was going to happen the second I stepped into that block. And they wanted more eyes on me in case I killed again. But I wasn't stupid enough to give up my freedom so soon. A few broken bones wouldn't hurt though.

We soon arrived on level four and energy flashed through my veins like lightning.

"How much restraint do you have, Eighty Eight?" Cain asked in a mocking tone. "One more death and I'll lock you in the hole for the rest of your sentence. And as you're in here for life, that's one hell of a long time to be alone in the dark."

"Monsters grow in the dark, Officer. Be careful what you do with me."

"Is that a threat?" he snarled, resting his hand on the baton at his hip.

"The day I threaten you is the day you die." I smiled brightly at him and he glowered, hauling me along toward Cell Block B where I-shit-you-not over thirty officers were standing around the door. "Is this welcome party just for me? You're a little sparse on the banners."

They said nothing and I gnashed my teeth at Officer Rind so he shrank back against the wall, drawing a manic laugh from my lungs. Cain shoved me toward the door and nodded to Officer Luscious who pressed her palm to the scanner. I smirked at her and a blush lined her cheeks as she looked down at her shoes.

I started bouncing on my heels as the door parted before me and the metal bridge extended over the void below. Convicts looked up to see what was happening and I grinned hungrily, doing a mental sweep as I hunted for the meanest assholes in here who were holding the top floor cells. I was ready to unleash the furious energy which had been locked in my veins for months.

"Hello pretties," I purred, stepping out onto the bridge. A bunch of the weakest Fae ran into the coop to hide and my smile stretched wider. "Daddy's home."

I stepped off of the bridge and it immediately retracted behind me. I spared a glance for the officers gathered by the door, keeping it open to watch me. And if they wanted a show, they were about to get one.

I headed to the stairs and Fae lurched out of my way as I raced up to the top floor and moved along the walkway as I picked out a cell. Well fuck it, why have one cell when I could have three?

I lunged at a shirtless fucker who resembled a walrus, snatching him by the throat and throwing him over the railing before he even knew what had happened. He screamed in alarm, hitting the metal floor below with a thwack that rang throughout the entire block. Fae came spilling out of their cells to watch as I moved to the railing, leaning over the edge and cupping my ear as I listened for signs of life. A grunt said the shitbag was still breathing and I tossed a wink at the guards in the doorway before turning back to my prey. Two girls and a towering bastard I was fairly sure was a Minotaur were approaching me. I rolled my neck as adrenaline surged into my limbs.

"Form a queue," I instructed, hoisting myself up onto the railing and standing there as I selected my next opponent from the line-up. I pointed at the girl with the pissed off eyes and tattoos covering ninety percent of her body. "Let's dance, sugar."

She shrieked as she lunged for me and I leapt over her head, landing behind her and catching her around the waist. I swung her around like we were in a dance before launching her over the railing without a backwards look. She screamed as she went and a heavy thump sounded her hitting the floor. Her yell of pain told me she was also alive though so that was just dandy.

The Minotaur came at me next with a snort of fury, sounding like the bull which lived in his flesh as he tried to mow me down.

I ducked under the first fist he threw, slamming my foot into his spindly knee and snatching him in a headlock as he buckled with a squeal of pain.

"It's called leg day, asshole," I spoke in his ear then threw him toward the stairs so he crashed down them, knocking people onto their asses.

The final girl leapt onto my back and I laughed as she tried to choke me out, her thighs clamping around my waist as she reared backwards to try and topple me. And if that was what she wanted, I was more than happy to oblige. I threw myself back onto the ground, my full body weight crushing her beneath me and she wheezed, her grip on my neck easing. I rolled over, catching hold of her throat and squeezing as I grinned down at her. She flailed beneath me, her legs kicking wildly as I pinned her in place and drank in the feel of her life in my hands.

"Dying is a good look on you," I said in a low voice. "Do you want to see how good you look dead?" I taunted.

"No," she rasped. "I give up."

I let her go, jumping to my feet and offering her my hand. She took it and I yanked her upright, throwing my arm into the air and pumping it with my victory as she scampered away.

"These three cells are mine!" I announced, pointing at them. "Any objections?!"

I swung my gaze to the Fae peeping out of their cells around me like little mice then twisted toward a huge guy as he strode out of one on the other side of the walkway. Several Fae followed him out of it and I recognised them as Oscura Wolves. I glanced around, looking for their Alpha, Amira, but she didn't appear.

I folded my arms, waiting for the group to approach and their leader halted a few feet away.

"Isn't your Alpha going to come and challenge me, kitten?" I purred.

The guy cocked his head to one side. "I'm Sonny Tribera, Beta of the Oscura Clan. And our new Alpha isn't in this block."

Everything clicked together in my head and I threw my head back with a laugh. I rushed forward and Sonny braced for impact, but I just clapped my hands to his cheeks and grinned. "It's her, isn't it? Rosalie's your Alpha."

Sonny nodded, shoving me away from him as his muscles flexed. "If you strike at us Wolves, I'll be more than happy to pass on that information to her and then we'll see how you fare against a Moon Wolf."

I moved nearer to him again, then dragged him into a firm hug which he didn't return. My heart thumped for joy at being so close to another Fae and I growled appreciatively at the heat of his body seeping into mine. "No need to run to Mommy. Me and her happen to be best friends. So I'll happily let you sleep on this floor as a favour to her."

I released him and he snarled, eyeing me like he wasn't sure what I was about to do next. Which made two of us because I wasn't sure either.

"It wasn't a request, but I'm glad we have peace." He nodded to me, heading away with his pack, being careful not to turn his back on me before he was far enough that it was no longer an insult.

I climbed onto the railing, sitting on the edge so my legs swung down beneath me. My eyes locked on Cain's beyond the door and he held my gaze for a long second before signalling another guard to shut the door.

The world was once again mine to take and taste and torture. And fuck did it feel divine.

Just as my growling stomach told me it was time for lunch and I prepared to pounce on Rosalie over a cheese sandwich, my plans were shattered by the bell ringing to announce time in the Order Yard. But this was even better. It was what I'd been dreaming about for so long. Fresh air, wide open spaces. I was going to be able to see the actual *sky* again. And more than that, I'd be able to flex my Order muscles and tame my little wild girl.

She wanted to recruit me to her plan? Then fine. But my terms and conditions involved her bent beneath me screaming my name. With the way she'd been panting in front of me, I didn't imagine she'd have many objections to that. Especially once I got a read on her sexual desires. Then I'd be like an irresistible piece of candy made especially for her.

I stood outside the elevators that led to the yard, waiting to ascend and not a single asshole wanted to get in with me when it arrived. Go figure.

I rose up in the elevator alone, my mind set on tracking down Rosalie and finding out what the rest of her name was. She'd forget it by the time I was inside her, so it was probably best to find out what it was before that happened.

As the doors opened on the surface, I took in a lungful of pure oxygen, laughing loudly as I took in more and more. I hurried out into the hollow building, hunting the groups of Fae around me as they hung their shit up in the lockers and shifted into their Order forms. A Vampire with pink hair gave me a hopeful look, her fangs bared and I offered her a mocking smile.

"You must be new," I said. "If you try and feed from me, I'll snap your legs like twigs and hang you in a tree so you'll be stuck there when the timer runs out."

"Noted." She tossed me a wink and sped past me in a blur, racing after a slow-ass Siren who quickly fell prey to her fangs. She hung on his back like a limpet, sucking at his neck then shot away before he could even figure out who had done it. Had to say, that shit was impressive.

I left my jumpsuit on, my Order not requiring me to shift fully, but I lowered the top half to tie around my waist and pulled my tank top off, tucking it in the back of my pants so I was ready to feel the sun on my skin.

I spotted a bunch of Harpies grouping together before the forest edge and made a path towards them.

I took in another deep breath of fresh air, letting my lungs expand with it as I tasted pines on the breeze. The sun kissed my skin like a whore and I drank in the feel of her licking my flesh. *It's been a long time coming, baby.*

I stalked towards the Harpies, setting my sights on a girl who was giving their flock leader hopeful glances. He was a tall fucker with long hair and a pretty boy face. I casually brushed my hand over the girl's arm and she turned to me in alarm as I read her desires and my form shifted before her eyes. I became just like the guy she'd been ogling, big white wings and all, but I held about fifty more pounds of muscle than he did.

I barked a laugh then took off into the sky before she could throw herself at me. I flexed my wings, holding her fantasy in my grip as I used it to my advantage, swooping over the forest as I hunted for Rosalie.

The thrill of flying was nothing in comparison to how excited I was to find her. I needed her naked body against mine, I had to feel how wet she was for me, needed the taste of her flesh coating my tongue. I'd take her like the monster I was and ruin her for all other men. My body was designed to please, but I liked to tug and rip and torture too. I'd leave her panting and destroyed.

I spotted a Wolf pack racing out of the forest led by an incredible silver Wolf with fur as bright as moonlight. I followed them, flying silently overhead as they headed into the tropical area of the forest and rose up towards a collection of shimmering rock pools.

They started shifting one by one and I bathed in the sunshine on my back as I waited for them to return to their Fae forms. The silver Wolf shifted last and I wasn't the least bit surprised when Rosalie appeared in her Fae form. A groan escaped me at the sight of her naked body and I was glad when she turned from her pack as they poured into the pools and she walked off into the trees.

I dove out of the sky, falling like a stone and landing in the canopy somewhere above her. I returned to my own form, dropping silently through the branches as I made my way down, anticipation crashing through my veins.

I reached the last branch of the tree, spotting her walking my way and I sat down, falling backwards and hanging from the branch by my knees as I hung down in front of her.

She gasped in surprise and I grinned satisfactorily. "Hey, wild girl."

"Sin," she breathed, walking closer as my gaze fell over her curves and a low growl fell from my throat.

"You owe me a kiss." I smirked, swinging forward to try and steal it.

She backed up, arching her brows. "I don't owe you anything. It's you who owes me. I was the one who got you out of the hole."

I released my hold on the branch, swinging my arms and using my momentum to flip over and land on my feet. I had plenty of height on her and I used it to my advantage as I stalked closer, refusing to blink as I took in her strawberry lips.

"Well I guess that means I owe *you* a kiss then…where do you want it?" I dropped my gaze to her pussy and she released a wolfish snarl.

"Eyes up here, asshole." She snapped her fingers beside her face and I looked up, hounding closer. I just needed to touch her, get a read on her desires. I was going to bury myself in that sweet body. I wanted to flip her over and ride her like a fucking cowboy. But I could see she needed some foreplay, and luckily for her, foreplay was my middle name.

"Let me plead my case for the kiss," I said, raising my hands in innocence. "I'll even give you my shirt so I don't eye-fuck you while I do it."

She thought about that for a second then held out her hand for it.

I chuckled, tugging my shirt from the back of my pants and tossing it to her. I didn't miss the way she was taking in the muscles on my torso or the tattoos lining my dark flesh. She had an ache in her eyes that said she wanted to explore me like a map to buried treasure. But it was clear she wasn't going to give in to my demands easily, even if she wanted me.

She pulled on the white tank top and it fell down to her thighs. She looked fucking edible in it and I had the powerful urge to rip it off again. I was already hard for her, but that was pretty much a permanent state I lived in these days.

"Let's hear it then," she taunted.

I placed a hand over my heart, my eyes locked on hers. "I, Sin Wilder, solemnly swear to tell the truth and nothing but the truth."

Her mouth twitched into a smile, but I kept my expression completely serious.

"I met a girl the other day who offered to break me out of this inescapable prison." I took a step forward, my pulse thumping solidly in my ears. "She looked like my perfect fantasy, my most delicious fucking desire. As an Incubus, I need sexual energy to thrive just like she needs to run under the moon." I took another step closer and her lips parted as she inhaled my dangerous scent. I tilted my head down as I approached my little predator, my gaze falling to her nipples hardening through my shirt. I drew in a breath, my magic reserves swelling as I sensed her need for me. I groaned softly, reaching out to take her chin into my grip and tilting her head up to look at me. "Would you really steal the moon from me, Rosalie?"

She licked her lips and I drew on my Order power, trying to get a sense of what she desired. I gripped her chin tighter, growling as my power failed to offer me any insight into what she liked in a Fae visually.

"No," she said and my thoughts tumbled away from me. "I wouldn't torture you like that, Sin."

I leaned down, ready to take and take from her until she filled me up, but she spoke again before I could.

"One kiss, that's all you get."

My throat thickened at the challenge. I wondered if spending so long without using my Order gifts had made them faulty somehow. I needed to use my power to become her fantasy, then she wouldn't be able to get enough of me. But I'd have to take this kiss as I was. Which wasn't ideal, but I could still make her feel things no guy ever could with just their mouth on hers.

"Better make it count then, huh?" I caught her hair with my free hand, yanking her head backwards and keeping her chin in my grip to control her. I took her bottom lip between my teeth and bit down until she gasped, then I plunged my tongue into her mouth, releasing her chin to drop my hand to her breast and skim my thumb over her pebbled nipple. She moaned, her tongue chasing mine for every stroke as I tasted her, drinking in her desire with every lick and bite I gave her.

I pushed her back against a tree, pressing my knee between her thighs and she ground against me keenly, her body so responsive to mine. I released her hair to torment her other nipple, making her pant against my mouth. She arched into me, letting me feed and feed on her arousal and I groaned with desperation as my cock throbbed with need. It had been so long since I'd touched a woman like this, and fuck if it had ever felt this good.

"How about we make it a full moon?" I growled against her mouth and she tipped her head back to break the kiss, a laugh falling from her lips.

She caught my wrists to stop me touching her, giving me a wicked smile. "I promised you one kiss. And you've had it, Sin. Don't be greedy."

"But if I was one of the seven dwarves, that would be my name," I purred.

I planted one hand on her arm, trying to draw her fantasy to me once more, but still nothing appeared to me.

"What is it you desire?" I demanded, growing frustrated that my Order powers weren't working. I didn't understand what was happening. Did she have some way of blocking it? "Let your barriers down," I urged and she cocked her head to one side. My knee was still between her thighs, keeping her pinned to the tree.

"Well right now..." She leaned in closer and I hung on her next words, aching to hear them. "I'm really thirsty, so I'm gonna go get some water." She shoved me backwards and raced off into the trees before I could even process that she'd left me there like a toy she'd grown too old for.

I stared after her with her taste still sitting on my tongue, her sugary sweet flavour like a drug kicking into my veins. I didn't know what the fuck had just happened, but I knew one thing. I needed to claim that girl. No one else was going to draw an ounce of my attention until I'd conquered her. So she'd better be ready for the troops to invade. Because I was declaring war.

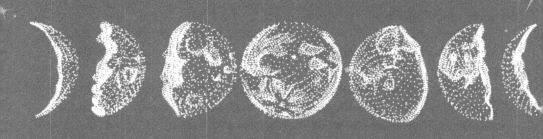

ROSALIE

PRISONER #12

CHAPTER TWENTY ONE

My pack was excited today. They'd heard a rumour that the next Order Yard visit would be at night and they were chomping at the bit to get out beneath the moon after three sessions held in daylight. In all honesty I was just as hyped as them. Not least because my magic was damn near tapped out and until I could replenish it by running beneath the moon, I couldn't do much more to progress my plans.

Ethan hadn't yet come calling for a turn with the cuff key, but I'd decided not to worry about that. He had to know that it would be damn near impossible for me to smuggle it out of my room while the searches were still being conducted so regularly anyway. Besides, he'd gone back to ignoring my existence for the most part. I still caught him glaring over at me from time to time, but he seemed to have no desire to confront me over his issues and I'd decided to leave him to dwell on them if that was what he wanted.

My gaze caught on Sin Wilder as he swaggered through the room clutching his tray. He approached a table filled with low ranking Fae and leaned close to say something to them which had them all leaping from the table and abandoning it for him to occupy alone as he began to eat.

My tray was piled up with various offerings from my pack as they handed me the best of their own food, but I was totally stuffed.

Banjo was getting excitable at the far end of the table and as usual, that led him to break out into song. Which perhaps wouldn't have been so bad if he could hold a tune or sang real songs, but he just made shit up and hollered it at the top of his lungs.

"There once was a Wolf whose fur went poof and her name was Rosa-leeee. She hollered to the moon, won't you come back soon and do a dance with meee?"

The other Wolves all started cheering and I rolled my eyes as I got to my feet, escaping the song as the pack started clapping their hands along to the nonsense and I grabbed a bowl of strawberries off of my tray.

Each of us had only been given one in our fruit pots today but the Wolves had gifted me all of theirs because they knew I loved them, leaving me with two full bowls which I hadn't been able to finish.

I waved the pack away as some of them tried to follow me and wound my way across the room towards Sin.

His eyes fell on me the instant I rose from my table and I teased him by training my gaze on some point at the rear of the room, acting like I was going to walk straight past him before veering off course at the last moment and dropping down before him.

"Hey," I said, offering him a warm smile.

"You wanna come back to my cell and see how many times you can scream my name before you lose your voice?" he offered, reaching across the table for my hand.

I moved out of his reach as I leaned back, tilting my head as I looked him over.

"You've cut your hair," I pointed out with a smile. The scruffy beard and hair he'd been sporting in the hole had been shaved down hard, leaving little more than a shadow along his dark skin. The harsher cut drew attention to the strength of his features and I found my gaze roaming over his face as I bit my bottom lip. His eyes drank me in just as keenly and I couldn't help but remember that kiss he'd given me in the Order Yard, my skin prickling with the memory of his touch. "It looks good on you."

"You know what would look even better on me?" he asked, his lips tipping into a filthy grin.

"Me?" I guessed, arching an eyebrow at him.

Sin barked a laugh, the rough edges of his voice making my toes curl. "I guess if we both agree then it's time we tried it out."

I rolled my eyes, flicking my long hair back over my shoulder and taking a strawberry into my grasp.

"Do you have a sweet tooth, Sin?" I asked him as I spun the bright red fruit between my fingers.

"I like to put sweet things in my mouth," he agreed. "And you're the sweetest thing I've seen all year."

I laughed, offering him a wide smile as I leaned a little closer, pushing the bowl of strawberries towards him. "I'm not on the menu. But these are, if you want them?"

His gaze fell on the fruit and he licked his lips in a way that had me seriously considering his offer to go back to his cell. But I'd been sent here to bust him out of this place. Sin Wilder was a job, letting myself get pulled into his charm would only complicate things.

"What do you want for them?" he asked seriously.

"Not everything is a transaction. It's just strawberries between friends." I pushed the bowl at him and his gaze narrowed in suspicion.

"Tit for tat. You give me strawberries, I gotta give you something. If you haven't figured out that's how this place works yet, wild girl, then you really are a pup."

I rolled my eyes at him, my gaze catching on a tattoo which he had inked onto the back of his hand. It was a clock hanging from a chain which wrapped around his wrist. Roman numerals were scrawled either side of the chain and the time on it was thirteen minutes past eight.

"Give me a story then," I asked, reaching out to tap the tattoo with my finger. "Why this tattoo?"

Sin inhaled deeply and turned his hand to capture mine, winding his fingers between mine as he groaned in satisfaction.

"That's the exact time and date of my very first kill," he whispered conspiratorially. "You wanna know how long it took for me to choke him out?"

"I want to know what he did," I replied instantly.

"What do you mean?" Sin asked, tilting his head to survey me as he pushed the strawberries into his mouth one after another.

"You only kill the bad guys," I said. "So what did number one do to push you over the edge?"

Sin finished his strawberries and smirked at me over the bowl. "What do I get for that answer?" he asked. "My strawberries are all gone now."

"I thought we said this doesn't have to be a transaction?"

Sin thumped his other fist down onto the table suddenly, making his whole tray jump. I didn't flinch but I did tug my hand back out of his as I raised an eyebrow at him.

"You weren't listening to me," he growled, the light in his eyes turning to shadows.

I pushed myself to my feet and placed my hands flat on the table before leaning down low to look into his eyes.

"You're the one who said we were exchanging things, Sin," I reminded him, letting my Alpha tone ring in my voice. "Just because I played along once doesn't mean I'm dancing to your tune now. I'll leave you to think about that."

I turned my back on him, offering up the insult of showing him that I had no respect for him as I stalked back across the Mess Hall to my pack.

His booming laughter suddenly ripped from his throat behind me and he started pounding his fist down on the table again and again.

"I love watching you walk away, wild girl!" he called after me.

I raised my middle finger and held it up for him to see as I kept walking and by the time I dropped down between my pack, the smile on my face felt etched on permanently. Sin Wilder may have had more than a few screws loose, but I was pretty sure I liked it.

Thankfully Banjo had called time on his song in my absence and I fell into thought as I listened to my pack chat and gossip around me. Their discussions were usually too small to interest me much. Their lives were so confined to this place that their topics of conversation almost all circled around who was screwing who or what minor fights had taken place. My mind still lived free, outside of Darkmore and its petty politics, and if I wasn't focusing on my escape plans then I preferred to think about my family who were waiting for me. The others tended to avoid that, not wanting to pine over the things they'd left behind and were missing out on.

"Twelve!" Cain's voice carried to me over the crowd of inmates, but I pretended not to hear him as I stayed in the thick of my Wolves.

I cupped my hands around my mouth and howled to the ceiling, encouraging my Wolves to start up a chorus of noise around me as I smirked to myself.

They circled me, touching my back and arms, nudging each other aside to get close as I found myself in the centre of the group and I encouraged them closer still. My smile was enough to urge them on and the pack of around a hundred Werewolves closed in tightly, keeping Cain away.

Sonny flexed his muscles and wrapped an arm around me as his dark eyes danced with amusement. He nuzzled against my hair and I gave in to my Wolf instincts as I snuggled closer to him for a moment.

"What are you up to, Alpha?" he asked in a low voice.

"Me?" I asked innocently. "When am I ever up to anything?"

I caught sight of Cain moving towards me through the throng of Wolves with a face like thunder, but I quickly looked away again.

"Why don't you transfer to our cell block, Alpha?" Brett asked suggestively as he moved closer to me, crawling up onto the table. He was tall and broad with rugged good looks and dark eyes which promised trouble but without the scent of an Alpha on him, he just didn't do anything for me. "We could do *anything* we liked in there whenever you wanted it."

The closest Wolves all started nodding in agreement, calling out suggestions for the ways they'd like to pleasure me and I rolled my eyes at them as I waved them off.

"Sorry guys, but like I tell you *every day,* I don't enjoy pack orgies. I need another Alpha to push my buttons," I teased. "But just keep giving Sonny all the pack love on my behalf, he's happy to join in."

"I am," he agreed with a smirk. "I'll gladly make use of your offer, Brett."

Brett's eyes widened with excitement as he moved around me to kiss my Beta. I laughed as Sonny failed to release me while they were making out and Esme started trailing her fingers through my hair.

"Would you like to watch instead?" she offered. "We could watch them together, or I could go down on you while you watch, or-"

Esme yelped as she was suddenly ripped out of her seat and I looked up at Cain's angry face with an innocent expression.

"Twelve," he snapped. "I've been calling you."

"Have you?" I asked with the hint of a smile playing around my lips.

Cain reached out and grabbed my arm, hauling me from my seat as he leaned down to snarl in my face. My pack all leapt to their feet, barking and growling as they swarmed forward to defend me but I raised a hand to wave them off. They didn't need to end up in the hole because of me.

"I know you heard me," he growled darkly, glaring into my eyes.

"Prove it," I breathed so low that only he'd be able to hear me with his Vampire ears.

Cain's dark eyes flared with the challenge I was presenting him and my heart leapt at the threat in his gaze.

"Your work assignment starts now," he snapped.

"But lunch isn't over yet," I complained half-heartedly. I'd finished eating anyway so it didn't really matter, but I wasn't just going to roll over whenever he gave me a command.

Cain reached out to my tray and snatched my half eaten pasta into his hand before shoving it straight into my face. Mac and cheese smeared over my skin before falling to the floor with a wet splat and every single Wolf around me fell utterly silent in shock.

My lips parted as I stared up at Cain in total surprise and his eyes dared me to flip out over what he'd just done.

"There you go," he announced. "All done."

Sonny started growling and my pack rose to their feet as the violent sound poured from a hundred sets of lips. From the corners of my eyes I noticed more guards shifting towards us as they sensed danger in the air and Cain just fucking waited to see what I'd do about it.

The balls on this stronzo!

After another beat of silence, my lips parted in a wide smile and I started laughing.

I dragged a finger down the side of my cheek, gathering cheese sauce onto it before pushing it into my mouth and moaning with exaggerated pleasure. "Mmm, that tastes even better now," I taunted and my pack all started laughing too.

Sonny grabbed my chin in his grasp and ran the pad of his tongue straight up the side of my cheek, licking off the cheese sauce as he moaned too.

"Oh fuck yeah," he groaned, panting like a dog as he put on a show for the others. "That tastes good enough to get me hard."

My smile widened as I looked up at Cain and I swiped more sauce from my chin onto my finger before offering it to him.

"Want a bite, *sir?*" I offered, batting my lashes at him and I could have sworn that for half of half a second, he almost smiled.

"Come on," he snapped, grabbing my outstretched arm around the wrist while ignoring my offer.

Before he could drag me from the table, I reached out and snatched up my unopened pudding pot.

"Pudding!" I yelled, spotting the enormous Bear Shifter in the crowd at the far side of the Mess Hall.

He raised his eyes from his food to look at me and I launched the pudding pot in his direction, throwing it over the heads of the other prisoners. His hand snapped out at the last second and he caught it, tucking it within his jumpsuit and looking back down at his own meal instantly as if it had never happened.

That guy totally loves me.

Cain yanked on my arm and pulled me out of the room at a fast trot and I fell into step with him rather than trying to resist.

We started walking down the corridor and he pulled a handkerchief from his pocket, offering it to me so that I could wipe the remains of the pasta from my face.

"Holy shit, Cain, do you carry a *hanky?*" I teased as I used it to remove the pasta. "Does your mamma tuck it into your pocket for you every morning just in case?"

He growled at me and I couldn't help but laugh as I pushed him further.

"Has she sewn your name into all of your shirts too?" I whispered conspiratorially.

"Shut up, Twelve."

"And what about your boxers? If I pulled them off of you would I find the name Mason Cain hand stitched into the waistband?"

"That's enough," he growled in a dark voice.

"When did I cross the line?" I asked. "Was it when I suggested that I'd take your underwear off or when I called you *Mason?*"

Cain twisted towards me in a flash of speed, catching me by the throat and shoving me up against the wall as he bared his teeth at me.

"Do you want another hit from my shock baton?" he threatened.

"Yes please," I purred in response.

He stared at me for a long moment like he was trying to figure me out then released me just as suddenly as he'd grabbed me.

I stayed silent as I started following him again but my tongue wouldn't remain tied for long.

"Where are we going?" I asked as we headed for the stairs.

"Isolation," he growled and I sighed dramatically. "Do you have a problem with your work assignment, *inmate?*"

"It's just so boring down there on my own," I muttered in a petulant tone. In all honesty I was perfectly happy with cleaning the isolation unit for work because it was where the door to the maintenance level stood and I'd been aiming to get down there to start the next part of my plan.

"Well it's not my job to make sure you're *entertained*," he said in a dark voice. "So just do what you're told or I'll write you up."

"Yes, sir," I agreed in a meek little voice which made him narrow his eyes at me suspiciously.

We headed down to the ninth floor and Cain unlocked the isolation unit where a mop and bucket already stood waiting for me. I was well used to the routine down here now so I headed away from him to dunk my mop in the water and started cleaning the floors.

Cain set himself up by the door as he watched me and I made a show of doing a good job to save myself from the complaints he liked to toss my way.

As I moved towards the far end of the corridor, his radio buzzed and I listened in as he answered it.

"Boss, I'm having a bit of trouble with the kitchen workers," Hastings' voice came over the speaker. "There seems to be a chopping knife missing..."

"For the love of the moon," Cain growled irritably before lifting the radio to his lips. "Hold on, I'm coming."

I paused in my mopping and turned to look at him with a hopeful expression. "Does that mean I'm done for the day?" I asked eagerly.

"No," he snapped predictably and I fought down the urge to grin as he fell into my trap. "Just keep working and don't go talking to any of the isolated prisoners again or I'll be forced to punish you."

"We wouldn't want that," I joked.

"I mean it, Twelve, don't cross me."

I nodded seriously and he grunted something beneath his breath before turning and heading out of the isolation unit. He locked the door after him, trapping me down here and I counted to ten as I waited to make sure he was really gone.

As soon as I was confident he wasn't coming back, I dragged my mop and bucket to the door at the end of the corridor. It stood open and a narrow staircase looked back at me, lit with dim yellow lamps which hung from the wall.

I super casually lifted my bucket into my grip and then headed on down.

My heart pounded with excitement as I jogged down the stairs and I found myself in a huge room at the base of them.

The maintenance level was at the very bottom of the subterranean building which made up Darkmore Penitentiary and it held everything they needed to contain over two thousand powerful criminals. From the power blocks which kept the various magical shields enforced to the vat of evermist they used to contain us in our cells. Not to mention water pump, boiler and oxygen tanks plus whatever else they needed to keep us all alive. But the thing I was most interested in were the tanks which held the Order Suppressant.

Unlike the magic which powered the shields surrounding the prison, the Suppressant tanks had to be running constantly and kept topped up with the ingredients required to create the gas and pump it up into the prison.

For my plan to work, I was going to need to neutralise the effects of the gas which meant I had to pump the antidote through the vents instead. Luckily for me, all that required was adding the right quantities of Nepula Weed, one Sunstone Crystal and the stone of a Nevercot Plum to the mix. *Un*luckily, the tanks were sealed up as tight as a duck's ass and getting into one of them without my magic was going to be a total bitch.

But I'd known that before I'd gotten myself locked up and so, with a little help from Roary's brother, Leon, I'd managed to get my hands on a tank exactly like the one they had here to practice on. I knew that motherfucker more intimately than the dude I'd given my virginity to, and I already knew exactly how I was going to slip my little ingredients into her when the time came.

I just needed to find the exact location of the tank and make sure that there wasn't a CCTV camera pointing at it so that I could find my way down here when I needed to.

The constant thrum of heavy machinery filled the space as I stepped down into the enormous room on the bottom floor and I placed my mop and bucket by the door with a grin hooking up my lips.

The room was lit with a dim red light and my heart pounded with excitement as I delved into it.

There were pipes and wires running along the ceiling and the scent of dust and smoke hung in the air.

My veins thrummed as I passed a huge glass cylinder filled with sparking white energy which was used to power the outer fence and my shadow danced around me as I moved beyond it.

I took a twisting path through the machinery, my eyes widening at the sheer scope of the things which were required to keep this place secure.

The space was huge, but there was so much crammed into it that it felt like a maze and I had to double back on myself more than once before I found the beast I was searching for.

I grinned as I hurried towards the enormous black tank but as I got closer, my heart fell right into the pit of my stomach.

"No," I breathed, reaching out to touch the machine just to make sure I was really seeing it. Because this couldn't be right. I'd found the purchase invoice from eight years ago when the prison had last upgraded this system. Or at least, when I'd *thought* they'd last upgraded. Because this wasn't the machine I'd spent countless hours working on and getting to know. It was newer, shinier, slicker and had a goddamn electronic control system instead of a manual one.

My heart fell and my pulse thundered in my ears. My entire plan hinged on me neutralising the Suppressant. I couldn't get us out of here without it. There was no other way. No other fucking way.

I tipped my head back and screamed my frustration at the stone ceiling before kicking the asshole machine for good measure.

What the fuck was I going to do now?

I can't believe this. I'm going to be stuck in here for the rest of my motherfucking miserable life with a bunch of psychopaths and nut cases…

I snarled and started pacing back and forth, clawing my hands into my hair as I tried to think of some way around this. There had to be something I could do, some way to overcome this issue. I wasn't going to give up. I was Rosalie goddamn Oscura and I'd survived the worst of fates twice over, I wouldn't be beaten by some damn hunk of metal.

I released a slow breath and smiled. It was going to be okay. This was just a speed bump. I'd call Dante and we'd figure it out. No big deal.

I ignored the little asshole voice in the back of my head who was wailing in despair and moved forward to get a look at the name stamped at the top of the machine. *ipump500.*

You're going down ipump.

"Twelve?!" Cain's voice echoed off of the walls and ice slid down my veins at the pure fucking rage in his tone. He was beyond pissed. Way, *way* beyond.

I looked around hopefully as I wondered if I might find something I could use as a weapon against him before realising that that was a terrible idea. I couldn't attack a guard. Which meant I was going to have to face his wrath.

"When I find you, you're going to be begging me for mercy!" he bellowed and my heart thumped out of rhythm.

There was one single thing which might just be enough to save me from his anger, but it also might be pushing him too far. Though at this point, it was pretty much my only option. I'd meant to continue mopping as I hunted around down here so that I could just play dumb and make out I'd still been cleaning, but of course that plan had gone to shit and I'd just abandoned the cleaning stuff by the door.

So I only had one hope. One crazy idea that I could try to cover for my own recklessness.

"I thought you liked the hunt, *Officer?*" I called in a taunting voice before turning and hurrying away from the tank, slipping down the next aisle of machinery. The general hum of magic and grinding gears should have been enough to cover the sound of my heartbeat and breaths even from his Vampire hearing and I was hoping that luring him into the hunt would distract him from any questions he might have about what I'd really been up to.

A deep growl echoed off of the walls and my heart leapt as I slipped between two huge machines and through a doorway which led into a massive storage room stacked with supplies from Mess Hall trays, to blankets and spare jumpsuits.

"You can run, Twelve, but I'm faster than you!" Cain yelled. "And when I catch you, you'll be sorry you disobeyed me."

"Are you going to spank me?" I called back before diving behind a mountainous stack of toilet paper. I was surprised the label on it didn't read *extra scratchy* because it sure felt like they went out of their way to get the horrible stuff when I was wiping.

I held my breath as footsteps sounded beyond my hiding place and Cain shot past, heading for the back of the room.

I rounded the toilet paper mountain and turned for the exit, breaking into a sprint just as a low snarl sounded behind me.

I raced out into the room filled with machinery again and skidded to my right before pressing my back to a huge generator which was roaring with power.

Cain burst around the corner a second later and lunged at me with his fangs bared.

My fist snapped out on instinct and I caught him straight in the jaw, busting his lip open in the process.

We both froze for half a second as the shock of what I'd just done washed over us then he shot towards me again with a manic smile lighting his face.

He caught my waist and whirled me back against the generator with a deep growl.

"Do you think you can fight me off, Twelve?" he purred, his eyes alive with the rush of the hunt.

"That sounds like you want me to try, *sir,*" I replied, tension coiling in my muscles at the thought of it.

"Oh you can *try.*"

The moment the words left his lips, I swung my fist into his side as hard as I could and after years of taking part in underground cage fights for fun, that was pretty damn hard.

He winced and I followed it up with an upper cut to his chin before lurching forward and slamming my shoulder into his gut.

He fell back as expected, but his arms locked around me and he dragged me down with him.

Cain rolled as we hit the floor, forcing me beneath him and snatching a fistful of my long hair into his grip.

He lunged forward and I cried out as his fangs drove into my neck a moment later.

Cain groaned in pure ecstasy as my blood spilled over his lips and he caught my left hand in his grip, pinning it to the floor above my head while running his other hand down the length of my body.

I gasped as his fingers moved over my breast and my nipple hardened through my thin clothes. I arched my back so that my body was pressed to his more firmly and I moaned as I felt how hard he was between my thighs.

This was so wrong on so many levels, but it just felt so fucking *good* that I couldn't even consider stopping it.

Always a sucker for an Alpha, Rosa.

I moved my hands to his chest and started unhooking his buttons as my body throbbed with pure need.

Cain groaned into my neck and dragged his teeth free of my flesh before leaning back to look down at me.

"Stop," he growled as I got half of his buttons open, though I could see the heat burning in his gaze. He wanted this just as much as I did.

"Are you worried about getting into trouble, Officer?" I mocked. He had me pinned to the floor while he drained my blood and dry humped me. It wasn't really like he'd be in any less trouble if he just gave in to what his body was craving anyway.

"You're the one who will be in trouble when I drag you down to interrogation to find out what the hell you were doing down here," he snapped.

I tipped my head back and laughed and he pushed himself to his feet before hauling me up behind him.

"Let's see how long you keep giggling once Dr Quentin gets to work on you," he growled.

I narrowed my eyes at him as I yanked my arm out of his grip. "Think again, *Officer,*" I purred darkly. "Because if I end up in interrogation with that freaky Cyclops, the first thing I'll be offering up are memories of your teeth in my neck and your hands on my body. Then we'll find out what upsets the Warden most. Do you think you'll last long when you're tossed into gen pop with the masses?"

Cain snarled at me but his gaze flickered uncertainly as he realised I had him over a barrel.

"In fact," I breathed, reaching out to fasten his buttons for him. "I'm pretty sure I only came down here because you told me to. Because you wanted to get me where the cameras weren't watching."

"You little bitch," he snarled.

I pouted at him and reached out to cup his cheek in my hand. "I can be your best friend or your worst nightmare, Officer," I said sweetly. "We can keep on playing these games you like so much and I can stay far, far away from interrogation. Or you can drag me down there and I'll start singing like a canary. It's simple."

"You don't want to go up against me, Twelve," Cain threatened, rage simmering in his eyes.

"No, *Mason.* I already told you once before," I purred. "You're the one who should fear making an enemy of *me.*"

ROARY

PRISONER #69

CHAPTER TWENTY TWO

I sat in my cell, brushing my hair to get the tangles out. It was a matter of pride for a Lion to keep his mane tended and I could hear my father's voice ringing in my head about upholding the Nights' reputation. Not that I was upholding anything anymore. Since I'd been imprisoned, my dad hadn't visited me once. I'd brought shame on the family. Even my three moms only came on birthdays and holidays. I'd once made my dad proud enough to burst. We were a family of thieves going back generations. And I was the first one to be put behind bars.

My gut twisted as I thought of them. My brother was coming to visitation today and though I always loved seeing him, it also dragged up the subject of my parents. And that was the sort of wound that wouldn't heal right. Lions needed their pride to feel content, but I was outcasted from that life now. And I'd never formed strong enough bonds with the other Lionesses in here to create anything that even came close to resembling a pride.

Male Lions didn't tend to socialise with each other if they weren't family and were instinctively pushed to fight for dominance. My gut twisted as I remembered the last male I'd gone up against. His bones cracking beneath my paws, his final roar which had echoed on through the Order Yard even after I'd sent him into death.

Darkmore had made me a killer. A monster. I was as black hearted as the worst convicts in this place now. And even though I knew I'd done my primal duty, it didn't make me feel any less shitty about it. In the real world, there was enough space for male Lions to live away from each other in peace. But in here, we were forced together. And since Rasheen had died at my hand, the rest of the males had bowed to me, keeping their distance as much as Faely possible. So long as they didn't challenge me, I wouldn't be forced to fight again. But if that day came, I knew I'd do whatever it took to maintain my position of power. And that was somehow worse than anything else. I wasn't just a Fae forced to defend himself, I was a killer who would kill again to keep his position. And with the amount of time I had left to serve in Darkmore, I was sure that day would come.

It would be another fifteen years before I'd be set free. I'd be in my late forties, I'd have missed out on half my life, and I'd have no home to go to. And what if my moms or dad got sick in that time? What if something happened to them and I wasn't there to say goodbye? To heal this rift between us-

My brush got stuck in a tangle and I ripped it free with a growl of frustration, tossing it across the room so it hit the wall. I immediately regretted it as the wooden brush broke in half and I sighed, dropping my head into my hands. What was the point anyway? Who was I doing it for? No one in here cared whether my mane was tame or not. I could shave it off for all it mattered. My gut tugged at the thought and I knew I could never really do it. I still had a vague hope that my father would find it in his heart to forgive me one day. That he'd show up at visitation with Leon. Maybe that was why I was trying to look my best today…

"What are you growling about?" Rosalie's voice carried from her cell.

I ignored her, fighting to unravel the knot in my chest. I only had an hour until my brother would be here and I was going to have a head full of tangles now. It would be just my luck that my father did turn up today and he'd see what had become of his worthless first born.

"Hey," Rosa's voice sounded to my right as she stepped into my cell. "Are you okay?"

I grunted in answer and felt her weight pressing down the bed beside me.

"Do you wanna talk about it?" she asked gently, her voice like sunshine breaking through the clouds of my mind. But I didn't want to tell her about this. It was shameful to have lost the respect of my family, especially when hers adored her to the ends of the earth and back. Even in here, she hadn't been locked in irons and carted away to Darkmore. She'd chosen to come on some crazy mission that would earn her even more respect if she pulled it off. I wanted that for her, I'd do anything to help her, I just hoped it was really possible.

"Is it because you broke your hairbrush?" she asked, a note of amusement in her tone.

I growled low in my throat and felt her leave the bed, but didn't lift my head to see what she was doing. A moment later, I heard her leave the cell and I sighed, dropping my head further.

I'd wasted too much of my free life being an arrogant piece of shit, only caring about my next big heist. But one day, when I got out of here, I was never going to take the people I cared about for granted again.

"This pity party is *wild*," Rosalie said as she returned to my cell. She dropped down beside me again and placed something on my knee. "Here." She leaned in close, her mouth moving to my ear. "Nothing a little earth magic couldn't fix."

I lifted my head, dropping my hands and gazing down at the wooden brush on my knee, now completely fixed. And not just that, she'd carved a Lion on the back of it and fixed all the bristles which had broken during the years I'd had it. I picked it up with a heavy sigh, glancing at Rosa with warmth in my heart. "Thank you, little pup."

Her eyes swallowed me whole for a moment and I reached out to tuck a lock of hair behind her ear, losing myself to her familiar presence. She was a piece of the life I'd lost. A constant reminder of the powerful, respected Lion I'd once been. And she still looked at me like I was that same Alpha beast. But she was wrong.

"What's got you so sad?" she asked, a frown creasing her brow.

"You wouldn't understand." I tore my gaze away from her and she released a growl of annoyance.

"I'm not a child anymore, Roary, stop treating me like one." She snatched the brush from my knee and reached out to comb it through my hair.

I caught her wrist at the last second, a snarl tearing from my lips. "Do you know what it means to brush a Lion's mane, pup?"

She rolled her eyes. "I don't know what *you* think it means, but I think it means I wanna do you a favour and sort out the bramble bush you're wearing on your head, Roar."

I cracked a smile, guiding her hand down to rest in her lap. "It's a big deal for Lions."

I'd never let anyone brush my hair since I was a kid and my moms had done it. My dad had taught me to wait until I found my queens, but I guessed in this hell hole, there wasn't much chance for real love. And Rosa was the closest thing to family I had, so maybe it wasn't the worst idea in the world.

"It can mean what we want it to mean." She leaned in conspiratorially as if we were sharing a secret and a smirk tugged up my lips.

"Alright, but you'll probably fall in love with me even harder if you do it, so I can't be held responsible for that," I teased and she shoved me in the shoulder as I chuckled.

I dropped down onto the floor and she shifted behind me, drawing my head back into her lap. Her legs hung down either side of me and I took hold of them, taking her bare feet into my hands.

"Tickle me and die, Roary Night," she warned and I snorted a laugh, sorely tempted to do it just to wind her up. But I lost all thoughts of that entirely as she ran the brush through my hair and pleasure skittered along my scalp and down my spine. A groan escaped me as she did it again and my eyes became hooded with every stroke of the brush. It felt so. Fucking. Good.

A deep purr started up in my chest and she giggled as she continued to tease the knots out of my hair and I tumbled into Lion heaven, letting my eyes fall closed as my whole body vibrated.

I started running my thumbs in circles on the pads of her feet and her toes curled up, but she didn't pull away.

"You're good at this," I sighed, relaxing completely.

I couldn't remember the last time I'd felt so at ease. You could never let your guard down in this place, but with her I didn't have to worry about being stabbed in the back. I trusted her implicitly. And I hoped she trusted me too, because having a true friend in here was the most valuable asset anyone could have.

"I used to braid my cousins' hair for them all the time," Rosa said. "And I always did Aunt Bianca's for parties. She said it was ironic that such a wild Wolf could tame the unruliest fur so well."

"She loves that you're wild," I commented, but what I really wanted to say was *I love that you're wild. And I'm so glad you never lost that.*

"Yeah…sometimes I feel bad though. I made her life so difficult, always breaking things or getting stuck places, getting into accidents. I'll never forget the time I fell from the porch roof and broke my ankle. She almost had an aneurism."

I squeezed her foot as a smile pulled at my mouth. "Life would be dull if no one ever got into trouble. Especially you."

"True, I guess there's just more consequences when you're an adult." She sighed and I sensed a heaviness to her which made my heart tug.

"Are you alright?"

"Yeah…I mean…not really. I miss home."

"You'll be able to have visitors after you've been here a month," I said gently, though I knew that wasn't the biggest comfort in the world. And with her plans to get out of here, I sensed there was more she wasn't saying, but as I went to answer she slid her hand onto my cheek.

"I'm so sorry I'm one of the reasons you're in here." She leaned down, pressing her lips to my forehead and my throat tightened. "I'll get you out," she breathed.

I turned around sharply, rising onto my knees and gripping her shoulders. "You're not responsible for me being in here, Rosa," I growled. "You don't owe me anything."

A part of me knew getting out of this place was impossible too, and though I desperately wanted her to escape this fate, I feared she'd signed away her life by coming here. Maybe she was starting to realise that now she was really here and it was no longer just some wild plan to get excited about at home, surrounded by her kin.

Her legs were still parted either side of me and her cheeks lined with colour under the intensity of my stare. I swallowed the lump in my throat as my eyes drifted to her lips and a feral part of me ached to claim them again. Her legs closed around me, her thighs tightening on my sides and drawing a low growl of desire from my throat.

I cupped her cheek and a ragged breath passed her lips as I pushed myself onto the bed and leaned over her. I let my gaze travel to the swell of her breasts and her legs locking around my waist. She was my little Rosa, my sinful temptation. Ten years had passed and forged her into the most desirable creature I'd ever known. But I'd aged in that time too, and no magic in Solaria could change that. I was always going to be that much older, always going to have loyalties to her cousin Dante. I needed to protect her in this place, not take advantage of her.

I hooked my hands beneath her and dragged her up into a firm hug. She clutched onto me with a whine in the back of her throat and I nuzzled into the side of her head in answer to it. I would always be here for her, but I could never cross the line drawn in the sand between us. I had to be strong, even when my body begged for me to betray that resilient part of myself. I would be her thief, her rock, her weapon, whenever she needed. But I could never be hers. And she could never be mine.

I headed up to level two with the rest of the inmates who had visitors today. We bypassed the Mess Hall and headed down a long corridor, guided by Officer Lyle toward visitation.

"I've got a good one for you today, old man," I teased as I fell into step beside him, feeling miles better after my time with Rosa.

Lyle had been my C.O. when I'd first entered Darkmore. I wouldn't exactly call us friends, but maybe on the outside of this place we could have been something that resembled that.

He chuckled softly. "It won't be funnier than the Medusa with the snake charmer one."

"It's better," I promised and he puffed out his chest as he waited for me to spill it. He was the only person in this prison who appreciated my Order jokes.

"A Tiberian Rat, a Pegasus and an Incubus walk into a bar," I started and Lyle rubbed his hands together in anticipation. "They sit down together and notice there's a huge pot of gold sitting on the bar. So the Pegasus calls out to the bartender, 'Hey, what's all that gold for?' and the bartender says, 'It's a prize for anyone who can drink an entire bottle of Sourache. Competitors have to go into that room over there and pull a splinter from a pissed off Dragon Shifter's foot in his Order form, then go upstairs and fuck the hundred year old lady up there until she's satisfied'."

Lyle was chuckling already but I wasn't done yet.

"'Alright, we'll give it a go!' the Tiberian Rat says enthusiastically and he stands up to go first. He drinks almost all of the bottle of Sourache then stumbles forward and collapses unconscious on the floor. The Pegasus steps up next, drinks the entire bottle of Sourache then staggers into the room with the Dragon Shifter. A tremendous roar sounds followed by a terrified whinny, and a second later the Pegasus comes running back out of the room in his Order form with one of his wings burned off.

Unshaken, the Incubus rises to the challenge. He grabs a bottle of Sourache off of the bar and drinks the whole thing."

Lyle gave me his full attention, his eyes wide as the punchline loomed.

"The Incubus strides confidently into the room with the Dragon Shifter and another tremendous roar carries to the bar, followed by another and another, then the entire bar trembles and shakes as a loud banging sounds against the door."

I grinned at Lyle, as he stared at me with undisguised delight in his eyes.

"The Incubus steps out of the room, bleeding and battered and says, 'Now, where is that lady with the splinter in her foot...'"

Lyle howled a laugh, clutching his side as honest to the stars tears glistened in his eyes. I smirked at him, shaking my head as he totally lost it.

"Is that better than the Medusa and the snake charmer one?" I asked and he nodded, unable to answer through his laughter. "I'd better up my game for next time."

He swiped at his eyes, still chuckling as we made it to visitation and slowed to a halt in front of the double doors.

"In you go, Night," he encouraged with a wide smile on his face.

I gave him a nod and filed through the doors, a scanner running over me before I stepped out into the corridor full of doors. The rest of the inmates followed me in and I noticed some of them were grinning at me so maybe my jokes weren't too piss poor after all.

A guard with a clipboard called us forward one at a time, directing us into the rooms and I waited my turn with anticipation racing through my limbs.

"Sixty Nine!" Officer Harding called at last, pointing me toward room fifteen. I hurried forward, opening the door and pushing through it. The room held a single table with four chairs at the heart of it and another door at the far end.

I smoothed down my hair, waiting to see if Leon had brought anyone else with him. The camera in the corner of the room glinted at me as I waited and waited, sweat beading on my brow.

The door finally opened and Leon strode in, his loose mane shining like pure gold around his shoulders. His smart white shirt and jeans were a far cry from anything I'd been privy to in a long time and a flashy watch adorned his wrist. I glanced over his shoulder once to be sure he was alone and my heart splintered before I pushed the feeling away and rushed forward to embrace my brother. He clapped me on the back, hugging me tight and the scent of fresh air and freedom clung to him like a drug.

"Looking sharp, brother." I stepped back, slapping on a taunting grin and he smirked right back at me.

"I would say the same to you, but it would be a total lie. Orange isn't really your colour," he laughed and I joined in as we moved to the table and dropped into seats opposite each other.

"How's our moms? And dad?" I tried to keep my voice level, but I always asked him this, hopeful that their disappointment in me might have finally started to subside.

Leon's smile fell away as he leaned back in his seat with a sigh. "Everyone's good. Dad is still…dad. I stole an emerald bracelet right off the wrist of the mayor's wife the other day and do you know what he said?"

"Shame it wasn't diamonds," I said at the exact same moment Leon did and we started laughing.

Our amusement soon faded away as a tightness filled my chest and Leon sighed. A heaviness filled the air and I reached out to my brother, patting him on the arm. Dad had always been harsh on us, and I'd once thought that was to make us better Fae. But maybe I was wrong.

"Pfft, I never liked diamonds anyway," Leon said, puffing out his chest and I nodded, withdrawing my hand as I fixed on a smile.

"Yeah, so dull." We shared a sad sort of smile that spoke of a lifetime of Dad's disappointment in us, but at least I knew he could never be more disappointed in my brother than me anymore. That was one good thing which had come out of this shitstorm. Because Leon had once gotten the shittier end of Dad's treatment, but now he'd taken the top spot as his golden boy. So I knew he wouldn't be bothered by Dad too much these days. Not when he had a failure of a brother to compare him to.

I dropped my gaze, wanting to change the subject. "Do they know about Rosa?"

Leon grinned. "*Everyone* knows about Rosa. Bianca is losing her shit even though Dante told her it's going to be okay." He gave me a meaningful look and I threw a surreptitious glance at the camera behind him, wondering how we were going to discuss this without giving away what Rosa was up to.

"She's got a lot of belief in herself," I said slowly.

"I know. Dante's got a lot of faith in her too."

"And what do you think?" I asked. "I mean...I'm worried about her."

He nodded then shrugged. "She's an Oscura, bro. They'll do what they wanna do. And they don't do anything without a plan."

My ears pricked up at that. I knew Rosa had a plan, not that she'd shared it with me. But maybe I wasn't giving her enough credit for how prepared she was for breaking out of here.

Leon's eyes caught the light and I smirked. "So how's the family?"

His whole face lit up as a smile split across his cheeks. "They're good, dude. The kids miss you."

My heart twisted sharply as I nodded. My little brother had found everything he'd ever wanted beyond these walls. And sometimes it was hard not to envy him, despite how happy I was for him and his wife. But the fact that my nephew and niece weren't allowed to visit here until they were sixteen was just plain painful.

"They've never even met me, Leonidas," I said, forcing a smile despite it hurting my fucking face.

"Well they *basically* have. I show them pictures all the time and tell them about their great Uncle Roary and all the crazy robberies he pulled off." He beamed and I nodded, trying to take some comfort in that.

"Hey er...out of interest, how did you know your wife was the one for you?" I asked, leaning forward across the table. We hadn't ever discussed it much seeing as I'd gotten carted off to Darkmore not long after he'd found her.

Leon's brows raised as he eyed me like a detective. "Whyyy?" he asked in a sing-song voice.

"Just wondering," I grunted.

He chuckled softly. "Well I guess I knew the first time she brushed my

252

hair. I couldn't even let my Mindys do that."

My heart jerked and I schooled my expression as I nodded. Leon used his Charisma to create a massive army of helpers he called Mindys. Although, I wondered if he still used them as much these days.

I pushed a hand into my hair and thought of Rosalie. Maybe I shouldn't have let her brush it after all. But being touched like that by her had felt so right, I didn't want to stop her doing it in future. Besides, just because that had meant something for Leon and his wife, that didn't predict anything between me and Rosa. I was strong-willed enough to keep my hands off of her.

"That's nice man," I said with half a smile.

"I'm sure you've got plenty of pretty things to look at in here, you could have anyone you want. Even that blonde guard with the nice ass who signed me in might be single." He winked and I sat up a little straighter. Leon smuggled stuff in to me through the guards, planting it in their pockets so I could steal it back off of them on the way out. So long as it was small enough to go unnoticed, he got me little bottles of shampoo, chocolate bars, candy. Treats that made life in here more bearable.

"Harding?" I guessed.

"Yeah, that's the one," he said with a smirk.

We soon fell into a conversation about Pitball as Leon caught me up on the League, jumping up from his seat and playing out the best moments in dramatized slow motion.

I felt miles better by the time visitation was over, but hugging him goodbye hurt like a bitch. These short moments we spent together were the highlights of my time in here, but beyond these walls he had a whole life to return to.

In Darkmore, life pressed pause. And by the time I got to press play again, I'd be in my late forties with no kids, no future, and returning to a world that had long since forgotten I was once a part of it. And I was starting to think, if Rosa really did have a solid plan to break out, maybe it would be worth the risk of getting caught and having another ten years slapped onto my sentence to gamble on my freedom. The old Roary would have rolled the dice. So maybe it was time for the new Roary to get back in the game and commit to this escape plan with all my heart.

ROSALIE

PRISONER #12

CHAPTER TWENTY THREE

"*A*gain."

I panted as I looked across the ring at Papà, my chest heaving as sweat coated my skin. His cold gaze slid over me analytically and I tried not to favour my left foot as my other ankle stung like hell. If he spotted the injury mid-round, I was done for.

"You hit like a little bitch," I hissed, spitting blood from my mouth. At eleven years old I could swear more colourfully than a sailor and I'd long since learned that Papà preferred it when I did. He might have been a cruel sonofabitch but there was method to his madness.

Every spiteful word, every snarl, slap, punch and kick were all aimed to toughen me up. To teach me a lesson about life and survival. Only the tough made it in this world. It was Fae eat Fae and a runt like me had to learn to fight twice as hard if I expected to make it out alive.

"I said, again!" Papà barked and I lurched forward despite the pain in my ankle.

His grey eyes flared with triumph as they flicked to my injured leg and I almost whimpered as he came at me.

But instead of giving in to the inevitable, I gritted my teeth and dove forward anyway.

His foot connected with my ankle and I yelped as something cracked within it and pain splintered through the limb.

But my momentum carried me forward all the same and I collided with his chest, punching, punching, punching as I aimed for every soft patch of flesh I could find.

Papà's arms closed around my waist and threw me off of him, my back slamming against the stone floor so hard that the air was driven from my lungs.

Agony crashed through me and a pained howl escaped my lips.

"Never show weakness!" Papà roared, losing his temper.

He reached for the hem of his wife beater, ripping it over his head before dropping his pants and shifting in the blink of an eye. His Wolf form was enormous and his fur was as grizzly as his facial hair in his Fae form. I always thought he looked half rabid as a Wolf, with his eyes bulging and saliva dripping between his teeth.

I tried to scramble away on my elbows but he leapt forward, two huge paws slamming down on my shoulders and pinning me beneath him. His weight crushed me and I snarled with fright and anger as I tried to wriggle out from beneath him.

His massive jaws filled with razor sharp teeth lunged for my throat and I screamed as terror flooded my small body.

Before those teeth could reach me, my fist snapped out and a snarl tore from my lips as my knuckles collided with his throat and I threw everything I had into the strike.

Papà fell back with a yelp of pain and he shifted again, landing heavily on his ass in his Fae form.

For a long moment silence rang out as we stared at each other. Even the members of his pack who had come to watch the runt get her ass kicked again didn't have anything to say this time. No more names or taunts or mocking calls. Just silence as Papà and I stared each other down.

A snarl escaped my lips as I fought to hold his eye. His glare intensified, his Alpha aura shining brightly with the desire to make me bow as I fought my hardest not to.

I bared my teeth as I fought it for another few seconds before it finally became too much and I dropped my gaze to my knees.

Papà barked a laugh and the sound of him moving to retrieve his clothes reached me as I continued to scrutinise my sweatpants. There was a hole in the knee but I didn't have any others.

"Better," Papà growled and I flinched as his hand appeared before me.

For a long moment I only stared at his dirty palm, not knowing what he wanted me to do with it.

He leaned down and snatched my hand into his, dragging me upright. I whimpered as I tried to put weight on my ankle and Papà suddenly hoisted me off of my feet.

He ducked beneath the rope which made up the ring we'd been fighting in and carried me out of the barn, up towards the house.

I didn't dare to move as he held me in his arms. Wolves were supposed to get a lot of physical contact with others of our kind like this but I never did. I slept alone in the room with no windows and I'd long since stopped caring about it. At least when I was locked up tight in there I didn't have to worry about where the next strike might hit.

Papà carried me up the stairs inside and kept going until we reached a room at the back of the house. I never came upstairs. Not once in the three years since he'd brought me here. He kept going until we reached a room with one tiny window and a mattress lying on the floor.

"Where are we?" I asked.

He dropped me onto the mattress and looked down at me with a calculating scowl.

"You just proved you're not a complete waste of space," Papà said in a low voice.

My heart beat faster at his words and I peered up at him hopefully. If I'd been in my Wolf form, my tail would have been wagging.

"Thank you," I breathed. That was the closest thing to praise which I'd ever heard crossing his lips.

"But you still showed me your pain when we began," he added, his tone darkening.

My lips parted but I knew better than to make excuses. Apologies wouldn't go down any better either. I licked my lips and tasted blood from my busted nose. If I kept quiet he might just tell me what I'd done wrong and leave it at that. Maybe... Hopefully.

"So I think it's time we worked on that, runt," he added.

"On what?" I breathed as I forced myself to hold my ground. Trying to run only made things worse.

"Your pain control," Papà said darkly as he slid his belt from its loops. "When you learn to master pain, you can master everything."

My lips parted on a protest and his eyes flared in warning.

I took in a shuddering breath and raised my chin as he wrapped the belt around his fist.

"Okay," I breathed, knowing that the only power I could claim over this was in owning it. "I'm ready."

"Then let's begin your next lesson," Papà snarled as his shadow fell over me.

I woke in a cold sweat as the sound of the bell ringing to announce the arrival of the guards pulled me from my nightmares. I scrambled upright in my bed as the ghosts of my past clung to my flesh with cold hands and dark memories.

The door to my cell was already standing open and I frowned to myself as I realised I'd slept through them opening for the day. I'd woken for the count a few hours ago but I must have drifted back off again.

"And I thought Nemean Lions were supposed to be the ones who slept too much," Roary's teasing voice came from the bunk beneath mine and I flinched in surprise.

"What are you doing in here?" I breathed.

"It's not particularly safe to be sleeping with your door open, little pup," he teased. "I thought I'd be a gentleman and keep watch over you when you failed to wake up."

My pounding heart softened at his words and I slid from my bunk, finding him sprawled on the mattress with his hands behind his head, looking totally at home in my space.

I bit my lip as I fought to push aside the nightmares, but I was struggling. The plan was going to shit. That Order Suppressant Tank could easily ruin everything and some part of me felt like that little girl who'd been locked in the cellar all over again.

Roary frowned up at me as he noticed something was off and he held out a hand in offering. "What's up, little pup?" he asked, taking my fingers between his and running his thumb across the back of my hand.

I had the most awful urge to cry sweeping through me and I suddenly just needed the reassurance of having my pack close. Of warms hugs and gentle touches. But none of them were in this cell block and Roary was all I had.

I dropped down suddenly, climbing into the bunk beside him despite the fact that there wasn't really room. He shifted over to accommodate me and I tucked myself in against his side, laying my head on his chest and winding my arms around him.

"Sometimes, this place makes me feel like I can't breathe," I murmured as I nuzzled into him, needing the contact like I needed to feel the light of the moon on my fur.

"I know the feeling," he replied darkly and those damn tears welled in my eyes again.

He was here because of me. I knew it, even if he wouldn't admit it. He was too good to get caught by the FIB. The only reason they'd managed to catch him was because he'd been trying to protect me. And when they'd hauled him away, I'd sworn to the stars that I'd find a way to get him out again. But it had already taken me way too long to set this right.

Roary's fingers began to move through my long hair and I shifted even closer to him, winding my leg over his hips. I'd slept in my tank and panties as usual, but Roary was already dressed in his orange jumpsuit so I hoped that barrier between us was enough to stop his *I'm too old for you* bullshit from pushing me away again.

"Do you want to talk about it?" he asked me softly.

"There's nothing to say," I replied. "The past is the past. That's where it should stay."

Roary hesitated for a moment before pressing on in a low voice. "Leon told me once what Felix did to you after I was arrested. He said he-"

"I don't want to talk about that," I snarled, my entire body tensing as screams rang in my ears and the scars along my side tingled with the memory of that pain. Even the memory of the agony was blinding, the taste of bile coating my tongue.

My breaths came faster and I made a move to push out of his arms but he pulled me closer, nuzzling against my hair as he tried to soothe me.

"Okay," Roary breathed. "Don't talk about it. But if you ever want to, I'm here, Rosa. I'm not going anywhere. You can tell me anything."

"Not that," I growled, though I relaxed back into his arms. I needed the comfort he was offering me then more than I needed to prove how big my balls were by throwing a fit and kicking him out. But he needed to know not to push me on this. "I'll never talk about that. Or *him*. I've locked all that shit up tight in a little vault which keeps company with the darkest parts of my soul and I *never* open it. There's no point in making old wounds bleed, Roar."

His silence said he didn't agree with me but he didn't push me either.

"Well slap my ass and call me Three Way Willy," Plunger's voice came from right outside my door and the two of us sat up with snarls as we found him peeking beneath the sheet I'd hung there. "You want some extra sausage in that bun, pup?" he offered, driving his tongue in and out of his cheek and making it bulge suggestively.

"Get the fuck out, Plunger," Roary warned, pushing to his feet and rolling his shoulders back in a clear threat.

"I could give you some pointers on some new things you could try," he said suggestively. "Or you could just pretend I'm not here and I'll watch in secret."

I snarled as I stalked towards him with my hand locked in a fist, but he dropped the sheet with a dirty laugh and moved away before I could punch his slimy face in.

I took a step to follow him, but Roary caught my wrist and halted me.

"Don't mix it with Plunger if you can avoid it," he muttered.

"Why?" I demanded. "I'm not afraid of him."

"It's not that. I know you'd wipe the floor with that asshole. He's just… depraved. That guy does messed up shit and if you get on his bad side he can do some pretty disgusting things in his vendetta against you. I'm telling you, it's not worth the aggravation. Why do you think he has a cell on the top floor?"

I gave up trying to pull out of his grip and turned to look up at him instead.

"Are you looking after me now then, Roary?" I teased, stepping closer to him.

"I promised Dante I'd look out for his kid cousin," he agreed casually.

I rolled my eyes at him as he went back to that age gap bullshit and moved away to get changed into fresh clothes for the day.

Roary didn't fall into the trap of watching me as I pulled my clothes off, but moved to the shelf which hung on the wall opposite my bunk and started looking through my things. Not that I had much. Dante had sent me a few family photos and Aunt Bianca and my cousins had written to me a bunch of times. I'd bought some wash stuff from the commissary and Sonny had leant me a pretty graphic erotica novel which I'd flicked through a few times, but that was it.

Once I'd pulled on my jumpsuit, Roary turned to look at me again with a smile playing around his lips.

"I have an idea for something we can do to help distract you from the shittiest things about being here…which, let's face it, are *most* of the things about being here," he said.

"Oh yeah?"

"Yeah. We can play, *I bet you won't.*"

I groaned as he named the ridiculous game my family had made up years ago. I remembered the night that Roary and Leon had been at our manor house, drinking around the bonfire we were having in honour of the winter solstice when they'd joined in with us. Dante had challenged Roary to use his Charisma on as many of the girls in attendance as possible and my cousins had all fallen over themselves as they threw themselves into his lap and practically crushed him in a dog pile. His Order gifts meant that he could draw weak willed Fae to him like moths to a flame if he wanted to, and they'd do everything and anything he asked of them to please him. I'd been the only one of my family who hadn't tried to climb into his lap and he'd smirked at me like that made me special somehow, but at the time I didn't know why. Now I understood. With a gift like his, it was hard for him to be sure if people's feelings towards him were genuine or just brought on by his talents. If I was immune to the

Charisma, then he knew anything I offered him was real. Although he liked to pretend it wasn't.

"Do we have to?" I groaned, though the idea of adding something fun to my day wasn't all bad.

Roary prowled towards me and I fell still as I looked up into his golden eyes. He had a smile playing around his lips and I couldn't help but think about the way it had felt when he'd kissed me. Not that he'd given me any indication that he was intending to do it again since.

He reached out and pushed my hair back behind my shoulder before leaning down and speaking into my ear in a rough voice. "*I bet you won't* start singing in front of everyone in the Mess Hall."

I snorted a laugh and turned my head to look at him, the space between us almost non-existent as electricity crackled along my skin.

"I can't hold a tune," I warned him.

"Even better. And no cheating," he added. "I want you to put on a proper performance."

I smirked at him and raised my chin at the challenge. "Okay then, Lion boy, I'll see what I can do."

I brushed past him and headed out of my cell just as the bell rang to announce breakfast.

Roary fell into step beside me as we headed for the stairs.

Thumping footsteps made the metal steps rattle behind me and let me know that Pudding was following too.

"Morning, Pudding," I said, turning my head to look at my cumbersome friend.

"No pudding at breakfast," he muttered, his brow low.

"That there isn't," I agreed, exchanging a smirk with Roary. "It's still nice to fill our bellies though, right?"

"No pudding, no pots," he grumbled before looking away from us and ending our conversation.

To be fair, the oatmeal we got for breakfast wasn't all that appealing, but I was getting used to it. There were usually little jars of honey to sweeten it anyway which made it a bit better.

As we reached the bottom of the stairs, I noticed Hastings was on duty and I slipped away from Roary as I headed for him.

"Buongiorno, ragazzo del coro," I purred, swaying my hips as I moved to stand before him. *Good morning, choir boy.*

"Why do I always feel like you're teasing me when you speak in Faetalian?" he asked, his lips twitching with half a smile.

"It's affectionate," I promised, painting a cross over my heart. "Are you walking us to breakfast today?"

"Er, yeah I'm on the breakfast run."

"Perfect." I reached out and took his arm, tugging gently to get him walking with me.

"It's not really appropriate for-"

"When do *you* get time to eat?" I asked him, looking up at him with an innocent expression. "You must need a lot of stamina…for a job like this."

A faint blush lined his cheeks and he cleared his throat as we started to walk up the stairs to the Mess Hall. "Well, I get up early, so-"

"I bet you get much nicer food than us, don't you?" I teased.

"We have a bit more choice," he admitted. "I like to have some fruit with my oatmeal."

I groaned with desire, leaning into him a little more as we continued to climb the stairs. "What I wouldn't give to have an apple with my breakfast."

"Well, *I'm* not a criminal," he replied with a smile as we made it up to the Mess Hall.

"Yeah. I guess that's what I get for being bad." I pouted at him as his gaze slid over me then released my hold on his arm, sighing dramatically.

I turned and walked away from him without waiting for a reply, collecting my bowl of oatmeal from the counter before dropping down in the centre of my pack's usual table.

I started eating my food alone as I waited for the members of the other cell blocks to arrive and my pack to show up.

Hastings did a slow sweep of the room before heading into the kitchen and my lips twitched with amusement.

The first prisoner from Cell Block B to arrive was Sin. He grabbed three bowls of oatmeal and six jars of honey for himself and no one dared to reprimand him for it as he stalked across the room and dropped down at the table he'd claimed for his own.

He started eating like a man possessed and I found myself smirking as I watched him. He'd tied his jumpsuit around his waist again so I had a clear view of his huge arms, the dark skin lined with more tattoos than I could easily count. He may have chosen his name for himself but there was something about him that made it suit him perfectly. And not just because he was an Incubus. Everything about him seemed designed to draw me in. He was temptation embodied, from his powerful build to the dangerous smile that played around his lips and the wicked glint in his eyes. Even the fear he inspired in the Fae surrounding him had my skin prickling with excitement. There was something about him that screamed of freedom, even though he was locked up just like the rest of us.

Hastings reappeared from the kitchen and walked along the side of the room at a casual pace. When he reached my table, he turned and walked along it until he made it to me where he leaned forward and placed an apple beside my bowl.

Sin looked up just as the guard walked away again and the smile he gave me was so heated that I felt it right down to my core.

"I thought I was the one who was supposed to embody everyone's desires?" he called teasingly as I bit into the gift with a smirk on my face.

"You do," I assured him, my gaze sliding over his muscular physique just as my pack appeared.

They flooded around me, blocking my view of the Incubus and I offered out welcomes and smiles as they brushed their hands over my arms and back and I continued to eat my apple.

The Mess Hall filled up around me and I waited until all of the tables were full before suddenly getting to my feet.

My pack looked around in confusion as I hopped up onto the table and I gave it an extra few seconds as inmates all around the room turned and looked my way, wondering what I was doing.

I caught Roary's eye and winked at him as I cupped my hands around my mouth and started singing It's Raining Men by The Weather Girls at the top of my lungs.

After a few beats of shocked silence, my pack all leapt up and joined in, dancing around the table and howling as they sang.

I fully gave myself to the song, closing my eyes as I belted out the song and strong arms suddenly closed around my waist.

I looked over my shoulder and found Sin grinning at me as he sang too, dragging my body back against his as we danced so that my ass was grinding into his crotch.

I laughed as I kept singing and the guards started to get antsy in their positions around the room.

Sonny got really excited as the chorus kicked in and grabbed a jug of water from the serving counter before leaping up beside me and pouring it over the two of us to make sure we genuinely were soaking wet.

I laughed as I swung my hair around my head and more and more prisoners leapt up to join us as we danced.

Sin's hands on my body had heat rising to the surface of my skin and the way he belted the song out with zero insecurity had a wide smile plastered to my face.

I reached my arm back over my shoulder, grasping the back of Sin's neck as we danced and he groaned as I drew him closer, his stubble catching on my hair.

We made it about three quarters of the way through the song before the guards ruined it, banging their batons on the tables threateningly and screaming about sending people to the hole if we didn't stop.

Sin released me and started leaping from table to table as he kept singing defiantly and the guards chased him.

I leapt down from the table with a heady laugh as I ran towards Roary, shoving through his gang members before leaning down to speak with him.

"*I bet you won't* steal a pudding from Pudding," I breathed in his ear and the grin he gave me in return sent my heart racing.

"Too easy," he said as my wet hair dripped onto his knee.

"*While* he's eating it," I added with a wink before shoving away from the table and heading for the exit.

I spotted Hastings as I stepped out into the hallway and paused to speak to him.

"Thank you for my gift, ragazzo del coro," I said in a low voice. "But do you think I could beg for another?"

"Isn't an apple enough?" he asked, frowning a little like he was wondering why he'd done that for me now. "And you just caused a scene in the Mess Hall, so I really shouldn't be giving you any preferential treatment now."

"I know," I agreed, shifting forward until I was right in his personal space and lowering my voice seductively. "It's just...I'm *so* wet."

Hastings stared at me for a long moment like he didn't know what to say to that and I stepped back, pointing at my drenched clothes.

"Oh. Right. Your clothes are wet," he mumbled, dropping his gaze to the floor.

"What else would I have meant?" I asked in a confused tone.

"Nothing," he blurted. "Nothing else." He waved a hand at me, using his water magic to pull the liquid from my hair and clothes and I grinned at him before turning away and heading for the row of phones at the far end of the hall.

There was a long line already waiting to use them but I ignored it, walking straight past everyone in the queue until I was at the front.

The guy there snorted angrily as I moved to stand before him and I turned my gaze to him lazily. He was about a foot taller than me and twice as wide. My gaze skimmed over the symbols on the lapel of his jumpsuit as I assessed him.

"Oh, you're an Experian Deer Shifter?" I asked curiously.

"What of it?"

"It's just that your kind are pretty rare. Probably because they were hunted to extinction...by *Wolves*." I bared my teeth at him and he flinched. "Is it okay if I take your turn on the phone?" I asked sweetly.

"Yeah, sure," he muttered. "Whatever."

"Thanks, poppet." I slapped his cheek a couple of times and moved to claim his turn.

The girl who was finishing up quickly ended her call and held the handset out for me. I smiled widely as I took it before dialling Dante's number and moving to lean against the wall.

It took a minute for the call to connect via the prison spy tech and I tapped my foot impatiently before my cousin's voice came down the line.

"Rosa?"

"Hey, Dante, how is everyone?"

"Good, everyone's good. Mamma is worrying herself sick over you and Fabrizio has another new boyfriend. Aunt Paula finally got that thing removed from her foot and Elaina's wedding was amazing. I drank your drinks too and I had to be carted home in a barrow."

I laughed, closing my eyes as I listened to his voice, letting it wash over me and transport me back home to the huge cream house overlooking the vineyards where there were more Wolves than you could shake a stick at and more love than you could ever drink in. He told me snippets about all of our aunts and cousins, his wife and the kids, more information than I could really take in in one hit, but there was only one thing which really counted. They were all okay. All happy. All waiting for me to come home.

"How are you, Rosa?" Dante asked eventually. "Is everything going well?"

"Yes," I said, falling straight into our rehearsed codes. "Everything's great, apart from my bed being uncomfortable." *There's an unforeseen problem.*

"Can you ask someone to fix it?" *Is it something you can solve from in there?*

"Unfortunately not. All the beds are the same. The guards don't care about us being uncomfortable," I sighed. *I'm going to need your help.*

"We miss you here," he said, waiting for my next coded message.

"I keep thinking back to that summer we spent fixing Nonno's car." I said slowly. *I'm having trouble with the Order Suppressant Tank.*

"You knew that engine inside out," he replied. "I was surprised it went wrong."

"Well, I *thought* I knew the engine inside out," I agreed. "I studied that manual night and day...but then when it came to me actually working on it, I realised I'd been studying the wrong model."

There was a beat of silence as Dante figured out what I was trying to tell him and I hoped he could manage it. He started laughing but I could hear the false tone to it. He knew as well as I did just how important it was that I could neutralise that machine. I wouldn't be getting out of here at all if I didn't.

I could hear him tapping on his keyboard as he quickly searched the internet to find out what other models the tank could be.

"I don't even know why I'd thought it was so old," I sighed. "It was a much newer model."

"Well Nonno always did like to have the best of things. Do you remember when he bought that *vat* for all the ice cream?" he asked, putting emphasis on the word vat which must have been a model of tank, though not the one I was faced with.

"No," I replied with a frown. "I don't think I was there for that."

"Well you must have been there when he got that *pump* for the well at the end of the vineyard?"

"Oh yeah *I* remember the *pump,*" I agreed.

"He must have moved about three hundred gallons of water with that thing," Dante added.

"More like *five hundred*," I said, scratching my cheek to hide my smirk.

"Yeah actually, you must be right," he agreed. "The thing looked really complicated...but once you understood it, it was actually pretty easy to use."

"It was?" I asked, my heart lightening as he referred to the tank.

"Yeah. I should really go now, though," he added. "I've got a lot of work to do today. But I'll write you tomorrow."

"Thank you, Dante," I breathed, clutching the phone tighter as tears pricked the backs of my eyes. "I don't know what I'd do without you."

"Good thing you'll never have to find out then," he teased.

"Ti amo," I whispered.

"Ti amo, Rosa. I'll see you soon." The line went dead and I released a shaky breath before opening my eyes and dropping the phone back onto the hook.

I strode away from the phones and headed back into the Mess Hall to rejoin my pack. There wasn't much that I could do about the tank until I heard back from Dante. But I *could* move on with the next part of my plan. Which meant I needed to locate a Polethius Mole Shifter.

ETHAN

PRISONER #1

CHAPTER TWENTY FOUR

"Number One, Fifty Eight, Thirty Nine, Three Hundred and Forty Six," the guard continued shouting out numbers from the bottom of my Cell Block, but I ignored the rest, my heart pounding with excitement as I headed out of my cell.

Every week, inmates were randomly selected to head to the Fate Room and today, my number was up. The most valuable part of being selected, was that those lucky enough to be sent there could access horoscopes, scrying bowls, tarot cards and more. And with a little insight into where the planets were sitting in my chart and a few forecasts, I could secure a month-long advantage in Darkmore.

The guards liked to keep these little visits randomised so the top dogs couldn't dominate the future. Especially considering that if anyone was planning shady shit, having a visit to the Fate Room prior to that could be very favourable indeed. The Warden insisted we were allowed access to it on occasion because it was a Fae's right. But the guards always got antsy afterwards, keeping a close eye on anyone who'd taken a visit.

I was soon out of my cell block, marching downstairs with the ten others who'd been selected, following the two guards. There'd be ten from every other cell block too so I wanted to get down there first and make the most of the two hours they gave us in the room.

We soon arrived on level eight and my heart thumped a hungry tune as I forced my way to the front of the masses gathered before the entrance. The huge, arching metal doors were engraved with the star sign constellations and three large iron bolts were slotted across to lock it.

Officer Cain stood beside it, surveying us all with his usual pissy expression. If it was up to him, he wouldn't ever let any of us in that room. But it wasn't, so he could rage out and turn into a fiery pile of soot for all I cared. It wasn't gonna change the Warden's orders.

His eyes trailed over me and a growl escaped his throat. That motherfucker hated it when the gang leaders got called into the Fate Room. It usually meant all hell was about to break loose. And he wouldn't be wrong. I had a score to settle with Gustard, one that preceded him attacking Rosalie, though that had sure as shit cemented his fate. And not just that, but he'd tripled the amount of pain I was going to rain down on him. And it had been a fuck load to begin with.

My breath caught in the back of my throat as her voice suddenly carried to me and I turned my head, finding Rosalie shoving through the crowd with that long-haired asshole Roary Night at her side looking like her fucking bodyguard. They were laughing and messing about together and jealousy burned a line through my chest at the sight. I turned my back on them again, a snarl rolling over my tongue. I hated that bitch with a passion, but I cared about her just as fiercely. I was a man divided down the centre, torn in half by this mate bond. I'd spent plenty of time trying to find a way to break it during library hours. But even if Rosalie died, it looked like I'd pine for her forever. And the mere suggestion of her dying made me want to kill everyone in this prison just so that no one was a threat to her.

I took a deep breath, pushing a hand over my hair and making sure it was perfectly styled as I focused on the task at hand. I needed to find out if the stars were in my favour this week. Because I'd been waiting for this for a long time, and Gustard had it coming. If fate was on my side, I was going to start executing the plan I'd been concocting against him.

Cain pressed his hand to the scanner beside the door and the thick bolts slid open at his touch. The doors opened inwards as the sound of heavy chains rattled through the air, drawing them wide.

"These doors will shut behind you," Cain growled. "They re-open again in two hours. You will be watched through cameras so any interference with the Horometer or tampering with the Arcane objects will result in one month in the hole. If any smartass thinks they can smuggle an artefact out of that room, think again. Even an attempt to do so will see you punished. Is everyone clear?"

A murmur of *yes sir* sounded around me and Cain clenched his jaw, stepping out of the way of the doors.

I hurried forward into the darkened room. The air was chilled and sent goosebumps prickling along my skin. A huge silver Horometer hung above us beneath the domed ceiling which glittered in mimicry of the night sky, each constellation twinkling down at me. The Horometer was a series of large silver orbs which represented the solar system, each of the magically suspended planets slowly circling the sun at the heart of it.

There was a metal staircase that led up to a walkway above it and I hurried through the room toward it, passing tables where scrying bowls, crystal balls and pendulums were chained to tables. Tarot cards and all manner of crystals sat waiting to be used, all of them magically linked to each surface so nothing could be taken a foot away from its place. I'd return to use them later, but right now, I wanted what every fucker in here wanted most. Their horoscope.

I raced up the stairs ahead of everyone else, my boots clanging against the metal. I reached the top, moving around the walkway to a large screen which was embedded in a podium. My pulse drummed harder as I pressed my right hand flat to it and a hum sounded as it scanned my palm.

My prison profile flashed up and I chewed on my lip as I read it, a loading bar at the bottom telling me my Horoscope was about to be revealed.

Prisoner Number: #1
Name: Ethan Shadowbrook
Crime: Kidnapping
Order: Werewolf
Star Sign: Cancer
Element: Water
Sentence remaining: Two months and fifteen days

I smiled at the sight of my sentence. I was so close to freedom, I could taste it. And if I made Gustard pay before I got out of here, then the world would be set right. I didn't dare let my mind wander to the idea of being parted from Rosalie. Maybe once I was far enough away from her, the moon would get the hint and break us apart for good. I sure as shit hoped so. I lifted a hand to scratch at the mate mark behind my ear, a growl leaving my throat. I'd had to promise pack protection to the guy who'd done it. He was a newbie who weighed a hundred and ten pounds. He'd also been facing the wrath of the Pegasus herd's hooves since he'd arrived, but he was one helluva a tattoo artist. So having him on side worked for me in more ways than one.

My horoscope finally loaded as a queue of inmates formed behind me and I turned to growl at the nearest asshole, making the guy back up several steps to give me more room. There wasn't a chance in hell I was going to let anyone see my horoscope. It could give vital insight into my future. What if I was due a spell of bad luck? I couldn't let that shit get out and be used against me.

Hello Cancer inmate,

The stars have spoken about your fortune.

A bond has formed between you and a Taurus and your compatibility is off the charts. Such signs can form a deep, loving relationship because of their mutual desire to build a home and family. However, you will feel split into two halves, one ruled by the war planet Mars and the other ruled by the love planet Venus. It is up to you to choose which planet's guidance you follow.

With the unbalance you hold in your soul, you may feel conflicted in other areas of your life too. If you lean towards the right planet, you will find all endeavours pay off, but be warned, a terrible fate could await you if you choose poorly.

I snarled, slamming my hand down on the railing as I drew away from the screen. So my fate hinged on the decisions I made about my fucking mate? That was just perfect. And if I chose wrong, I was screwed up the ass with cherries on top. So which side of me was I supposed to follow? Which fucking planet could make everything right for me? The raging asshole that was Mars or that lovestruck whore of a planet Venus?

I shoved people out of my way as I headed back to the stairs, hurrying down them. I needed to use this time to hunt for clearer insights into my fate. Maybe the tarot cards could see which choice I needed to make, but even the idea of giving in to Venus and trying to make it work with Rosalie set my veins alight. She was an Oscura. My mortal enemy. I'd fought against her family since I'd followed in my mother's footsteps and joined the Lunar Brotherhood.

Rosalie started marching up the stairs, bypassing the queue and I drew to a halt, barring her way forward.

"It doesn't matter what your horoscope says, love, there's only one fate coming for you. You're going to bow to me."

She rolled her eyes, throwing her shoulder into mine as she tried to get by, but I caught her arm in a painfully tight grip to stop her. She bared her teeth and I released a breath of amusement, leaning in close to her ear so no one would hear my next words. "I'm going to show the moon where you really belong then she'll see sense and unbind us."

"Good luck arguing with the moon, stronzo," she said coolly and her dark eyes carved a path all the way to my soul. My grip softened on her arm and my mouth became dry as her heavenly sweet scent rolled under my nose.

She smirked then ducked under my arm, running on up the stairs and I cursed her as I continued down to the ground floor.

I strode over to a table at the back of the room, snarling at a guy who was about to pick up the tarot deck there and he backed off fast, dropping his head and scampering away.

I cracked my knuckles one by one before picking up the cards and shuffling them.

Fucking beautiful fucking Wolf with her stupid fucking Bambi eyes and those tits that follow me into my dreams.

I swept a hand over my hair, checking it was in place before laying the cards out in three piles in front of me.

I'd been perfectly happy being a polyamorous sex god, and now look? She's in my brain. Even when I try to jerk off about other girls, they always end up looking like her in my head.

I'd asked several girls into my cell this week with the intention of fucking my mate out of my mind, only to freak out the second they started undressing and shoving them out again. There were rumours going around about me. My pack knew something was up. I'd tried sleeping with them in one cell, but as soon as things turned towards an orgy, I had to excuse myself like a fucking No-Dick Daniel. They were gonna think I had *problems* down there. Like Faemidia or Centyphilis.

Shitballs, I needed to come up with a good excuse and fast. But what?

I snarled as I turned over the first card on the closest pile, my mind not nearly focused enough for this. Predictably I got a card about my one-and-fucking-only.

The Lovers.

I tossed it aside with a growl, turning over the next card.

The Lovers.

"Fuck you, who's mixed up this deck?" I turned the last card over and threw the whole lot at the wall as The Lovers stared up at me again. The cards were flung back by the magical shield keeping them bound to this table and half of them slapped me in the face.

"Having a little trouble there, Shadowbrook?" Roary Night swept past me, plucking a card off of my shoulder and tossing it down onto the table in front of me. The *Lovers*.

"Nothing I need your help with," I said coldly.

"Are you sure? I've never seen a pack of cards attack someone before."

"Ha. Ha," I said dryly, shoving away from the table and heading toward another one and swiping up the tarot deck there. How had someone even tampered with that pack? And by the stars, why would they do it?

Roary headed over to a scrying bowl on the table beside mine and I pointedly ignored him as I laid out the new deck, focusing on Gustard and his bunch of asshole followers. A few months back, Gustard had taken something precious from me. My Wolves in his Cell Block had told me that the picture of my sister was now hanging in his cell above his bed. My fucking baby sister. And if I even let my mind stray to the thought of what he used that picture for, I wanted to tear his head off with my bare hands.

It wasn't just that though. My pack had had one too many run ins with The Watchers of late. I didn't know what their vile gang had done to Kayla, but she hadn't been the same since and she refused to talk about it. One guess about what had happened had my blood burning. And after what they'd done to Rosalie, I could say that guess was pretty solid. So Gustard had written his own death by touching my Wolves. And I was going to make him regret it.

Rosalie soon joined Roary at the table beside mine and I couldn't help but let my attention drift to their conversation as I tried my hand at another tarot prediction.

"What do you need next, little pup?" Roary asked in a low voice and my brow creased at the intensity of his tone.

"I need to buddy up with a Polethius Mole Shifter," she said, dipping her finger into the water in the bowl and swirling it around. "But there's only two in the prison. Sook Min and Norman Hitchcock."

My frown increased as I listened. What did she need a Polethius Mole for?

"Well Norman Hitchcock is out," Roary said with a grimace.

"Why?" Rosalie questioned.

"That's Plunger. And I'll let you befriend him over my dead body."

Rosalie cringed full bodily and I hid my smirk with my thumb. I not only knew Sook, she even worked for me. She wasn't part of the Lunar Brotherhood, but she was strong and I liked to keep her sweet with luxuries while she ran Veiled Wall jobs for me.

"Yeah, wasn't planning on it, Roar," Rosalie laughed and irritation crackled up my spine at how over-familiar she was with the Lion. I didn't have a right to be jealous considering my fucking stance on our mate bond, but Venus was having a good go at tugging on those strings.

I realised I suddenly had leverage on Rosalie for the sake of that cuff key and I abandoned the tarot deck, walking up behind her and gazing down into the obsidian bowl over her shoulder. Roary was resting his elbows on the table, looking into the water and I cocked my head as I waited for them to realise I was there.

"Wait, is the bowl showing me-" Rosalie started.

"The hottest guy in Darkmore?" I finished for her and she snapped around in alarm.

I smirked, folding my arms as Roary stood upright, his eyes narrowing on me.

"Here's a twist of fate, love…Sook Min is under my control. So if you want her, you can buy her."

Rosalie's lips parted and I couldn't help but remember my cock pressed between them as she knelt before me in the mud. *Shit, must concentrate.*

"You can't own people, Ethan," she said scathingly, arching a brow. "I'll just offer her a sweeter deal than you so she comes and works for me instead."

Roary smirked at me and I had the good mind to throw my fist into his face. But I didn't think Rosalie would trade anything with me if I broke her bestie's face.

"The thing is, love, loyalties in here are hard to find and even harder to keep. I've built up a rapport with Sook. She's my girl. And I look after her, she gets pack protection and a decent cell. And as she's in *my* Cell Block, what more could you offer her than I can? In fact…" I moved into her personal space, devouring the air around her. "If she crossed me to work for you, I'd make her life all kinds of hell in our block, so you could offer her the sweetest fruit in your basket for all I care, but she's not going to take a bite."

"What do you want in exchange for her?" Roary growled, but I ignored him, keeping my eyes trained on my mate.

"I know what he wants," she said, her lips pursing and a smile spread across my face.

"Good," I purred. "Give it to me in the Mess Hall tonight."

I moved to walk away and Rosalie caught my arm, yanking me back to face her. "I can't just walk up to you in the middle of dinner, idiota."

Her accent made my dick jerk happily and I growled, dragging my arm free of her. "You're a smart pup. Figure it out. Or you don't get your Polethius Mole."

I marched away, heading to a tarot table far away from her so I could finally get a good reading done which wasn't tainted by her driving a wedge into my head.

If I got that key tonight, I could start my war against Gustard. So the stars had better be on my side.

I waited for Rosalie to come to me at dinner. Part of me wondered what she wanted Sook for, but I wasn't going to fall into that little mind trap. In Darkmore, everyone's business was their own. So if she wanted her to dance naked with nipple tassels on to the tune of Baby Shark then that was her concern. Not mine.

I queued up behind Rosalie, even spent some time away from my pack as I waited for her to approach me, but she never did. She just sat with Roary Night and her pack and they all laughed together like life was so fucking hilarious.

The guards finally ejected us from the Mess Hall and I glared over at Rosalie then to Sook who was sitting with a couple of Griffins. She was covered in tattoos and the long, dark hair that fell down her back was completely straight. She was size extra, extra small but had the kind of dangerous look about her that said she'd murder you in your sleep. My kind of friend.

Her almond shaped eyes flashed my way and she raised a brow, waiting for an instruction, but I just pressed my lips together and walked away. Maybe Rosalie was going to recruit Plunger for whatever it was she wanted done after all – so I really hoped the naked Baby Shark tassel dance wasn't what she had planned- but was lending me that key really so bad that she would rather spend time with that lecherous creep than do a trade with me? Plunger was currently bent over in the doorway as he fished for something on the ground, forcing unsuspecting Fae to accidentally trip over him and brace themselves on his ass.

"Oh pardon me, excuse my little fanny," he called as a guy walked straight into him dick to ass.

I shuddered, heading toward the exit and forging a path around him with my pack in tow. They were all hyped up and Harper kept brushing her hand over my back hopefully. It was clear what was gonna happen the second we got back to our cell block, and I was running out of excuses to refuse them.

I was furious by the time I reached our block and Rosalie was long fucking gone. How dare she refuse me? I'd made her a fair offer, but she clearly didn't trust me. So why had the girl fucked me in the Order Yard like she was trying her hardest to make the moon take notice, dammit?

"You seem tense, Alpha." Harper tip-toed up to rub my shoulders and I sighed. "Come join us for some fun."

"I'm not in the mood," I said, shrugging her off and refusing to look back as I jogged upstairs to my cell. My pack howled mournfully after me and a low whine escaped me at displeasing them.

By the stars, how long was I gonna be able to keep this up? I had to give them some reason for this soon enough. And I swear on the moon, if I had to tell them I had Manticrabs, I was going to take my rage out on Rosalie. Because this was *her* fault.

I slipped into my cell, hanging a sheet over the bars and stripping down to my boxers before dropping onto my bed with a huff.

I sat in the quiet for a long time and the doors eventually rattled shut for the night. I growled under my breath in annoyance. The tarot cards had given me the all clear, promising me good fortune. But maybe I'd read them wrong, because my fortune seemed pretty shitty to me right now.

I shut my eyes, giving up on my plans and trying to get some sleep. My mind wouldn't let me rest for a long time, but just as I was falling away into oblivion, someone jabbed me in the ribs.

I lunged upwards with a snarl and Rosalie's hand clamped over my mouth a second before I attacked her. Her eyes sparkled with mischief and my heart thundered in my ears as my gaze flicked to the hole she'd carved through the back wall of my cell. It took me half a second longer to realise she was only wearing a white tank top and black panties.

She pressed a finger to her lips then I felt her silencing bubble slip over me and she smirked. "Made you jump."

"Made me nearly kill you," I grunted, my heart twitching at the idea. "You can't come crawling into my cell whenever you like, love. You don't have an open invitation."

She pouted mockingly then lifted a shining silver key before my eyes. "I suppose I'll just head back to my cell then."

I lunged for the key, but she spun away from me like a fucking ballerina with a musical laugh. Despite the silencing bubble, anxiety still filled me at the idea of a guard finding her here and I threw a cautious glance at the sheet covering the bars.

"Give it here then." I held out my hand and she rolled her eyes.

"As if I'd let you take it, Ethan. You can *borrow* it, but I'm going to be right here next to you while you do an engorgement spell on your dick or whatever it is you need it for."

A growl rumbled in the back of my throat. "I think you're quite aware I don't need one of those, love."

She shrugged innocently. "You could have a tiny todger for all I know and just spend your Magic Compound time engorging it."

I released a hollow laugh, holding out my hand. "If you're just angling for me to show you it, you're gonna be disappointed. I have zero intention of ever fucking you again. Now give me the key."

She tutted, approaching me on her tip-toes and cocking her head to one side. "How romantic my mate is."

She rested her hands on my shoulders with a hunter's smile pulling at her mouth. She leaned in close, trying to make me blink, but I refused, waiting for her to stop playing games and give me what I was owed. Her mouth came within a centimetre of mine and her intoxicating scent tried to lure me into the

277

trap of her body. But I wasn't going to be fooled this time.

"You can have the key when you tell me what you're going to do with it," she purred, her tits pushing against my chest and drawing all of my attention for a long moment.

I cleared my throat, standing my ground as I considered wrestling her for it.

"That's not your business."

"It is actually," she said sweetly. "This is *my* key. And if you do something that gets you caught with it, I'm going to be more than a little pissed. So I need the details before I agree to it."

I tsked. "I want the key for the night. You're not staying with me."

"No," she said immediately.

"Then no deal," I snarled.

"Then no key," she tossed back, dropping her arms and walking away toward the hole.

I lunged at her in fury, snatching her around the waist and dragging her back against me. She fought like a banshee as I tried to get hold of her fist with the key in it. She stuffed it into her little panties then withdrew her hand with a wild laugh.

"Stronzo," she taunted.

I shoved my hand into her underwear without thought and she gasped, stilling against me as I got hold of the key. I left my hand there, my nose pressed into her hair as her breasts rose and fell with her ragged breathing.

"Don't underestimate me, love," I said against her ear, slowly extracting my hand and brushing my thumb across her clit as I did so, making her release a breathy moan. My free hand was splayed across her stomach and I found myself unable to let her go. For an endless second, I needed her more than anything. More than I needed water to live.

"You can come with me," I agreed out of nowhere, releasing her. The moon fucking knew why. But right then I wanted her close and she deserved a little revenge on Gustard too, so fuck it.

"Where are you going?" she asked as I stuck the key in my right cuff and twisted it. Magic rushed to my fingertips and I sighed contentedly before freeing the other one.

"Well I *was* going to fuck with Gustard in the Mess Hall, but now I have to improvise. So we're going to pay him a little visit."

She paled at the mention of his name, though her spine straightened with resilience. "I want him dead."

My stomach knotted and I immediately reached for her, skimming my knuckles over her cheek.

"You can't take a king down without destroying his empire first, love. Otherwise there'll always be pawns ready to replace him."

"So what's your plan?" she whispered, excitement flickering in her gaze and setting my pulse racing.

"Well…" I thought about it for a moment then a slow smile spread across my face. "Rumour has it he never sleeps without his mistress, Wet Wendy, so whatever I do, I'm gonna blame it on her."

"Why's she called-" Rosalie halted herself mid-sentence, wrinkling her nose. "Never mind, I don't wanna know."

I stepped forward in the direction of the hole, but she planted herself in front of me, holding out her hand. "Promise you'll keep your word about Sook Min. By breakfast tomorrow I want her to know that she belongs to the Oscuras, deal?"

I eyed her hand before taking it in my grip and shaking firmly. "Deal."

Magic clapped between us as the stars bound us to the vow. If I broke it, I'd be paying for it with bad luck for a long time to come, so I wasn't about to risk that shit.

I released her, heading to the hole at the back of the cell and dropping to a crouch. "Come on then, looks like I need you after all."

"Hm, I'm not surprised. Earth magic *is* better than water." She dropped down beside me, elbowing me aside and crawling into the hole ahead of me.

"Wrong." I caught her ankle, freezing her skin with a blast of ice and she yelped in anger.

She kicked me as she crawled away and I pulled myself in after her, my shoulders almost getting stuck on the way through. But hell if I was gonna ask for her help. I forced my way into the small space, moving to stand with my back hunched over.

"I'm guessing you know his cell number and block?" she asked.

"Twenty Seven, level three, Cell Block C," I said with a smile. *We're coming for you, Gustard.*

Rosalie kept the silencing bubble around us as we hurried along, following the narrow passage to Cell Block C.

A guttural roar made my blood chill and both of us stopped moving at the exact same time. I turned my head toward the wall to my right as adrenaline rippled down my spine. The Belorian was close, roaming the corridors at night in case of any escapee prisoners. Just like us.

"It can't get into the walls, right?" Rosalie breathed and I swallowed the lump in my throat.

"Don't think so, love."

"Comforting." She threw me a scathing look and I snorted a laugh.

Another roar sounded further off in the prison and my shoulders relaxed as we continued moving.

"Have you ever seen it?" she asked.

"Nope, and I don't plan to," I said firmly. "A few years back a guy in my block hid in the Mess Hall while everyone was counted in for the night. When they realised he was missing, they released that monster to hunt him down. When they finally called it off, all that was left of him was blood. They had to bleach the walls to remove the stains." I grimaced and Rosalie shuddered.

"Thanks for the bedtime story."

"You're welcome. You can listen to more on my website at www dot Ethan's cockle warmers dot com."

She tried to stop herself from laughing, but it slipped out and a satisfied grin pulled at my mouth in response.

When we arrived behind the top row of cells of Cell Block C, I slowed to a halt in front of the wall parting us from Gustard's cell and dropped into a crouch. I rested my hand on the bricks and smirked as Rosalie knelt down beside me. I extended a silencing bubble into his cell as she started to cut a hole through the wall. I whistled while she worked and she threw me an irritated look so I whistled louder as she continued.

When it was done, she went to crawl in and I caught her arm, yanking her backwards with a swell of protectiveness.

"I'll go first, love." I pushed her away from me so she didn't get any ideas about me being a gentleman and I crawled into Gustard's cell. A sheet hung over the bars which meant we were safe from any midnight-snacking nosey inmates looking in here. My gaze swung to the bunk to my left where Wet Wendy's lithe, naked body was wrapped around Gustard's muscular frame. His cell was kitted out with extra blankets, pillows and even a fucking television.

I rose to my feet, extending the silencing bubble around me and over Rosalie so I could approach undetected, keeping Gustard and his girl out of it so they couldn't hear us. I spotted a line of photographs stuck to his wall and had the feeling none of the girls pictured were anyone he knew. I leaned over him and snatched Eisha's photo off of the wall with a snarl.

"Who is that?" Rosalie asked as she moved to my side.

"My sister."

"You can't take it, he'll know it was you," she said firmly. "Is this really your big plan?"

"What did I say about underestimating me?" I shot at her before, moving to a notebook on Gustard's nightstand and ripping out a page. I shut my eyes as I focused, extending my will into the page and casting an illusion on it so it was a double of my sister's photograph. Then I ripped it into pieces and tossed it on the cell floor.

Rosalie glared at Gustard as I took each of the photographs from the wall, ripping them to shreds and tossing them on the floor like confetti. Wet Wendy was going to get *all* the blame for this. Jealousy was a good enough cover, but it wasn't going to be enough for Gustard to cut her off. And that was what I wanted. I needed him to lose trust in each and every one of his slimy followers until he was all on his lonesome. Then, when he had no mean fuckers to hide behind or avenge his death, I'd finish him. The main problem was, as a Cyclops he could interrogate anyone he liked in the Order Yard and find out the truth. But Wendy was the only possible culprit here so I didn't see why he'd bother. And even if he did, it still wouldn't lead him to me or Rosalie.

"I imagine Wet Wendy went on quite the bender when she got mad about those photographs…" A malicious glint entered Rosalie's gaze and I offered her a real smile, unable to help falling for those big browns of hers. She strode across the room, grabbing the neat piles of spare tank tops and underwear Gustard had claimed for himself and started tearing them apart.

I barked a laugh, opening Gustard's bedside drawer and hunting for more things Wet Wendy might have gone to town on. A porn magazine entitled *Zodiass Weekly* was stashed beneath an Astrology book and an electric blue dildo sat beside them. I hooked the magazine out with a grin, avoiding touching the dildo at all costs. I scanned my eyes down the columns listed on the front and snorted as I pointed one out to Rosalie.

"How to make a Werewolf howl," I read the title. "I think I could give them a few tips, don't you, love?"

"I'm pretty sure *you* were the one howling," she said lightly as she finished destroying Gustard's spare clothes.

I bit down on the inside of my cheek, unable to deny that and my eyes drifted down to her bare legs. "Why did you show up without your jumpsuit on tonight?" I purred.

"Because this is what I sleep in and if I have to run back to my cell, then it would look pretty weird if I was found in my jumpsuit by a guard."

"Hm…either that or you wanted me to see you like this."

"Ethan, if I wanted you to fuck me again, all I'd have to do is snap my fingers."

"Pfft." I waved the magazine at her before creating a blade of ice and sheering it apart down the middle. "I've got my whole pack to please me," I said, grinning through the lie.

"You could have the whole prison trying to please you, stronzo, you'd still be thinking about me." She turned her back on me and I hated how right she was as I glared at her perfectly round ass.

She grabbed hold of the television, tossing it onto the floor between us and my mouth fell open.

"What? Wet Wendy was *really* mad." She shrugged and I fought the urge to kiss that delicious looking smile off of her lips.

"Right, one more thing and then we're done." I moved back to the drawer, melting the blade in my hand and grabbing a tissue from a box on top of the nightstand. I used it to pick up the bright blue dildo in the drawer with a low laugh.

I moved over to the bed, cautious as Gustard stirred a little in his sleep. But this was definitely gonna be worth it. It was just a shame I was gonna miss his reaction when he woke up.

I gently reached down and picked up Wendy's hand, placing it beside Gustard's head on the pillow.

"Are you crazy?" Rosalie hissed.

I ignored her, the adrenaline too keen in my veins to ignore. I loved the rush of doing dangerous shit. My mom had berated me all through my teens for taking up cliff diving, Pegasus air-jumping and my favourite game 'poke a dangerous Order with a pointy stick'. I loved riding that line, always coming so close to the edge that one slip could end me. But life wasn't worth living without taking the risks and riding those highs.

I rested the dildo in Wendy's palm and gently touched the end to Gustard's lips. He mumbled something incoherent, but I didn't stay to hear what. I turned sharply, snatching Rosalie's hand and shoving her into the hole before diving after her. She turned as a grunt sounded in the room and my heart pounded madly as adrenaline coursed through my bloodstream. Rosalie worked fast, closing up the hole while I pulled the silencing bubble in around us. The second it was closed, she lunged at me, her hand locking around my throat.

"Don't do stupid shit like that ever again!" she snarled.

I rested my head back against the floor, laughing madly and taking hold of her waist. "Do you know how many highs I get to chase between these walls, love? Zero."

She released her grip on my throat, her features softening and I leaned up, winding my arms behind her and holding her close.

"I felt alive again in there, didn't you?" I breathed and her lips parted as she nodded. "Ride the high," I commanded, lifting her hand and placing it against her heart. "Enjoy it."

I kept my hand pressed over hers and felt the thrum of her heartbeat pounding right through it.

"I've always done crazy shit for fun too, Ethan," she admitted. "But I can't risk getting caught and losing this key."

282

"Why?" I murmured, my hand drifting into her hair of its own accord. "What is it you're using it for that matters so much?" *Mind your own business, asshole.* But I just couldn't with her, no matter how hard I tried, she circled through my brain a thousand times a day. I wanted to know everything about her, what she dreamed of, what she lived for, what she loved. And I equally wanted to cut out the piece of me that felt that way.

She leaned down, brushing her lips over mine and the taste of temptation flooded my tongue, begging me to kiss her.

"That's none of your concern," she breathed, then jumped off of me and darted away down the tunnel.

I growled as I headed after her, but paused as I heard Gustard yell, "By the stars, Wendy, get Christopher's dildo away from me – it's for safe keeping! Wait – *fuck!* What have you done to my room, you bitch!?"

I burst out laughing, racing after Rosalie as her laughter joined mine and we fled the scene of the crime. And holy shit did it feel good to be breaking the rules with her by my side.

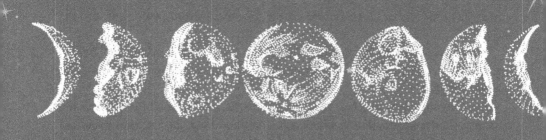

ROSALIE

PRISONER #12

CHAPTER TWENTY FIVE

D inner in the Mess Hall was the loudest meal of the day. Everyone got overexcited about having a few hours of free time to use the gymnasium, library and generally make their own decisions about where they spent their time. There was always some fight or drama which had taken place somewhere during the day, and the prisoners loved the opportunity to spread the stories and rumours between the different cell blocks like a bunch of school girls who'd just found out that Justin Beiber had come for a visit.

I didn't bother myself with rounding up the information, letting members of my pack do the running about and report back to me while I ate. If there was anything I took a particular interest in, they'd happily dig up as many details as Faely possible on the matter just to please me.

There wasn't a whole lot going on today anyway. There had been some more scuffles over bunks in the Oscura cell block now that Sin had laid claim to a chunk of the top floor for himself, but he was keeping his word about not mixing it with my Wolves and I wasn't really interested in the other Fae he was pissing off. A girl from Ethan's pack had been hauled before the Warden for trying to smuggle a love potion into the prison from someone who came to see her in visitation. Not exactly the kinds of things that meant much to me.

Sonny had scraped his bowl clean and was leaning forward over the table as he eyed the remains of my meal. He reached out to steal a fry and I growled half-heartedly.

Sonny gave me his most pathetic whimper, widening his brown eyes in a plea and I snorted a laugh before picking up the fry and pushing it into his mouth.

He smirked triumphantly and I shoved the rest of my meal his way before the Wolves descended on it. They could fight him for my scraps if they wanted them that badly.

I got to my feet, tussling Sonny's hair affectionately while he growled over my food and practically inhaled it. I walked away at a casual pace and felt the eyes of my pack on me as I headed away from them. They'd finally learned not to follow me around everywhere. But I'd had to tell them about fifty times that I only wanted them to follow me if I asked them to before it stuck. It wasn't like I could make much headway with my subtle escape plans with an entourage following me about all the time.

Sook Min was sitting with a group of her friends and I caught her eye as I moved through the crowd in her direction, beckoning her over to join me. My little Mole seemed unimpressed with me taking ownership of her, but I was willing to bet she'd forgive me when we escaped this place. Her jaw tightened and I could tell she didn't much like being bossed around and I smirked to myself as I turned towards Sin's table.

He looked up as I approached, a broad smile lighting his features as I walked up to stand opposite him.

"Do you mind if I sit here?" I asked him in a sweet tone.

"That would make my day, kitten," he purred.

"Thanks. You're a doll." I winked at him then moved to sit at the far end of his table, pointing at the seat opposite me for Sook to sit down too.

Sin laughed loudly as I abandoned him and I couldn't help but smirk to myself as I waited for Sook to join me.

She fell still as she eyed Sin, pushing her tongue into her cheek as she considered what to do before lifting her chin and stalking forward to join me.

"Hi," I said with a wide smile.

"Look at me, I'm building a harem," Sin teased from the far end of the table.

I rolled my eyes and Sook cut him a look. "You've got a bit too much going on between your legs for my taste," she said boldly and I snorted a laugh.

"I bet I could convince you otherwise," Sin countered.

"Don't mind him," I said, waving a hand at Sin dismissively. "He's just figuring out how to function amongst company again after spending so long alone. You may be able to tell he's not doing so well at it."

Sook's eyes widened like she thought Sin might attack me and I turned to him with a taunting look, daring him to do his worst.

"My wild girl just wants to make sure you're not tempted by me so that she can keep me all for herself," he replied, his eyes dripping over me.

"Keep dreaming, sinner boy," I replied dismissively before turning back to my newest friend.

"I know Ethan said that he wants me to be aligned with you now," she said slowly. "But I don't really understand why. I mean, making a deal with the Brotherhood can't be something you do regularly. Which must mean you *really* want me for something. But I'm having trouble figuring out *what*."

"Well at least you're bright enough," I said easily. "As for *why* I want you to be Oscura aligned, that's simple: I want to have the strongest gang in here. Which doesn't mean having just any member join. I want the best of the best. And you make the cut, Mole girl."

"Bullshit," she replied, arching a brow at me and I had to admit that made me like her a whole lot more.

"Okay then," I said conspiratorially. "How about this? I have my own reasons and I don't trust you enough to share them yet."

Sook smirked. "Better. I guess I'll have to wait and find out your motivations then."

"In the meantime, I feel like we make a good pair. So why don't we try out something simpler than trust? Friendship."

She eyed me for a long moment then shrugged. "You seem cool enough. So I guess it wouldn't kill me to give that a shot."

I barked a laugh and leaned back in my seat. "Perfect. So how about the next time we head up to the Order Yard, you show me just what you can do in your shifted form."

"And what do I get out of that?"

I grinned at her. She was ballsy and I liked that. "Have you ever ridden a Moon Wolf while they run beneath the stars?"

Her eyes lightened at the idea of that. Her Order form wasn't exactly built for speed and fun was pretty hard to come by in here.

"Deal," she said, offering me her hand.

"Deal," I agreed, slapping my palm into hers.

"So, when you're not leading one of the biggest packs in the prison, what else do you like to-"

A high pitched scream interrupted our conversation as a guy on the other side of the Mess Hall suddenly leapt out of his seat and raced across the room with his head bowed down like a charging bull.

My eyes widened as he swerved right towards us, still shrieking as he clawed at his face, drawing blood down his cheeks with his fingernails.

I sprang to my feet as he closed in on me and Sook but before he could reach us, Roary suddenly appeared in front of me, slamming his fist straight into the guy's face.

He howled as he was knocked to the ground and I exchanged a shocked glance with Roary before the lunatic leapt up and started charging down the aisle between the tables in the Mess Hall, running for the exit.

"They're inside me!" he howled desperately as the guards took chase, releasing their batons from their belts and setting them to stun, electricity sparking along their lengths.

I shifted closer to Roary, gripping his arm to catch his attention. I glanced up at him and he gave me a tense look as the guy started tearing at his clothes in a desperate bid to rip them off.

Hastings was racing after him at the front of the guards, his jaw set with determination as he swung his baton straight for the guy's back.

Electricity poured from the weapon and the crazy convict shrieked as his body jerked and spasmed and he fell to the floor with a crash.

Hastings stowed his weapon and dropped onto the guy's back a second later, wrenching his arms behind him and securing his cuffs with a magical chain.

The convict thrashed and flailed, trying to fight off the effects of the baton and he suddenly threw his head back, catching Hastings straight in the face with a sickening crack as his nose broke. Blood pissed down over his mouth but he didn't even flinch, driving his weight down on the convict's back as he tightened the cuffs before wrenching him to his feet again.

Sin started laughing loudly at the far end of the table, pounding his fist on the wood as he shouted out for an encore.

A couple of the other guards congratulated Hastings on the take down and I smirked as he forced the crazed convict out of the room.

"Forse non è così innocente come sembra." *Maybe he is not as innocent as he seems.*

"Tut, tut, tut, Rosa, are you trying to corrupt that guard?" Roary asked me in an undertone, his eyes sparkling with understanding.

"What makes you say that?" I asked, batting my eyelashes at him.

"There isn't a whole lot to do in here, little pup. You can take all kinds of courses once you're in the correctional program, including conversational Faetalian."

My smile widened and I leaned closer, tiptoeing up to his ear. "Quindi mi capirai ogni volta che sarò cattiva?" *So you'll understand me whenever I'm being bad?*

"Non puoi nascondermi niente, Rosa," he replied and I bit my lip at the sound of my language on his lips. *You can't hide anything from me, Rosa.*

"Beh, dovrò solo provare ed essere brava." *Well, I'll just have to try and be good.*

"Non credo che tu sappia come." *I don't think you know how.*

I smirked to myself and shrugged as I stepped back. "Probably not," I agreed.

Roary laughed but his expression hardened as he looked towards the door. "There's something unnatural about the way these people keep losing it," he muttered.

"Like what?" I asked.

He glanced at the Guards who remained in the room and shrugged before he headed away from me again, clearly not wanting to voice any more in public.

Sook looked a bit unsettled as I turned back to her and I raised an eyebrow curiously. "Are you okay?" I asked.

"Yeah," she replied slowly. "I just used to work with that guy in laundry and he was so laid back...I can't marry that up with the dude who just got dragged off to Psych."

I pursed my lips as I glanced towards the door, wondering if there really was something to Roary's suspicions about the crazies or not. But it wasn't like I could do much about it if there was. We just needed to get out of here. Then whatever was sending people psycho could stay locked up in Darkmore Penitentiary with the rest of the criminals.

"Alpha?" Amira's voice interrupted us and I turned to her with a sigh. Her less than thrilled attitude towards me hadn't gone unnoticed and I was pretty close to having to beat her down to remind her who ran this pack again.

"What?" I asked, not bothering to hide my irritation with her.

"Sonny asked me to ask you to meet him in the library," she said in a timid voice.

"Oh. Okay then. Thanks."

She scurried away and I almost felt bad about being short with her. Almost.

"I'd better go and see what that's about before we're all herded back to our cells," I said, offering Sook an easy smile. "I'll catch you later."

"Okay. See you in the Order Yard," she said with a smirk, clearly meaning to hold me to my promise.

I nodded in agreement and headed away from her, waving goodbye to the members of my pack who still sat at our usual table.

There was only one guard on duty out in the hall after the group of them had headed off to escort the prisoner to Psych. I walked away from her and headed down the stairs to the library with my mind turning over the different parts of my plans.

I'd been looking for an excuse to head to the library anyway. I needed contingencies in place just in case things went wrong with my plans which meant I needed weapons stashed in various places. I was hoping to find somewhere suitable in the library before I created a shank with my earth magic. It was simple enough to create blades from wood and with enough magic I could even create metal, but I wouldn't do it until I could be sure that I could hide it. If I was caught with a weapon then that was an automatic two weeks in the hole. Minimum. And I had no intention of wasting any time in there. I had things to do and plans to push forward.

The library was quiet as I entered it, the rows of wooden shelves filled with dog eared, dusty books which met the approved reading material list. As in, the no sex, no violence, no adventure, no fun kind of literature which drove me to tears.

"Sonny?" I called, frowning into the dim room.

He didn't reply but the room was huge, the stacks sprawling away from me with various areas splitting them up and small tables for inmates to study at.

I picked up a book for the sake of the CCTV and wandered further through the stacks before returning it to a shelf. I continued to do that as I cast surreptitious glances at the cameras and figured out the blind spots.

Because of the tall shelves, there were plenty of them and I headed down a long aisle as I began to hunt for a good hiding place for a weapon while shouting out for Sonny again. It wasn't like him to call on me and then mess me about.

The library door opened and closed again in the distance and I stilled as a prickle of apprehension ran down my spine. My Moon Wolf instincts never failed me and I wasn't about to ignore them now.

I fell still, straining my ears as I listened for the sound of someone approaching and heard several sets of footsteps moving towards me.

My instincts sent a shiver along my skin and I bared my teeth as my inner Wolf raised her hackles.

Those same instincts had saved my life more than once.

Instead of heading back the way I'd come, I slipped to the end of the aisle and crept around the shelf, heading deeper into the library as the footsteps drew closer.

I wet my lips as I kept going, wanting to see if I was right about this being an enemy before I showed myself. I was always more than ready for a fight, but I liked to know what I was going up against before I stepped into the ring.

I tiptoed to the end of the next row and carefully leaned out into the aisle to get a look back toward the door. My heart fell as I spotted The Watchers and

I quickly ducked back out of sight again. Gustard's cowardly followers would no doubt come at me in a group again and I had no intention of letting them. I'd happily take them out one by one like real Fae, but I wasn't fool enough to think I could do it if they all attacked me as one.

Bunch of un-Fae stronzos.

I cursed them beneath my breath and darted away down the aisle to escape them. I'd find Sonny then get my pack and teach them exactly who they were messing with. They might not want to fight like a Fae, but I had the numbers to force them to.

I sprinted to the far end of the aisle, gripped the edge of the shelf and swung myself around it.

"Running, pup?" Gustard mocked as I damn near crashed into him.

I only gave surprise a moment to freeze me before I lunged forward with my hand curled into fist. I punched him square in the jaw and he staggered back with a snarl of fury as I chased him with a strike to his temple and a solid kick to his chest.

He crashed back to the floor with blood spilling from a cut to his brow but as I leapt forward to finish the job, strong arms locked around me from behind.

I released a stream of Faetalian curses as I kicked and fought to free myself, gouging my nails into the arm of the big bastardo who was holding me and tearing his flesh open.

He threw me to the floor between the stacks and I rolled over twice before slamming into the bookshelf.

I snarled as I leapt to my feet, ripping books off of the shelf closest to me and throwing them at the gang as they surrounded me.

A hardback caught a Sphinx right between her eyes and she dropped like a sack of shit.

They got too close for me to throw things at and I started swinging the fattest book I could grab at them, using the only weapon available to me as they swarmed forward to overwhelm me once more.

"You're a fucking coward, Gustard!" I shrieked as I was knocked to the floor again.

Boots slammed into me left, right and centre and I was forced to wrap my arms around my head and take it as I felt bones crack and flesh split.

Pain consumed me while inside I was screaming, promising vengeance in any and every way that I could dish it out.

When they finally stopped, I couldn't even move. My heart was racing and the taste of blood overwhelmed my senses.

A foot shoved me roughly and I rolled onto my back, my swollen eyes cracking open just enough for the fluorescent light of the library to burn into my brain. I coughed out a breath, blood slipping from the edge of my mouth as I lay beneath them.

Gustard's face swam into focus as he leaned over me and he smirked like he thought he'd won something with this pathetic display.

The bell rang to tell us all to head back to our cell blocks, but the sound of it was off and it took me a moment to realise I couldn't hear out of my left ear at all.

"Let's hope the second time's the charm," Gustard mocked. "But if not, I can happily teach you this lesson again."

A breath wheezed between my lips as I forced my swollen tongue to bend around the words I wanted to spit at him. He moved out of sight and all of The Watchers' footsteps rattled through the floorboards beneath me as I struggled to get them out.

"Your face looks…like a toddler took a sharpie…to it. You…ass munching…*stronzo*," I hissed as the library door fell shut and silence enveloped me.

The second bell rang as I listened to my pulse hammering unevenly and I tried to force my broken body to move. I had five minutes to get back down to the cell block for the count. And if I wasn't there then they'd lock the doors without me. And I'd be stuck out here when they set the Belorian loose for the night.

I cursed as I tried to roll over and my vision darkened. The pain only grew sharper as I tried to move and the shadows surrounding my vision thickened.

I drew in a breath as I gave up on trying to keep my eyes open.

Maybe the Belorian wouldn't find me in here. Or maybe I was about to find out exactly what it looked like.

Fear skittered through me as I remembered the last time I'd lain crippled in agony, my body betraying me as a monster stalked closer. But this wasn't like that. The last monster who'd hunted me had craved my pain. At least this one would only require my death.

The agony in my body was all consuming and a whimper escaped my lips as it devoured me.

I couldn't count the amount of people I'd be letting down if I died. But the thought of them grieving me tore me in two.

The pain in my heart matched that in my body and the darkness finally took me.

I'm sorry...

CAIN

COMMANDING OFFICER

CHAPTER TWENTY SIX

I headed into Cell Block D for the count, folding my arms and waiting as everyone filed into their cells.

Hastings moved up beside me, his arm rubbing mine and I instinctively took a step away, not that he seemed to notice. A Cerberus like him was all about making friends, but as a Vampire I didn't need company, let alone a friend.

"Hey, so I noticed our shifts finish at the same time tonight," he said, throwing me a hopeful look and I frowned, wondering where the fuck he was going with this. "I thought maybe we could head out to Silvertown and grab a few beers. The Blueshine vs Starfire game is on. Which Pitball team do you support?"

My eyes narrowed on him. "I like to watch the game in my quarters."

"Oh cool, so maybe I could go grab some beer and swing by later?"

"I like to watch it alone," I said coolly and I could almost see his little mutt heart breaking as he bowed his head.

"Oh…okay."

I clenched my jaw, turning away from him and trying to ignore the stirring in my chest, but it wouldn't quit. He'd made friends amongst the guards so I didn't know why the fuck he thought *I* was a good candidate to cosy up to. We might have been paired for work, but I didn't get close with people. Not since I was a kid…my heart twisted at the painful memories waiting for me in the past and I forced them away, refusing to let them in.

A buzz sounded to signal the doors closing and the inmates were soon locked in their cells or in the huge coop on the bottom floor. I headed upstairs with Hastings while the other guards split off toward the coop and the second floor.

On the top level, Hastings headed away from me as we moved systematically around the walkways, using our scanners to take the count.

I reached Sixty Nine's cell and found his expression anxious as he rested his hands on the bars. I lifted the scanner to his face with a scowl.

"What is it, inmate?" I growled.

He ran a hand into his long hair, refusing to answer me and I moved away from him toward Twelve's cell.

I banged on the bars when she didn't appear and leaned forward to hunt for her in her cell. My throat tightened with rage as I found it empty.

"Hastings!" I barked over at him as he tried to scan Twenty Four's face while the pervert twirled the long grey hairs of his chest, standing butt naked before him.

Jack turned to me in surprise, raising his brows. "What's up, boss?"

"Have you counted Twelve? Is she in someone else's cell?" I strode around the walkway to join him, looking in all the cells I passed, fury coiling around my heart.

"No, sir," he said instantly.

I growled, hurrying around to finish the count, scanning faces while hunting their cells for Twelve.

Where the fuck is she?

When it was done, the total flashed up on my screen with an alert saying we were one short.

"Fuck!" I rushed to the railing, taking hold of it and staring down at the guards. "Everyone is on high alert. We have a prisoner missing. Find Twelve *now*."

Everyone rushed to obey including Hastings and I snatched the radio from my hip to alert the Warden. "Ma'am we have a code red. Potential escapee."

The static crackled down the line then she answered in a clipped tone. "Follow protocol. You have fifteen minutes to search the prison, if she's not found dead or alive, release The Belorian and send a team to the perimeter."

My throat tightened at the word *dead*. "Yes ma'am."

I hung the radio back on my belt, turning and finding Sixty Nine watching me too closely for my liking. I narrowed my gaze, striding towards him with a snarl.

"Where is she?" I snarled. "You live on her back like a fucking limpet, so if anyone knows where she is it's *you*."

Sixty Nine glowered at me, folding his arms. "I don't know where she is, asshole. She left the Mess Hall to go and look for her Beta." Worry flickered in his gaze, but he hid it quickly behind a steely mask.

"Where?" I hissed, reaching for my baton, tempted to have his cell opened and beat the answer from his lips. I was sure he knew more than he was letting on. The guy had made a living on deceit before he came here.

"She went to the library!" someone called from down below and my heart juddered. I abandoned my line of questioning and rushed down the stairs to the second floor, landing with a heavy thud on the walkway.

I headed down to the bottom level and sprinted out of the block, slamming my palm on the security panel to retract the bridge.

Guards were racing through the halls, splitting off in different directions as they hunted for her. I rushed into the elevator in a burst of Vampire speed as an armed unit moved out of it and my jaw clenched as I slammed my finger on the button for level six. My heart thundered in my ears as I descended. If we had to let that fucking Belorian loose in the halls while she was out of her cell block, she wouldn't stand a chance if it found her. I'd never known an inmate to survive an encounter with it in all my years at Darkmore.

The doors slid open and I rushed out with the speed of my Order, the quiet pressing in on me as I shot into the library.

"Twelve!" I yelled, heading down an aisle and hunting the stacks. I forced myself to be quiet, extending my Vampire hearing into the space and picking up a soft heartbeat.

I pivoted around, tearing down the next aisle and finding her at the end of it. I almost stalled at the sight of her battered body, but I couldn't stop. She had multiple injuries and the thought of who had done this set rage burning a passage through my heart. And in that instant I was transported back to my past, replaying the moment I'd found my friend in a pool of his own blood.

I was moving so fast that as I dropped to my knees, my radio fell from my belt, skittering across the floor and slamming into the nearest shelf. I ignored it, resting my fingers to her shattered collar bone and closing my eyes as I released wave after wave of healing energy into her body. I took away her pain and fixed bones and bruises as my magic flowed into her, giving her everything I had to offer.

Whoever had done this would pay in blood. I didn't care what rules I had to bend to make it happen. And I had a feeling I knew exactly which gang was targeting her because there weren't many fuckers in this prison tough enough to face her. The assholes who didn't respect Fae on Fae fights. Who discarded their pride to get the upper hand in this prison. But she'd never admit it, and I'd never get a confession from any of them.

Twelve groaned softly and relief spilled through me as she lifted her head, her eyes fluttering open as she gazed up at me. I schooled my expression, refusing to let her see how much it killed me to find her like this. But this was why I didn't let people in. It was happening all over again. As soon as I cared for anything, it withered and died before my eyes. I couldn't protect her.

"Every time I get hurt, you show up, Mason," she whispered and I swallowed thickly.

"I'm just doing my job," I growled.

She reached up, brushing her fingers over my cheek. "Sure you are."

For a moment, I fell into the warmth in her eyes and a deep, primal need unfolded in my chest telling me to hold her close and protect her. But I wasn't her saviour. I was a guard with a corrupted soul and me helping her meant nothing. It *had* to mean nothing.

Warden Pike's voice sounded across my radio and I was jerked back to reality. "All personnel please move to the nearest elevator and return to the Guard Barracks. The Belorian is releasing in thirty seconds."

I cursed, jumping to my feet and rushing forward to pick up the radio. I lifted it to my lips, holding down the call button and static hissed out of the receiver. "I've found Twelve, ma'am. Keep the beast in its cage." I released the button and static flared down the line. I pressed it again as my heart thudded harder. "Ma'am, inmate found. Confirm." I pressed the button again, swearing as the light didn't come on. It was fucking broken.

"*Cain,*" Twelve breathed, the fear in her tone making me fall still.

I turned to her, finding her pointing at the glass doors to the library where a hulking shadow was cast against it. A grunting, sniffing noise reached me and my blood turned to ice.

I lifted my hand, casting a silencing bubble around us, but I couldn't do anything about our heat signature. And that was how this thing hunted best.

The door to the library pushed open and the scrape of its spines against the glass made me wince as the Belorian entered. I caught Twelve's hand, dragging her down the next aisle as my pulse thrummed in my ears.

We pressed back against a bookshelf and I gathered flames in my hands.

"What are you doing?" she hissed.

"It hunts by detecting heat," I growled.

"That sounds like a good reason not to start a fire, asshole."

I ignored her, snatching her around the waist and throwing her over my shoulder at the same moment as I launched the fireball towards the far end of the library. A shriek sounded as the Belorian raced after it and I used a burst of Vampire speed to race out of the room and tear towards the elevator at the end of the hall. I nearly crashed into the wall as I came to a halt, dropping Twelve to her feet and slamming my hand against the scanner.

Another shriek sounded behind me and I turned, casting a fiery wall before us as the monstrous creature came for us on its six spiny legs, its eyeless face angled toward us. Its skin was grey and its grotesque, spidery body took up most of the space in the hall. The fire sent it into a frenzy, chasing us down at high speed and I jammed my thumb on the call button again and again.

"Unlock my cuffs!" Twelve demanded, shaking my arm.

My flames couldn't penetrate the Belorian's iron-like skin and I knew we were fucked if the door didn't fucking op-

The doors parted and Twelve dragged me inside. I slammed my finger on the button to shut them again and they slid over, closing just before the monster collided with them, releasing a horrible wail.

I leaned back against the wall with a heavy sigh, sweat trickling down my brow.

"Thank fuck you found me," Twelve said heavily, giving me an intense look.

I shrugged, dropping her gaze but I could practically feel her rolling her eyes at me. I stepped forward to the call panel on the wall and typed in the code to patch me through to the Warden.

"Yes?" she asked sharply.

"Ma'am, my radio broke. I found Twelve on level six. We had a run in with the Belorian."

"Goodness, are you alright?"

"Just about," I said in a low tone. "I'm taking Twelve down to Medical, we need a lockdown on level six to keep it contained."

"I'll have it done immediately. Well done, Officer."

"Thank you, ma'am." The call cut off and silence stretched between me and Twelve as the elevator headed down toward level eight.

"You should've killed that thing," she commented with a shudder.

"That *thing* is a bio-weapon. And it's made specifically to withstand Fae magic."

"Well whoever created it is an idiota." She pursed her lips.

"In what way?" I asked dryly as the doors slid open.

"If you make an unkillable monster, then one day…" She stepped out of the elevator and turned back to me with a dark look. "It's going to kill you. Better to put it down now before that happens, don't you think, Mason?"

"Don't call me Mason." I strode after her, snatching hold of her arm and dragging her in the direction of the medical bay. "And that monster is controlled. It has a collar which will drive it back to level seven where it lives."

"You've got a lot of trust in a thing that nearly ate you," she said lightly, attempting to thread her fingers through mine.

I shoved her forward, making her stumble and she laughed. We reached the ward and I moved to open the door, but before I could, Twelve leaned in close to my ear and whispered, "Thank you for coming to save me, my valiant knight."

"I didn't-" I started but she opened the door and slipped inside, blowing me a kiss before shutting it behind her.

I pressed my lips together tightly as a smile tried to carve itself into my face.

Damn that girl knows how to get under my skin.

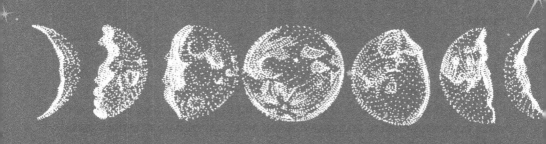

ROSALIE

PRISONER #12

CHAPTER TWENTY SEVEN

I lay in my bunk with my lips pursed and a scowl on my face. Fucking Gustard. I'd let the first encounter with him slide, partly because I'd gotten my revenge by setting up Two Hundred and partly because I didn't have time for his shit. He wanted to teach me a lesson and I'd taught him one instead. Or so I'd hoped.

But now it had happened again. And I couldn't let that kind of disrespect slide. I needed to strike at him hard. *But,* I had to admit that Ethan had a point when we'd snuck into Gustard's cell the other night. Just killing him wouldn't solve the problem for me. First off, I'd have to be sure that I could get away with that kind of thing anyway as I couldn't afford to waste time stuck in the hole. And secondly, death was too easy for him now. I wanted his reputation annihilated, his followers abandoning him and his spirt broken.

So I was going to pick apart his empire brick by brick. And if that meant working with Ethan to do it then all the better. Because that would only further my plans to unite our packs and seize control of the prison anyway.

Officer Lyle had escorted me back to my cell first thing this morning and I couldn't say I was sad to be away from Mother Brenda. That woman was a straight up whack job. Though I was happy to have eaten more of her chocolate.

I was cranky after missing out on a lot of my sleep and I'd spent way too much time going over the events that had led to The Watchers beating the shit out of me again. And one particular detail just kept on twisting through my thoughts.

Amira was the one who'd sent me there. She told me Sonny was waiting for me and yet he clearly hadn't been. I intended to ask him whether or not he'd been in the library at all last night when I saw him, but I was pretty damn sure I already knew the answer.

And if that bitch had sold me out she might as well have slit her own throat, because if I had to do it myself I was sure as shit going to make a messy job of it.

Not yet though. I'd had time to think it over and let my temper cool. If Amira had decided to sell me out to Gustard then I might just be able to use that to my advantage and lay a trap of my own for him in return. Which meant I was going to have to bide my time, act like I had no idea that ass munching whore had sold me out and let her believe I hadn't figured it out. Then, when the time was right I'd pounce and she'd be praying to the moon for mercy long before I was through with her.

"Tell me how it feels on the inside, baby," a rough voice carried to me from somewhere beyond my cell and I frowned as I was almost certain that I'd recognised Pudding. He groaned enthusiastically and I shuddered, wondering who he'd brought back to his cell last night. I guessed grumpy old Bear Shifters got urges too, but I didn't really want to become too familiar with them.

"I bet it tastes so sweet. Did you use cinnamon this time?"

My frown deepened. That was damn strange pillow talk.

"And did you bake it until it was *just* golden brown?"

Okay, he was definitely talking about food which was a relief, except I couldn't hear anyone replying to him. Which either meant he was talking in his sleep or doing something *much* more exciting.

"Think of me when you eat it," he growled urgently. "Can you put Guntar on now?"

My heart stilled. I sat up straight and held my breath as I listened for more.

"Hi. I'm just checking in, I wanted to make sure you're doing okay with the Aborini job?"

Oh yes, yes, hell to the fucking yes!!

I jumped out of my bed and moved towards the cell doors with my heart in my throat. The guards had done the count already and it was almost time for us to be let out of our cells. Which was perfect because I needed to make a stop off with my favourite Bear ASAP.

I listened as he continued to talk to whoever he was on the phone with for another few minutes then everything fell silent.

Or at least it did until the all too familiar sound of Plunger using his home made pube trimmers reached me alongside his commentary on his progress.

"Come here you scruffy duffy…"

Bleugh.

I moved away from the door and dropped into a set of push ups, hoping that if I concentrated hard enough on a workout then I might be able to block him out.

By the time the doors rattled open for the day, I was coated in a layer of sweat and panting from my exercise. I hadn't entirely managed to cut Plunger's trimming efforts out of my head, but I'd done a good job of distracting myself.

I headed straight out onto the walkway before turning left and stopping outside cell eleven.

"Pudding?" I called in my sweetest voice through the sheet he'd hung over the door.

He grunted in response and I took that as an invitation to twitch the sheet aside.

It took my eyes a moment to adjust to the darkness in his cell as he'd managed to pile his hoard so high that it covered the light fitting in the ceiling. I couldn't even see him amid the carefully heaped pudding cups and other accrued crap he'd used to decorate the space.

"Can I come in?"

"Just don't touch anything," he replied.

"Okay." I stepped inside, letting the sheet fall back into place behind me and the darkness deepened.

I looked around for Pudding but I couldn't spot him anywhere amid the mountain of shit. There was a hole carved into the side of the mound which looked like it led in towards the bunk and I crouched down to look through it into the dark, wondering if Pudding would actually be able to fit through it.

"Get to the point, hound," he grunted from within the heap, giving me my answer.

"I'd like to use your cell phone," I said, doing as he'd asked and cutting the shit.

"We're half a mile underground, pup," he scoffed. "There's no service down here for cell phones."

"So how did you do it?" I asked. "I heard you talking to someone on the phone earlier."

"I want more pudding cups."

"What?"

"If you want something from me, I want something from you. You've got the followers required to get me mass quantities."

"You want my pack collecting pudding cups for you?" I asked in surprise. "That's a hell of a lot of sugar, even for a guy your size."

"I don't want to eat them. I just want the cups."

I paused for a long moment at that. "Can I ask, why?" He had a fucking ton of them already so it wasn't like he was short on them.

"You want to speak to someone on the outside. I need pudding cups. Simple."

"Okay then. Any chance you'll take my word on it and let me make that call now?" I tried my luck, wondering if I might be able to use my abundance of charm on him to get my way.

"Why are pretty girls always so stupid?" he grunted.

"Hey! I don't know whether to be offended or complimented by that," I joked.

"See? Stupid."

Pudding fell silent and I shifted uncomfortably, wondering what that was supposed to mean.

"Erm, at the risk of sounding *more* stupid... I'm not entirely sure if we've made a deal here or-"

Pudding's face suddenly loomed in the dark tunnel between the pudding pots and I gasped as I shifted back out of his way, standing upright again.

"I'll show you. Then you'll see how stupid you are," he muttered as he emerged from the hole and stood too. He towered above me, his broad frame taking up most of the space left available in the cell around the pudding pot mountain.

I shifted back against the wall as he passed me and he moved towards his sink before picking up an unopened pudding there.

He tossed it to me so suddenly that I almost didn't catch it.

"What do you see?" he demanded.

"Erm...vanilla pudding?" I said slowly, knowing I was about to be told I was wrong, but not really having any clue what he wanted me to say.

"Stupid." His big hand closed over mine and he uncurled my fingers, making me lay my palm flat before him as he plucked the pudding pot from my hand.

I watched as he peeled the foil lid off of it and he abruptly upturned the cup, dumping the wobbly vanilla goo onto my hand.

"What the hell?" I demanded angrily as it slid between my fingers, but Pudding wasn't listening.

He stuck his finger into the bottom of the empty cup and pushed down until a snap sounded and he held the cup up for me to look at.

I frowned into the empty tub at the crack he'd split in the bottom of it.

"You see it?" Pudding asked.

"Stronzo, all I see is a crack in the plastic and a crazy motherfucker who

306

just filled my hand with pudding," I growled, wondering if this was all some weird ass joke or something.

"Stupid," he stated again and I growled at him.

"Keep calling me that and you'll find out why my name is being whispered all over this prison," I warned.

My hand was full of gloop and I was beginning to think he was just messing with me for some weird Bear joke or something and I wasn't laughing.

Pudding rolled his eyes at me before fishing his finger back into the pot again and hooking something out from the crack in the bottom of the plastic.

"These puddings are spelled to stop them turning bad," he explained as he held a little white square of plastic before my eyes. "They all have one of these hidden in the bottom of the pot to store the magic that keeps them fresh well after they should go off."

"Eww. I eat these things. How old are they then?" I demanded.

"The card holds *magic,* hound," he emphasised like I was being intentionally dense.

"Yeah. That's great and all but the minuscule amount they'd place in there wouldn't exactly be enough to-"

"That's why I need lots of them," he said impatiently. "One hundred of these cards combined with a stick of blueberry gum, a length of dental floss, a few mint leaves and the everflames they use in the lightbulbs can make a powerful transmitter."

"A transmitter?" I asked curiously, my interest one hundred percent piqued at last. "So you just combine the little scraps of magic from a load of old shit in just the right way and you can make a phone?"

"A *transmitter,"* he growled irritably. "There's no cell service down here. A transmitter takes the sound of your voice and replicates it elsewhere. My brother made a receiver so he can open up the line of communication between us."

I stood staring at him in silence for a long minute before a grin broke over my face. "You're a fucking genius, Pudding," I announced. "Can I use it?"

"Stupid girl," he sighed. "The charge from the pudding cups burns out after three minutes. That's it. It takes me weeks to collect the cups I need for one conversation."

"But my pack can get a hundred a day," I said, grinning as I realised how I could fit in to his little scheme. "I get you those cups, you make the transmitter thingys then we take turns to make calls."

"I can't bring a hundred pudding cups back here every day. I'll need cards only. But don't be obvious in taking them out like stupid pups."

"Okay. We can manage that," I said enthusiastically, moving to shake his hand before looking down at the pudding which still sat in my palm.

"Go wash your hand now. Let's see if you can manage this plan." Pudding waved me away and I didn't even give a shit about the dismissive attitude. If he could open up a line of communication with Dante for me which the Guards couldn't spy on, then I could pass vital information back and forth so much more easily than trying to use codes over the phone or during visitation.

I hurried back into my cell and quickly washed the pudding from my hand before grabbing my wash bag, fresh clothes and towel from my shelf and heading down to join the queue of people waiting for the guards to let us out for a shower.

I spotted one of Gustard's lackeys ahead of me and narrowed my eyes as I prowled straight towards her. She was a tall fucker with mean eyes and a Griffin symbol shining on the lapel of her jumpsuit. And her boot had most certainly connected with my body when their group of cowardly stronzos attacked me last night.

"Twenty Seven," I barked, spotting the Siren amongst the crowd.

"Yes?" she asked, looking around at me nervously.

"Hold my shit." I shoved my wash stuff and clothes into her hands without bothering to stop as I stalked towards the Griffin.

She looked around just as my fist flew and she crumpled like a sack of shit as my knuckles impacted with her temple. I gave her a solid kick to the kidney while she was down and she groaned from her position on the ground.

Six more of Gustard's little bitches suddenly raced towards me as they realised what I'd done and I lifted my chin, cupping my hands as I howled to the sky.

"Anyone who wants to join the ranks of the Oscura Clan will make sure that Gustard's cowardly stronzos fight me one on one like true Fae!" I shouted before the first asshole reached me.

He was a little fucker, a Tiberian Rat Shifter, but he was fast as hell as he dodged beneath my first punch and drove his fist into my side.

I moved with the force of the punch and whirled around, kicking him in the ass as I made it behind him. I aimed a punch straight at the back of his head, taking the pain in my knuckles for the reward of seeing him fall beneath me.

Several Oscura hopefuls had reacted to my offer, moving to intercept some of Gustard's lackeys so that they couldn't all attack me at once.

I whirled towards a Manticore next, racing forward and slamming my shoulder into her gut as I took her down. She shrieked in defiance as we fell to the floor, but I managed to maintain my advantage as I pinned her beneath me, punching, punching, punching until her blood coated my fists and she stopped trying to fight back.

A hand locked in my hair as another stronzo made it to me and he ripped me backwards off of the defeated Manticore.

I snarled as he dragged me across the floor by my hair, swinging my leg around and taking out the backs of his knees. He dropped me as he tried to stop himself from falling and I used my low position to swing my fist straight up into his junk.

I leapt to my feet as the final two bastardos came for me at once. The pair of Minotaurs looked similar enough to mark them out as brothers and I ducked and weaved between them, using my speed to my advantage as I landed swift blows and avoided most of theirs.

One of them swung a meaty fist at my face, busting my lip open as he caught me in the jaw and I snarled as I leapt at him. I grabbed a fistful of his hair, driving the knuckles of my other hand into his face five times in quick succession before using my hold on his hair to swing him towards his brother as he charged at me.

Their heads collided with a sickening crack and the two of them fell unconscious at my feet.

I wiped the back of my hand across my bloody mouth as I panted, looking around at the crowd of onlookers to make sure there were no more assholes looking to dance with me.

"The Watchers are no longer welcome in this cell block!" I yelled. "So pack up your shit and request a transfer over to stay with your good friend Gustard. Anyone who doesn't heed this warning will answer to my fists again and again and again until you get the fucking message. And tell your cowardly leader that if he ever locates his balls and wants to fight me Fae on Fae, I'm more than ready to wipe the floor with his smug face too."

The bell rang to announce the arrival of the guards to take us to the showers and I stalked through the crowd to the front of the line. Fae scurried out of my way as I moved between them and I couldn't deny the rush that gave me.

Twenty Seven hurried over with my stuff and I took it from her with a grunt of acknowledgement before elbowing my way to the front of the crowd.

Roary smirked at me as I moved to join him, leaning down to speak into my ear. "Making rules now are you? Do you think this cell block belongs to you, little pup?" he asked, the hint of a warning in his voice.

I licked my busted lip as I looked up at him, the iron tang of blood coating my tongue. "Do you like having The Watchers in here, Roary?" I asked innocently.

"No."

"Then maybe I was just doing you a favour."

He snorted a laugh and I smiled in response.

"Just don't forget who runs this cell block, little pup," he said in a firm tone.

"Every king needs a queen, Roar," I teased as the bridge slid into place before us and the doors parted to let us out.

"You want to be my queen, Rosa? Some things never change I guess."

"Well if the crown fits…" I winked at him and walked away, striding over the bridge as the guards came into view.

Cain caught my eye as he took in my slightly bruised and beaten appearance and I smirked at him as I kept walking, putting a little extra swagger into my step as I went. No doubt Gustard would try to come at me twice as hard now, but that was fine by me. I'd never been one to hide in the shadows unnoticed. Not since I'd broken free of the cage my parents had built for me. And I'd survived much worse monsters than Gustard in my lifetime.

I strolled down the corridor to the showers and a blur of motion in my periphery signalled Cain shooting ahead of me.

He was standing just inside the locker room door as I passed through it and he reached out to press his hand to my bleeding lip as I stepped inside.

My eyebrows rose in surprise as I looked up at him and the tingle of healing magic swept beneath my skin as he cured the cuts and bruises I'd gotten from my brawl.

"Keep moving, Twelve," he said in a rough voice as he pulled his hand back just as quickly as he'd touched me. "Or you'll cause a blockage."

"We wouldn't want that," I mocked, watching as he pushed his thumb between his lips to lick my blood off of it. My heart leapt at the sight and I couldn't stop myself from staring at his mouth for a long moment. Officer Off Limits was starting to give off some seriously tempting vibes and I was beginning to think it was time we did something about this tension that was building between us.

I moved away from him and he stayed by the door as the rest of the convicts appeared, but I could still feel his eyes on me.

I moved to place my things on a hook, kicking my boots off as the sound of the showers starting up filled the open space.

Plunger strutted past me, tossing his clothes off haphazardly as he went and I slowed my movements. I'd long since learned to wait for him to pick a shower before choosing my own as far from him as physically possible. He liked to get into all sorts of weird and wonderful poses beneath the flow of tepid water and I did *not* need to see that before I ate my breakfast.

As expected, Plunger instantly dropped down to press his palms flat to the floor and thrust his ass up under the flow of water like he was hoping to fill it up or something.

I shuddered as I looked away from him, just thankful that his back end was pointed at the wall so that I didn't have to endure the rear view of that particular horror show.

"What the hell is wrong with you, you twisted freak?" a male voice came from my left and I looked around in time to see the new pup who'd arrived yesterday striding towards Plunger like he meant to force him upright again. The guy was fairly big but he hadn't challenged anyone for a cell the moment he'd arrived, which was enough to tell me he wasn't going to be on my radar much.

"There are ladies present," he snarled. "They don't wanna look at you doing that!"

Plunger flipped upright, smiling like a creepy ass clown and silence fell amongst the convicts in the shower room.

I glanced around to see if Cain was watching this, but he'd stepped outside again. No doubt he was listening in with his bat ears, but the guards wouldn't intervene unless they absolutely had to anyway.

"Say that again, *friend,*" Plunger said in a low tone which had my hackles rising.

Roary moved to stand at my side and we exchanged a glance as we waited to see how this would play out.

"I'm asking you to stop bending over with your asshole in the air," the pup growled.

Plunger raised his hands innocently and moved back to his shower. "Didn't mean to offend you, *pup,*" he said in an overly innocent tone.

The pup smirked as he moved to stand under the next shower along, but the tightness in my gut didn't ease.

Plunger picked up a bar of soap and began to scrub it under his armpits vigorously. He started moaning and groaning as he scrubbed it down his hairy belly and rubbed it all over his junk with way too much vigour. He kept moaning, sounding like he was about to come and the pup growled angrily from the shower beside him.

Plunger turned and bent over, pointing his ass at the new pup while he scrubbed the soap between his cheeks, causing suds to froth up all over his body as he groaned loudly in exaggerated pleasure.

"Oooooh yeah, that's the business," he moaned.

"What the fuck are you doing?" The pup stepped towards him with his shoulders pressed back and Plunger lunged. He flipped around so quickly that the motion was practically a blur.

The pup swung a fist at him but Plunger ducked beneath it, wrapping his arms around his waist and knocking him off of his feet to the wet floor.

The pup cried out as Plunger punched him over and over with the fist holding the bar of soap. Suds flew everywhere and the rest of the inmates in the shower scattered.

The pup tried to fight back but Plunger was like a savage beast, his eyes wild with fury as he punched and punched.

They rolled across the wet tiles and Plunger scrambled on top, slamming his bare balls down on the pup's chest.

I cringed at the mere thought of it and glanced at Roary as his upper lip curled back.

Plunger suddenly grabbed the pup's face, forcing his mouth open before driving the soap down his throat. I caught sight of a curly black hair sticking to it before it disappeared into his mouth and I damn near threw up.

"For the love of the moon," I growled in disgust.

"Do we still have a problem, *pup*?" Plunger snarled as the new kid kicked and choked beneath him while he slapped a hand over his mouth to keep the soap in there. "Or can I resume my daily routine in peace?"

The kid was turning blue, his thrashing limbs losing power.

"Holy shit, he's going to kill him," a girl muttered behind me.

The door banged open and Cain shot into the room, skidding to a halt behind Plunger and the pup. He ripped his baton from his belt, set it to stun and drove it into the puddle of water at his feet.

The rubber soles of his boots protected him from the blast but Plunger, the pup and several Fae who were still standing in the water all fell prey to the blast.

"Get the fuck out of here!" Cain bellowed at all of us. "No showers for you today! If you behave like animals in here then you can stink like them too!"

He strode towards the new pup and shoved him over with his boot before smacking him on the back with his baton which he'd switched off.

The pup heaved the soap out of his mouth and started coughing his guts up after it as he lay his cheek down in the puddle of water on the floor and tried to catch his breath.

"Whoops," Plunger gasped, covering his mouth in exaggerated horror. "Seems like that little shock made me wet myself!"

The pup cried out as he tried to scramble out of the puddle and Cain snarled angrily as he strode out of it himself.

"What are you all still doing here?!" he bellowed. "Get dressed and fuck off up to breakfast. Unless you want me to ban you from that today too?"

I snatched my clothes from my hook and quickly pulled my jumpsuit on as we all hurried to follow his commands.

Missing showers was a pain in the ass, but missing breakfast was unthinkable. The mail slot was only open in the mornings for inmates to collect their letters from home and I was expecting a letter from my cousin today. A very important letter which should help me figure out my issues with that Order Suppressant tank.

I fell into step with Roary as we headed out of the showers and nudged his arm with mine, nuzzling his shoulder for a moment affectionately.

"What's got you so happy, little pup?" he asked, drawing me under his arm.

"Things are all coming together," I replied, offering him a smirk. "Today is gonna be a good day."

He laughed at my happy mood and didn't release me as we started up the stairs. And the feeling of his arm wrapped around me had my smile growing even more.

S IN

PRISONER #88

CHAPTER TWENTY EIGHT

I heaved myself up onto the pull-up bar in the gym as sweat dripped down my bare back. A grunt of effort passed my lips as I forced my arms to work harder, pulling myself up and down faster than any other fucker in the gym. When I worked out, I was a soldier, a fucking mercenary. It didn't matter if I was the biggest guy in the room or the smallest, I'd still beat every asshole in here because I had no mental barriers, no walls to hit. I could push into pain until it started to feel like ecstasy. And that was my favourite place to live.

When I was done with my set, I climbed up onto the bar, sitting there as I gazed over the huge gym. Voices caught my ear behind me and I turned my head to look at the boxing ring. Ethan Shadowbrook was sparring with his pack, taking them on one by one and laying them out as flat as pancakes every time. He was the sort of Fae I could admire for his strength. And the lifestyle he led made my blackened heart tug. My kind were solitary by nature, but we craved the warmth of other bodies. I could never form connections beyond the bedroom so what Shadowbrook had was something I wasn't capable of. Incubus's were made for lust, not love. But I couldn't help but wonder what it would have been like to have family who would go to the ends of the world for you. My mother had taken one walk for me, the one which had led her to the garbage can where I'd been left to die. A real funeral for a king. *Oh well. C'est la fucking vie.*

Rosalie caught my eye across the room, benching two hundred pounds like a pro. It was boner city, especially the way her bare stomach muscles flexed beneath her sports bra. The Darkmore gym clothes were black, plain, dull. But she wore them like a rainbow. And I wanted to turn into a Pegasus and ride right through her.

Shadowbrook whistled to catch the attention of the whole gym and I turned my gaze in his direction again as he directed the nearest Fae to line up and challenge him in a spar. Apparently defeating every member of his pack wasn't enough for him. Despite the fact that his chest was gleaming with sweat and his tattoos looked like they'd turned to liquid ink. The sight brought a smirk to my lips. This fucker had no limits. And I could relate.

I was about to drop down from the bar and show him what the mat beneath him tasted like, when my little wild girl saved me the bother. She strode past the forming line and ducked under the rope, climbing up to face Ethan with a dark smile on her lips. Fuck, I wanted to lick that mouth right off her face sometimes. And though I was about to bust a ball with how desperate I was to get laid, I'd decided to bide my time with the silver Wolf and hold out for her. Isolation had taught me the one skill I'd never thought I'd have. Patience. With how long I'd waited and dreamed and hoped for the day I'd be able to claim someone's body again, I deserved for it to be someone special. And Rosalie Oscura was the definition of special.

"How high is your pain threshold, love?" Ethan asked loudly as he and Rosalie began to circle one another. His Wolf pack were crowding around the ring, howling and pounding their fists on the mat as they urged him on; Rosalie's pack were gathering on the other side of the ring too, crying out their own support.

"It's higher than yours," Rosalie answered and a grin twisted up my lips.
Pound his pretty face, kitten.

Shadowbrook made the first move, throwing a bare-knuckled punch at Rosalie's gut. She deflected it then darted around him, throwing a sharp punch into his jaw.

He jerked back a step with a growl and adrenaline seeped into my blood as he swung around, catching her by the throat. Neither of them were playing by the rules and it was clear Ethan wasn't going to go easy on her. He kicked out her legs and threw her to the ground. She was almost up again when he dropped over her to try and pin her down. She threw her head up, her forehead colliding with his so he lurched backwards just enough for her to wriggle free. She leapt around and knelt over him, catching his blonde hair in her fist and slamming his face into the mat.

I barked a laugh, rocking back and forth on the bar as I waited for her to finish him.

Ethan reached behind him, catching her calf and hauling her off of him with a fierce strength. He crawled over her, grabbing hold of her throat and my jaw tightened as she lifted her hips, grinding against him. His eyes became hooded and jealousy hit me like a fucking hurricane. They were trying to hide it, but no one could conceal lust from an Incubus. I was finely tuned to pick up on that shit like some sort of sex radio.

She jammed a punch into his side and he released her throat with a pained oomph, but pressed his weight down harder to keep her pinned. He caught hold of her chin in an iron grip and she slapped his hand away as they continued to fight, but I started to notice that every blow only brought more light to their eyes. They were evenly matched. And they were enjoying this like a good fuck.

They finally called a truce and feigned some pissy looks at each other while I read the truth behind their eyes.

The two of them soon headed toward the locker room, passing the guard manning the door and I dropped from the bar, landing on my feet with a hard thud.

I moved across the room with purposeful strides and shoved through the door, passing the rows of empty lockers and benches as I hunted for them. A moan caught my ears and my hands curled into tight fists.

I rounded the final row of lockers and found Ethan holding my wild girl against the wall. Their bodies were moulded together and the noises leaving Rosalie filled me with the sudden urge to join in. I mean hell, I'd been in plenty of orgies before but something about Shadowbrook claiming her before I had was a kick in the teeth.

I leaned my shoulder against a locker, folding my arms and waiting, because I may have been pissed. May have even been as jealous as a fat kid watching a pig eat pie. But I was also the most notorious assassin in the whole of Solaria. And no one ever saw me rattled.

When Ethan dipped his hand into her waistband, I decided to clear my throat and let them know this secret show had a one man audience.

Ethan twisted around and Rosalie inhaled sharply, her lips reddened and swollen from the force of Ethan's kiss.

I smiled like a clown as I gazed between the two of them, holding their fates in my palm. "Well if it isn't an Oscura and a Lunar settling their differences," I mused. "The stars must be playing games…"

I moved away from the locker, striding closer and enjoying the power I held over them.

Ethan squared his shoulders at me. "Tell anyone and I'll-"

"You'll what, kitten?" I purred, continuing to walk forward until I was nose to nose with him. "Will you bite me like a bad dog?"

"Ethan's embarrassed about us," Rosalie said and I shifted my gaze to her, not moving an inch out of Ethan's personal space. She tucked her hair behind her ear and I lunged forward as I caught a glimpse of something. I grabbed her chin, forcing her head to one side and examining the mark behind her ear. Ethan started growling as my teeth clenched and rage spewed through my chest like an overflowing volcano.

I shoved Rosalie back against the wall, lowering my head to snarl in her face, "Did you forget to tell me about your *mate*, wild girl? I've fucked plenty of wives and even the odd husband, but a mate chosen by the moon? Astrology is rather working against our fate, baby."

Rosalie shoved me back a step with a growl. "I pick my own fate."

"Tell anyone about this, Wilder, and I'll have you castrated," Ethan snarled behind me.

I whirled around with a crazy as fuck smile that didn't even unsettle the bastard. I'd had bigger men than him cowering when I looked at them like that and it quietly earned him a few more respect points from me. It also made me want to force him to heel.

"You're starting to sound like a broken record, Ethan," I said with an eye roll. "I'm not going to tell anyone."

"You'd better not," he hissed.

"*If*," I added, letting that word hang in the air like an oncoming storm.

"If what?" Rosalie asked, sounding like she didn't really care whether I told anyone or not. And that shit intrigued me like a horse who'd just found out his mother was a swan called Deborah.

"If…" I smirked. "I get a pet Wolf for my troubles."

Ethan's upper lip peeled back and Rosalie growled low in the back of her throat.

"What exactly is that supposed to mean?" she demanded. "I'm no one's pet, and frankly you can go tell the whole prison for all I care." She started forward but I pressed a hand to her tits to stop her. She shoved my hand away with her lips pursed and I gave her an innocent smile.

"No," Ethan said simply. "She's mine."

"I'm not yours," Rosalie replied immediately.

"The moon chose you for me," Ethan growled.

"Then why don't you go tell your pack who your mate is, Ethekins?" I asked sweetly and he glowered at me while Rosalie smirked at him.

"What do you want from her?" Ethan demanded.

I laughed sinisterly. "I'd never try to tame my wild girl. I want to collar and leash the other big bad Wolf in this prison."

Ethan's eyes darkened and he stepped forward into my breathing space, the scent of a hurricane hanging around him. "I'd die before I was owned."

"That's a shame, because I have *really* loose lips and I can see this secret spreading through the entire prison before the day is out." I feigned my horror at the idea. "What will your pack think? I think they'll do more than stop sucking your cock, don't you? By the stars, they could even outcast you for something like this, kitten." I tipped my chin up to emphasis my half a centimetre of height on him and his jaw ticked with rage.

He finally opened his mouth to respond and a Wolf inked on his arm appeared to snarl at me as his muscles flexed. "I won't be made into anyone's bitch in front of my pack."

"No…you'll do it in private though." I grinned and I swear a breath of laughter escaped Rosalie. I reached out, petting Ethan's hair before locking my fingers into it, making him growl. "If I need something then you get it for me, understand?"

He shoved me off of him, clearly working hard not to fight me. "Fine, asshole."

I caught Rosalie's hand, twirling her under it and yanking her against my hip. "And that goes for her too."

Ethan glared at me, testosterone burning through the air between us so fiercely I was surprised I couldn't taste his man fumes in my mouth.

"Fine," he bit out.

"You know, there is something I need actually," Rosalie said, amusement sparkling in her eyes.

"What's that, kitten?" I purred, sliding my arm around her waist.

She leaned forward between us, beckoning Ethan closer and he bent his head to hear her whisper. "Nepula Weed."

My eyebrows arched at the same time Ethan's did.

"What for?" we asked in unison, but Rosalie mimed zipping her lips.

I clapped Ethan on the arm hard enough to leave a mark. "The next time we're in the Order Yard, leave your pack and meet me by the Fortune Pond."

"Even if it grows there-" Ethan started.

"It does grow there, I've seen it," I spoke over him.

"It's poisonous to touch and even if we could get some out of the pond, there's no way to get it past the guards on the way back into the prison." Ethan folded his arms.

"We just need to think outside the box," I echoed Rosalie's words from the first time we'd met and she smiled.

"I'll leave it to you guys then," she said with an angelic look. She played innocent so well, it almost convinced me at times. But I saw the beast living beneath her eyes and she saw the beast in me looking right back. And those dark creatures were destined to meet in the flesh one day soon.

"See you in the yard, Ethan," I said as I turned toward him sharply, catching him off guard as I slammed my mouth to his. He threw me away half a heartbeat later and I roared a laugh as he wiped his mouth in anger. A kiss from me was a threat as often as it was an invitation. And he knew exactly which one I'd given him.

Rosalie looked between us in surprise and I tipped an invisible hat to her before pivoting away from them and heading toward the exit. I had Ethan Shadowbrook's secret in my grasp. And for now, the bitch was mine.

I waited by the Fortune Pond in the Order Yard as rain rushed down around me. I'd scared off the Sirens and Heptian Toads so the place was reserved just for me. Ethan was taking his sweet time to arrive so I took the opportunity to strip down naked and wade out into the circular pool. Raindrops sent ripples out around me in every direction and I bathed in the moment of calm. I had a ziplock bag stashed under my tongue courtesy of a job on the Veiled Wall and a plan was locked down in my mind.

I swam to the centre of the pool, turning to float on my back and stare up at the dark clouds swirling beneath the dome. It was magically created, the weather in here constantly changing to suit the various Order forms. Heptian Toads needed the rain to regenerate their magic and I was more than happy to enjoy it too, the splashes against my cheeks reminding me of how long I'd been in the dark.

"Wilder!" Ethan's voice carried to me and I shifted upright to tread water as he approached the pool butt naked.

He swam out to join me with a scowl on his face. "Let's get this done, shitbag. Are you going down or am I?"

I took the plastic bag from my mouth with a smirk. "You look like a guy who's not so used to going down. Maybe you need the practise." I held out the bag for him and his eyes narrowed.

"At least I get laid by my own virtue, Wilder, I don't rely on my Order gifts to get a fuck out of anyone." He snatched the bag from my fingers and I tried to ignore the sting of truth in his words.

"Off you go," I snarled and Ethan took a breath before diving under the surface.

I swam back to the edge of the pond, leaving him to it as I pulled on my clothes and accepted they were going to be wet as shit when I returned to the prison.

Ethan finally resurfaced, heading out of the water to join me with a blade of Nepula Weed in the clear bag. "Now what, asshole? If one of us swallows this and that weed leaks out of the bag, we're fucked."

"That's why you have to put it up your butt," I said casually, tying my open jumpsuit around my waist.

"I'm not putting anything up my ass," he scoffed. "You can do it." He held out the bag and I ignored it.

"I can't, that's why I invited you along, pretty boy. They still strip search me after every yard session because I'm a 'high risk' inmate." I air quoted the words which were a total lie.

Ethan's jaw locked as he glared at me. "I'm not doing it."

I strode forward with a sideways smile, holding out my hand. "Give it here then."

He passed it to me, his shoulders visibly relaxing just before I whirled him around, intending to do it myself.

"Hey motherfucker!" he barked, trying to fight me off.

"I'll just use my little finger," I insisted as he twisted sharply and slammed his knuckles into the side of my head, making my ear ring with the impact.

I stumbled back before coming at him again, throwing my full weight against him. His leg caught on a log and we tumbled to the ground so I fell on top of him in the mud.

"Wilder!" he roared as I sat on his back.

"Just the pinky," I promised.

Movement in my periphery made me look up and I found an Experian Deer Shifter staring at us with wide eyes, her mouth parted so a pile of half chewed grass hung out of it.

I started laughing and Ethan threw an elbow back, catching me in the gut. I wheezed as pain splintered through me and he shoved me off, leaping to his feet and slamming the heel of his foot into my side. The deer scampered off into the woods in horror and my laughter continued as I got to my feet and Ethan swung a fist at me again. I avoided it, stepping back and raising my hands in innocence.

"You have to swallow it then," I said with a shrug. "There's only a ninety one percent chance you'll die."

"Fuck off," he growled. "*You* swallow it."

"Alright," I sighed, folding up the bag as small as I could in my palm. "I'll just tell Rosalie what I risked for her and get all the glory. I bet she'll be *real* grateful. The last time I agreed to help her I got a sexy as fuck kiss for it, I wonder what she'll give me this time…"

I tilted my head back, preparing to swallow that down like a baby bird would a worm, but Ethan suddenly locked a hand around my throat and plucked the bag from my fingers.

"One day, Wilder, you're gonna get yours in here. You're gonna be found alone and bloody in your cell and no one will remember you ever existed." He pushed me back a step, turning and heading into the woods while I grinned after him.

"You're gonna put it up your butt, aren't you?!" I called after him. "Aren't you!?" I shouted louder when he didn't respond.

It wasn't long before the fifteen minute warning flashed up on the timer high above the forest and I made my way back to the elevators soaking fucking wet, coated in mud and as smug as a cow in a three piece suit.

I spotted Ethan filing into an elevator with his pack and I caught his eye. I made a circle with my index finger and thumb then pushed my other index finger into it with a raised eyebrow. He answered by lifting his own finger and running it across his throat.

A grin bit into my cheeks as I headed into another elevator.

It's totally up his butt.

ROSALIE

PRISONER #12

CHAPTER TWENTY NINE

There was something about being an apex predator which meant that I was always supremely aware of my surroundings. Specifically of the other creatures in close proximity to me. I'd asked my cousins about it once while I was still growing into my nature and they'd all cocked their little puppy dog heads at me like I was insane. So I'd dropped it.

Maybe it was one of my mythical Moon Wolf powers. There were rumoured to be as many of them as there were faces of the moon, but I still had no idea what most of them were. I was a rare breed of a common Order. Special. But not special enough for anyone to have done too much research into. The only books I'd ever come across which mentioned the powers of a Moon Wolf had been Children's fairy tales. And as much as the idea of me granting wishes while looking into a still pool of water with the full moon reflected on it sounded cool, it was also bullshit. I'd spent fifteen separate full moons trying that shit for my cousins and it didn't work. They still liked to suggest I *wish for it* any time I wanted something too. And that joke got old ten years ago.

I also didn't have the ability to run across the sky or put myself into an un-ageing slumber for years at a time like the Moon Wolf in the fairy tales.

The few gifts I *had* discovered were pretty cool in their own ways, though none were so magical as the stories. For example, I could run faster than any other Wolf I knew, I was stronger and more agile too, though that *could* be down to my overall fitness. But I couldn't explain away my sharper senses without assuming they were additional gifts. In fact, I had an uncanny ability to sense trouble before it hit. It was like a shiver that would run down my spine, instincts screaming at me to buck the hell up and take note just before the shit hit the fan. Not just sometimes. *Every* time. Even when there were zero warning signs. If shit was gonna go down, I was always ready for it. It was just a shame I only got the sense for it a few moments before it happened instead of a few hours, but I'd still take it.

So, despite the fact that none of my Werewolf cousins had ever experienced the awareness which I could claim of my surroundings, I'd learned not to doubt the knowledge those gifts gave me. But I *was* surprised that I was still able to access what I'd termed fondly as my ultra-wolf instincts in the main prison considering that the Order Suppressant was keeping my inner beast firmly chained down. But perhaps that was looking at it too literally. Sin may not have been able to shift into the form of another Fae while his powers were locked down, but he still oozed sex with every move he made. Our Orders were more than just some power we wielded: they were *us*. Which I guessed meant that despite my Wolf's currently subdued state, I was still all animal. And I wasn't going to complain about that.

And as such, I was always acutely aware of any threat which came too close to me. A threat, like the eyes of another monster honing in on me while I ate. Especially when that particular monster was growing so damn fond of watching me.

It was tempting to look up at my favourite guard and let him know that I'd caught him, but it was more tempting still for me to put on a show if he was so inclined to watch.

I placed my spoon down as I finished my little pot of vanilla pudding and reached into it with my fingers to wipe the last of the sugary goodness from it. While my finger was in the pot, I made sure to crack the bottom open so that I could access the little square of magically imbued plastic for Pudding too.

I raised my sticky finger to my lips and pushed it into my mouth, drawing it out again slowly as my eyes fell closed and I moaned in a way that was really damn sexual.

"Mmm…" I groaned enthusiastically. "Mmmason…" My eyes snapped open and I trained them on Cain as he raised his chin and tried not to react to what he'd just snooped on. As I'd guessed, his gaze was fixed on me and with his Vampire bat ears I was sure he'd heard the way I'd just moaned his name beneath my breath too.

His jaw ticked angrily, but with the clamour of voices in the Mess Hall and the game of sucker punch my pack were currently enthralled in, I was confident no one else had heard me. He still looked angry enough to spit though. Poor guy really needed to get laid.

I held his eye and slowly ran my tongue up the length of my finger as he damn near snarled. Was that lust or hate? Though in all honesty those lines were easy to blur and I was willing to bet he wanted to blur them real good.

A group of convicts passed between us, blocking my view of him and I quickly dropped my gaze, moving the pudding pot to my lap so that I could retrieve the magical chip from it. I caught my Beta's eye and pretended I'd never even looked over at Cain at all.

"Can you help me out with something, Sonny?" I asked in my sweetest voice.

I could feel Cain's eyes on me again but I tossed my hair innocently, pretending that nothing at all had just passed between us while I could practically hear his teeth grinding as he glared at me.

"Anything, Alpha," Sonny agreed, knocking Brett's hand off of his thigh as he gave me his full attention.

"I need help locating some Mernwood essence and I heard a rumour they use it in the laundry where you work?" Mernwood essence was one of those hippy juice cure-all bullshit things that moronic Fae liked to attribute magical powers to. That particular herb was said to be a terrific libido enhancer and I certainly had no need for it, but if Mr Nosy Asshole wanted to spy on me then I was happy for him to hear all kinds of nonsensical shit. That way, if he happened to hear me asking for help with one of the real ingredients I needed to neutralise the Order Suppressant then it was all the more likely that he'd dismiss it as more crap. Hopefully. I was already certain that I'd gotten away with obtaining the Nepula Weed from Ethan and Sin and it was currently stashed in my wall where no nosey Vampires could find it. I just had to be sure that he couldn't figure out what I was making.

"Yes, Alpha," Sonny agreed with a dirty grin. Brett started kissing his neck and Sonny's dark eyes hooded with pleasure, letting me know exactly where they'd all be heading after this. "Are you gonna come and join us for some pack fun once you've got it?"

Several of my other Wolves all looked up hopefully at that and Esme even popped open a few buttons to give me a look at her rack. And good on Esme, she had some pretty spectacular boobs, but even with those buoyancy aids included, the idea just didn't float my boat.

"Sorry guys," I said with a small shrug. "But I prefer to be thrown around in the bedroom and there aren't many people who can match me like that." Certainly not any of my underdogs.

Alphas are more my flavour, and there does happen to be more than one of them in this place though...

My Wolves all whimpered a little in disappointment and busty Esme even let out a soft howl.

I snorted a laugh and Sonny leaned closer conspiratorially. "So have you found anyone in here to give you what you crave, Alpha?" he teased, though the hunger in his eyes said he really wanted to know. It was the job of a Wolf pack to ensure their Alpha was satisfied in every way, so I guessed it was causing them concern to think of poor little Rosa all alone in my cell at night burning up with sexual frustration.

"I've managed to hunt down a candidate or two," I assured him.

I flicked my gaze to Cain and sure enough at the mention of the word *hunt* the intensity of his gaze had upped considerably. There was an Alpha who might be able to give me what I needed, assuming he even knew how to loosen up. But I was willing to bet a real monster was waiting to be unleashed beneath that uniform and I'd had more than a few fantasies about setting it loose recently.

More convicts were leaving their positions around the room and I stood too, leaving my pack to clear my tray away and palming the little magical chip from my pudding pot.

I set my gaze straight on Cain as I began to weave across the room towards him, twisting a finger around a lock of my long, black hair. His eyes narrowed and I bit into my bottom lip as I kept going, closing in on him with each step.

Ethan left his table and his pack instantly stood to follow him as he headed for the exit.

My mate's gaze cut to mine as I drew closer and his jaw tightened as he looked me over for a long moment. I winked at him and a snarl of warning escaped his lips which only served to draw a laugh from me.

The pack blocked Cain's view of me as they surged by and I changed course, passing Pudding and dropping the chip into his pocket. The rest of my pack would deliver their chips to him throughout the evening and as a sweetener to our deal, his brother on the outside was going to meet up with Dante and help him construct the receiver he needed to make our contact possible. Within another week or so I should be able to make private calls to him regularly and my plans would be able to progress even faster.

Pudding grunted as I turned away from him which I took to mean thanks and I moved towards Sin's table.

He sat in the centre of it, eating mashed potato like it was going to run off of his plate if he didn't hurry up. I smirked as I closed in on him.

I approached from behind and Sin's broad muscles tensed like he could sense a Wolf at his back.

Before he got the chance to turn towards me, I hopped up onto the table, my ass taking the spot beside his tray as I rested my feet on the bench.

Sin twisted sharply, one hand gripping my knee to keep me in place as a plastic fork pressed against my stomach with his thumb bracing it so that it wouldn't snap.

Death by disposable cutlery, now that really would be tragic.

Sin looked up at me in surprise as he stayed his hand and I growled softly to warn him back.

"You shouldn't sneak up on a man while he's eating, kitten," he said, shifting the hand with the fork so that it slipped between the open buttons of my jumpsuit and the plastic prongs dug into the flesh below my navel.

"Are you going to fork me, Sin?" I asked, leaning forward so that his funny little weapon dug in a bit more as I reached out to wipe an imaginary crumb from the corner of his lips.

He shifted suddenly, drawing my thumb into his mouth and sucking on it. "I could fork you all day long, sugar. I might even spoon you a bit too."

"Does your lust generally make you sloppy or am I special in that regard?" I purred, leaning closer to him so that my hair cascaded over my shoulder, shielding us from the world.

"Sloppy?" he asked with a frown.

"Yeah...I mean, a fork to the gut would hurt like a bitch and all. But I've gotta think I'm winning with a knife to your jugular." I shifted my other hand so that the plastic knife scraped along the stubble at his throat to draw his attention to it and his smile widened with excitement.

"Well, shit," he purred. "Looks like I'm done for. You wanna grant a dying man a final request?"

"Un desiderio prima di morire?" I teased. *A death wish?*

"Fuck, keep talking like that and I'll come in my pants without you even needing to touch it," he said with an exaggerated groan.

My smile grew as I looked into his dark eyes. "That doesn't sound like I'd be getting a lot out of the exchange."

"How about I bargain for my life then? I'll pay a ransom in orgasms. I can give you one before you leave this table as a down payment and no one would even notice...aside from the fact that you'd be screaming my name loud enough to rock the foundations of this underground hell of course."

"Perché dovrei fidarmi di un uomo in punto di morte?" I breathed, shifting even closer to him so that the space between our lips was reduced to almost nothing. *Why should I trust a dead man?*

Sin opened his mouth to reply just as a bang shook through the table.

I looked up to find Officer Cain standing over us, his baton in his hand from using it to strike the table.

"Am I going to have to put you back in the hole for trying to stab someone with a fork, Eighty Eight?" he demanded, glaring at Sin.

"No one's stabbing anyone," Sin replied casually, easing the fork away from my stomach and tossing it on the floor with a clatter. "This is just foreplay."

A smile tugged at my lips as I drew back too, tossing the plastic knife aside as I looked up at Cain with my most innocent expression.

"Poor Sin just looked so lonely over here all by himself," I said. "I thought he might like a new friend."

"Eighty Eight doesn't have friends because he is immensely unlikable," Cain growled.

"I have friends," Sin replied, clutching at his heart like he was mortally wounded by Cain's words. "What about Alf?"

"If you're referring to Ninety Six then you know full well that he's dead. Someone beat the shit out of him and drowned him in a toilet before writing the words *don't fuck with my pencils* on the walls in his blood," Cain snapped.

"That does sound familiar, now you mention it," Sin said thoughtfully.

"It was the same day that you were reprimanded for hoarding all of the pencils in the library so that you could build a nest out of them," Cain growled.

"It was a wigwam – side note, pencils aren't great for building wigwams." Sin sighed like that was supremely disappointing and I laughed.

"Fuck off, Eighty Eight. Work assignments are starting and as you don't qualify for a job, you need to get back to sitting in your cell and staring at the walls." Cain pointed towards the door with his baton and I glanced around as the rest of the convicts filed out of the room.

"I've had a lot of practice staring at walls," Sin replied casually as he got to his feet, his gaze sliding over me hungrily. "And luckily for me, my little wild girl has given me plenty of fantasy ammo to keep my imagination busy."

I laughed again and Cain growled, giving Sin a shove to get him walking.

He swaggered from the room, looking casual as fuck and I let my eyes wander over his broad frame as he walked away.

Cain slammed his baton down on the table beside me again to draw my attention back to him and I flinched as I turned to look up at him innocently.

"You'll keep away from Eighty Eight if you know what's good for you, Twelve," he growled. "People who get close to him have an unfortunate habit of ending up in body bags."

His dark hair had been cropped closer on the sides and the product he'd slicked through the top of it kept the style in perfect position. The closer cut brought the strength of his features into sharper focus and I found myself smiling as I appreciated it.

"Have you had your hair done, sir?" I asked as my gaze travelled over him. "It looks good."

His eyes lit with anger and he stowed his baton back on his belt as he glared at me. "You seem to have a problem with your ears, Twelve. Did you listen to what I just said?"

"Yeah… You're jealous of me hanging out with Sin."

His lip pulled back and I eyed his white teeth, wondering how much it would take to draw his fangs out to play.

"The day I'm jealous of an inmate will be a cold day in hell. I'm just being a good C.O. Eighty Eight is only after one thing from you. Once he's had it, he'll cut you up and dump you in a trash heap alongside the rest of his corpses."

I nodded thoughtfully as I looked up at him, gripping the edge of the table with both of my hands as I leaned forward. The angle offered him the perfect view down my shirt, but he kept the stick firmly up his ass as he refused to fall for the bait. "The thing is, Sin may only be after one thing... But so am *I.* So unless you know anyone else who wants to help me scratch that itch, I might just find out why everyone makes such a fuss about Incubuses."

Cain growled but he dropped the subject, refusing to get pulled any further into my net. He reached out and grabbed my arm and I *accidentally* lost my footing as he pulled me from the table, stumbling into him and resting my hand on his chest. He stepped back instantly, his growl deepening and sending a shiver down my spine.

"Vuoi inseguirmi, Vampiro?" I breathed. *Do you want to chase me, Vampire?*

I was pretty sure he had enough grasp on my language to understand the offer and the way his eyes lit made me certain of it.

"You're late for work," he snarled. "You're cleaning down on the maintenance level again today."

I bet I am.

Cain hadn't brought me back down there since the last time he'd lost control and bitten me. I was pretty sure he'd been meaning to stop our little arrangement since I'd threatened to tell the Warden all about it if he sent me to interrogation. But seduction was one of my specialities and I knew he was running out of excuses to stop himself from taking what he wanted from me. I'd have to be careful down there now though, he was on to me and I couldn't afford to let him figure out my plans.

I wasn't ready to make any moves down on Maintenance anyway and after Sin had interrupted me and Ethan the other day, I was more than a little in need of something to get my blood pumping. If that meant playing chase with a dark and dangerous hunter then I was prepared to make that sacrifice.

"Get moving, inmate, or I'll write you up on an infraction." Cain gave me a not so gentle push and I smirked at him before trotting ahead and making my way to the doors.

We headed for the staircase where the distant echoes of other inmates' feet moved away from us as they either headed to their jobs or went back to their cell blocks.

I hesitated on the top step and turned to Cain, placing my hand on his chest to halt him. He snarled at me in warning but I just shifted closer, tilting my head so that my hair slid away from my neck.

My fingertips were pressed against his black shirt right above his heart and I felt the strength of his desire in the way it pounded for me.

"Why don't you give me a head start?" I suggested in a low voice. "There's no cameras on the stairs, right?"

His eyes lit with that dark hunger again and I shifted a little closer, sliding my hand up his chest.

"Maintain your distance, inmate," he growled.

"How much distance?" I breathed, moving closer so that my chest brushed against his and I had to tip my head back to look up at him.

Cain growled and adrenaline trickled through my limbs. I knew I should have been afraid of him, but I was mostly excited by his anger. I *really* wanted to see him when he let go entirely. A beast like him didn't belong on a leash and that was what the rules of his job were. They were caging his true nature and I wanted to set him free.

"A *lot* of distance," he snarled. "You should probably run."

A wide smile pulled at my lips as I looked into his eyes, the heat of his fire magic dancing in their swirling grey depths.

"Give me a ten second head start and don't use your gifted speed," I murmured.

"Why?"

"Because you'll catch me too easily with it and that's not really the point, is it?" I challenged.

"No promises," he growled and my smile widened.

"Start counting then." I backed up and he locked his jaw, refusing to play along.

I laughed as I turned away from him and ran down the stairs. My heart pounded with the game as I raced down flight after flight, gripping the handrail and swinging myself around on each level before racing down again.

I laughed as I ran, adrenaline flooding my limbs as I raced on and on. Cain's heavy footsteps soon pounded after me on the levels above. I glanced up between the railings just as he looked down and the hunger in his eyes had my heart thumping harder as I was captured in his gaze.

I gasped and ran faster, my footsteps and heavy breathing blocking out all other sounds. I kept going, feeling Cain drawing closer behind me with every step.

But it wasn't in my nature to run from a fight and the Alpha in me was begging to turn and meet him.

As I made it down to level nine, I rounded the steps and pressed my back to the wall as his pounding footsteps drew closer.

Cain rounded the corner and I snarled as I leapt at him, my shoulder colliding with his chest as I aimed to knock him from his feet.

A bark of laughter escaped him and he absorbed my blow like a pro, whirling us around to make use of my momentum as he grabbed my arm and twisted me away from him.

I stumbled back but before I could leap at him again, he shot forward with his gifts, catching hold of my waist and lifting me clean off of my feet before slamming me back against the wall.

His gaze met mine as he bared his fangs and I growled right back at him. His hips pinned me in place and I wound my legs around his waist, locking my ankles behind his back and pulling him closer.

He snarled hungrily and I panted in his arms for several seconds before tilting my head aside to give him access to my neck.

Cain groaned with undisguised lust as he lunged at me and I cried out as his fangs pierced my flesh. His body crushed me against the wall and I arched my back to press my breasts against his chest as he fed, reaching out to run my hands over his muscular body.

He caught my wrists with another flash of speed and slammed them against the wall either side of my head as his body continued to press against mine.

I moaned at the heady feeling of him drawing my blood and magic from my body, shifting my hips so that the firm ridge of his dick ground between my thighs.

"Di Più," I demanded breathlessly. *More.*

Cain groaned against my neck as he shifted between my thighs, grinding against me, sending flames of desire racing through my flesh.

I flexed against his grip on my wrists, wanting to touch him, to explore his broad frame but he wouldn't relent, using his gifts to keep me immobilised at his mercy.

Footsteps sounded behind us and Cain stilled, pulling his fangs from my neck and dropping me suddenly so that my legs fell from his waist.

My blood stained the corner of his mouth and he glared at me in a clear warning to keep my mouth shut.

"Erm, sir?" Hastings' voice came from behind him and I offered him the dirtiest smile in my arsenal before dropping my gaze to the huge bulge in his pants.

"If you try to run from an Officer again, you'll get more than a bite for it, Twelve. Do you want to spend a week in the hole?" Cain snarled at me.

"No, sir," I said in my most innocent voice, biting my bottom lip.

He growled at me in warning before snatching my arms in his grip and spinning me around so that my back was to him and my wrists were pinned at the base of my spine. He whirled us to face his colleague and I fought a smirk, knowing full well why he was holding me in front of him like that. I couldn't say I'd ever been used as a boner shield before, but it was pretty damn hilarious.

I pouted as I looked up at Hasting and he cleared his throat uncomfortably. I was willing to bet he'd noticed the way my legs had been wrapped around his boss's waist as he damn near screwed me up against that wall, but my choir boy didn't have the balls to mention it. I guess Officer Cain had been too deep in the bloodlust and plain old flesh lust to listen out with his bat ears for anyone sneaking up on us.

"What is it?" Cain demanded angrily.

I flexed my fingers and brushed them down the hard length of his erection behind me and his grip tightened in what could have been a warning for me to stop or just plain shock.

"Warden Pike has decided to change the Order Yard time to now," he said. "Just a heads up, before-"

A distant bell started ringing and I couldn't help but smile at the announcement of Order time. We'd only been up there yesterday evening and it was never a guarantee that we'd get to go again the following day.

"I'll escort Twelve up then," Cain announced.

"Are you going to heal this shit on my neck?" I asked petulantly as Cain twisted me away from his colleague and shoved me towards the stairs.

Hastings watched us go with a look on his face which said he almost wanted to say something, but he turned and hurried away again without a word.

Poor little choir boy, afraid of the big bad Vampire.

As soon as he was gone, Cain hoisted me off of my feet and shot to the top of the stairs toward the elevators that led to the Order Yard. He spun me to face him before we left the stairwell where the cameras couldn't see us and leaned down to glare at me.

"I already told you, I can be a *really* good friend to you, Officer," I purred

334

as I looked up into his eyes.

"We aren't friends," he snapped. "I'm your guard and you're my blood bag."

"Do you get a hard on for everyone you bite, or am I special?" I asked, drawing closer to him.

He pushed me back a step so that my spine hit the wall and his palms landed against the bricks on either side of my head as he stooped down to glare at me.

"You're not *special*, Twelve. You're a number. And a means to an end. Don't go thinking this is about anything aside from how powerful your blood is."

Instead of cowering like he wanted, I shifted closer, so close that our breaths mingled and my mouth was just a tip of his head away from a kiss.

"You don't need to keep warning me, Mason," I said, my blood heating from the way his eyes flashed with rage at the sound of his name in my mouth. "But next time we play your game, maybe we should do it somewhere really private. Just in case you're tempted to break a few more rules?"

"You're deluded if you think I'd ever fuck an inmate."

"Okay," I replied innocently, my gaze dropping to the bulge in his pants.

Footsteps were pounding closer as the rest of the convicts made their way up to join us.

Cain snarled as he backed away from me, not so subtly rearranging his dick to try and hide his arousal from everyone else.

I was *super* convinced that he didn't desire me beyond my blood.

He pointed towards the elevators and I slipped away from him without another word, waiting for the doors to open.

Cain turned away from me with his jaw ticking and I couldn't help but smirk to myself. He clearly thought he was still in charge of this situation, but I was taking the reins from him inch by inch and he'd be my own personal pack mule before he even realised it had happened.

The other convicts began to appear and I found myself surrounded by the inmates from Cell Block B. My pack started to arrive but Sin made a beeline for me as soon as he appeared, snarling at them to warn them back. I offered a smile to let them know it was fine and set my gaze on the Incubus as he approached me.

"I've got a surprise for you when we get up there, wild girl," Sin said in a deep voice that had me trailing my eyes over his muscular frame.

I seriously had no idea why he'd ever make use of his shape shifting powers from the point of view of getting people to lust after him. The guy *was* lust, his voice alone had my stomach writhing with excitement and the few times he'd touched me, my flesh had come alive for him. Not to mention the fact that he looked like a Demigod poured into a slice of I'm-gonna-have-double-of-this.

He moved to tower over me and I raised my chin to hold his dark gaze.

"Is it your dick?" I asked. "Because you keep trying to give me that surprise and my answer hasn't changed." Although as my gaze trailed over him, I was beginning to wonder if I'd been right to make that decision.

Is it a full moon or something because I'm feeling way too hot today...

Still, I got the impression he'd never had to work for a girl before so this would be character building for him. And if he put up a good enough fight then I might even let my judgement slip at some point.

"Well, it does always surprise girls with just how big it is," he said thoughtfully. "But I've been working on something a little more to your specific tastes."

"Is that so?"

The elevators slid open all around us and I backed into the closest one. Sin stalked after me, his eyes alight with all kinds of dark promises and my pulse elevated as I wondered just what he was thinking.

Some of the other convicts began to follow us inside, but Sin growled in a low tone that had the hairs lifting along the back of my neck. He didn't even turn to look at them, didn't so much as raise a hand, just growled like a damn monster and sent a group of the world's most hardened criminals scuttling away like ants.

And *fuck* if that just didn't make him hotter.

"You're such an ass," I murmured as the doors slid closed, leaving us alone.

The Order Suppressant antidote fell over us and I sighed as my inner Wolf was released from her chains.

"Funny thing is," Sin began, stalking closer to me. "I can taste lust on the air all around you. Which must mean that you quite like me being an ass."

A smile blossomed on my lips and I inched closer like I was going to share a secret with him. "You might just be right," I breathed.

Sin's eyes lit with excitement at that revelation but before he could reply, the doors slid open and I ducked around him, jogging straight out into the building filled with lockers to deposit my clothes.

I kicked my boots off and shrugged out of my jumpsuit before Sin caught up to me again, knocking my locker door shut and leaning against it to halt my progress. I pouted at him as I stood in my white tank and black panties, waiting for him to move aside so I could get my Wolf on.

"I want to show you something before you shift and run off on me," he

336

rumbled, folding his muscular arms so that his tattoos stood out against his dark skin.

"And I want to shift and run off, so…"

"It'll take five minutes to show you. If you don't like it, you can run off to your heart's content."

"Thanks, but-" I shrieked as Sin lunged for me, scooping me off of my feet and throwing me over his shoulder like a sack of potatoes.

"Five minutes. You're gonna like it," he growled as he strode straight out of the building and into the jungle to the north side of the dome.

"Put me down!" I snarled, wriggling against his grip as I tried to figure out how to play this. I could absolutely fight my way out of his hold and give him a good kicking to teach him a lesson too, but that wouldn't really serve me well in the whole making friends tactic I was employing with him. But I also couldn't let him push me around. I wasn't going to get knocked off of my top spot by some peacocking sex addict.

"Shh, your complaints are killing the mood."

"Seriously, Sin, I don't wanna have to kick your head in but if that's what it takes to-" Sin's hand collided with my ass and I gasped in surprise as I clutched his broad shoulders. "Did you just *spank* me?" I snarled.

"Yeah. And you liked it, wild girl."

I opened my mouth to protest and he did it again. The gasp that escaped my lips that time had the hint of a moan to it and I cursed as I found myself half wanting him to do it again.

"That's not the point," I growled and Sin laughed.

"If you're into BDSM I can give you one hell of a party, especially with your earth magic to help us create a few things…"

A laugh burst from my lips too and I sagged forward as I gave up on fighting him. My hair swung back and forth beneath me in time with his steps and my gaze lingered on the curve of his ass which should *not* have looked that damn good in a prison jumpsuit.

The world suddenly flipped right way up again as Sin set me on my feet in a clearing surrounded by thick vegetation.

He smirked at me like a dog with a bone and I arched an eyebrow as I waited to find out what his surprise was.

"I'm not sure how much you know about my Order," he said slowly. "But basically, once I've read someone's deepest desire and taken on a skin, I can access it whenever I like."

"What does that mean?"

He smirked at me, running a hand over his face, but as he dropped it I found myself looking at Jason Mamoa instead of Sin.

I stepped back, cursing as I stared at him and he ran his hand over his face again, this time appearing as Dwayne Johnson.

"That's…insane," I said, shifting closer again and reaching up to touch his face.

It felt exactly like it should have, there was no way to tell it was an illusion. I'd known this coming in here but seeing it in the flesh was something else.

"Have your *bones* changed shape?" I asked as my brain tried to process exactly what I was seeing.

"I guess so. Never gave it much thought. Point is, it works." The moment he stopped speaking, his features shifted again and I found myself staring up at Ethan Shadowbrook. "Do you know how many members of his pack lust after this guy? It was too easy to get hold of his skin."

I withdrew my hands, frowning as Sin's words came out of Ethan's mouth. Hell, even his voice was Ethan's - but it wasn't him at the same time.

"This is too weird," I murmured, stepping back.

"Don't you like your surprise?" Sin asked cockily, hounding after me as I continued to retreat.

A fat silver beetle buzzed around my head and I batted it away.

"Change back," I said with a frown.

"I thought you were into the pretty boy?" Sin asked, giving me a smoulder. "Think about it this way, you can play out all of your fantasies about him with me and you won't be breaking any of your little pack rules. It's a win win."

"Ew," I held a hand up. "That's twisted. Besides, *I* make the pack rules so I can screw whoever the hell I like. And why would I want to be with you while you look like someone else?"

Sin growled menacingly, falling still in his advance and I realised that I'd just seriously insulted his entire Order.

"I just mean, I don't want a fake version of Ethan. Or a fake version of you. If I'm with someone I want to be with *them*. Not some fantasy version. Change back," I added, trying to fix my mistake.

Sin's/Ethan's brows lowered and he moved closer again. "Give me your hand."

"Why?"

He reached out and snatched it without asking again and I could feel the press of his gifts against my skin before he suddenly shifted back into himself.

I sighed with relief as I looked up at him but he only seemed to be getting more pissed at me.

"This is bullshit," he snarled, looking down at his own arms. "What are you doing to block my gifts?"

"I don't know what you mean."

338

"Well, unless the real me just so happens to be your perfect fucking fantasy, you must be doing something to stop me from getting a read on you. And as I can count the amount of times that I've been someone's ideal fantasy in my Fae form on a closed fist, I know for a fact that you're doing something to fuck with me."

"Sin, I have no idea what you're talking about-"

"Don't feed me that horse shit."

My lips popped open and I stared at him in surprise.

He lunged at me suddenly and gripped my upper arms as I felt his gifts brushing against my skin again.

"Stop it!" he demanded. "Sin, I promise you I'm not doing *anything*. Maybe you can't get a read on me because I'm not attracted to guys based on looks alone."

"What does that mean?"

"It means that half of what I look for in a guy is that he's a true alpha," I snapped, shaking his arms off of me. "And the other half might be looks, but my preferences for that change pretty regularly. I like variety. And for the record, when you're not being a total ass, I *do* happen to have fantasies about you just the way you are. So maybe you should stop doubting whether or not I prefer you as you, because if there's one thing I know I *don't* find attractive, it's pretty lies."

Sin stared at me for a long moment like he was trying to figure out whether or not he believed me.

"*Bullshit,*" he snarled eventually before turning and storming away.

My lips parted as I watched him go. Was he seriously pissed that I found him attractive as he was and didn't want him dressing up as anything else for me? What kind of sense did that make?

"Who'd have thought an Incubus would have such massive insecurities?" I yelled after him. "And for the record, pouting like a little bitch when things don't go your way isn't attractive either!"

Sin raised a hand above his head and flipped me off without looking back. The trees soon closed around him, swallowing him up and I grumbled to myself as I turned in the opposite direction.

Fucking idiota.

The silver beetle made a reappearance and I swatted at it angrily as a warning shiver raced down my spine. I wasn't worried about Sin lashing out though. He'd just have to get over himself.

I reached for the hem of my tank and made to pull it off. Before the material made it higher than my chest, the leaves before me parted and I snarled as I came face to face with Gustard.

My lips parted in horror as I spotted the single, huge eye in the centre of his forehead but before I could run the fuck away from him and his creepy Cyclops Order form, the power of his gifts slammed into me.

I cried out as I fell to my knees and the urge to vomit consumed me. I tried to fight back but without access to my magic, I couldn't keep my mental walls as strong as they needed to be to fight off his kind of power.

I gasped as I tried to summon the energy to call for help, but darkness was pressing in on me.

If he got beyond my mental defences then he'd be able to root around in my brain for anything he wanted. His power required him to hunt for specific answers but if he got into my head, I wouldn't be able to control what he found. He just had to be creative with the kinds of questions he asked in his search and I could give up everything. He might discover my plans to escape this place. Hell, he could find out every deep, dark and ugly thing there was to know about me given enough time to hunt.

My fingernails clawed the mud at my feet as I tried to fight him off but the darkness was closing in on me regardless and I couldn't tear my gaze away from his big fucking eye.

I bared my teeth and hissed a final curse which passed between my lips as oblivion came for me.

"I bet...you'd look really...fucking...stupid...with...*glasses...*"

I fell into a pit of darkness as he forced his way into my mind and all I could do was pray that he didn't find anything I needed to keep secret.

ETHAN

PRISONER #1

CHAPTER THIRTY

I pulled on my clothes by the elevators, stretching my arms above my head as satisfaction spread through me from running in my Wolf form. The timer on the wall dropped to fifteen minutes and I turned to my pack as they filed into one of the elevators.

Man, one day soon I was going to get out of this place and run in my Order form whenever I liked. The short time we got out here was never enough and as much as the magic in this fake landscape was powerful enough to feel real, it was still just an illusion of the outside world. One look up at the dome was all it took to remind me that I was in a cage. And for the past five years, I'd remained in it for something I didn't even do. Not that I regretted it. So long as I was in here taking the blame for my sister's crime, I was content enough.

Apart from anything else, Darkmore didn't take pregnancies lightly and she had just found out she was carrying her first pup the day I'd given myself up to the cops in her place. If you didn't perform the monthly contraception spell in the Magic Compound then that was on your head. But the fate of bearing a child in here was far worse than anyone would ever risk it for. The kid would be taken into the system the moment they were born and raised without knowledge of you or your family's existence. Convicts didn't have the right to parenthood. And there was no way in hell that I would have let my baby sister face that fate.

I just had to be grateful we weren't all sterilised upon processing, so at least when I left this stars-forsaken place in a couple of months, my junk would be intact and I could father an army of mini Ethans. Small wins and all.

"Come on Alpha!" Harper called from the elevator and I headed toward her, throwing a glance over my shoulder as some part of my soul sought out my mate. I hated that I was always looking for her. Every free space in my mind was taken up by Rosalie Oscura now. Which was why I always had to keep myself distracted.

"Hey, pretty boy," a voice caught my ear and I turned to find Gustard and his unFae band of fuckers moving toward one of the elevators. "You'll have less secrets to hide in a few minutes."

His gang sniggered as they filed into the elevator and I frowned, halting in the doorway as my instincts sent a sliver of ice down my spine.

I moved away from my pack, hounding after Gustard and my Wolves called after me in concern.

The elevator doors started to close and I caught them at the last second, forcing them wide as I glared in at Gustard.

"What the hell is that supposed to mean?" I demanded.

He gave me a creepy ass smile, stepping closer to me. "It means, you can repay me later when she's dead." He threw his hands into my chest, forcing me back a step and the doors slammed closed between us.

Panic crashed through my veins as my mind turned over what he was insinuating. The only secret I had to hide was Rosalie. And if Gustard had been with her, used his Order powers on her and sieved through her mind then that meant he *knew*.

"Alpha!" my Wolves called desperately. "We need to go!"

Elevators were closing all around me and panic was slicing my heart to shreds. I hadn't seen her come back, but I assumed I'd missed her. She often spent time away from her pack out here so they hadn't been worried. But was I really going to gamble my life on the chance that she was still out there somewhere?

I turned away from my pack, looking to the forest beyond the building as my pulse thumped solidly in the base of my skull.

"Alpha!" my Wolves begged.

I rounded on them, making a decision that must have been total fucking insanity. "Go!" I barked, using my Alpha tone so they all bowed their heads in compliance. Fear clutched their features as the doors closed and I turned around to face the exit, pulling my jumpsuit back off as I raced out of the building.

I dropped it to the ground and leapt forward, shifting into my huge black wolf form, my paws hitting the ground hard. The air whipped around me as I sped into the trees, throwing a cursory glance up at the timer as it dropped to twelve minutes. *Fuck a duck!*

I sprinted through the forest, sniffing the wind as I tried to catch any scent of her. The world was dipped in an ominous red glow as the entire dome turned red in warning and panic seared my insides.

I lifted my head and howled to the sky, my voice filled with concern that begged her to reply to me.

I strained my ears, but no sound came in response.

What if she's not out here? You're gonna kill yourself for a girl who tricked you into being her mate!

A snarl ripped from my throat as I powered on, forcing the thought away. Enemy or not, Rosalie was deep under my skin. She lived in my blood like another channel of magic and if there was even a single chance that she was out here, I had to find her. The mate bond would never let me get over her if she died. I'd pine until my heart was nothing but dust and I longed to follow her into the afterlife.

A howl caught my ear and I practically tumbled down a muddy hill as I tried to stop and listen for her. I came to a sharp halt at the bottom, twisting around as I listened for it again. The noise reached me once more, Rosalie's voice hoarse in her Fae form.

I doubled back through the trees before taking another path in the direction of her howl, lifting my head as the timer dropped to just seven minutes above me.

I soon broke into a clearing and found her on the ground, her hands braced in the mud as she heaved like she was going to cough up a lung.

I barked to let her know I was here, rushing to her side and shifting out of my Order form so I crashed to my knees beside her.

"You gotta move, love." I caught her waist, trying to pull her upright but she shook me off, retching once more, though nothing came out.

"Fucking…Cyclops," she wheezed.

Anger scored a line through my chest. Hell if I was going to let that bastard keep breathing for much longer.

I'd only been interrogated by one Cyclops in my life, but the sickness the mind invasion had left me with had been immobilising for several minutes. And we didn't have that time to spare.

A siren suddenly filled the dome as the timer hit five minutes and I growled in panic.

"Ride me," I commanded.

"Five minutes isn't much time for an end of days fuck, Ethan," she panted, pushing herself back onto her knees with a dazed smile.

"Dammit, Rosalie!" I snapped, turning away from her and shifting into my Wolf form.

I snapped my teeth at her and she tried to get up. I rushed forward, pressing my muzzle against her chest to help her and she made it to her feet. I lowered down so she could climb on and her fingers knotted in my fur as she pulled herself up.

I took off into the trees, my heart thrashing wildly as I carved a path in the direction of the elevators. Rosalie's arms slid around my neck as she held on tighter, her cheek resting against my fur as she placed her life in my hands. And I couldn't fucking fail her.

My heart knotted and my lungs laboured as I tore up the ground, feeling so horribly far away from safety that I feared it was already too late.

I threw a glance at the timer and found it sliding onto one minute. I pushed my body to its limits, weaving through the trees so fast they became nothing but a dark green blur on either side of us.

I finally broke out of the forest and the building became visible up on the hill. I howled in desperation as I charged toward it.

It was too fucking far. We weren't going to make it.

Rosalie's fingers tightened in my fur and I felt true fear in her grip as she clung to me.

"Ethan," she breathed in horror.

I growled, refusing to accept that this was it. That I couldn't save my mate. That I wasn't fast enough or strong enough. I was Ethan Shadowbrook, the most powerful Alpha Wolf in Solaria. And I would *not* fail.

The timer dipped to ten seconds just as my paws collided with the concrete floor of the long building. The air seemed harder to breathe already as I raced for the nearest elevator, all of them standing open, ready for anyone who was stupid enough to run this late.

The first doors slammed closed before I made it and I crashed into them, sending Rosalie flying from my back.

I wheeled around in terror as the elevators all started closing in succession.

Rosalie tried to get up, but her legs trembled violently beneath her. The air suddenly stopped flowing into my lungs and the world closed in around me.

I shifted out of my Order form, my lungs burning for air as I scooped Rosalie up, hugging her to my chest and racing past the closed doors of the elevators to the only one standing open at the far end of the building.

Rosalie gasped for air in my arms and I wished I had some to give her as my own body roared with need.

Blackness curtained my vision as I closed in on the final elevator, the doors sliding shut before my eyes.

No!

I used every last ounce of energy I had, leaping toward it and jamming my hand into the inch of space left between the doors. With a grunt of effort, I forced them wide and stumbled forward into the empty space. I hit the ground and Rosalie clutched onto me as the doors closed behind us and the elevator started to descend.

A hiss sounded as air was pumped in through the vent above and I gasped in relief as I breathed in the crispest lungful of oxygen I'd ever tasted. The subtle scent of the Order Suppressant tingled my senses and my Wolf was locked away deep within my chest.

I cupped Rosalie's cheek, forcing her to look up at me and wasn't remotely prepared when her lips collided with mine. I felt the heat of her flesh against my naked body like a fire had sparked beneath my skin. I wanted her like no other Wolf. Like no other Fae. I'd never craved a creature like this. She was chosen for me by the moon. My fucking perfect match. And yet who she was made it impossible for me to ever truly have her in front of the world and that tore me apart inside.

"Why did you come back for me?" she breathed as she broke the kiss.

I brushed my fingers up her neck until my thumb caressed the crescent moon behind her ear. "Because you're mine, love. Not even death can take you from me if I decide against it."

We reached the lower floor and I pushed Rosalie off of me, setting my jaw as I prepared to return to my cell, my pack, my life. She may have been mine, but only in secret. And even the moon couldn't force my hand in that.

The doors opened and two guards turned toward us in surprise. Officer Cain turned ashen pale as Officer Hastings rushed forward in alarm.

"Holy shit, you must have almost died," he exclaimed, sweeping a hand into his baby blonde locks.

"Almost," I agreed. "Unfortunately the Oscura bitch was fast enough to save her ass too."

"If you hadn't been staring at my tits for so long, you might have gotten back sooner, right Ethan?" she taunted and I ignored her, though my heart swelled at hearing the strength in her voice once more. She was power personified, but even she didn't stand a chance against Gustard and The Watchers when they united against an individual. It made my gut churn.

"Get him a new uniform and take him to his cell block," Cain commanded and Hastings took my arm as he nodded.

I glanced back as I walked away, frowning as Cain took hold of Rosalie's arm and a flash of healing magic flared under his touch. That Vampire was as hard skinned as a boulder, but for a moment he almost looked soft. It looked like my mate could sway even the moon to her favour if she wanted to. But if

347

she thought she could go around cosying up to any asshole she liked in here, she was dead wrong. I may have kept her as my dirty little secret, but I was a selfish fucker and when something was mine, it remained so. Indefinitely.

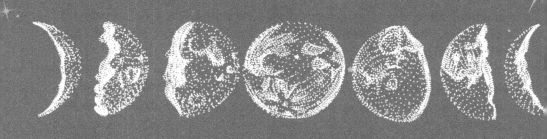

ROSALIE

PRISONER #12

CHAPTER THIRTY ONE

Time in the Magic Compound wasn't as precious to me as it used to be now that I could access my powers outside of this place, but I still had to make a show of using my earth magic all the same. Every other Fae in here would come and use up as much of their power as they could the second it was let loose, and it would look pretty damn suspicious if I didn't join in.

However, tonight, I really needed to get back into the vents and keep searching for a way out of the cell block levels. My last escapade had led me to the drainage pipe system which dove down to level five beneath the cells, but I hadn't had enough magic left in me to spend the time checking for sensors in the space between floors and I couldn't risk setting off any alarms. So I needed to have as much magic left in my veins as possible for later. Relying on running beneath the moon to replenish my magic was so frustrating. We only got out in the Order Yard five times a week and that meant two night shifts one week and three the next. Back home I could run every night to replenish my magic and hardly ever burned through my power. Here, I felt like I was in a constant struggle to replenish and keep a hold of it for when I needed it.

And today I couldn't afford to waste a drop.

I strolled across the Compound, ignoring the Veiled Wall and the Fae who were playing with the message carrying balls which constantly slammed against it.

I twisted my fingers in the simple patterns required for basic earth magic, but I didn't allow any of my power to flow forth and carry out the commands I was making. I had to be careful that no one noticed, so I was only faking casts with minimal effects like underground tremors.

"Tut, tut, tut, Rosalie Oscura can't even perform a basic spell, whatever would her Aunt Bianca think if she found out?" Roary's mocking voice carried to me and I looked up to find him sitting on a bench to the side of the Compound.

A few of his Shades lingered nearby but with nothing more than a slight flick of his fingers, they scattered.

I raised an eyebrow at him and his crazy control over his followers. His Charisma had to be stupid powerful for its effects to linger in them for so long while he was cut off from his Order gifts.

"What's the craziest thing you've ever convinced someone to do for you?" I asked him as I drifted closer, my gaze trailing over the way his long hair fell around his broad shoulders.

"They don't need convincing, they do things for me because they enjoy pleasing me," he said arrogantly.

I snorted a laugh and moved to sit beside him, my leg pressing against his as my inner Wolf took the reins and made me forget about personal boundaries for a moment.

He cut me a sidelong glance and I smirked as I nuzzled closer, refusing to back down like an embarrassed school girl now that I'd gone and done it.

"Do you wanna just climb into my lap, Rosa?" he teased.

"Well this bench *is* cold on my ass," I commented lightly.

"You might cause a Lioness riot if you do," he joked.

"Is that a challenge?"

Roary's golden eyes fixed on mine and a mischievous glint flashed in them as he leaned towards me. "*I bet you won't...*" he purred.

Gah that damn game!

"Be careful what you wish for, stronzo," I muttered, battling against the blush which was clawing at my cheeks.

I got to my feet and he looked up at me as he waited to see if I'd go through with the dare or not. The most infuriating thing was that on paper this should have been the simplest of dares that either of us had been given and yet as I stood before him, a dark tension crackled in the air.

This felt like standing up and yelling from the rooftops that I really did have a crush on Roary Night, and I half expected him to start laughing in my face the moment I did.

I internally snarled at myself as I hunted for my big girl balls and strapped them on tight. I was long past the days where this man could slay me with a single dismissive comment and puncture my heart with an amused smirk at my expense.

I wasn't a little girl with a crush anymore and it was past time Roary realised that too.

"You don't have to look so desperate for it, Roary," I mocked as I stepped towards him. "Anyone would think you haven't gotten laid in a long time."

"Is that so?" His gaze slid over me and I rolled my eyes as I stepped forward purposefully.

I wasn't just gonna perch in his lap like a little love struck pup. If he was going to go around making dares like that then he could suck up the full consequences of it.

I gripped his shoulders as I approached him, pushing him back so that he was forced to look up at me, his eyebrows raising as I dropped into his lap, straddling him in front of every stronzo in this place.

"Non dovresti sottovalutarmi, Roary," I purred. *You shouldn't underestimate me, Roary.*

He opened his mouth but I didn't give him a chance to respond, pushing my hands straight into his hair as I leaned forward like I might kiss him.

A growl escaped his lips but it wasn't the kind to warn me off, more the type to draw me closer.

His hands fell to my waist and he looked up at me for a moment that seemed to stretch as neither of us moved any closer.

My heart fluttered at the mere fact that I was even in this position after spending so many of my growing years daydreaming about things like this.

My fingers pushed deeper into his soft hair and his grip on my waist tightened like he was caught between dragging me closer and pushing me off.

"Rosa..." he said slowly and my jaw tightened as I felt yet another rejection hovering on his lips.

But fuck that. I refused to let him make me feel like a stupid little kid ever again.

"You need to work on your dares, Lion boy," I said with a snort of amusement before shoving off of him as quickly as I'd taken my seat.

I dropped down on the bench beside him again, leaving a nice healthy gap between us this time as I ignored the stares we were drawing from around the Compound. Two of the prisons gang leaders hooking up would definitely be worthy of gossip, but me and Roary Night were not worth discussing. He was just my *old* friend.

I snorted a laugh at my own joke and Roary cut me a look that said he hadn't quite decided whether to hit me with the *I'm friends with your cousin and far too old for you* horse shit or not.

"I was talking to Dante about some old family stories," I said casually before he could, like my heart wasn't racing from climbing on top of him like that and I didn't care about it at all.

"Oh yeah?" he asked, clearly deciding to give his tired routine a rest. Probably because the only thing I'd done was follow the dare he set out anyway. "My brother's been going on about a few old stories with me too actually. Maybe they think that if we dwell in the past together we can forget about what's going on in the present…"

I smirked at him as I tucked my legs up beneath me, meaning to swap the details of these so called memories which would hold more details about the way the ipump500 worked and therefore teach me how to fix my problem with the Order Suppressant.

But before either of us could say any more, a maniacal laugh interrupted us and I looked up in surprise as Sook ran across the yard in front of us.

As I watched, she dropped to the ground and started calling out.

"Sausage, sausage, I'm a sausage rolllll!"

She stuck her arms up above her head and began rolling across the concrete doing an impression of a sausage.

My lips parted in surprise as more than a few of the surrounding convicts started to laugh.

"What's she doing?" I asked, a smile twitching the corner of my mouth as she rolled away from us.

Roary didn't reply and I looked back to him, finding a frown pulling at his brow.

"What's up?" I asked in confusion because he seriously looked like someone had just taken a shit in his ice cream and I was left feeling like I was absolutely missing something.

"Exactly how much do you need a Polethius Mole Shifter to pull off your plan?" he asked me in a low tone.

"What?" I shifted closer to him as I caught on to the seriousness of his mood. "Why are you asking me that? Do you doubt her capabilities now that you know she likes to spend her down time playing sausage? Hell, I might like to play sausage from time to time, though my rules would be pretty different to hers, and-"

"This is serious, Rosa," Roary cut me off, catching my arm and drawing me to my feet as he pulled me away from the bench and headed to the back of the chamber.

He looked over to Claud, the leader of his Shades, and within moments we were shielded from the guards or any other nosey fuckers by a wall of his followers as he drew me into a corner.

"You're worrying me, Roar," I said, trying to keep my voice light as his gaze darkened and he threw a silencing bubble up around us to keep our conversation private.

"Sook has never acted like that before as far as I've seen and she's been in here six years." he said seriously.

I frowned as I considered his question. "You think she's losing the plot like that guy who Hastings tackled in the middle of the Mess Hall?" I asked with a frown. "I mean, she's just mucking about - he cracked harder than a teapot hitting concrete."

Roary didn't laugh which was ridiculous because that shit was funny.

"Yeah, he was in the last stage."

"The last stage of what?" I asked, the smile slipping from my face as I realised he wasn't joking.

"The guards call it *under stimulation.*"

"And what's that?"

"They say that some Fae can't take being cut off from their magic and Order forms as much as we are. As in, their minds can't take it. So they just lose the plot, start acting crazy and eventually they snap hard enough to pose a danger to themselves or the other inmates. After that, they're hauled off to Psych and never seen again." Roary looked around like he expected someone to be watching us through his wall of Shades.

"You think Sook is going to end up in Psych?" I asked anxiously, chewing on my thumbnail as I considered that.

"Undoubtedly."

For my plan to work I absolutely needed a Polethius Mole. There were only two in the entire Prison and I would only be asking Plunger along for the ride over my cold, rotting corpse. Which meant we needed Sook Min to keep her shit together.

"Alright, I'll go talk to her, see if I can coax her back from the brink of crazy and-"

"It won't matter," Roary growled. "I've seen people try and help Fae when they go Under before. Nothing works. Once they start showing symptoms it's only a matter of time before they're relocated to Psych."

I bit my tongue against a pointless argument with him over it. He'd been here a hell of a lot longer than me and if he said that that was what always happened then I was willing to take his word for it. "Then we need to hide her freak flag long enough for us to escape. Once she's free, she can get to her magic and Order form twenty four seven and she'll be fine. Problem solved."

"You aren't going to be able to hide her Under tendencies if she keeps up the sausage impersonations," Roary growled. "Not to mention what she'll do when she fully snaps."

"So what do you suggest, oh great and powerful convict king? Because I'm trying to come up with solutions and all you're doing is shitting on my parade like a pigeon with diarrhoea."

He didn't laugh at that either which was a fricking travesty and I rolled my eyes as I tried to think of some other way to stop Sook from being carted off to the crazy capital.

"So how come *you've* never gone Under then?" I asked casually, like we were chatting about the weather not suggesting he might lose control of his shit at any moment.

"That's another weird thing about the Fae who go Under," he muttered. "There's no rhyme nor reason to it that I can see. I've seen a guy get hauled off to Psych in his second week here for going Under but there are also bastards who had served a long sentence before I even showed my face here ten years ago and they're still swimming in the main tank. I don't get why some people snap after a few days, others a few weeks, months or even years. And some never snap at all. There's no pattern to it either. Young, old, Dragon, Siren, Harpy or Polethius Mole, it can strike anyone. And something about the whole thing just reeks of wrong to me."

"How so?"

"Well, for example no two people ever snap at once. They don't ever exhibit symptoms at the same time. We get one crazy at a time and once they're gone, that's it. Then maybe two weeks later, the show starts again. It's like some weird cycle that's a little too irregular to really be irregular."

"Merde," I cursed. "I need my Mole. I don't wanna lose her to Psych or anything else. Who else might know more about this Under stuff than you?" I demanded.

"No one. Well, none of the convicts anyway. Who knows what the guards know? They wouldn't tell us anyway so what's the point of asking?"

A smile tugged at my lips at that suggestion. "Well, they wouldn't tell *you...*"

"You think you've got enough sway on a guard to get answers from them?" Roary scoffed.

"Maybe," I replied slowly. "Only one way to be sure."

Roary shook his head at my ego, but I caught the smile hooking up his lips too.

"Go on then, oh mighty Oscura Queen," he challenged.

"Maybe I will. And in the meantime, *I bet you won't* lick Officer Lucius."

I left Roary with that challenge hanging in the air as he finally laughed and I turned away from him to find my little choir boy. I was sure it wouldn't be too hard to squeeze a little information from that wet cloth before he even realised what I was doing. Although, that said, Hastings was new here, almost as new as me and that probably meant he didn't know a whole hell of a lot about things that had been happening within the prison for years.

I moved towards the exit, my gaze skimming over the guards who were gathering beyond the magic proof glass which blocked our way out of here so that they could escort us to our work places once our session ended.

Cain was waiting out there already, ramrod straight with his hands clasped at the base of his spine as he scowled out at us. The other guards were chatting amongst themselves, smiling and laughing in their camaraderie. But not my dark souled Vampire, he stood separate from it, his gaze scouring the convicts like he was hunting for his next meal and as his eyes fell on me, they lit in a way which said he'd found it.

But if I expected to get any information out of my C.O. he was going to be a hell of a lot harder to crack than the choir boy.

Instead of holding his gaze with a provocative look like I usually would, I dropped my eyes and let my bottom lip slide into the barest hint of a pout.

I didn't stay before the glass either, but twisted my fingers into my hair nervously and released a soft whimper as I wandered away.

The first of my Wolves arrived within moments, a low whine escaping her lips as she raced towards me.

"Are you okay, Alpha?" Esme asked, reaching out to embrace me and I let her, enjoying the contact with another of my kind.

That was enough to draw the whole pack running and I sighed again as hands slid over my body and I was pulled from Fae to Fae as they all worked to comfort me against my mystery problem.

Sonny got hold of me and wouldn't let go, muttering curses as he tried to figure out what had me so upset.

Whispers and murmurs filled the air around me as they all asked what was wrong and made multiple guesses.

"I think she stubbed her toe."

"She broke up with Roary Night."

"She needs to get laid."

"She needs the moon."

"I'm going to get her more pillows for her bed."

"Let me sing her a song."

"She's missing home."

"I can give her a foot rub."

"She's sad she can't fix her hair nicely in here." *That one was rude.* I cuffed the offending Wolf around the ear and he had the good grace to look mortified as he scampered back with his tail between his legs.

Amira lingered amongst the pack, offering words of concern while managing to hold back. I had to force myself not to growl whenever I was in her presence and I turned my gaze away from her now. That bitch wouldn't know what hit her when I exposed her betrayal to the pack. But for now, I was biding my time. Revenge was a dish best served cold and I planned on serving hers up at sub zero.

The buzzer finally sounded to mark the end of our time in the Magic Compound and I stayed amongst my Wolf pack as they pressed closer still, desperate to soothe me.

I would have felt bad for causing them so much heartache if it wasn't so important that I did it.

The rest of the inmates all filed back inside to have their magic cut off and head for their cell blocks or jobs until finally, it was just me and my pack left.

Sonny kept trying to get me to confide in him, but I just shook him off with a sad whimper which made him howl in frustration.

I made them all leave ahead of me too and the guards ensured none of them waited for me on the other side either.

So when it was finally my turn to step through the first door and present my manacled wrists to the guard inside the booth, I raised my hands like an obedient little pup and let him cut off my access to my magic without a word of complaint.

The second door opened the moment my magic was secured and I headed out to find Cain waiting for me like I'd expected.

"Come on, Twelve, you've got work to do on Maintenance again today," he said, drawing closer like he expected me to resist in some way.

"Yes, sir," I murmured without looking at him before heading along the corridor towards the stairs.

His clipped steps soon joined mine and we walked side by side towards the lowest level of my underground tomb.

Cain was silent for a long time, but I could feel his curiosity and irritation rising the further we went.

It took everything I had not to start smirking as he slowly fell into my trap.

I waited as he unlocked the isolation unit doors and led me inside. We kept going, heading down the stairs to Maintenance until we were finally in the enormous room and the sounds of the whirring machinery filled the air.

"Spill it, Twelve, why do you look like someone just pissed on your grandma?" Cain snarled.

I kept my gaze on my feet and didn't answer him.

Cain growled menacingly. "I asked you a question, inmate."

I kept my lips sealed and he reached out to grab my chin, forcing my gaze up to meet his.

"You wouldn't give a shit anyway," I muttered, looking away from him again so that my eyes fixed on a point over his shoulder.

"Probably not. But you're still going to spill it."

I hesitated just long enough for him to know I was unsure. "I shouldn't be talking to a guard about this," I said eventually.

"I think by now, we've shared enough secrets for you to offer me one more," he pressed. "Besides, if you start bitching about the other inmates being mean to you, I'm not going to give a shit anyway. I certainly wouldn't do anything to help you."

"If only my problems were so simple," I muttered.

"Spill," he demanded.

I shook his grip from my chin and stepped back. "What do you know about the inmates they keep carting off to Psych?" I asked vaguely.

A fire lit in Cain's eyes and he shot forward, shoving me back against the closest wall as he looked at me like I'd just offered him some kind of gift.

"Tell me *everything,*" he insisted.

I shook my head, my heart pounding at the contact of his body with mine. "Why would you give a shit about what's happening to us anyway?" I hissed.

Cain snarled, leaning down to force my gaze to meet his again.

"Tell me what you know about this, Twelve."

"Why?"

An endless moment passed between us where I refused to speak another word and he glared at me.

"Maybe I've noticed some things about the inmates taken to Psych too," he said eventually in a low voice.

"Really?" I breathed, inching closer to him.

"Really. So why don't you tell me what you know and I'll give you the same curtesy?"

I looked at him for another long moment, mistrust filling my gaze as I held my tongue.

"Fine," Cain snarled eventually. "I'll tell you what I know first."

Jackpot.

"There's something strange about the way they do things down in Psych. They won't even let me inside and the only person who outranks me in this place is the Warden herself."

"So you think they're hiding something?" I asked carefully. If he caught on to me now then I'd never get anything else out of him.

"Why keep everything about it so secret if they don't have something to hide?" he muttered and I chewed on my lip as I thought about that.

"Maybe they're just trying to protect the privacy of the inmates down there…Or maybe they don't want people knowing that the things you subject us to in here make Fae snap," I suggested.

"What's that supposed to mean?" he growled.

"If the inmates are only losing their shit because we're cut off from our Orders and Magic too much then that doesn't exactly look good, does it? It kinda suggests we're maltreated."

Cain barked a laugh. "You don't get it, do you? You were sent here to rot. The rulers of Solaria don't give one shit about you. You're only lucky that executions were banned after The Savage King died. There was so much bloodshed during his reign that the people demanded an end to it, so the Celestial Councillors gave in. But that doesn't mean they suddenly started giving a shit about the scum of the earth murderers and rapists who they send here. No one gives a fuck if you all go insane and have to be locked up in padded cells for the rest of your miserable existences. Why do you think this place was dug beneath the ground?"

"To make it harder to escape?"

"No. Because down here it's easy to forget about you. Out of sight, out of mind. No one cares what happens to any of you down here. They just want to forget you exist," he growled, his eyes alight with his belief in those words.

"I guess so," I agreed, though it left a bitter taste in my mouth. "But that means there's some other reason for the secrecy…" I held my tongue as I waited to see what else he might know or suspect about Psych.

"We don't mix with the staff there or even know their names. And whenever an inmate is processed into their system we never hear from them again," Cain growled, clearly irritated by the fact.

"You mean, no one ever comes back?" I breathed. I'd been hoping that I could at least try and get Sook returned to gen pop if she was sectioned, but it sounded like that plan could fester and die.

"*Never.* And the way the Warden guards that place from us is…suspicious."

"Why?" I asked, tilting my head slightly to give him a better view of my throat as my pulse hammered against my skin.

His gaze caressed my neck for a moment before slipping over my mouth and back to my eyes.

"She never lets any of us put a single toe over the threshold. The excuses she gives are poor at best. There's clearly something else going on down there and…"

"What?" I asked, inching closer to him as he hesitated.

"We get a fair few deaths in this place," Cain said slowly. "And because

360

so many of our inmates are lowlife scum, they often don't have anyone who gives two shits about them."

"I don't understand what this has to do with-"

"When a Fae has no one who wants to bury them, it's the responsibility of the prison to dispose of the body safely so that there is no chance of the remains being stolen for use in Dark Magic."

I nodded in understanding. A Fae's magic remained in their bones after death and some dark practices allowed it to be wielded by a living soul in addition to their own power. It was dangerous as fuck and even more illegal than murder, but there were always stronzos willing to risk it all for power. So by law, all Fae bodies had to be disposed of properly which either meant cremation so that the magic could be released back to the stars. Or burial in a high security graveyard which cost a fucking fortune. My family could afford the plots to bury us, but most Fae weren't so well off.

"As a fire Elemental, I sometimes lend my power to the furnaces in the crematorium. And on more than one occasion, there have been additional bodies to burn. I'm the chief officer here. No inmate dies without me filling out the paperwork so I know *exactly* which bodies should be arriving for cremation. And which ones have been tossed on the heap in hopes that no one would notice."

"You think they come from Psych?" I asked, wondering what the hell could be going on down there to have a regular body count. As far as I was aware, the prisoners kept there should be housed separately and suicide was pretty difficult to achieve in a padded cell.

"I *know* they come from Psych. There's nowhere else down here. I just don't know why or what happened to them. There's never any stab wounds, ligature marks, signs of suffocation or anything else that would point towards the kinds of deaths I'm used to dealing with in here," Cain growled. "Which means there's something else going on down there. And I want to get to the bottom of it."

I looked up into his grey eyes for a long moment before reaching out to take his fingers between mine.

"Thank you for telling me," I breathed.

Cain's jaw locked at the contact and his large fingers certainly didn't curl to encircle mine, but he didn't snatch his hand away either.

"Now tell me what you know," he demanded.

I batted my eyelashes as I looked up at him innocently, biting my bottom lip. This was the part where he would probably lose his shit.

"Today, I noticed Sook Min acting kind of crazy," I murmured.

"What of it?"

"So I asked Roary what it meant…and he said she'd be taken to Psych soon and wouldn't come back."

"And what else have you figured out about that?"

"Well…I just got a guard to tell me quite a lot about it…"

Cain blinked at me as my words sank in and I smiled as he realised he'd just been played.

"Are you telling me you don't know anything?" he growled, sending a shiver of fear dancing along my spine as his gaze darkened and he suddenly gripped my hand with his gifted strength, crushing my fingers in his grasp.

"I'm telling you I didn't…before our little chat."

A growl tore from his throat and my heart leapt as rage filled his eyes.

"You'd better run, Twelve," he snarled. "And if your worthless life means anything to you, you might wanna make sure I don't catch you this time. Because like I said, *I'm* the one who files away the deaths in here. So how easy do you think it would be for me to fake a form with your name on it?"

I inhaled sharply as he released me and he shoved me back a step.

I hesitated for another moment as he snarled at me, revealing his lengthening fangs in the dim red light of the maintenance room.

Oh fuck.

I whirled away from him and started running, his footsteps pounding after me in the next second.

I didn't even make it five steps before he collided with me, grabbing a fistful of my hair and bending me over a huge chest which sat against the wall. He slammed my face down against the rusty metal, wrenching my head to the side a moment before his fangs ripped into my neck.

I cried out as he crushed me beneath him, snarling like a beast as he took what he craved from my blood and my heart raced in panic. His fangs stayed deep in my skin and he drew my blood from my body with such vigour that for a moment I feared he wouldn't stop.

But as his growls slowly quietened and he fell into the full grip of the bloodlust, the panic faded from my limbs.

Cain may have just assaulted me and I might have pissed him off to no end. But he wasn't going to kill me, he liked the taste of my blood too much to give it up. And the risk was worth it, because now I knew that Sook wasn't coming back out of Psych if she was hauled down there and I couldn't afford to let that happen.

So I was going to have to work doubly hard at completing my plans before they took her away. And in the meantime, I'd try to figure out a way to keep her insanity hidden from the guards.

I wasn't going to let this destroy my plans. It was just time to up my game.

362

ROARY

PRISONER #69

CHAPTER THIRTY TWO

"Ah! Shark Shifter!" Sook Min jumped out of her seat across the Mess Hall and I looked over at her with a frown. She dropped to the floor, crawling under the table with a plastic cup in her grip. "You won't get in my water. Where will you swim? Ha -ha! Where will you swim you shifty shark?!"

She chugged the water then wiped her mouth, a manic gleam in her eyes as she peaked out from under the table. Several inmates moved away from her and the guards exchanged glances around the room. She wouldn't be sent to Psych unless the Warden ordered it, but if she carried on like that, one of the guards was surely gonna write her up.

Rosalie gave me a concerned look from amongst her pack, biting down on her lip. I rose from my seat, pushing a hand into my hair and moving towards the table where Sook was holing up.

I'd seen too many inmates go crazy in this place. Whatever it was that fucked them in the head must have been in the air. And that was just one more thing to worry about. I could survive my sentence so long as I didn't lose my mind in the process. But if that shit ever happened to me, I'd be forcing Rosa's plans into action tomorrow. No fucking way was I gonna go crazy in Darkmore. I'd already sacrificed too much to this place.

I dropped down to a crouch and cocked my head to one side. "Hey Sook, there's no sharks about right now, so come on out, yeah?"

She cleared her throat, wiping a line of sweat from her brow. "Right…

yeah. Of course there's not." She laughed nervously then crawled out from under the bench.

I slung an arm around her shoulders, chuckling as I led her back to her seat. "You're such a prankster, Sook."

The guards eyed us closely but soon lost interest as I planted her on the bench and dropped down beside her. She picked up her fruit pot, picking at her grapes, her eyes watering. I frowned, nudging her with my elbow to catch her attention, but she didn't look at me.

"You alright?" I asked in a low tone.

"No," she whispered. "Nothing's alright. They're going to come for me."

I didn't tend to make emotional connections in here if I could help it, but I couldn't deny the tug in my chest at the broken expression on her face.

"Hey," I breathed, leaning forward to catch her eye. "You're ninety percent saner than Sin Wilder and no one's calling him crazy. The guards aren't going to come for you."

"Do you promise?" she asked, her eyes burning with emotion. She was a tough girl, I'd seen her take out a Bear Shifter in the Magic Compound once without getting up from her seat. But Darkmore was designed to break everyone in here eventually. I was gonna get out before I fell prey to that fate, but Sook? I didn't know how much time she had left. I wasn't gonna crush what was left of her spirit though.

"Promise," I agreed and her shoulders relaxed a bit.

Free time was coming to an end soon so I parted from Sook and headed back to my cell block. Rosalie appeared at my side as we reached the bridge and she arched a brow at me.

"Is Sook okay?"

"I guess." I shrugged and she reached out to cling onto my arm, her nails digging in.

"Nothing can happen to her, Roar," she said seriously and my brows lowered. "I got something out of Cain."

"The guard?" I balked.

"No, the happy-go-lucky sea turtle who lives under my bed – of *course* the guard." She rolled her eyes at me and I fought a grin, gesturing for her to go on. She drew in a deep breath and I could see the stress of this situation was eating at her. "He said the Warden doesn't let any of the Darkmore guards in there. It's run as its own unit. And bodies come out of there regularly without a mark on them."

I ground my jaw as I worked over that piece of information in my mind. There wasn't much we could do about it if the Warden decided to send Sook for analysis. And it killed me that I couldn't do more to help ease Rosa's mind.

I was tempted to reached out and brush her hair behind her ear and tell her everything would be alright. But I couldn't lie to Rosa in that moment. She would see right through me anyway.

"We just have to hope we have enough time before she's taken away. How close are you with the plan?" I asked as we headed up to the top floor of our cell block.

"I'm getting closer," she said and a gleam of hope entered her eyes. I felt that gleam right through to my soul. It was my salvation. My one chance at a way out of here before I lost half my life to this place.

"The closer the better," I murmured as we parted.

She headed into her cell and I headed into mine, trying not to stare at her ass as she went but fuck, I lost that bet with myself. I dropped down onto my bed and grabbed the tattered copy of *A Pride To Be Proud Of* and flipped it open to the page I'd last been reading.

I didn't know why I still clung to the ways of my kind when I'd lost the one thing that made me a true Lion. My family. I didn't have a pride. And I certainly couldn't be proud of what I *did* have; a criminal record which tarnished my family's reputation. My name was probably whispered behind hands between the Nights and the Oscuras. My father would throw sharp looks every time the subject came up.

Leon would never tell me the whole truth about what went on at home, he was too damn upbeat for his own good. So when he said Dad was 'not nearly as upset about me as he used to be', that was code for, he'd stopped talking about me. I'd bet my mane that any pictures of me in the house were hastily stuffed in drawers any time they had guests over. And maybe, after time, they'd stopped coming back out of those drawers.

My brother wasn't supposed to come and visit me. When a Lion brought shame on their family, they were meant to be ostracised from the pride. But Leon and his wife came anyway because they'd never been ones to follow the rules. And I was more grateful to them for that than they could ever really know.

A growl rumbled through my chest as I read the passage on the page for the hundredth time. It was a code I'd once lived by, a way of life I'd embodied, taken pride in. But now…

A Lion is a king in every aspect of life. A king is firm, patient and fair. To use one's Charisma for selfish gain is the way of a cub. To become a true Lion, the gifts of your Order must be wielded to build a clan of powerful followers. To bend their will gently in the name of your kingdom. Once a true king is made, his first queen will appear. And only a true test of Lionship by courting her without the aid of Charisma will prove you to be worthy of your Lioness and prepare you to earn the love of more queens and build your pride.

I sighed, continuing to read until a heavy weight descended on me. I didn't know why I tortured myself with this book. It only served to remind me of my fall from grace. But some part of me hoped I could have another shot at becoming a true king of my kind one day. And breaking out of here with Rosalie would certainly make my dad sit up and pay attention.

The bell soon rang to announce the cell doors closing and the headcount started up throughout the block.

"Get up Sixty Nine!" Officer Cain barked and I pushed myself to my feet, yawning broadly as I moved to the closed door and waited to be scanned. His eyes slid down me like I was a piece of shit on his shoe and I pressed my tongue into my cheek.

"Problem?" I questioned.

"You just have a really punchable fucking face, Sixty Nine. Anyone ever tell you that?" he asked coolly, lifting the scanner so it counted me.

I rubbed the stubble on my jaw, feigning a thoughtful expression. "That's funny, I was just thinking the same about you, Officer."

He lowered the scanner, shifting closer to glare in at me. "Well the difference between you and me, inmate, is if you punched me, I could throw you in the hole for a month. If I punched *you*, I could keep punching until my knuckles busted." He sneered and I growled.

"I guess this job makes you feel like the big man, huh? Does it compensate for your tiny dick, sir?"

He released a derisive breath, lowering his hand to rest on his baton. "Just give me one more reason to come in there, inmate, and I'll leave you bloody and bruised until morning."

I clenched my fists, almost tempted to goad him further. That book had put me in a pissy mood and I would have relished a fight to burn off some of this energy.

"I don't think he needs to compensate for anything," Rosa's voice came from her cell and Cain looked away from me, his eyes narrowing on her. I knew she'd saved my ass and maybe it was for the best. Though why the fuck was she bigging the guy up to do it?

A twinge of jealousy made my fists tighten as Cain stepped toward her, clearly fixated. And why wouldn't he be? To any warm blooded man, she was a fucking Siren calling them in. Even I was a slave to it at times. But I had logic on my side, even though my dick had a whole lot to say to the contrary sometimes.

"Always flirting," Cain taunted her. "Does that mouth of yours do anything other than weave pretty words and give adequate blowjobs?"

"They're not adequate, are they Roar?" she called over to me and I snorted a laugh.

"They're supreme," I answered and Cain shot me a glare that could have melted glass back into sand.

"I'd rather put my dick in a blender than in some Wolf whore's mouth," he said coldly and a growl rumbled through my chest. I was about to step in when I remembered Rosa was perfectly able to fight her own battles.

"I didn't realise you had a thing for kitchen appliances, sir," Rosa mocked. "You will be careful to keep them unplugged while you dip your dick in them, won't you? My Uncle Ricardo got a nasty shock off of a toaster once when he shoved his finger in it, I can't imagine the mess it would make of your-"

"That's enough, Twelve." Cain scanned her in and I headed back to my bed with a chuckle, pulling my jumpsuit and tank off and lying down in my boxers.

I snatched up the book again, flicking to the front page where my dad had written a message for me back when I was a teenager. It had been a gift for my sixteenth birthday and Leon had sent it in to Darkmore after I'd been incarcerated. Part of me regretting asking him to do that now, but back then I'd still had hope that our dad could forgive me. These days, I knew my Lionhood had been flushed down the drain the second the FIB had slapped me in cuffs.

I ran my thumb over the strong strokes my father had inked on the inside of the cover, my throat thickening as I read them.

My boy, it's time you became a man.

My father gave me this book as a cub, and it helped transform me into the Lion I am today. I hope it can do the same for you, son.

The Nights can't shine without stars. Always aim to be the brightest one in our sky.

All my love,

Dad x

My heart hurt as I closed the book and put it back on the shelf above my bunk and wondered if he even still loved me. Or if I was just a dark space in the sky he'd wished for me to shine in one day.

"Hey," Rosa's voice carried through the vent and I was half tempted to pretend I was asleep. I had a reputation to uphold in this prison and right now I could feel it cracking, letting out the weakness in me.

"What's up Rosa?" I asked, a heaviness to my tone.

"Hang a sheet, I'm coming in," she breathed and I sensed a silencing bubble slipping around the cell.

I heard her setting to work and I was forced to obey, jumping up and hanging a sheet over the bars before her head appeared through the vent she'd forced open. She crawled through, rising to her feet and brushing down her jumpsuit.

She immediately cocked her head to one side and a low whine escaped her. "What's up?"

Dammit, how the fuck can she read me so well?

I shrugged, dropping down onto my bed and she followed me onto it, folding her legs up beneath her. Her jumpsuit was tied around her waist, revealing the gym sports bra beneath it and my gaze automatically traced the curve of her spine. My fingers itched to follow the path it made up to her neck and I blinked hard, forcing myself to look away.

"You know you can tell me anything, right?" She turned to me with her eyes glimmering and I leaned toward her on instinct.

"I know," I said, dragging my gaze away from her again. "It's just the past. And I don't want to dwell there anymore."

She'd said something similar to me not long ago, so I knew she'd respect my wishes. The problem was, I knew what haunted her in the night. I knew her father, Felix, had hurt her. My brother had told me about what he'd done to her that night at the Letterman farm all those years ago. I'd beaten the hell out of several Fae the day I'd heard. It had cut me up inside, made me want to tear through these walls and rip her father limb from limb.

My gaze dropped to the tattooed rose vine running up her side and my heart twisted as I could just make out some of the scars hidden beneath it. One day, we needed to talk about it. But today was not that day.

"How about I cheer you up?" she suggested conspiratorially before reaching into her pocket and holding out the cuff key. My heart thumped harder as she offered it to me and I quickly grabbed it and unleashed my magic. My power rushed keenly to my fingertips, purring beneath my skin like a hungry beast.

"Fuck," I breathed as ecstasy coiled through my blood. "I've gotta use it."

I caught Rosa's hand as an idea occurred to me and I dropped back onto the mattress, dragging her down beside me. Her breathing hitched as I pressed against her and I knew if I turned my head, I'd find a blush lining her cheeks. I smirked as I raised a hand, feeling better already with the heat of her arm flush to mine.

I brought ice to my fingertips and sighed as it rippled against my palm. I encouraged it towards the ceiling and let the frost grow all across it in a shimmering blue coat. The temperature dropped quickly and Rosa shivered beside me, making my pulse quicken as I continued to wield the magic. I'd graduated from Aurora Academy with flying colours and one thing I'd excelled at in particular was my Astrology classes. I'd memorised every constellation in the heavens and I urged them into existence now, painting them across the ceiling in shimmering ice that glittered like starlight.

Rosa inhaled deeply as the night sky spread out above us and despite the cold, warmth flooded my veins.

"Do you like it, little pup?" I asked in a deep tone.

"It's beautiful," she breathed.

I dropped my arm between us and my hand grazed hers, her fingers twitching in response to my touch. With magic racing through my limbs, I felt high, all caution abandoned as I ran my thumb across the back of her hand, painting an icy trail there. She shivered again and I kept my gaze trained on the ceiling despite how much I wanted to turn toward her and decorate more of her flesh with my magic.

"Do you trust me, Roar?" she asked in a seductive tone that had my cock paying way too much fucking attention.

"Of course I do," I growled.

I felt her magic press against the barriers of my skin and knew what she was asking of me. I wanted to power share with her so badly, it hurt. But doing that was wrong if I had even the slightest inclination towards claiming her. Her power would call to me, drive me crazy with need. But it had been so long since I'd felt anything at all and she was suddenly offering me so fucking much.

Power sharing wasn't an easy thing to do with just anyone, but with her it felt as natural as breathing. So I gave up fighting it and let my barriers down, welcoming her magic into my blood.

I groaned as her power tumbled through my veins like an earthquake. She was nature itself, humming through me and making every hair on my body stand on end.

"*Rosa*," I choked out and she sighed in response as my own magic rushed under her skin.

"You feel like a waterfall," she said breathily.

"You feel like a fucking landslide." I rolled towards her, intertwining my fingers with hers, seeking more of her flesh as I lost myself to her power. Everywhere our skin touched, our power connected and thrummed with even more energy.

I hooked one leg over hers, catching her other hand and pushing it down into the mattress. She gazed up at me through hooded eyes and her full lips parted just for me. A blush painted her cheeks the perfect colour of a rose and I groaned again as another wave of her magic washed into me.

"Rosa," I rasped, like saying her name could do anything to stop me. But I knew I'd made the decision before I even did it. I had to feel those lips against mine, I had to fall into this wild storm which held us in its grip.

She tilted up to meet me, her back arching before I crushed her down into the bed and drove my tongue into her mouth. We'd kissed before, but not like this. Not like the world would stop turning if I didn't keep going.

I shifted on top of her so my weight held her immobilised as her tongue met mine for every stroke. She tasted like every bad idea I'd ever had. She was so off limits, so forbidden and so, so fucking delicious.

Her teeth grazed my lower lip, then she bit down like a wild animal and my rock hard dick throbbed between her legs.

"Roary," she moaned and I growled into her mouth, the sound of my name on her lips driving me crazy.

I ran my mouth down to her throat, sucking, devouring, possessing. She tasted like a summer's day, like the sweetness of my past, like every good thing in this world.

Fuck, this is so wrong. I have to stop. I must fucking stop.

I dug deep for the tiny shred of resilience I had left and released her hands, forcing my barriers up between us to block off the flow of her magic. Our heavy breaths tangled between us and I didn't move as I pressed my hands into the pillow either side of her head. My hard on was a dead giveaway to how much further I wanted this to go, but if I crossed that line I could never go back.

I rolled off of her with a sigh that let her know just how pissed I was at myself. My dick was gonna start a war with me if I didn't get laid soon. But since Rosa had arrived at Darkmore, my gaze never seemed to stray to another girl.

"Pussy," Rosa teased and I rammed my elbow into her ribs.

"Magic gets me hard, not you," I lied, but with enough edge to my tone that it sounded like the truth.

She snorted like she didn't believe me and sat up as if to leave. I caught her waist, following her upright and dragging her back against my chest. I dropped my mouth to her ear, winding my hands around her so she couldn't escape. "I don't want you to go."

I heard her swallow and could sense that she was about to refuse so I turned and placed a kiss against her temple, tasting the sweetness of her skin once more.

"Stay," I urged.

"On one condition," she said, turning her head to gaze at me with that Alpha look which said she was in control. Her eyes swallowed me up and I nodded without question. She could have asked for a star right then and I would have found some way to knock one out of the heavens for her.

"Admit you want me." She raised a brow, a challenge in her eyes despite the fact that her cheeks were still red and I could see so much of the girl who'd crushed on me all those years ago shining out at me.

My gaze fell to her lips and I wet my mouth before scraping my eyes back up to meet hers. "You're a beautiful girl, Rosa, but I'll never tarnish you."

"What if I want to be tarnished? Maybe I like a little tarnishing." She smirked and I tossed her down onto the bed, pushing the covers down and wrapping them around us.

"Not by me," I said defiantly as she rolled away to face the wall and I spooned the fuck out of her, my hands winding around her waist

My dick was still making a good effort at convincing me to change my mind, and it was sure as hell making itself known to Rosa as I held her close and was forced to own my hard on like a straight up Fae.

"Whatever you say, Roar," she giggled and the sound got me even fucking harder.

By the stars...

"Tell me about the time you and Dante broke into the crystal farm," I asked in a strained voice, shutting my eyes and willing my blood to make a path north.

"You mean when I accidently spilled a whole tank of melted ammonite and turned an entire road into a rainbow lake?"

I chuckled, winding my hands tighter around her. "That's it," I encouraged.

"Aunt Bianca nearly evicted me for that one."

"She never would," I chuckled. "She loves you too much."

"If the FIB had caught us, I might have ended up in here sooner," she laughed then started telling the story. The familiarity of it soothed my aching heart and with her in my arms, every worry I'd had in here suddenly seemed so far away. With her, I didn't have to be so alone anymore.

I woke to a cold drip on my face then the sound of the bell alerting me to the morning count. I swore sharply, bolting upright and Rosa lurched up too.

"Get back through the hole," I hissed, lifting a hand and siphoning away the water which had dripped over us from the melted ice on the ceiling during the night. I sent it all down the sink as Rosa scrambled to put on her jumpsuit which she must have stripped out of during the night.

She ran to the hole just as a baton tapped against the bars beyond the sheet. "Sixty Nine! Get up!" Officer Cain barked and panic swept through me.

Rosa gave me a wide-eyed look then directed her hands at the hole, closing it up before twisting the key in her cuffs. I expelled the silencing bubble around us with my heart in my throat. *Holy shit!*

"Sixty Nine!" Cain shouted, reaching through to grab the sheet just as Rosa tossed me the key.

My heart pounded wildly as I twisted it in my cuffs, blocking off my magic before doing the only thing I could think to do and placing the key in my mouth. The warm metal pressed against my tongue just as Cain ripped the sheet down and I lunged at Rosa, throwing her onto the bed and hooking her leg up around my thigh.

Fuck fuck fuck. She isn't supposed to be in here!

The sheet tumbled to the ground and Cain glared in at us, his brows pinching together as he spotted us on the bunk in the compromising position. Rosa wriggled out from beneath me and I took the opportunity to turn my head and swallow that motherfucking key down. It hurt like a bitch, but it went down and I tried not to think about how I was gonna get it back out.

"Oopsie, sorry Officer, we were a bit busy." Rosa batted her lashes as I moved to her side in front of the bars and Cain looked between us, shaking his head in confusion.

"No...you weren't in there last night." He pointed at Twelve and my gut clenched tightly, but I'd lied my way out of trickier situations than this. Maybe not many, but still.

"What? That's ridiculous," I laughed and Cain's eyes narrowed on me.

"Are you questioning my sanity, Sixty Nine?" he snarled, a furious beast leering out from behind his eyes.

"No sir," I said with an innocent shrug.

Cain growled dangerously, taking the radio from his belt. "Open cell thirteen on three."

A buzz sounded a few seconds later and the door slid open. We stepped back as Cain moved into my cell menacingly, his eyes roaming over our faces as he hunted for answers.

My heart thudded in my ears as I held my ground, having no choice but to front this out and pray he'd buy it.

"*Strip,*" he snapped at us both, pointing to the wall. "Then turn around and spread your legs."

I glanced at Rosa before dropping my boxers and moving to the wall, placing my hands flat on the surface. Rosa joined me a second later and I glanced at her as adrenaline surged through my blood.

Cain set about destroying my room, upturning everything with his Vampire speed and hunting every crevice he could find.

"What are you looking for?" Rosa asked sweetly.

"You know what I'm fucking looking for." He shot up behind her, grabbing a fistful of her hair. "Don't play stupid with me, Twelve." He tugged her head back sharply then growled as he spotted the hicky I'd left on her neck last night. For a moment I could have sworn a flash of jealousy entered his gaze.

"Let go of her," I snarled dangerously and Cain's fury shifted onto me. He took the baton from his hip and slammed it into my back. "*Motherfucker*," I hissed.

"You question my authority again and the shock function will be switched on next time," Cain warned.

The sound of him trashing my room ensued then a beat of silence passed before he growled in frustration. "Get dressed!"

I turned, grabbing my boxers and pulling them on while Rosa slipped into her underwear and tugged on her jumpsuit. Cain fixed me with a dark stare, striding forward as an innocent smile spread across my face. "If you're hiding that key, maybe Dr Quentin can loosen your tongue down in interrogation. Either that or I'll get Hastings in here to conduct a full cavity search."

"I wouldn't do that if I were you," Rosa said in a whisper so quiet I almost couldn't hear it, but Cain's Vampire hearing could definitely pick it up. He whirled toward her with a snarl, then lifted a hand, casting a silencing bubble around us in an instant.

"Dare to threaten me again," he said in a deadly tone.

She pressed her shoulders back, a wild glint in her gaze. "You can't send him anywhere or conduct any more searches because he knows all about the way you like to hunt and bite me."

I nearly lost my cool, my mouth dropping open but I managed to slam it shut again just as Cain glanced over his shoulder at me in a rage.

"You little bitch-" Cain took a step toward her and I lurched after him, catching his shoulder and yanking him backwards. He shoved me off of him with a snarl, raising his baton to point at me. "Stand down or I'll-"

"You'll what?" I cut over him. "Do anything and I'll tell the Warden about your filthy little secret."

His upper lip peeled back to reveal his fangs and I gave him a smug smile. Hell, I kinda wanted to floor him for the mere fact that he'd sunk his teeth into Rosa. But if the other guards came over here to help, there wouldn't be much I could do to stop *them* throwing me in the hole.

Cain moved to the door of my cell, his features twisting as he raised a finger to point at Rosa. "I'm going to find that key, Twelve. Mark my words." He disbanded the silencing bubble then shot away across the walkway to Plunger's cell who was doing a naked yoga routine while Hastings tried to scan his face.

I turned to Rosa with a punishing look, anger unfolding in my chest. "That asshole bites you?"

She shrugged.

"We can go to the Warden, he's not allowed to-"

"And then where would my leverage be?" she asked with an eyeroll, heading out the door. She glanced back at me with a wicked smile. "Besides, maybe I like it." She tossed her hair over her shoulder as she headed back to her cell and I was hit with a rush of jealousy so fierce, I almost went after her.

I'd obviously noticed the way Cain looked at her, but I'd never thought Rosa was looking back. I'd dismissed the way she talked to him as an act; she was just playing him for info. But apparently I'd been wrong about that. And that fucked me off for a deep, dark reason I didn't want to admit to. I liked the way Rosa idolised me, she made me feel like a king again. But apparently I wasn't the only king she was making.

I clutched onto the bars beside the open door, taking an even breath as I stared at Officer Cain across the walkway. That fucker was competition for a girl I couldn't have. And hell if that didn't make me want to forget the rules I'd made and claim her for my own.

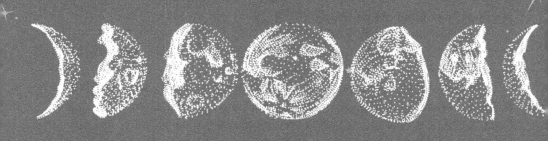

ROSALIE

PRISONER #12

CHAPTER THIRTY THREE

My stomach was satisfyingly full even if the taste of the plain oatmeal left a lot to be desired. I'd had a little jar of honey which should have improved the taste, but Cain had snatched it from me before I could add it to my meal. I'd considered going head to head with him over my morning sugar, but it wasn't worth the hassle so I'd just eaten it plain. Yuck.

But if the price for a night in Roary Night's arms was a grumpy Vampire then I would happily pay it. The memory of his kisses still burned against my bruised lips and the heat he'd lit beneath my flesh wasn't fading any time soon.

And sure, he'd tried to brush me off again, but I wasn't buying it anymore. Spending a night locked in his arms while his hard on drove into my ass was a sure-fire way to convince me of his interest, and if he wanted to keep fighting what was happening between us then that was okay. I could wait. When it came to Roary Night, I'd been doing that for a hell of a long time anyway. And the idea that he was hungering for me now too was more than I'd ever even dreamed of happening before. So if he needed some time to get over his age gap issues, he could have it.

After Cain and the other guards had done the count, I'd held Roary's hair for him while he stuck his fingers down his throat and brought the key back up. A little clean with some of his water magic and I'd managed to hide it away again in my cell, though I had to admit that it didn't feel so secure now that Cain was on to us.

But it wasn't like I had anywhere else to hide it so I just had to hope that my sway over him held him back.

In the meantime, I had work to do.

I sauntered out into the corridor and turned right towards the line of Fae waiting to retrieve their mail from the slot.

Plunger's voice rang out as I passed the queue and I frowned as Officer Hastings' voice replied angrily. "If you don't stop, I'll close down the mail hatch for the day and no one will get their letters for a week!"

Anger flushed through me at that suggestion. I was expecting another letter from Dante today with the final pieces of information I needed about the ipump500. I was already under pressure to get my plans moving with Sook acting crazier and crazier each day and I couldn't afford a week's delay on that damn letter.

"I don't know what you mean, Officer," Plunger purred. "I'm not doing anything except airing the fairy and trying to collect my post."

"I won't warn you again," Hastings snarled, sounding a lot more like a force to be reckoned with and a lot less like my little choir boy than usual. If he kept that up, he might just become a decent guard after all.

I made it to the front of the queue and stopped dead as I found Plunger facing off against Hastings. He'd unbuttoned the bottom of his jumpsuit and had flopped his junk out through the hole, hanging a sock over it to mostly shield his flesh but making my stomach turn all the same.

"These uniforms are not made with organic cotton," Plunger pouted. "Only the socks give me the gentle caress I need on my happy hose. And it's not like I have it on show, is it, Officer?" He thrust his hips about so that the sock flapped between his thighs and I cringed.

What the hell was with this guy?

"That's it!" Hastings bellowed, throwing the shutter down over the mail collection point. "The mail slot is closed for a week and if any Fae has a problem with that then they can take it up with Twenty Four!" He pointed at the number on Plunger's uniform and I damn near snarled in rage.

Plunger sighed dramatically and flounced away with his hands in the air and his sock swinging. I tried not to look at it, but I swear the damn thing was trying to catch my eye and I caught sight of a tuft of hair poking out above the sock before I could force my gaze away. More than a few of the Fae in the queue chased after him, offering threats and insults and the rest stalked away, muttering in disappointment.

I was left alone with Hastings as his eyes flashed with a steely determination and the power of his victory. But there was no way in hell I was leaving here without my damn letter.

"Are you hard of hearing, Twelve?" he asked in a dark tone, turning his ocean blue eyes on me as he puffed his chest up. Someone was riding high on a wave of power. I'd have to play this just right if I wanted my letter.

I bit my bottom lip and moved towards him, swaying my hips just enough to draw his gaze to my movements.

"Thank you, sir," I breathed, looking up at him from beneath my lashes. "I don't think I've seen anyone put Plunger in his place like that before."

The edge of aggression slipped from Hastings' stance as his spine straightened at the compliment. "Just doing my job, inmate."

A smile tugged at my lips and I moved a little closer still. "You'll be chief guard before we know it."

"I don't know about that," he replied, pushing a hand into his beach blonde hair, though his eyes twinkled with the idea.

"Oh I do. I've always been able to spot a powerful alpha when I see one," I murmured, reaching out to slide my hand over his bicep before squeezing lightly.

"Is that so?"

"Sì. E tu non sei uno," I purred in a low tone which brought the hint of a smile to his lips. *Yes. And you're not one.*

Why were so many men a sucker for Faetalian? I swear I could talk some guys into anything while insulting them in my language and it never even occurred to them to ask what I was saying.

"What are you after, inmate?" Hastings asked, suspicion colouring his words though his eyes still sparkled from the compliment he thought I'd given him.

"Maybe I just enjoy your company…"

He raised an eyebrow at me and I shrugged innocently.

"I know your game, Twelve-"

"You can call me Rosalie, if you like."

Hastings cleared his throat. "Fine. I know your game…Rosalie."

"What Academy did you attend? I know you weren't at Aurora because I wouldn't have forgotten a face like yours."

"Starlight. I graduated three years ago, but that's not really-"

"I always did like the guys in the year above me. Did you play Pitball by any chance, ragazzo del coro?" I asked in my most seductive voice.

"I was a Waterback," he admitted, his chest swelling again as I caressed his bicep.

"Maybe we met on the pitch then," I suggested. "Although I think I'd remember if you'd ever pinned me down in the dirt."

"You played?" he asked with interest. We really could have faced each other in the academy league at some point but I certainly didn't recall if we had.

"I was the Aurora Academy Earthraider," I purred.

"We lost to Aurora in my third year... You're not the girl who caused a landslide which wiped out our whole team in the final round, are you?" His eyes suddenly glimmered with recognition and my smile widened. That had been a pretty epic play. We'd been at a draw but my genius move had secured the win for Aurora and buried his team beneath a foot of soil for good measure.

"I like to play dirty," I teased, though we both knew that shit hadn't been against the rules.

"*Fuck.* You know, the guys on our team had a nickname for you after that..." Hastings pushed his hand into his hair and a little colour touched his cheeks.

"Oh yeah?" I asked, wondering what it could have been to make him blush for me.

"It was dumb," he hedged, clearly not wanting to tell me.

"Don't leave me in suspense, ragazzo del coro." I pouted at him and he cleared his throat as he gave in.

"We just called you the filthy little wolf." Hastings cleared his throat and I could tell that they hadn't called me filthy because of the earth magic I'd covered them with.

"Was that because you all hated me for beating you or because you liked the idea of getting dirty with me?" I teased as my grip on his bicep tightened a little more.

Hastings didn't seem to want to answer that and I laughed teasingly.

"Who knew I was looking after a legend in here?" he joked.

My smile widened but I withdrew my hand before I pushed him too far.

"I'd better get back to the Mess Hall before breakfast finishes," I said in a soft voice. My gaze slid down his admittedly muscular body before crossing to the closed mail slot.

I released a disappointed sigh, biting down on my bottom lip before turning and heading away from him with my head down.

Three, two, one-

"Wait," Hastings called and I looked back over my shoulder with my eyebrows raised.

"Yes, sir?"

"Are you waiting for some news from home?" he asked, his brows pulling together like he felt bad about denying me my letter.

"My Great Aunt Mable is sick. She's one hundred and seventeen...I'll see if I've got enough tokens to call home for information instead though." I turned away again and brushed a hand across my cheek as if I'd just swiped at a tear. In all honesty, I'd missed my calling to be a movie star.

I started walking slowly and the sound of the mail slot opening behind me drew a smirk to my lips, but I didn't turn back.

Footsteps pounded after me and Hastings' hand landed on my shoulder as he pulled me around to face him.

"Twelve…Rosalie…don't tell anyone else but, here." He pressed Dante's letter into my hand and I widened my eyes as if I was surprised.

"But-"

"You weren't the one with a sock on your cock," he teased, curling my fingers over the letter. "I hope your aunt is okay."

I offered him a genuine smile and pushed up onto my tiptoes to press a kiss to his cheek. "Thank you, ragazzo del coro," I breathed and I almost felt bad about calling him choir boy right to his face. Almost. "This means the world to me."

I hurried away before he could reply, taking my seat back in the Mess Hall amongst my pack as I read over Dante's letter, decoding the information he'd sent me about the ipump500 with a lightness filling my chest.

A shadow loomed over my table and I looked up from my letter as my Wolves started growling.

"Can I have a word, kitten?" Sin purred and I sighed as I waved my Wolves off.

"Here or in private?" I asked, tucking Dante's letter into my pocket.

"I'll take this conversation to go," he confirmed before turning and striding away from me.

I rolled my eyes at Sonny as he frowned with concern and pushed myself to my feet as I followed Sin back out of the Mess Hall again.

Just before I stepped out into the hallway, my gaze caught on Gustard where he held court with The Watchers in the back corner of the room.

His lips tilted up in a way that made my blood run cold.

He hadn't said a word when I'd been at breakfast after his attempt to kill me had failed, but the dangerous look in his eyes every time I'd seen him since said he held my fate in his hands. He'd been rooting around in my head with his psychic gifts and I had no damn way of telling whether or not he'd stolen my darkest secrets unless he brought them to light.

Ethan had told me that Gustard knew about us and I was just hoping that he'd been satisfied with that secret. An Oscura and a member of the Lunar Brotherhood mating was a pretty big deal and he was no doubt hoping to use it against both of us. But I wasn't overly concerned about that. I'd deal with any disquiet in my pack if it came to it. My main concern was that Gustard hadn't gotten anything else from my mind when it had been under his control.

But the way he kept looking at me said he knew something else. Something bad. And I could only hope that he didn't do anything to screw up my plans with the knowledge he'd stolen before I had the chance to use it.

I looked away from Gustard dismissively, refusing to show him that he'd rattled me. There was nothing I could do about the things he'd stolen from my mind so I just had to try and forget about it unless it caused me a problem.

Sin led me out of the Mess Hall and down the stairs, maintaining a quick pace so that I couldn't walk beside him.

"If you insist on leading me along like a dog pulling its owner, I'll start treating you like one," I commented.

Sin whirled around so suddenly that I almost lost my footing on the step above him and he reached out to grasp my waist to stop me from falling.

"I just saved your life, kitten," he said in a low voice. "What do I get for a debt like that?"

"My eternal gratitude," I said with a smile. "And a pat on the head."

Sin huffed irritably and released me. "I'll take a pass on that. Don't you want to know why I've lured you down into an abandoned stairwell on your own?"

"Is this the part where I'm supposed to tremble in fear?" I teased.

Sin moved up a step so that we was towering over me and I licked my lips as I looked up at him.

He leaned down, sweeping my hair away from my ear as his mouth brushed against the shell, sending a shiver darting down my spine.

"Are you ready for your answer?" he purred.

"Enough with the foreplay, Sin. Just give it to me."

He growled at my choice of words and I smirked as I tipped my head to look into his dark eyes, inhaling the smoky scent of his flesh. There was something sweet and something spicy to the smell which had my toes curling as I wondered if his skin would taste like that too.

"Your Mole got taken to Psych this morning," he breathed seductively and it took me a moment to process what he'd said.

"What?" I gasped, jerking back as I looked up at him. "Sook? When? How-"

"They dragged her out of the showers when she attacked another inmate for having perkier tits than her."

"Be serious, Sin, this could fuck up everything. Tell me what happened!" I slammed my hands into his solid chest and he snarled at me as he caught my wrists, keeping me there with my palms against his pecs.

"She tried to drink shampoo then took a running jump at a wall," he growled. "Busted her nose up real good, there was blood everywhere. Then

384

she tried to attack the guards who came to help her and bought herself a one way ticket to crazy town."

My hands fisted in the material of his tank top and I tried to shake him, but he was too damn big to move.

"Do you understand how fucked we are now?" I hissed, glaring into his dark eyes as he fucking laughed at me.

"Yeah, I think I've got a grasp on it," he said, surveying me keenly.

"So why the hell are you smiling like it's Christmas Day and you just got a hamper full of dildos?" I snarled.

"Because this right here is the point at which I'm gonna find out what you're made of, wild girl," he purred. "It's all well and good being the crème de la crème when everything's going to plan. But I prefer to judge a Fae on how well they react when the shit hits the fan. So what's it gonna be? Are you going to roll over and admit defeat? Or are you ready to prove just how much of a badass you are?"

I snarled at him angrily as my grip tightened on his tank top. "What do you think, stronzo? I'm going to show you what a badass I am, obviously."

"Fuck yeah you are," Sin replied enthusiastically. He yanked me close and stamped his mouth to mine before I could see it coming. My breathing hitched and for half a second I wanted to melt into the pure temptation that was Sin Wilder. But I didn't have time for that shit. I had work to do.

I shoved him back with a snarl while he grinned in a way that said he'd known how much I'd liked it despite my reaction.

I huffed irritably and turned away from him as I pounded back up the stairs. I had a plan to salvage. I just had to figure out how the fuck I was going to do it.

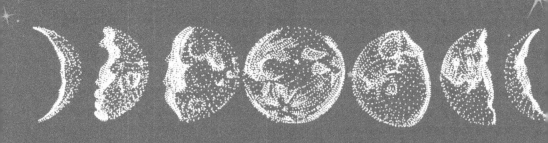

CAIN

COMMANDING OFFICER

CHAPTER THIRTY FOUR

Twelve couldn't be trusted. And I'd been played by her for the last time. I didn't become a Commanding Officer because I was a weak willed piece of shit. I should never have fallen for her bullshit. But I settled scores the way I fucked. Hard, mercilessly and without emotion.

She'd returned from wherever she'd headed with Eighty Eight and my gaze was fixed on her across the Mess Hall as she played a card game with her Wolf pack, each of them standing before the table and tossing cards down onto it. Whenever a pair or more of cards appeared, the whole band of them dropped onto their seats and started howling. It seemed to be some twisted version of musical chairs because whoever sat last was forced to leave the game.

Twelve laughed her ass off as she and her Beta went for the same seat and the two of them crashed to the floor. The rest of her pack dove forward to help her up, but she looked like she was having way too much fun to need it. She was a different person to the miserable sucker she'd been yesterday, pushing out her lower lip like the world was gonna end. But that was what made me watch her harder. She wore her emotions like masks, easily exchanging one for the next without blinking. I wondered which of them really touched her heart, or if there was just a stone cold rock living in her chest. And if that was the case, I could definitely relate.

My eyes narrowed as I observed her, a sweet kind of satisfaction filling me at knowing I was going to be the one to wipe that smile off of her face today. No one made a fool of me and got away with it and I'd been biding my time deciding on exactly how I was going to handle it.

When breakfast finally came to an end, I moved to the door to wait for her, ready to take her down to Maintenance for her morning's work. She was amongst the last to leave, sauntering through the door like she had all the time in the world and I snatched hold of her elbow, catching her by surprise as I shoved her towards the stairs.

"Morning, Officer Grumps, did you get out of the wrong side of the bed again today? Maybe you need some signage to remind you which way to go."

I clenched my jaw, saying nothing as I led her downstairs and I felt her surveying me from the corner of my eye.

"What do you eat for breakfast, sir? Uncheerios?"

My jaw locked harder until my face started to ache. My fangs were tingling with the anticipation of the hunt and I couldn't wait to impact her mood like a fucking meteor crashing into her world.

We finally reached level nine and I guided her past the isolation cells to the door that led down to the maintenance level. I'd ordered one of the janitors to leave cleaning supplies down there every day so I didn't have to bother fetching it anymore.

We reached the bottom of the stairs and I released Twelve, moving to the trolley of cleaning supplies and folding my arms.

"Start scrubbing the floor," I commanded, pointing to it and she gave me a confused look.

"Don't you want to hunt today?" she taunted as she moved toward me with her hips swaying.

"Get cleaning. Now," I snarled and her brows pulled together. She didn't question me again though which was an improvement on her usual cocky behaviour and I watched as she grabbed a bucket and scrubbing brush from the trolley, placing them on the floor.

She turned away from me, unbuttoning her jumpsuit and letting it fall to her feet.

"What are you doing?" I growled.

"I just don't want it to get wet," she said innocently, stepping out of it in nothing but her boots, a black sports bra and panties. I dragged my eyes away from her as she turned and laid the jumpsuit across the trolley.

She dropped down onto her knees then started scrubbing the floor, her hair falling around her. As she worked, she moved across the ground on all fours, her perfectly round ass drawing my attention again and again.

I cleared my throat and shifted my gaze up to the ceiling, clasping my hands behind my back. I wasn't going to let her distract me again. I had a plan in place and this was the first part of her punishment.

I let her work for over an hour until she was gleaming with sweat before I told her to stop.

She rose to her feet before me, pushing her hair behind her ears as she bit down on her lip. "Do you like watching me work for you, Mason?"

"Use my name again and I'll write you up for an infraction, Twelve." I bared my fangs. "Do you think I'm a fool you can twist around your little finger?"

She batted her lashes, shaking her head. "No, sir."

I stepped forward with a low growl, moving until I was right in her face as I leaned down to glare at her. "I think you do. I think you play games to get men to do what you want. But I'm not your prey, Twelve, I'm the hunter. So you'd better run before I prove it."

She swallowed thickly, her pupils dilating at my words like she was actually into this. But I wouldn't hold back today. She was about to find out what it was like to make an enemy of an apex predator.

"*Run*," I hissed and she turned, speeding away into the labyrinth of machinery with a wild laugh.

I took a breath to slow my racing pulse, training my ears on her as she fled. I could catch her blindfolded and half asleep if I wanted to. I was an expert at this, but I was going to let her have a longer leash today. My prey always tasted better when they thought they'd won.

I headed into the first passage, making a slow path through the room as the bloodlust rose in me. "It's going to hurt this time, Twelve!" I called to her, her footsteps still reaching me from the far end of the room. "You're going to learn exactly who you're messing with."

Her footfalls fell quiet and I smirked as she hid somewhere to my right. I made a path that way, my pounding boots ringing through the room and telling her how close I was getting.

I rounded the next corner and my heart lurched as I found her leaning back against a large pipe which extended up through the room. Her hand was in her panties and she bit down on her lip as a moan escaped her.

"What the fuck are you doing?" I snarled, my dick hardening with need as she disarmed me entirely.

"This game is so *hot*," she panted, her eyes hooded as she beckoned me closer. "Come here, Officer."

I swallowed the jagged ball in my throat, refusing to move an inch as I simply stood there with a raging hard on and the need to claim her devouring me.

She tipped her head back, sighing my name and I sure as shit wasn't gonna be writing her up for it.

"Twelve," I rasped as she panted. "Stop."

"I need you," she begged and I shot toward her, losing myself to this fucking beautiful sight before me.

I caught her waist with a growl of desire and she reached for my belt buckle, tugging it open and slipping her hand into my boxers. She stroked my aching length and I cursed under my breath at the feel of her soft palm tightening into a fist. I yanked her hand free from her panties and closed my mouth around her fingers, sucking them to taste her and making her eyes widen in surprise.

I smirked then twisted her around, crushing my chest to her back and forcing her head to one side with a handful of her hair. She ground her ass back against me as my fangs grazed her neck and she moaned my name once more.

"I need you," she begged and my heart thundered in my chest as I kicked her ankles wider.

"You're going to scream for me, Twelve," I said against her ear and she nodded keenly.

I didn't fuck inmates, that rule was hardwired into me, but she had me by the balls. I couldn't stop thinking about her, dreaming about her. Every time I tried to force her beneath me, she rose her head and bit back. And it was driving me to insanity. One fuck wasn't going to change things. If anything, it would fix my problem. I'd screw her out of my system. She already had enough ammo to get me fired with the hunting games we played, so what was the point in holding back?

"I need this, Mason, I've been so worried. So alone. Please give me this."

"Why are you worried?" I murmured against her neck, sliding my hand onto her stomach and running it down towards the edge of her panties.

"I'm scared of going crazy...what if I get sent to Psych?"

"You won't," I growled, brushing my fangs over her shoulder and making her shiver. "I'll protect you." Fuck, what was I even saying right now? Did I really mean that? It sure felt like I did. But I didn't get attached to anyone. And it had been a long, long time since I'd felt *protective* of someone.

"So you can decide if people get sent there or not? Even if they're crazy?" she asked breathily, reaching back to caress my dick.

I groaned, running my knuckles over her panties and making her arch back against me with a gasp. "Not everyone. But you're mine," I growled fiercely. The idea of her getting taken away from me made fury bubble under my skin. I wouldn't let her be sent to Psych. Ever.

"So C.O.'s have that power?" she asked just as I was about to dip my hand into her panties.

I lifted my head away from her throat, my thoughts clearing for a solid moment.

Holy fuck...she's playing me again.

I released a roar of rage, yanking her away from the pipe and throwing her to the floor. She inhaled sharply in fear as she looked up at me and she should have been afraid. Very fucking afraid.

She scrambled upright and I lunged forward, throwing her to the ground once more.

"Mason!" she gasped.

"How dare you?!" I bellowed, my pride wounded as much as my fucking dignity.

She leapt upright again, trying to run and I shot in front of her, shoving her back over a control panel and holding her down by the throat.

"I'm just some cog in your wheel, right?" I snapped. "So what is it you're planning, Twelve, because I'll face the Warden's wrath to bring you down if I have to, mark my words."

She clutched my arm as she choked then threw a sharp kick into my side, forcing me back a step. She scrambled backwards over the other side of the console and started to run, but I leapt after her with my Vampire speed, taking her to the ground beneath me. I pressed her face into the cold floor and she threw an elbow back into my gut with the force of a battering ram. I snarled as something cracked and I was forced back, but I didn't let go.

"What are you planning?" I demanded again.

"You're crazy!" She thrashed like a wild cat and managed to get free, jumping upright with a skill that could only have been learned. I rushed up after her just as her foot slammed into my gut. She lifted her hands like a pro fighter and I barked a laugh, raising mine too.

"You wanna fight me, Twelve?" I rolled my shoulders. "Go ahead."

She lunged at me once more, throwing a punch at my head which I deflected at speed. She launched a kick to my side and I caught her ankle, flipping her off her feet so her back slammed to the ground. She was up again in a flash and I darted forward with a burst of Vampire speed, catching her arm and wheeling her around so she smashed into one of the machines. She came at me again with a burning intensity in her eyes and my heart thrummed with the excitement of fighting an equal. Even without magic, she was a powerful creature and I tried to ignore how much I liked that about her.

She yelled in anger as she threw another perfect punch toward my gut, but I dodged it with my speed, rushing around her and kicking out her legs.

She crashed to her knees, hissing between her teeth as she came at me again.

"What are you planning?!" I shouted, grabbing her hair and yanking her to her feet by it.

She slammed her knuckles into my chest in quick succession and I growled, holding on by sheer force of will.

"I'm planning to kick your ass!" she laughed and I threw her back against another pipe with a snarl.

She recovered fast, running at me once more. I didn't bother to evade her, wanting to feast on her anger. I needed this outlet. She'd been driving me crazy for too fucking long.

Her fist impacted with my jaw and my head snapped back. I bit my tongue and blood oozed between my teeth, the sting of pain only driving me on. I knew part of me was refraining from using my fists against her, but I didn't know why I held back after everything.

She swung at me once more and I caught her wrist, yanking her into my chest and locking my arms around her.

"Tell me what you want with me or I'll force it from your lips," I snarled.

She looked up at me as the pounding of her heart thumped solidly against my own chest. "Do you wanna know what I want? What I really fucking want right now?"

"Yeah," I spat.

She tip-toed up and pressed her mouth to mine. My heart stopped beating for a full fucking second as I tasted the desire on her lips. Real fucking desire. For *me*.

I caught the back of her neck and pushed my tongue into her mouth, crushing her against me with the force of my Order. She groaned, running her hands down my bruised arms and clinging to me like her life depended on it.

I whirled her around to press her back against a pillar, not being the least bit gentle as I claimed her mouth with fierce strokes of my tongue. My fangs sliced into her lip and both of our blood washed between us, making my pulse spike with hunger.

I ran my hands down her sides, her naked flesh making me ache in places I hadn't known existed. I released flashes of healing magic from my palms, taking away her bruises, while leaving my own injuries intact. I wanted to feel the bite of her hate, the heat of her lust and drown in the hurt she left in my soul.

Her fingers knotted in my hair and her breathing quickened with the truth of how much she wanted me.

I finally broke the kiss and the spell between us shattered like falling glass.

I took a step back, wiping away the blood that was coating my lips. Our eyes locked as we stared at each other and reality came crashing in around me. She was never going to tell me the truth. She was a criminal I was employed to contain. And I'd crossed so many boundaries already that my badge was probably going to be stripped away if I didn't stop this soon. I needed this job. I had nothing else beyond this prison. No home, no nothing. I couldn't sacrifice the only life I had for a girl.

"Get dressed," I snapped, pointing down the passage to my left.

She licked her lips, shaking her head at me before heading away. "Fuck you, Mason Cain."

I turned my back on her, scraping a hand through my hair and finally healing myself of the wounds she'd inflicted on me, knowing I needed to try and forget this had ever happened. I had to act like a damn professional from now on.

I sighed, doing up my belt with shame rushing down on me like a rainstorm. "Fuck you too, Rosalie Oscura."

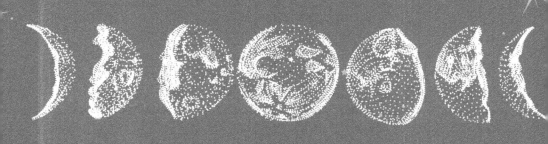

ROSALIE

PRISONER #12

CHAPTER THIRTY FIVE

The routines of this damn place were pure agony with so much pressure closing in on me. I needed to progress my plans, but there was absolutely nothing I could do about it while we were herded between our jobs and meals.

I was granted one small mercy after our work finished for the morning and we headed back to the Mess Hall though; Cain's break was starting too. He ditched me amongst the masses without a word and headed back to the staff quarters to get his own food. I wasn't sure how soon he'd be back working again, but with a bit of luck he wouldn't be hounding me so closely anyway. Following our kiss he'd turned full asshole, barking instructions at me about the cleaning I was doing and refusing to look at me without a scowl on his face aside from that. Who knew someone who bent the rules as often as he did would be so afraid of breaking a few?

If I knew anyone who needed to relieve a bit of tension then it was definitely him and I could have done a spectacular job of helping out. But if he enjoyed the feeling of that stick up his ass, who was I to try and loosen it for him? That said, this heat between us wasn't going anywhere, but if he wanted to torture himself with it he could be my guest. In the meantime, I'd happily use his distracted state of mind to further my plans. I had a clear few hours to work on my issues without the added worry of a Vampire listening in on me the whole damn time and I was going to make use of them.

I was growing more anxious as the day progressed though and as I headed into the Mess Hall, I was writhing with anxious energy. I had to find out what was going on with Sook in Psych. Which meant that tonight I had every intention of heading through the vents and tracking her down.

I was pretty sure I could break into Psych if I had to and bust her ass out before we escaped. Even if she was crazy, she'd still have her gifts and I was plenty used to working with crazy in my family. But I needed to do a recon trip down there beforehand to make sure I had her exit strategy ready. I had to find her exact location and figure out how I'd be getting her out of her cell.

The problems with that were uncountable though, not least because Cain was on to me and if I was out of my cell for too long after lock up, he could easily come looking and discover me missing. All the detection and concealment spells in the world wouldn't let me move as fast as a damn Vampire.

I huffed dramatically as I dropped into my seat at the centre of my pack and my Wolves instantly swivelled towards me as they picked up on my mood.

"What's wrong, Alpha?" Brett asked, reaching out to grip my thigh.

I growled at him half-heartedly, knocking his hand back off. The guy was way too keen to solve my problems with group sex and I was getting sick of reminding him that I only wanted Alphas.

"I have an issue," I said, glancing around the room to see if anyone was lurking too close to us.

My pack instantly hustled, leaning close and forming a wall of Wolf flesh all around me three Fae deep to keep my words private.

Amira was amongst them and I fought the ripple of anger which raced through me as her hand landed on my shoulder in a comforting gesture.

La vendetta sta arrivando, bitch. Revenge is coming.

She moved away quickly and I relaxed as Sonny nuzzled against my neck.

I was also bombarded with fruit cups and pudding pots as more than half of the pack offered up what little gifts they could to try and lighten my mood. I gave them a grateful smile for the gestures as I looked around, wondering if there was actually anything they could do to help.

"I need…" My tongue stalled. I couldn't risk compromising myself by allowing my plans to slip through the pack. I trusted them, but secrets only stayed secrets when they were your own and I already had two other Fae in here guarding my plans. Possibly three if Gustard had stolen the knowledge from my mind. But I refused to worry about that unless he made a move.

My thoughts snagged on Roary and Sin. They were as invested in this as I was. Which actually made them the ideal Fae to ask for help.

"I need…to get laid," I finished, smirking as I quickly formed a plan.

"Yes!" Brett exclaimed, releasing a howl of excitement.

Busty Esme was already unhooking all of her buttons and a few of the others started making out as they got overexcited.

I growled lightly but before I had to make it clear that I didn't mean a pack orgy, Sonny got to his feet and snarled at them, slamming his hands down on the table.

"She doesn't mean she wants to join in with *us*," he said, glaring at Esme as she got her boobs out. She really did have a nice rack, but I wasn't looking for nipples with my cheese sandwich.

"Yeah, sorry guys," I said, offering them a shrug. "I'm still after Alphas."

Brett whimpered and Esme slowly put her tits away again.

"What do you need our help with?" Sonny asked, cutting to the point as his eyes sparkled with excitement.

"Well…" I looked between my pack and offered them a teasing smile. "I need a bit of privacy to-"

"We can clear out the library for you!" Banjo exclaimed.

"Yeah, the back corner has no cameras between the stacks."

"Shall I try and find you some blankets?"

"I got a scented candle from commissary…but I have no way to light it so you have to just sniff the wax."

"I got some lacy underwear from commissary too!" Clive shouted and I looked around at him with a laugh.

"I could cut my hair off and fashion a whip out of it if you're into that kind of thing-"

"Stop!" I gasped as a laugh tore from my lips. "I'm not in need of anything aside from an Alpha to throw me about."

"Okay, we can go and get an Alpha for you, but the only true Alpha Wolf in here is…"

"Ethan Shadowbrook," Banjo murmured in horror.

A chorus of gasps and growls sounded all around me at the mere suggestion of me fraternising with our sworn enemy and I bit my tongue as I looked around at their horrified expressions.

"I have a thing for Alphas," I said slowly. "But that doesn't have to mean an Alpha *Wolf…*"

My pack released a collective breath and I offered them a laugh which I hoped didn't sound as false as it felt. When they found out about me and Ethan I'd have a lot of damage control to do, but that was tomorrow's problem.

"How about Roary Night?" someone suggested and I smirked.

"Yeah, Roary could give me what I'm after," I agreed, ignoring how weird this whole conversation was.

"I'll go and tell him he's required!"

"The rest of us will go and clear out the library."

My pack began to disperse and I cleared my throat to draw their attention back.

"Maybe get Sin Wilder for me too," I said, my lips twitching with that idea. In all honesty if this wasn't just a lie to cover up my meeting with the two of them, I wouldn't be complaining. A three-way with Sin and Roary would be a pretty spectacular way to spend my afternoon.

My pack hesitated as more than a few of them looked over to Sin where he sat alone on his table devouring his lunch. They were clearly afraid to approach him and I didn't really blame them, but I was pretty sure they'd be okay once they told him what I wanted.

"If it's too much bother…" I began with a pout.

Sonny shoved himself to his feet, squaring his shoulders as a growl escaped his throat. "I'll get the Incubus," he announced, his dark eyes flaring with determination. "The rest of you just sort the library."

My pack scattered and I leaned back in my seat with a laugh as I looked at the abandoned lunch trays all around me and the mountain of fruit and pudding cups which still lay heaped in front of my plate.

I reached out and peeled open the closest fruit cup, popping a strawberry between my lips as I watched Sonny cross the room and approach Sin.

A few of my other Wolves trailed after him, but they hung back as my ballsy Beta strode forward to interrupt Sin's meal.

I watched with interest, wondering if I might need to step in on his behalf.

Sin looked up from his plate with a wicked grin on his lips and threw a sandwich straight at Sonny's face. He deflected it at the last moment, growling as he leaned down over the table and got right in Sin's personal space to speak to him.

My hackles rose at the murderous look on Sin's face but I refused to move, pushing another strawberry between my lips as I watched his fingers curl around the edge of his tray. If Sonny didn't get to the point soon, I was pretty sure he'd have a tray to the face within seconds.

Sin's dark eyes suddenly snapped to me and a filthy grin lit his features as his gaze dropped over my body.

I pushed another strawberry into my mouth, biting down slowly as he watched with unconcealed desire. I almost felt bad about misleading him, but it would be worth it when I figured out how to get Sook out of Psych.

I pushed out of my seat, taking my fruit pot with me as I walked and eating the rest of it as I crossed the room. I caught Roary's eye as I went and he smirked as he got to his feet and headed out of the Mess Hall before me.

I hesitated by the door as I finished my fruit then passed the empty pot to one of my Wolves so she could toss it in the trash for me.

I headed downstairs with excitement trickling down my spine as I passed several pissed looking Fae on their way back up. My pack had clearly made good on clearing the library for me and as I reached level six, I found half the pack guarding the doors to keep everyone out.

I brushed my hands over their arms and backs gratefully and they smiled at me, clearly proud of themselves for sorting out this whole three-way Alpha hook up situation for me. Which was actually seriously weird, especially considering that I was related to more than a few of them. But oh well. Wolves *were* weird. We were okay with it.

Brett pulled the door open for me and I headed into the huge library with a smirk on my lips.

The smell of books enveloped me as I moved further into the vaulted space and I breathed it in deeply. Aunt Bianca had a library at the manor and after I'd moved in with her, I'd formed a habit of reading there every evening when I got back from running beneath the moon. She'd found me asleep in there so many mornings that she'd even made up a reading corner for me filled with soft blankets and pillows so that I was comfortable when I inevitably drifted off.

My cousins thought the joy I took in reading was bordering on obsessive but in the years I'd spent living with my mamma and then my papà, I'd never been given the opportunity to learn like that. When I'd first come to live with my aunt I'd been damn near illiterate, but I'd been determined to learn. So between Faetube videos online and the family library, I'd caught myself up on everything I would have learned if I'd been able to attend school. And I'd done it all without anyone ever realising.

So the scent of the library actually felt safe to me. It was somewhere that I was used to being when I took control of my destiny and I was about to do that again now.

I rounded the final stack and found Roary leaning against a little table which sat by the far wall. He was reading a thick book entitled *Making the most of your incarceration* and his lips curved like he found something amusing in its pages.

He didn't look up as I approached and I reached out to tug the book from his hands as I made it to him.

"What's so interesting that you can't even say hello to me?" I asked, flipping the book around to look at it.

Roary snatched it back, laughing as he slammed it shut and held it above my head. "Maybe I don't want you to know."

I eyed the book above me and half considered tackling him for it, but I was pretty sure that was what he wanted.

"Fine. Keep your secrets, Lion boy, I don't need tips on enjoying my incarceration anyway. I don't plan on it lasting long."

Roary slid the book onto the top shelf out of reach and I skirted him to take a seat on the reading desk behind him, crossing my legs beneath me.

"I'm guessing you didn't actually want me to meet you here for a hook up…" Roary said slowly as he turned to look down at me.

My lips parted on a response, but the Library door banged closed before I could get it out. Roary frowned in confusion but before he could ask, Sin's voice filled the space.

"I'm ready to find out just how wild you are, kitten," he called.

I snorted a laugh as Roary raised his eyebrows at me and Sin's heavy footsteps approached our spot at the rear of the library.

"I'll warn you that after all that time in isolation, this isn't going to be quick. I'm rough at the best of times but you might have done well to bring a helmet today... I'm going to take my time making you feel absolutely every kind pleasure and by the time you're done screaming my name, your throat will be rubbed raw-" Sin paused in his promises as he rounded the corner and spotted Roary with me.

His jumpsuit was tied around his waist, leaving his dark arms bare for me to appreciate and I bit my lip as I looked him over. One day, I was going to spend some serious time studying his tattoos in depth.

"Hey," I said innocently as his heated gaze drank us in.

"I didn't get the message about the extra player," Sin growled, looking at Roary for a long moment. "But I guess it just means you'll scream louder." He stalked forward, yanking his tank off and exposing the ripped muscles of his abs.

My mouth dried out as I watched him coming for me and the wild part of me was seriously tempted to indulge in this fantasy.

Before I could give it nearly enough consideration, Roary stepped between me and Sin, stopping his advance as he planted his feet and folded his arms.

"The three-way was a cover, asshole," he snarled. "Rosa brought us here to talk about something, not get naked on a stack of books."

"There could be time for both," I joked. Although it might have been a genuine offer too.

Sin licked his lips as his hungry gaze burned into mine and my pulse thrummed at the idea of doing what we were pretending to do.

"I'm guessing you had good reason to call us down here aside from eye-fucking an Incubus," Roary growled and heat licked down my spine at the sound.

He turned to look at me and I surveyed him curiously because that had sounded a hell of a lot like jealousy.

"Calm down boys, there's plenty of me to go around," I promised and Sin's smile widened. "But sadly, I did ask you to meet me for a reason aside from getting naked together."

"What is it?" Roary asked.

"As it stands, the three of us are the only ones in on the plan for us to escape this place."

Roary and Sin exchanged a dark look and I bit my lip, wondering if I should have given them that little nugget of info before now.

"Why him?" they both asked at once and I laughed.

"I was paid to come and rescue Sin," I explained. "And the Fae who booked his ticket out of here is essential to making this plan work."

"That doesn't explain why the Lion is coming," Sin growled.

"*Roary* has already proved his worth by securing something I needed to do all of this. Besides, he's the only reason I agreed to this job. Either Roary comes with us or we don't escape at all." I raised my chin defiantly, daring them to question me but after a tense moment, they both seemed to accept it.

"So what's this meet up about?" Roary asked.

"I'm still up for the three-way," Sin added seductively.

I ignored the heat that lit beneath my flesh and got to the point.

"Sook Min. She's in Psych and I need her if we want to get out of here. Which means I need to get into Psych, check she's okay and then set up a plan for getting her out when we leave."

"Sounds like a bitch of a problem," Sin said disinterestedly. "What's it got to do with me?"

"You want to get your ass out of this dungeon too, don't you?" Roary snarled.

"I've got a bed, regular meals and a girl who I'm gonna claim all day every day for the foreseeable future," Sin replied, eyeing me like that was a foregone conclusion. "What more do I need from the outside world?"

"For a start, if that girl is *me,* then I can assure you you won't be claiming anything all the time we're stuck down here."

"Are you saving it for a reward when we escape?" Sin asked excitedly.

I rolled my eyes at him, but if he wanted to play that game then why not? I might have been resisting his charms to keep him on the hook, but there was nothing wrong with adding a little extra incentive too.

"You want a night with me as a reward for breaking out of here?" I teased.

"For starters," Sin purred.

I paused for a long moment and Roary tensed beside me. But in all honesty,

I already knew I was going to be giving in to Sin's demands sooner or later. My body ached for his and I was already captivated by the promises he made. What was the harm in putting a date on it?

"Done," I agreed, biting down on my bottom lip.

Roary growled like that pissed him off and I looked up at him from beneath my lashes.

"What's wrong, Roar?" I teased. "You don't want me, but no one else can have me either?"

"Oh he wants you," Sin interrupted. "I can taste so much lust on him that it's giving me belly ache."

I laughed as I looked up at Roary, tossing my long hair over my shoulders as his jaw ticked with irritation.

"Are you going to tell us what you want our help with or not?" he demanded.

"I need you to keep the guards distracted while I head into the walls during our free time this evening." We were given four hours of free time following on from dinner in the Mess Hall each night where we could wander between the cell blocks, library and gym. As we had so many options, the guards couldn't keep as close of an eye on us and it would be easy for them to lose track of little old me.

"You're going to chance it while everyone is awake?" Roary questioned.

"Yeah. Cain is on to me and I can't risk him coming looking for us during the night again. It's too obvious that I'm up to something if he comes to my cell and finds me missing. But during free time, I could be in any number of places. It's a lot harder for him or any of the guards to keep track and I can make use of that."

"So you want a riot or something to keep them distracted?" Roary asked.

"What if the Belorian got loose in the corridors?" Sin suggested darkly.

"Are you crazy?" I hissed, staring at him. "That thing could kill half the Fae in here!"

"Yeah...and it would be a pretty epic distraction," he replied, like the idea wasn't entirely insane.

"Fuck no," Roary snarled. "How the hell would you even get to it anyway? You're not even thinking straight."

"I could get to it easy," Sin said, rolling his eyes. "I know more shit about this place than you could ever dream to."

"I've been here longer than you, asshole," Roary reminded him.

"Yeah. But some of us haven't relied on gangs and bullshit to carve our place here. I've got more knowledge about this prison than you could ever claim."

402

"Stop it," I snapped before Roary could respond. "This is a pointless discussion. We aren't setting the fucking Belorian free. I don't actually want to be eaten by a soulless monster, thanks all the same. So we need to come up with something better."

"I've got something," Sin announced.

"What?" I demanded.

"You'll see." His eyes lit with danger and I pursed my lips as I looked at him.

"You expect me to trust you based on *you'll see?"*

"Yeah. It'll be epic. You'll see," he repeated and Roary growled.

"Sin," I began but he turned and started walking away from us, giving me a look at the huge Sagittarius tattoo he had inked on his back. The ferocious centaur had his lips parted in a battle cry as his long hair billowed out behind him and his muscular arms tensed in their position holding a bow and arrow ready to fire. He looked wild and fierce and dangerous. Just like Sin.

"I'm on it, beautiful. Consider your distraction sorted." Sin snatched his tank from the ground as he went, shrugging it back on and leaving me alone with Roary again.

"Are you going to trust him?" he asked me, the suspicion in his eyes clear.

"Yeah," I replied. "But it can't hurt to have a backup plan in place too…"

He smirked as he looked down at me and nodded in agreement. "Okay, little pup, I've got you covered. Just make sure you don't get caught."

"Are you worried about me, Roary?"

"I'm worried about being stuck in here if you can't pull this off," he hedged.

"Well don't concern yourself over that," I said cockily. "I *always* get what I want."

And today that would be Sook Min.

SIN

PRISONER #88

CHAPTER THIRTY SIX

I had my eyes shut, meditating the shit out of tonight's plan as I sat in the Mess Hall with three lemons lined up before me on the table. If my wild girl wanted a distraction, she was going to get the biggest one this prison had ever seen. Getting down to level seven wouldn't be an issue, but I needed to lure a guard down there with me. Then, I just had to force them to open the Belorian's door and hope to hell I could outrun a hungry monster. Or at least outrun the guard.

Sure, Rosalie had told me releasing the Belorian was insane. But I knew exactly what she'd *really* meant by that. She'd practically given me the old wink-wink nudge-nudge treatment. She wanted this to happen, she just couldn't say it in front of Roary Night who was as straight as a knife. He was a thief, not a killer. He didn't know how to let blood run when it was needed. But I knew how and so did my sweet little candy cane of a treat who'd promised herself to me after we pulled off this escape. Fuck, I was going to make her hurt in all the right places. I could wait a little longer for that. But in order to live out that dream, I had to let my psycho loose.

Meditation was supposed to calm the mind, but I didn't have an ordinary mind. So my brain was sparking like a car ignition, ready for me to press the throttle and take it for a wild ride.

I cracked open my eyes, scanning the guards in the room as I made my selection. My gaze landed on Officer Nixon. He was a tall fucker with a mean face and a bald head. I knew for a fact he was a lech who took sexual favours from the inmates in exchange for him smuggling shit into the prison for them. He also left bruises on their skin and had left more than one Fae with a broken look in their eyes after his time with them. It wasn't common knowledge, but with my sense for lust, I always picked up on who was fucking who in this place. So Nixon was overdue a quick death. Or a slow one if I could manage it. I'd just make him open the Belorian's door then make sure he got eaten by it to cover my ass.

"Hell yes!" I announced, slamming my palms down on the table. A Pegasus walking past nearly dropped his tray in alarm as he looked to me then scampered away.

I was about to get up and wing the rest of my plan to get Nixon to take me downstairs when Rosalie dropped into the seat beside me.

"Hey kitten," I purred, letting my eyes trail down to her cleavage peeping through the open buttons of her jumpsuit.

Her hand dropped onto my knee and my dick jumped to attention. A dirty growl escaped me and a smile twisted up my lips. "Do you wanna check out the goods before you buy? You'll need to go a little higher, but not that high if you catch my meaning." I smirked and she rolled her eyes.

"Gimme your hands," she asked and I instantly dropped them under the table to give them to her despite not knowing why. But she could have any piece of me she desired. Intact or cut off. Whichever way my wild girl preferred. I mean, a severed dick dildo wasn't nearly as fun as when it was attached to a sex god like me, but who knew what she was into?

Her fingers coiled around my wrist then something clicked faintly before she moved to my other hand. Magic flooded into my fingertips and I groaned like I'd just come in my pants.

"Holy shit baby," I sighed. By the stars, she was per-to-the-fect. I'd heard the rumours that someone in this prison had obtained a cuff key and I'd been fucking stupid not to realise it was her before now. "You really know how to get my juices flowing." I tugged my sleeves down to make sure the unlit cuffs weren't on show to the guards and resisted the urge to bring a coil of flames to my fingertips immediately. *Man* I loved burning things.

"Are you all good?" she asked innocently, but what she was really asking was *are you ready to give me my distraction, lover boy?*

I turned to look at the clock on the wall as it ticked its way up towards a quarter to six. *Thirty seconds to go.*

"I'm all good, wild girl. Here, take this and keep it on you for luck." I held out a lemon for her and she frowned in confusion but took it all the same. I leaned in close, tucking a lock of hair behind her ear and murmuring softly so only she could hear. "Brace for impact."

I picked up the other two lemons just as the clock ticked onto a quarter to and an empty table at the back of the room exploded, smashing into the ceiling and sending a fiery blast out around it. That shit had cost me hard on the Veiled Wall to get it done today, but I was gonna be a free man soon. Who needed tokens for commissary when I was going to have my life back and Rosalie Oscura moaning my name within a few days?

Rosalie gasped as debris soared overhead and the two of us ducked in sync. The guards from all around the room started running forward to put out the fire as the inmates surged away from it in a stampede. In the chaos, we could all slip away to where we needed to be tonight and now that I had my magic, I had no need for Officer Nixon. Which was a crying shame as I'd been looking forward to watching his head get eaten by the Belorian.

I stamped my mouth to Rosalie's cheek and jumped to my feet. "See ya later gladiator."

I backed away and she stared after me in surprise with a whole lot of lust dolloped on top. I smirked before turning into the crowd and striding through the hall, juggling the final two lemons in my hands. As I passed Roary, I tossed one to him with a wink and he caught it at the last second. "You'll thank me later."

I pocketed my own before he could reply and jogged toward the unmanned open doors. Rosalie probably thought this was my entire plan, but a little flash bang wasn't gonna keep the guards occupied for long. And if my baby was going into the vents tonight, I sure as shit needed to keep anyone from looking for her for as long as I possibly could.

I raced down the stairs, taking them two or three at a time as I pranced down them like a fucking pony. With my magic free, my plan had gotten a whole lot easier, but not much less dangerous. I'd always been a whore for danger though. I flirted with her on a daily basis. And this might have been one of the crazier things I'd done in my time, but it was also the most exhilarating.

I ran and ran until I reached the darkened floor where they kept the beast. Seven. The doors to this corridor were always left open, but no fucker was crazy enough to spend their free time hanging around outside the Belorian's house aside from me. It was as cold as my mother's heart down here and creepy as shit. A low light at the far end of the brick walled corridor illuminated the huge sun steel door that kept the Belorian contained. I stood back in the stairwell, lifting my hands and letting my air magic spread out into the room. I pushed my will into it to create a whip and slammed it into the top left corner of the ceiling beyond the archway. A satisfying crack sounded the camera there breaking and I smirked to myself.

I walked forward with adrenaline charging my veins. Tension was building in my body like an orgasm waiting to unleash. And with every step I took toward that door, I drew closer and closer to release.

I snapped my fingers so sparks flashed between them as I approached. As a double Elemental, I was the most powerful Fae in this prison. An overlord, if you will. And that was lucky for me. Because when this beasty was free, all hell would break loose and who knew what I'd be needing all my magic for in the chaos?

I reached the door, placing my hand against the cold metal, the sensation lifting the hairs on the back of my neck.

"Here kitty kitty." I made kissing noises as I moved along the door, trailing my fingers across it. My gaze fell to an air vent that sat to one side of the door and I moved to crouch before it with a smirk. I ran my thumb across the bolts, pouring heat into my touch until the metal melted. I weakened each corner before tugging the grate free and tossing it on the ground with a clatter. A guttural groan sounded from somewhere beyond the door and shivers chased each other up and down my spine.

"Come to daddy," I purred as I dropped onto all fours and crawled into the narrow space.

My shoulders pressed against the metal walls, but I could just about manage to move along. I'd been in a tighter space than this when I'd hid behind Lady Cherisse Needham's bedpost butt ass naked when her husband had come home.

A heavy scuttling sounded somewhere above me and I realised this vent must run under the room the Belorian was housed in. That meant I needed to pop up like a jack-in-the-box, scramble the collar on its neck so the Warden couldn't control it and blow the doors off Italian Job style to set it free.

Simple.

A cold wind whistled through the vent and I shuddered as I reached a grate above me. I rolled onto my back awkwardly, reaching up and melting the bolts holding it in place as I hummed under my breath. A horrible shriek sounded out in the room and I stilled, my blood running cold at the sound. But I was Sin Wilder, I didn't get scared by anything.

I took a breath and broke the final bolt then reached down into my pocket, taking out the lemon and bringing it to my lips. I sank my teeth into it, taking a good old bite and swallowing it down rind and all while my face screwed up like a cat's asshole. *Fuck, this better work.*

The Belorian released another toe curling screech and I shoved the grate open at the same time to cover the sound. Low red lights lit the space above and I quickly willed three fireballs into existence, sending them flying out in different directions. The thunderous sound of the monster's footfalls sounded as it chased after one of them, picking up the heat signature and racing to devour it.

With my heart thrashing in my chest, I sat upright, getting myself half way through the hole and pressing my hands to the icy concrete either side of the vent. A shriek caught my ear and I heard it coming for me in the dark. My heart pounded like mad as I tried to pull myself out of the narrow gap.

I raised a hand as a roar raked against my ears and released another wave of fireballs out around me, sending them toward the outer walls. I heard it change direction behind me and I scrambled out of the vent, sweat sticking my jumpsuit to my back.

As fast as I could, I pushed the grate back into place and leapt to my feet with my fists raised and my breaths ragged. *Where are you, you Jurassic Park bastard?*

I wheeled around as I hunted for it, my eyes falling on the huge fucker with its six legs and smooth, greyish body as it devoured the fireballs with its wide, fang filled mouth. It was a monster pure and simple. A creature made from nightmares and fear.

I lifted my hands, forcing myself to focus on the large collar around its bulbous throat. I had to do this. Had to pull this off for my wild girl. My crazy ideas always landed me in trouble, but I may have just led myself to my death this time if I didn't act fast.

Just relax and keep to the plan. You're Sin fucking Wilder.

I released a shield of air and guided it toward the beast as it gnashed at the remaining fireball. I could cast with the gift of a god and I quickly wrapped that air bubble right around the collar until it blocked off all transmission and the green light on it turned red.

"Gotcha." I grinned, pivoting toward the door and spotting the manual override lever half way up the wall. I'd been called into Warden Pike's office once and gotten a glimpse at the designs for this place proudly presented on her wall. No one would suspect an inmate would wanna let this creature out. But I'd tucked that nugget of information away for a rainy day. And it looked like today it was pouring.

I sprinted towards it then jumped into the air, catching hold of the lever and hanging my full body weight from it. The whole thing dropped down with a heavy clunk and a loud buzzzzz sounded the doors opening, the noise setting my brain on fire. I fell to the ground on my feet, lifting my hands fast and casting a blazing line of fire out into the corridor beyond. My heart thumped madly as the Belorian twisted around and ran toward the open doors with a shriek of exhilaration. I guessed even creepy ass bio-monsters liked being free. And this one was about to attend a feast.

The fucker's eyeless face looked my way before heading out and my throat closed up.

I scrambled for the half eaten lemon in my pocket and hoped to the fucking stars I knew what I was doing. I'd once heard the guards talking about the lemon sprays they wore to repel the beast if they ever accidently ran into it during their night shifts. But it could have been superstition as easily as fact...

The Belorian bared its fangs at me and panic skittered under my skin as it took in a rattling breath which made its fleshy nostrils flare. It rushed towards me and real fear tore through me as I backed up until my spine hit the wall. Its clawed foot smashed into my side and I was thrown to the ground, tumbling across it as my bones bruised and broke.

Fuck no no no.

I raised the lemon as pain clutched hold of my insides, lifting my other hand to cast magic, but if I attacked this fucker it was never going to leave me alone. I held my breath, ripping into the lemon with my nails and praying I wasn't as crazy as my reputation.

The Belorian dove over me, its talons slamming into the concrete either side of my head and its acrid breath rushing over me. I was a hair's breadth from death. The closest I'd ever come. And in the face of it, I realised the terrifying reality of never tasting freedom again. This was my life. I'd spent most of it alone. I'd clawed my way through it, tasting the darker flavours it had to offer, but barely any of the sweeter. And I'd never got to have the one thing I'd always craved. *Love.*

The Belorian lunged for me and I squirted that lemon in its face, squeezing my full fist around it so it popped like a balloon. The monster reared backwards as the scent hit the air, spitting and hissing as it backed away from me.

Hell to the fucking yes.

"Off you go like a good beasty," I begged.

Miraculously, it turned its head towards the flames beyond its cell and I took in its towering height and the drool leaking from its pale lips. It didn't spare me another look as it raced through the open doors and out into a prison full of fresh meat. I only killed bad motherfuckers with hearts made of coal, and this place was swarming with them. Who was I but a vigilante cleansing the world?

I wet my dry mouth as I healed my body of my injuries and slowly got to my feet. That bastard had shown me something no other opponent ever had. It had pressed my face against the door to death and now I knew I had so much more life to live. So many more flavours to taste in the world. And I was going to make damn sure I sampled every last one of them before I went out of it.

The hulking creature rounded onto the stairway at the far end of the corridor and I hurried out of the room. I kicked the vent grate upright on the floor so I could fix it back in place and no one could ever figure out that someone had let the beast out from the inside.

A blood-curdling scream reached me from somewhere far above and a manic laugh tumbled from my throat.

Run free beastykins. Kill like it's your birthday.

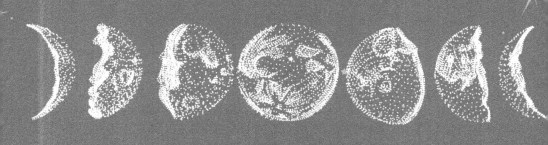

ROSALIE

PRISONER #12

CHAPTER THIRTY SEVEN

I hurried up the stairs in our cell block with Roary by my side and the thrill of the job racing through my veins. This was why I'd always been on the front line of every job I'd ever pulled for my family, not because I had to be but because I *needed* to be. I craved the rush of doing something I shouldn't like a Killblaze addict craved a high.

But I didn't need drugs to get me off, hell I'd never even bothered with alcohol much. This was what pressed my buttons. Adrenaline, fear and danger. If I could live on a diet of that, I'd be one happy Wolf.

We kept going all the way up to the third floor and headed straight for our cells. The cell block was pretty empty while everyone had free time, but there were always a few nosey fuckers hanging about. I kept an eye out for them, wondering if anyone might notice me going into my cell and not coming back out.

As we approached my door, Roary suddenly caught hold of my waist and tugged me around to face him. He growled softly as he dragged me into his arms and I gasped as his mouth fell against my neck, brushing a line up to my ear.

"Come on, Rosa, let the nice criminals know that we're going to be busy in here for a while," he purred as his hands pushed inside my open jumpsuit and caressed the inch of bare skin between my panties and my tank top.

I gasped as his fingers chilled with water magic as he channelled ice into them, raising goosebumps all over my body.

"Apart from the bit where you'll leave again in a minute," I murmured as I ran my hands up his sides, gripping the broad slope of his shoulders.

"I'll have to make out I got a bit too enthusiastic and finished quickly," he teased, nipping my earlobe. "Although I'm sure I could keep you satisfied even in that situation."

A moan escaped my lips and I fisted my fingers through his long hair as I arched my back, my breasts pressing against his chest.

"Or you could just be that fast for real and we could stop playing this stupid game," I dared.

Roary growled again, deeper this time as he damn near lifted me off of my feet and backed me into my cell, pushing the sheet I'd hung aside as we entered.

He kept backing me up until we reached the rear wall and I gasped as my spine collided with the bricks.

I drew back but he lingered close, eyeing me for a long moment which made my heart pound.

"We should get going," I breathed.

"Yeah."

Neither of us moved.

I swallowed thickly and his gaze trailed to my mouth.

Roary pulled back suddenly and I released a breath of frustration as I turned from him, ducking low so that I could remove the bricks from their hiding place beneath the sink.

Roary moved back towards the door as he set up a strong repellent spell outside my cell. If anyone got it into their head to come and visit me, they'd find themselves in desperate need of a shit before they could cross my threshold and go scurrying off to relieve themselves instead.

I made quick work of the bricks, revealing the tunnel beyond them. I shrugged my arms out of my jumpsuit and tied it around my waist. The lemon Sin had given me in his madness got in the way in my pocket and I took it out, tossing it onto my bunk before tying my long hair in a knot on the top of my head for good measure. It was hot in the walls and we needed to move fast.

Roary finished his spell and started working on an illusion next.

A false version of my voice filled the air as I cried out in pleasure and I snorted a laugh as he filled the room with fake sex noises, adding the sounds of the bunk crashing against the wall repeatedly a moment later.

"Believe me, stronzo, you'd be shouting my name too," I purred as I dropped down onto my hands and knees.

"You think so, little pup?" he teased in a low voice and I growled right back at him.

414

"You might find out if you choose to stop with your I'm-too-old-to-do-more-than-spoon-and-make-out-with-you bullshit."

Roary rolled his eyes as he dropped down beside me. "I would have made out with a sock that night, pup. You caught me in a bad moment and I wanted a distraction. Don't go thinking I've suddenly got a thing for you now."

I swore at him in Faetalian and waited for him to crawl into the tunnel. I followed close behind him, pausing to replace the bricks and hide the hole in the wall.

As soon as we made it into the maintenance gap, I threw a silencing bubble around us and quickly led the way through the walls to the pipes I'd discovered which led down to the lower levels. This next part of my plan was either genius or fucking insane, but I was willing to take a bet on it being the former.

We stayed silent as we scrambled through the walls, the seriousness of our situation pressing in on us. If we were caught here, that would be the end of it. We'd be thrown in the hole for the stars knew how long and all of the work I'd done would be for nothing.

When we finally reached the pipes which led to the lower level, Roary reached out and pressed his palm to the biggest one. It was the water waste pipe and it led down through every level and split off to run into Psych too. I could use it to get down there, but I'd have to come back through the vents and return to the corridor on level eight. Luckily I'd scouted a vent in the stairwell so I'd just have to exit from that one to avoid the CCTV then head back up to my cell. Simple. Not. But then what was the point in an easy existence?

I waited in silence as Roary gritted his teeth, pushing Water magic into the pipe and freezing it solid in the space beyond his hand. Blue crystals began to form all over the metal pipe and my breath rose in a cloud of vapour before me as the temperature plummeted.

A shiver raced along my spine and the constant rush of running water within the pipe was abruptly cut off.

Roary continued to work at freezing the water within the pipe for another long minute as I watched his muscles bunch with energy.

"There," he panted, withdrawing his hand when it was finally done. "That will last half an hour tops. But don't be in there when the water breaks through."

"I'll be in and out just as soon as I've sealed the wall in my room behind you," I swore to him.

We hurried back through the maintenance gap as fast as we could, climbing up through the levels until we were back outside my cell.

I quickly dismantled the wall and the sound of my pleasure filled screams flooded over us from Roary's illusion.

I rolled my eyes as he smirked at the sound of me begging for more. "You wish, stronzo."

Roary snorted a laugh as he squeezed back through the gap and I quickly replaced the bricks.

When there was just one brick to go, he caught my gaze, his golden eyes glittering with concern. "Be careful, Rosa," he growled. "And don't linger in that pipe."

"Lo prometto," I swore. *I promise.* I pulled the cuff key from my pocket and passed it to him. "You might need to cut your magic off again before I get back. Sin's too. Don't lose it."

"Cross my heart," he swore, painting an X on his chest.

Roary gave me a tight smile and I shoved the last brick into the wall, sealing the mortar again so that no one would be able to find it.

The muffled sound of my voice thanking Roary for the best sex of my life reached me and I snarled irritably.

Asshole.

His voice followed a moment later as I guessed he stepped out of my cell and my scowl deepened at his words. "I think I wore her out." He even fucking chuckled like a cocky bastardo. He'd be the one who was worn out after a night with me.

Pudding's deep laughter came in response and I scuttled away as a blush bit at my cheeks. One day, Roary Night would be pinned beneath me, begging for more while I toyed with him and I'd remind him of this shit as I let the torture stretch.

I ran along the maintenance gap as fast as I could, dashing for the pipes again as my heart pounded adrenaline through my limbs.

I practically fell down the holes which led to the lower levels and finally skidded to a halt beside the pipe once more. There was already less ice coating it than there had been when he'd cast it and panic bled through me as I wondered whether I was about to do something really fucking stupid.

I reached out to a spot beneath the ice and used my earth magic to carve a hole in the pipe just big enough for me to fit through.

I peeled the metal back with trembling fingers, relief spilling through me as no water appeared.

I threw my hand out into the space, casting an orange Faelight into existence and letting it sink down the sheer drop by a few meters so that I could see.

My heart hammered to the beat of a war drum in my chest as I leaned out over the space. That pipe led all the way to the bottom of Darkmore and beyond. It was a six floor drop which would kill me on impact if I fell and the smooth pipe had no handholds.

I took a deep breath and lowered myself into the tight space, pressing my feet against the right side of the pipe and managing to wedge my back against the left.

The wet walls were slippery and slick. This was a terrible fucking idea.

I reached out carefully and bent the metal back across to seal the pipe up again with me inside it before pressing my hand to the edges of the cut I'd made.

I shivered as the chill of Roary's ice kissed my freezing skin and I concentrated on forging the metal back into one smooth piece. Metal was the hardest thing to create with my earth magic and I gritted my teeth as I concentrated on sealing it back up perfectly. If I didn't do it right, the pipe would burst when the water was set loose again and the guards would figure out that someone had tampered with it.

The metal slowly fused back together and I sighed in relief as I felt out the last bumps and ridges to repair.

A cold drip fell on my stomach and I flinched as I continued to work.

A second drip slid into my hair and a third raced down my bare thigh.

My breath caught in my throat as a dull crack sounded above me.

I tipped my head back slowly as fear took me hostage and the orange glow of my Faelight illuminated the tight space.

The ice plug Roary had created to hold back the water sat a foot above my head and as I looked at it, more drips fell down to splash against my skin.

Another dull crack echoed through the pipe and I flinched as a spiderweb of lines splintered across the ice above me.

I choked on a scream as I half expected the whole thing to break in that moment, my heart skipping a beat as my life flashed before my eyes. It was brief and all too unhappy in places. I'd barely even begun to find my place in this world and I sure as shit wasn't going to lose it now.

I did the only thing I could and relaxed my posture, shrieking as I instantly began to fall. My back and feet were still pressed to the slick sides of the pipe but as I plummeted downwards, I began to doubt whether I'd be able to stop myself again at the junction to the pipe which ran into Psych.

I pressed my hands to the walls either side of me as I fell down the world's deadliest water slide, my stomach swooping as real fear consumed me and I hardly even slowed at all.

All of a sudden, the pipe to my left opened up and I cried out as I threw my weight that way, my heart leaping as I scrambled to catch hold of the hole.

My fingertips clawed onto the lip of the edge and I swung around as I held on for dear life, my legs slamming into the pipe with a dull thump which echoed around the space.

I grunted with effort as I scrambled to gain purchase on anything at all so that I could heave myself up.

A loud crack echoed down from somewhere above me as the ice continued to give way.

With a snarl of determination, I swung my leg up and managed to hook my knee over the edge of the pipe.

I grunted in effort as the rest of my body followed and I fell to my hands and knees, panting as fear sliced my soul apart.

I started crawling, directing my Faelight ahead of me as I moved as fast as I possibly could on all fours.

Another crack sounded in the dark behind me and I felt it right down to my core.

I kept going. I had to make it down the corridor which led away from the main prison and into Psych if I wanted to get into the vents there.

My pulse pounded against my eardrums as I crawled and crawled, another crack sounding somewhere far above.

My knees slipped and skidded against the smooth surface of the wet pipe and I trembled as I fought to get far enough through it.

An ear splitting roar exploded behind me as the ice suddenly gave way and I screamed at the sound of the water coming for me.

I slammed my hands against the wall, not caring if I'd made it far enough or not as my earth magic punched a hole straight into the side of the pipe.

I threw myself out, tossing a look over my shoulder as a tidal wave of water raced into the pipe from the main flow and charged straight towards me.

I fell into a metal vent and leapt back up, throwing my weight against the flap of pipe I'd bent open as I directed my earth magic into it, channelling everything I had into sealing that hole.

The magic glowed green with the force at which I commanded it and my limbs trembled in utter terror as water began to seep through the cracks.

My wet boots slipped on the smooth metal beneath me as I fought to hold the pipe closed and my magic worked to seal it off.

With a grunt of determination, the final gap sealed over and I fell back onto my ass, panting as the adrenaline shuddered through my body.

"Fuck you, Roary Night," I hissed as my heart remembered how to beat normally again. "Half an hour my ass."

ROARY

PRISONER #69

CHAPTER THIRTY EIGHT

I headed down the stairs in the cell block, my boots clanging against the metal as Plunger rushed to my side.

"What does she feel like?" he purred and I growled in warning.

"Get the fuck away from me," I snarled and he gave me a pouting look, staying at my side.

"Come on, just a few details. Was she *moist*? How did her *folds* feel?"

I lunged at him as we reached the next level down, throwing him back against the bars of a cell and a metallic dong sounded around the space.

I opened my mouth to threaten him when a scream caught my ear followed by the thundering of footfalls. I loosened my grip on Plunger, turning toward the noise and confusion pinched my features as inmates raced across the bridge into the block with fear in their eyes and screams on their lips.

A group piled into the cell beside me and Plunger, trying to force the door to shut.

"Please! Lock us in!" one girl cried and I followed her gaze to Officer Lucius who was running into the block with everyone else. She pulled her radio from her belt as she leapt off of the bridge, her honey blonde hair falling loose from her usually perfect bun. "We need lockdown in Cell Block D. Close all cells and retract the bridge immediately!"

The bell started ringing to announce the lockdown and Plunger shoved away from me, darting back up the stairs with a wild giggle.

"What's going on?!" I called to Lucius as inmates poured into the cells all around me.

"Back in your cell!" she commanded, taking her shock baton from her hip.

My heart pounded unevenly. I had to get to level eight to meet Rosa. If I wasn't there to cut her magic back off and she was found with her cuffs switched off, she was gonna be screwed.

I strode towards Lucius as more and more prisoners raced into the block. The bridge started to retract and my heart lurched as people leapt off of it into the block with screams of panic.

"Go back!" Lucius commanded, her eyes wild as more and more prisoners started jumping across the gap.

I ran forward with my heart in my throat, knowing I was facing loss of privileges and maybe some time in the hole by ignoring a direct order. But fuck it. I wasn't going to abandon my little pup.

The prisoners piled up on the bridge and screams rang out as the front row were forced forward. My gut wrenched a second before a line of them tumbled over the edge, falling into the void with shrieks of terror.

"Wait!" Lucius screamed, raising her hands and casting a bridge of ice between the gap. The inmates poured over it, racing into the block. I took my chance, running forward and pushing through the crowd to get to the other side.

"Sixty Nine!" she yelled after me. "Return to your cell *now*!"

I made it out of the block, adrenaline crashing through my veins as I ran against the tide. I didn't know what the fuck had happened to cause this kind of panic, but I had the awful feeling I was about to find out.

I spotted more guards trying to direct the prisoners towards their cell blocks and I ducked my head to hide as I darted into the stairwell and sped down it. The flow of bodies thinned out until there were just a few stragglers running up the stairs. I spotted the pink-haired girl Bullseye coated in blood as she sprinted up the steps with her sling-shot in hand.

"Hey – what's going on down there?" I called to her, but she just shook her head in warning and ran on.

My throat thickened as I descended, the sounds of racing footsteps moving far away from me. As I reached level six, a clamour of voices carried from beyond the glass doors of the library. A man was hammering his fists on it, jumping frantically up and down. "Let me in you assholes!"

I moved to run on down the stairs but my heart turned to a solid lump of ice as I spotted a vile creature below me. The Belorian's head was bent down on its long neck as it lapped at the blood of a dead inmate beneath it. Its talons were ripped deep into his chest and the man's lips were parted in a silent scream, painted there even after his death.

I drew in a shuddering breath as fear made a passage down my spine, backing up a step and waving at the guy who was trying to break into the library to try and catch his attention. *"Shut the fuck up,"* I hissed.

He finally noticed, turning toward me as I pressed a finger to my lips. His face paled as he realised the Belorian was close.

I side-stepped into the corridor and crossed to the other side, pressing my back to the wall. I had to get downstairs. Had to get past that fucking beast. I knew it hunted by heat and luckily for me I had water magic on my side. I just hoped this guy didn't turn out to be a damn snitch when this was all over, but I didn't have much choice but to use my power. My gaze shifted to a camera up on the wall which was aimed toward the library doors. I twitched my fingers, casting ice against the wall behind it. It grew outwards into a sharp spike, reaching through the metal cage around it before puncturing the wires and cutting the feed.

I hurried into action, raising my palms and casting a wall of ice across the archway that led into the stairwell, concealing us behind it. There was still a lot of noise coming from the library so I quickly cast a silencing bubble over the door too. The guy stared at me in surprise, looking to my cuffs.

He rushed over to me with desperation in his eyes. "Hey, do you have a key? Give it to me. Open my cuffs. I'm Dirk, you know, me right? I gave you my honey pot once, remember?"

He caught my arm and I shoved him off of me with a snarl. I wasn't going to start unlocking people's cuffs like a fucking idiot. I was risking enough as it was for someone I actually gave a shit about. He lunged at me again, tearing at my jumpsuit as he tried to get into my pockets. I threw him backwards with a growl and his spine hit the opposite wall.

"Fuck you, man!" Dirk spat.

A deep growl sounded beyond the wall of ice and my spine prickled as the Belorian's towering shadow appeared behind it.

I used my magic to chill my blood, shivering as a wave of cold ran over me and ice started to form on my skin. I couldn't stay like this for long, but it would give me a chance to run if I had to.

Come on, move upstairs you fucker.

A sound like a knife scoring against a plate filled my ears and a claw sliced through the centre of the ice, ripping a hole in it.

Dirk panted heavily and I raised my hand, telling him to stay where he was, sure he was about to do something stupid.

The Belorian lowered its head to the hole and I caught a glimpse of the flaps on its face lifting. *Holy shit.* It was using its heat sensors to see. Panic clutched my heart and I directed my magic onto Dirk, urging his body to chill. He gasped in surprise and the Belorian growled in response, its talons suddenly ripping at the entire wall.

Dirk ran at me with terror in his eyes, throwing a fist that I deflected with a growl of fury. He lunged for my pocket once more and I shoved him back a step, but he kept coming like a mad man.

I caught him by the collar, and hissed in his face, *"Shut the fuck up!"*

I threw him toward the library door, backing up and raising my hands to cast another wall of ice to conceal us, goosebumps rising across my flesh. A crash like breaking glass sounded as the beast broke through the first wall of ice and I stilled as silence fell once more.

The monster drew in a shuddering breath that set off a gurgling noise in its chest and I stilled in horror as it inhaled deeply again.

It could smell us.

"Let us in!" Dirk jumped up, hammering his fist on the library door.

The Belorian shrieked and I frantically threw a silencing bubble around Dirk to quiet him, my magic stretching towards breaking point. I hadn't laid in the sun to restore my power since yesterday morning and I'd used too much in the Compound since then. Freezing the pipe for Rosa had depleted my reserves even more so. If I'd known I was going to need it to fight the fucking Belorian, I would have been more careful.

The beast threw its whole weight against the wall and I swore, raising my hands to cast more ice to keep it intact. A deep tug in my chest told me I was getting close to the last of my power and fear scratched at my heart.

Fuck what do I do, what do I do?

I came up with the only solution I could. I reached into my pocket for the key to free Dirk's power. I was going to need help if I was gonna survive this. As I tugged it loose, the lemon Sin had given me fell from my pocket and rolled across the ground between us. It hit me with an absolute clarity that Sin had done this. He'd let out the Belorian like a fucking maniac despite Rosa telling him not to.

I ignored the lemon, holding the key out to Dirk as I fought to keep the wall intact.

"Here!" I called and he ran toward me with hope in his eyes. I unlocked his cuffs, refusing to part with the key before stuffing it back into my pocket. Fire magic flared to life in his palms and I opened my mouth in warning not to use it just as the Belorian ran at the wall full force. The monster burst through it, sending a shower of ice shards everywhere. With a yell of alarm, I transformed them into water before they hit us and they splashed over me, melting away some of the ice coating my skin.

The Belorian dove toward Dirk as fire flared in his palms and he fell to the ground with a cry of fear. Dirk directed a huge flame toward me, casting it above my head and the beast lurched away from him, racing for me instead.

"Motherfucker!" I cursed, coating my skin in more ice and darting away from the charging beast.

It crashed into the wall beneath the flame, unable to find me, but my magic was stuttering and I could feel the ice melting against my flesh already. *Fuck!*

Dirk scrambled to his knees and started to run but the beast lurched around, blocking his exit. The Belorian dove at him then jerked away with a shriek as its face came close to the lemon on the ground. It turned its head to the ceiling, shaking it violently as if the fruit had hurt it somehow.

My eyes locked with Dirk's as we both realised the power of that lemon and he snatched it into his grasp, jumping to his feet. He held it out in front of him and the Belorian backed up with a roar of anger, its spiny tail whipping through the air and slicing across my forearm. I released a yell of pain, clutching the wound as I stumbled back. The beast swung its vile head around, its eyes locking on me and I dove away from it, using the final drops of my power to coat my skin in ice once more.

It lunged forward blindly, hunting me by scent alone as it snapped its vicious teeth in the air. Dirk tried to run past it, but the Belorian's spiny tail caught him in the stomach and knocked him to the ground with a thwack. He wailed as blood leaked from the wounds on his gut and the Belorian twisted toward him, the metallic scent filling the air. The guy screamed in agony and the lemon fell from his hand, rolling toward me. The monster lunged, tearing into Dirk's chest with sharp teeth and I grimaced at the sound of crunching bones.

I went to heal my arm but my magic stuttered out before I'd even started and the spells around me died with it. My heart lurched at the clamour in the library filling my ears and I knew I had no more seconds to waste.

I darted forward and snatched the lemon into my grasp, racing past the beast with my heart jack-hammering in my chest. Dirk was fucked, but I had a whole lot of life yet to live so I couldn't look back.

I ripped into the lemon with my teeth, squeezing the juice all over my arms and neck as I sped into the stairwell with his dying screams following me. I stuffed the lemon back into my pocket, leaving enough juice for Rosa and focusing on what I had to do as the adrenaline in my blood hit a peak. I held my hand over the wound on my arm and tried to ignore the burning sensation that was racing through my bloodstream.

I had to find her. I had to get her back to her cell. And I had to beat the living hell out of Sin Wilder for freeing that motherfucking monster.

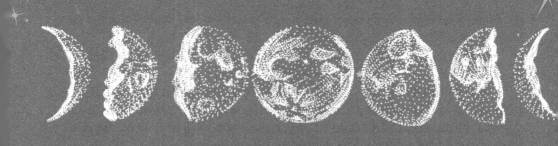

ROSALIE

PRISONER #12

CHAPTER THIRTY NINE

The vent narrowed as it headed into the Psych unit and I pushed aside any thoughts of claustrophobia with an iron fist. I wasn't turning back now. Hell, I *couldn't* turn back considering how tight this damn shaft was. It was forward or nothing. My hips and shoulders were firmly rammed against the sides of the metal shaft as I crawled along and the only light that reached me was through the sporadic grates which looked down into the empty corridor below.

Everything in Psych was white which seemed super cliché to me, but there it was. White floor, white walls, white doors. Not that I could see much beyond floor level.

The vent continued to tighten around me and I fell still as I reached another grate. I couldn't go on. Which meant I had to go down.

But that was easier said than done when the corridor beneath me was likely monitored by CCTV.

I craned my neck as I tried to get a look beyond the thick bars which blocked the grate beneath me, but it was no good. I couldn't see anything other than the floor and a few inches of wall on either side of the corridor.

I cursed beneath my breath and cast an amplifying spell to make it easier for me to hear anyone close by.

For a long moment there was nothing at all, but then a high pitched scream came to me from far away. A shiver danced along my spine at the sound, but I clenched my jaw against the fear which wanted to take root in me. This wasn't the time to let useless emotions take hold. To get the job done, I needed to keep my head clear and my emotions out of it.

I needed to escape this prison. For that I needed a Polethius Mole Shifter. And my Polethius Mole Shifter was in this damn unit.

I reached for the grate, curling my fingers around it and unleashing my earth magic so that the metal bowed to my commands and released its hold on the vent. I lifted it out of the hole it had occupied and dropped it on the far side of the vent, my silencing bubble hiding the sound for me.

I blew out a breath and lowered my head down as slowly as I could manage until I could see more of the corridor.

Windows ran along the walls on either side of the space, the edges of white rooms showing through the glass. A heavy door stood at the far end of the corridor leading back into the main prison and above it, a camera sat watching the hallway.

Luckily for me, it was trained down the corridor not up at the ceiling and I lowered my arm as I took aim at it. A vine shot from my palm, snaking along the ceiling before dropping down to encircle the camera. I tightened my fist and the vine snapped back, ripping the camera from the roof and dropping it inside the cage that contained it with a clatter.

I froze, listening to the sounds from my amplifying spell to see if anyone had heard that.

The screams came again in the distance and I chewed on my lip as I listened to them.

Someone somewhere close was in a shit load of pain.

I wriggled forward on my stomach until I made it through the hole in the vent, clinging to the edge as I swung my legs down beneath me. I pulled the grate back into place above me, balancing it so that no one would notice it had been loosened without a close look, before dropping to the floor.

I landed in a crouch and stilled as I took in my surroundings.

The windows which dotted the walls on either side of me drew my attention as I straightened and I looked into the first one curiously.

Inside the room were padded walls, a single mattress and a hole in the floor which I guessed served as a toilet.

A guy lay sleeping on the bed, his features pinched like he was in pain and his lip curled back in a snarl.

I glanced at the symbols which were painted on the top right corner of the glass. They matched those which decorated the lapels of our orange jumpsuits. A magic Element, Order sign and prisoner number. This guy was a Harpy with fire magic. Number eighty three.

I moved away from him, heading deeper into the unit as I searched for

Sook.

Most of the cells I passed held sleeping Fae, but as I turned a corner, I found a girl who was racing back and forth, bouncing off of the padded walls while screaming at the roof. I couldn't hear her voice through the walls though and I had to guess that the rooms were spelled to keep sound in.

I upped my pace as I hurried down the corridor, using my vines to disable any cameras ahead before they could catch sight of me.

Another Psych patient spotted me and raced up to the window, shrieking something I couldn't hear.

I took a step back as she pounded her fists on the glass in frustration, frowning as I wondered what the hell was wrong with her. There was something truly disturbing about her eyes. Like there was nothing where her soul should be.

I backed up until I bumped into the far wall and turned as another Fae leapt up before the glass.

The guy in there was a Manticore and as his eyes fixed on me, tears welled in them. He pressed his hands to the glass, his mouth forming two words which were impossible to mistake. *Help me.*

I shook my head uselessly. The door beside the glass didn't even have a handle, just a keypad and magic scanner to allow entry. There was nothing I could do to open it. And nowhere for him to run to even if I could.

I shrugged apologetically, shaking my head as I backed away from him.

He dropped to his knees and clasped his hands together as he begged, but what could I do? I didn't have access to that door. It would only open for someone who's magical signature was in the system and that definitely wasn't me.

"I'm sorry," I breathed, my gut twisting guiltily as I turned away from the desperation in his eyes.

The next window held a woman with the same hollow expression who started waving her arms anxiously, pointing me back the way I'd come like she was trying to warn me to run. But I didn't need her to tell me that. My instincts had been telling me to get the fuck out of here since before I'd climbed out of the vent. But I refused to let myself turn back. I had to escape this fucking prison. And to do that I needed Sook Min.

I hurried on, refusing to do more than glance in each cell to make sure Sook wasn't there. I couldn't take the emptiness in their eyes. I couldn't bear to think about the fact that I wasn't saving them too.

The screams came again from up ahead and I stilled as I recognised Sook's voice.

"Merda," I breathed.

I upped my pace, only pausing to wait as my vines sought out the next camera and destroyed it before I headed around the corner.

I stepped under the broken camera as it swung from a single bracket above my head and jogged down the hall as the screams got louder.

A set of double doors stood at the end of the hallway and as another scream cut through the air, I was sure that it came from beyond them.

My heart was pounding, my magic spinning through my limbs as it hunted for an outlet, even my inner Wolf was aching to break free of her chains. Everything inside me was screaming at me to run the fuck away from those doors instead of towards them.

But that was Sook in there. I knew it. And whether she knew it or not, when I'd decided to give her a place on my escape team, I'd welcomed her into my pack. And a true Alpha never abandoned one of their own.

A snarl tore from my lips as she screamed again and my instincts screamed at me in turn. I had to find out what was happening to her. I had to help her. I had to-

The door swung open suddenly and I gasped as I leapt to my left in a panic. The stars were shining on me. The guy who came out of the doors had his back to me as he dragged a trolley along behind him.

A door stood ajar on the wall beside me and I dove inside it without bothering to think it through. It was my salvation or my doom. Either way, staying out in that corridor meant getting caught which meant the hole or worse. So screw that.

I stumbled into a dark room, only sparing it enough attention to make sure it was empty before hurriedly pressing the door almost closed behind me. I used the gap to peer back out into the corridor with my heart thundering. Thank the stars I still had my silencing bubble in place.

The guy pulling the trolley kept backing up with it. Sweat coated his bald head and blood splattered his green scrubs. His gaze was dark and his jaw tight with tension.

Whatever was on the metal trolley he was pulling had been covered with a white cloth, but curiosity begged for me to get a look at it.

My heart pounded as I opened my hand, twitching my fingers as I commanded the thinnest vine I could conjure into existence. I directed it after the guy and his creepy bloodstained trolley until it hitched itself around the corner of the cloth and I yanked it off.

My lips parted in surprise as I stared at the huge glass jar which sat on the trolley. It had a gold lid inscribed with runes and whatever the hell was inside it twisted and danced like bright blue starlight. Something about it called to me in a desperate kind of way, like it was aching to be set loose from the jar.

I flinched as moisture slipped along my cheek and it took me a moment to realise that it was a tear tracking down my skin. But I didn't know why.

The guy cursed as he moved to pull the cloth back over the jar and I flinched back into the shadows of the room I'd used to hide.

I backed up, dispersing the magic that had created my vine as I sank into the shadows of the room.

I turned around slowly as my eyes adjusted to the darkness after so much white.

There was light spilling into the space from the furthest wall and I moved towards it as I realised it was a window looking into the room with the double doors.

The one way glass was tinted, letting me see into the huge operating theatre while hiding me from those inside.

The lights were dimmed and men and women in scrubs were moving around the room as they cleared bloody scalpels and trays away, their faces covered with surgical masks and their hair beneath nets.

I swallowed thickly as I looked through the glass at the figure who was laid out on the operating table.

Sook's eyes were open as she stared up at the ceiling and her lips moved in a repeating pattern as she murmured something over and over again.

A shiver crept along my limbs as I looked at her. Blood stained her naked skin, but whatever they'd done to her body had been magically healed already.

I wasn't concerned with her flesh. I was more concerned with the empty look in her eyes as she stared up at nothing and everything at once.

There was something wrong with her. Something hopelessly, endlessly, *wrong*.

I moved closer to the glass, aching to understand what I was seeing. Because despite the fact that she lay there right before my eyes, it felt like there was something I *couldn't* see.

Sook jerked on the table and the Fae in the room all turned to look at her. She jerked again and one of the men cursed, hurrying forward with healing magic flashing beneath his palms.

"Shit, not again," he snarled.

Sook jerked once more and the man grabbed her shoulders, driving her down onto the table as one of the women raced forward to help too.

My heart squeezed as I watched, unable to tear my gaze from the room as they scrambled around her.

Sook's head fell back, her mouth wide as she screamed at the top of her lungs. The sound was filled with a grief and pain so pure that it cut right into my soul.

A snarl left my lips and fear unlike anything I'd ever felt raced through my body.

I backed away as Sook fell still, her eyes glazing over in death. The worst part of it was that a piece of me was glad. Because whatever they'd just done to her had been too much for her to bear. In death she might claim some solace from it. And the pain of that scream had sounded like the worst of fates.

I kept backing away from the window as my mind scrambled to catch up to the desperate need to flee which was taking hold of my body.

I was an Alpha. I didn't run from anything. This feeling was alien and terrifying in its own right, but I knew I had to obey it or my own fate would be tied to the dead girl's in that room.

Heart pounding and tears blurring my vision, I lunged for the door and without even bothering to check if the coast was clear, I ran.

ETHAN

PRISONER #1

CHAPTER FORTY

I rammed my shoulder against the door to the library as that motherfucking son of a worm's asshole tried to get in from the outside. Some of my pack were hunting for movable furniture to barricade us in, but everything was bolted down. They didn't want inmates shutting themselves in here, but apparently the Warden hadn't considered the possibility that we might have a star-damned reason to.

"I'll take over Alpha, you need to direct us," Harper said firmly, pulling me away from the door and pressing herself into my spot.

Sweat beaded on my brow and I frowned, hating to step back. But she was right. If anyone was gonna get us out of this mess, it needed to be their leader. Unfortunately, me and my pack weren't the only ones who'd been in here when that freak had attacked. Gustard and his Watchers were gathered together on the far side of the room, not helping us block the door for shit while they talked in low voices.

I jumped up onto the nearest table and howled to grab my pack's attention. I caught The Watchers' attention too and they sidled closer, eyeing me like I might be the answer to their problems. And something about that did nothing to put me at ease.

"We have two options," I said loudly so everyone could hear. "We let it in here and lure it to the back of the room while we make a run for it. Or, someone goes out there to lure it away from here."

"We're not letting it in, I won't allow it," Gustard growled, his tattooed features twisting into a snarl. I eyed his group; there were as many of them as there were of us. And though part of me was aware that now might be a good time to kill the fucker while the guards weren't watching, I also knew that with the Belorian knocking at the door and four cameras pointing at us from every direction, it probably wasn't worth the hell I'd pay for it.

"Well either it gets in before we make a decision, or we act now to give us a chance," I demanded, pressing my shoulders back.

Gustard ran his tongue across his teeth, nodding in seeming agreement. He caught hold of a guy with a large gut, shoving him towards the door.

"Move aside!" he barked at my Wolves and I snarled at him for ordering them about. They looked to me for a command, ignoring him and I glanced at the man Gustard had chosen for the job.

"Are you willing?" I asked and he looked at Gustard with fear in his eyes.

The guy swallowed hard then nodded. "For my master," he breathed.

Gustard sneered in some semblance of a smile and I directed my Wolves away from the doors.

Before I could give the guy any pointers on how to handle this or how quickly we should all run after him, Gustard wrenched one door open and shoved him out.

My pack quickly threw themselves into place once more, closing ranks and laying their weight against the frosted glass doors. Shadows moved beyond the glass before the guy screamed in terror and blood splattered all over it.

"Holy fuck," I breathed.

Gustard turned to his people, pointing at another girl. "You next."

"Wait! We need a fucking plan," I barked at him.

"I have one. Feed it enough bodies to keep it satisfied enough for us to stroll on past it," Gustard said simply. "My people will happily die for me."

"So would we for our leader!" Harper called to me with a plea in her eyes.

"That doesn't mean I'd choose to send them to their deaths!" I snapped and my Wolves howled together, their voices filled with love. "Besides, the more blood you spill, the more you're going to send that thing into a frenzy. We have to lead it away from here."

"So pick the fastest of your people and I'll pick the fastest of mine. We'll draw straws to decide who goes," Gustard suggested.

I jumped down from the table, landing with a hard thud in front of him, nose to nose. "A true leader faces danger for the sake of his people. I'll go for my pack, but will you go for yours?" I slammed my shoulder into his and walked toward the door. My Wolves cried mournfully, brushing their hands over my arms.

Gustard rolled his eyes, stuffing his hands in his pockets in a clear show that he wasn't going anywhere.

"Please Alpha, let me go for you," Harper begged and every other member of the pack started offering the same thing.

I cupped Harper's cheek, shaking my head. "I'm the fastest. I can do it. I'll lead it downstairs then howl when it's time for you to run. Get to our cell block, don't look back."

She bowed her head in agreement, a tear tracking down her cheek which I quickly wiped away.

"Let's see what you're made of, Shadowbrook," Gustard taunted, moving up beside me with a psycho smile on his lips.

One of my pack handed me a table leg they must have broken off and I took it with a nod of thanks. It wasn't much against the Belorian, but it felt better to have the weight of it in my hands.

My Wolves readied to open the door and Gustard leaned in close to me, whispering in my ear. "I'm looking forward to seeing your innards splattered on the walls. You can't be a king beyond the grave, but I'll be sure to send your queen to you soon."

I growled, ignoring the flash of heat in my gut that told me to destroy him here and now. I didn't have time to respond to him as the doors were tugged open. Harper was glaring at Gustard like she might just murder him and the second I darted through the doors, she shoved him out with me.

"Fuck!" he roared as the doors closed and the beast came at us in an instant.

Its eyeless head swung toward me, its huge mouth full of serrated teeth ready to devour me whole. I smashed the table leg into its face with a cry of effort, making it shriek in pain and back up a few steps. I raced around it, my heart thrashing like a wild animal in a cage as I tore towards the end of the corridor.

Footsteps behind me said Gustard had made it away from the monster too and I cursed my luck. If the Belorian finished him, it would save me the damn bother.

His weight collided with me from behind and I slammed to the ground, the makeshift bat skittering away across the floor as I lost my grip on it.

"What the fuck?" I snarled as Gustard leapt off of me, laughing as he ran towards the stairwell.

A spiny foot slammed into the ground beside my head and I rolled in alarm as the Belorian lunged for me with its teeth bared. I scrambled to my feet, ducking half a second before its spiny tail whipped out to the side and almost decapitated me.

With my pulse elevating, I snatched up the table leg, swinging it around with a wild cry of defiance and slamming it into the monster's ugly face.

It screeched so loud my ears felt like they were bleeding as it raised up onto its back legs and tried to regain its senses. I ran before it took chase again, powering along the corridor to where Gustard was rounding into the stairwell. I threw the bat with all my might and it crashed into the back of his head, knocking him off balance. He stumbled with a groan of pain and I put on a burst of speed as the sound of the Belorian came right behind me. I could feel its hot breath on my neck as I tried to outrun it, but it was a fast piece of shit. I needed my Wolf, but I couldn't reach it now. I had to rely on nothing but flesh and bones, not even a hint of magic at my aid.

I dropped down to skid into the stairwell and a snap of teeth sounded above me. Gustard threw a kick at my head and I yelled as his foot impacted with my jaw and knocked me down the steps to my left. The Belorian raced between us and as blood coated my tongue and the smell of it hit the air, I knew which of us it was going to chase. It turned towards me with a hungry growl and I forced myself upright, half falling down the stairs as I fled. Gustard's manic laughter carried to me as he ran up the steps in the opposite direction.

I lifted my head, cupping my hands around my mouth and howling as loudly as I could to let my Wolves know they could flee. The sound of a crowd surging above me filled my ears and relief flooded me.

Now I just have to escape this asshole of a slug and I'll have songs sung about me until the end of time.

I had one small advantage in the stairwell. That fucker was huge and its legs weren't made for running down steps. It slipped and skidded, its teeth gnashing blindly as it hunted for me. I leapt down the stairs, taking them four, six, seven at a time. If I missed my footing once, I was fucked. I'd be just another number in this prison, another statistic. *Fifty three die in Darkmore Penitentiary after an accidental outbreak of their bio-weapon.* Fuck. That. I was not gonna be a headline in the news. Not like that anyway. If I was going to make headlines, it was because I'd won the biggest dick competition, or hottest Alpha Werewolf award. I wasn't going in print like this. *Not like this!*

I rounded onto level eight where Medical was and spotted a store cupboard across the hall. I raced for it, shoving it open and practically fell inside. I got the door shut before the fucker saw where I went and it charged on down the corridor, turning left towards Psych.

Fuck. Yes.

"Hey, asshole," a voice made me jump and I turned, spotting Roary Night looking like death warmed up, his face pale and blood pissing from his arm.

"What the hell happened to you?" I asked.

"That creep's spines cut me when I ran from it. Looks like they're fucking

438

poisonous," he wheezed. "I need to get to Psych but I can hardly walk."

"Trust me, you don't wanna go to Psych right now." I leaned back against the wall as I tried to catch my breath.

"What? Why?" he demanded, panic flaring in his eyes.

"Because there's where I just sent the monster."

"What?!" he roared, trying to get up, but his body gave out and he slumped back down again. "*Fuck.* I've gotta help her."

"Help who?" I asked, folding my arms.

"Doesn't matter," he said through his teeth. "Like you'd give a fuck anyway. She's your damn enemy."

"Who?" I breathed, my heart beating out of rhythm. "Fucking *who*!?" I strode toward him, dropping down to a crouch and grabbing hold of his collar as anxiety bled through me.

"Rosalie Oscura," he ground out, making my whole world fall to pieces in an instant.

"She's down there?" I rasped, fear gripping me in its fist.

He nodded, fear flashing through his eyes.

"I'll help her," I said immediately and he frowned at me.

"Why would you?"

"Because I just will, alright?" I spat and he growled deep in his throat protectively.

"Bullshit," he spat, catching hold of my arm like he was really gonna try and keep me there. "You're more likely to hurt her than help her."

I huffed, clenching my fists as I made a decision I prayed I wasn't gonna regret. I turned my head and pointed to the crescent hidden within my tattoo. "We're mated. But if you tell a soul I'll rip your kidneys out and stuff them down your throat, got it?"

He stared at me like I'd just punched him in the face then released me, reaching into his pocket and produced a cuff key. My lips parted as I went to take it, but the sound of the door opening halted me.

Roary quickly twisted it in his own cuffs until they glowed blue then stuffed it back in his pocket.

"Inmates!" Officer's Cain's voice cut through the air. "Back to your cells – now!"

"Wait, sir-" I started, getting to my feet but he rushed at me, taking hold of my arm. His gaze fell to Roary on the ground and a low noise of frustration left his throat. Cain dropped to a crouch, releasing me and ripping Roary's sleeve away before pressing his fingers to the swollen wound to heal it.

I backed up toward the door, adrenaline seeping through my blood. I had to get to Rosa. I had to make sure she was alright.

"Move another inch and I'll throw you in the hole, One," Cain warned without even looking around. But Rosalie's life was worth some time in the hole. I had to get to her.

I lunged for the door but Cain slammed into me with his Vampire speed, dragging my hands behind my back and connecting my cuffs together with a chain of magic.

"You dare refuse a direct order?" he snarled in my ear.

Cain yanked the door open and threw me out of it so I stumbled forward into the corridor. He directed Roary up next, pulling him out of the door by his arm.

Three more guards were standing on the stairs and Cain shoved us towards them, sending panic daggering through my heart. They marched us up towards our cells and I shared a look with Roary, unsure what to do. As we reached level four, Roary shoved his way out of the guards' grip with a snarl.

"Rosalie's in trouble," he blurted at Cain. "She's down in Psych, where that *thing* is headed."

My heart beat out of tune as I looked to Cain, wondering if he really might help.

"Do you think I give a fuck?" Cain growled and my heart sank. "Take them back to their cells!" He directed the Officers and they shoved us along. Cain turned around and shot down the stairs with his Vampire speed and I gazed over my shoulder in confusion.

I was hauled along and my breaths came raggedly from my lungs. I shared an anxious look with Roary beside me, seeing the same panic in his own eyes. We shared a nod and threw ourselves at the guards, forcing our way free of them in seconds. We made it two steps away before a net of vines crashed over us and my knees hit the floor as the power of the earth magic weighed me down.

"Up. Now!" Officer Rind barked.

Strong hands gripped my shoulders and me and Roary were dragged to our feet once more. Rind had his shock baton on, pointing it at us as the other two guards shoved us towards the cell blocks and my heart started to ache.

But as I was dragged away and Roary's bellows of protest rang out around us, a tiny flower of hope started to bloom in my chest. Because Officer Cain had headed in the direction of Rosalie. And he may have been a bastard who had the temper of a Dragon Shifter with a hot poker up its ass, but he was powerful as fuck. And it was his job to get that freak back in its cage. I just prayed he managed it before it got its teeth in my mate.

ROSALIE

PRISONER #12

CHAPTER FORTY ONE

I fled down the white corridors with my heart pounding and my stomach churning. I'd come here to figure out how to save Sook from Psych and was leaving with both the knowledge that she was dead and that they were doing something really, really bad to the prisoners they sent down here.

So much for thinking losing your mind was the worst that could happen to you in this place. You could lose your damn life to some kind of magical butchery too.

How the hell is this allowed?

I understood that as the worst criminals in Solaria, we didn't have a whole lot of rights but chopping someone up because they went a bit bat shit? What the actual fuck?

Sook was a money launderer, not a psychopath. What the hell kind of fate was that for her?

I sped towards the next corner which led to the final corridor with nothing on my mind aside from wanting to get the hell out of here and I gasped as my Moon Wolf instincts almost floored me with an intense wave of warning.

My breath caught, my skin prickled and hairs raised along the back of my neck.

In my desperation to escape, I'd almost run right up to the guy with the trolley.

I crept closer to the corner, thanking my silencing bubble once again for saving my life. I owed this piece of magic my ass ten times over and I sent silent wishes of good fortune to my old Cardinal Magic Professor. She was a mean bitch with a better moustache than Freddy Mercury and the temperament of a horse trying to walk in stilettos. I'd made it my mission to fuck with her on more than one occasion without her ever figuring out it was me. But now I owed that mean old hag a life debt. I'd be telling Dante to send her a gift basket filled with moustache grooming products if I ever made it out of this little slice of hell.

My chest rose and fell heavily as I reached the corner and the porter's whistles reached me. The tune was familiar and it only took me a moment to recognise Hickory Dickory Dock. That was such a psychopath thing to do. Was it because their mammas never sang to them so they felt the need to entertain themselves with a childhood tune or two when the demons in their minds were resting?

But if that was the case then surely I'd be in the habit of whistling nursery rhymes too. My mamma certainly never sang me a song. I'd often wondered how I ever made it past the baby stage at all. Maybe back then she'd loved me. Or more likely I'd just been a determined little fucker as a baby too and refused to die from neglect just as surely as I had as I'd grown.

The whistler moved further and further away until I felt confident that he'd left the next corridor and I stepped around the corner.

A door swung shut at the end of a corridor on my left while the thick doors which led back to the main prison stood down the corridor to my right.

I hesitated for a moment, the desire to find out what the hell was in that jar gnawing at me. It was an itch I needed to scratch. But delving deeper into the secrets of this place to satisfy my own curiosity seemed like suicide.

The vent I needed to escape was right there.

I'd come here for Sook and I'd failed.

I didn't even want to consider what that meant for my escape plans yet, but it did mean I had no further reason to stay down here.

I clenched my teeth and pushed all thoughts of that creepy jar from my mind as I ran towards my escape route.

I quickly made it to the spot beneath the grate I'd broken and I tipped my head back to look up at it as I created vines in my palms and sent them snaking up into the vent.

They grew and strengthened, hunting down something to secure themselves to before leaving me with the means to climb out of here.

I leapt up as soon as they were ready and heaved myself skyward with a grunt of effort.

My fingers curled around the lip of the hole in the vent and I began to hoist myself inside.

Footsteps clicked along the tiles behind me and I gasped as I fought to heave my legs inside.

I reached forward to grasp a raised bolt as I used it to pull myself higher, but my slick palm slipped against the cool metal.

One moment I was half way up into the vent and the next I was falling.

My back slammed into the tiled floor and I gasped in pain and panic as the footsteps drew closer.

"I always feel so drained after surgery," a woman's voice reached me.

"I know. I can't wait for a bit of down time now," a man replied.

I rolled over, scrambling to my hands and knees as I hunted around for some way out, some plan I could implement or way for me to escape. I dispersed the magic in my vines so that they disintegrated.

There was nothing around me besides the door back to the main prison and no time to climb back up into the vent.

My heart crashed against my ribs painfully as I backed up, throwing my hands up as I fought to construct a concealment spell around me.

But those spells were designed to shroud me in shadow so that I might go unnoticed in the dark. They weren't for stupid girls in white corridors wearing a motherfucking *orange* jumpsuit.

My back hit the wall beside the door as I threw more magic at the spell and the light twisted around me as my power tried to do what I needed it to.

Hide me! Don't let them see me! I have to hide!!

Panic swept through me as tension coiled in my limbs. If they caught me here, they'd throw me in the hole for years and let me rot... assuming they didn't decided to take me back to that operating theatre and give me a dose of what they gave Sook.

The two doctors rounded the corner, their eyes widening as they fell on me and I sucked in a sharp breath.

I've got to hide!!

My limbs started trembling with something that had nothing at all to do with fear and a flood of silver light like a pure moonbeam suddenly erupted from my flesh, coating me in a hazy glow of warmth.

I froze, my eyes fixed on the two Fae who could ruin all my best laid plans as they slowly turned away from me.

"I've lost track of the time again," the woman muttered. "Is it dinner now?"

"Yeah. I heard there's a new chef at that curry house in town, maybe we can grab some dinner there?"

"That sounds like heaven," she groaned hungrily and they walked straight up to the doors like they couldn't see me at all.

I didn't know what the hell this stuff coating my body was, but I did know it wasn't magic of mine. That said, it did feel like a part of me, like something linked to the very fibres of my being.

The doctors moved to unlock the heavy doors which led back into the main prison and I waited as they had their magic scanned and entered a code into the reader. A low buzz sounded and the door swung open to admit them.

I didn't know if it was bravery, madness or if I was just plain stupid, but I scurried behind them before the door could close again.

They walked on down the corridor which led back to the main prison and I fell still as the doors closed behind me and the silver light coating my body faded away.

I sagged forward, my hands falling to my knees as exhaustion tugged at me and my eyes flickered with fatigue.

I felt like I'd spent the night running beneath the moon, my limbs trembling from the power of my Order form.

I paused as that thought occurred to me. Had I just tapped into one of my Order gifts? It shouldn't have been possible with the Order Suppressant flooding through the vents in the main prison but now that I thought of it, I could feel my Wolf shifting beneath my skin. And my Moon Wolf status *was* rumoured to come with all kinds of strange and wonderful gifts…

A frown tugged at my brow. Why wouldn't they be using the suppressant in Psych? I could feel it creeping over me again now that I was back in the main prison, my Wolf snarling in displeasure as she was locked away again.

A scream echoed down the corridor ahead of me and I stilled as a deep growl followed it.

The screams got louder and I started running towards them, not wanting to end up cornered in this dead end by whatever the hell was happening up ahead of me.

I rounded the corner, spilling out into the corridor of level eight just as the male doctor threw his hands up into the air, an enormous fireball exploding from his palms.

The wave of heat slammed into me and I staggered back a step as the walls were charred and everything from the signs hanging on the brickwork to the cameras suspended from the ceiling were incinerated instantly.

But it didn't slow the monster which came for him.

Six huge, scaly grey legs burst through the wall of flames and a shriek of triumph erupted from a mouth lined with row upon row of razor sharp teeth as the Belorian pounced.

The doctor's scream barely passed his lips before the creature was on him, its jaws snapping closed over his head and ripping it clean off in one bite.

The fire licked around the creature's hideous body as it feasted, stuttering out of existence as the Fae who had summoned it was devoured.

I choked on the scream which wanted to escape me and started running as fast as I could.

I skirted the beast, ignoring the horrendous crunching, and chomping sounds which came from it as it ate. My sneakers slipped in a puddle of blood and my arms whirled as I fought to keep my balance.

I raced on, spotting the other doctor running ahead of me as I sprinted for the stairs at the far end of the corridor and the possibility of escape.

How the hell had that thing gotten out? Who in their right mind would...
Sin.

I snarled with rage as I ran for my damn life. I was gonna kick that Incubus's ass so hard he'd be crying real tears by the time I was done with him. I'd told him. I'd fucking *told* him that this was a terrible goddamn idea!

A deep roar sounded behind me and my heart leapt with terror as the sound of the Belorian's clawed feet rattled against the concrete floor behind me.

I was damn fast, but not fast enough to outrun that thing.

The doctor who had killed Sook raced ahead of me, wailing in terror as she closed in on the stairs.

The Belorian roared right behind me and I shrieked in fear as I dove aside. It slammed into the wall where I'd just been running a second later and I screamed again as I scrambled to get moving once more.

The doctor looked back at me, raising her hands before throwing a wall of dirt up between us, blocking me in the corridor with the monster as she ran for freedom.

You ass feasting whore!

I screamed again as the Belorian dove at me and I summoned wooden spears into my hands as I ducked beneath it, slashing at its soft belly with them.

Grey ichor spilled from the wounds and the creature bellowed in rage.

One of its taloned limbs slammed into me and I was hurled away from it as pain sliced through my arm and blood ran hot against my skin.

I hit the dirt wall the doctor had created to trap me and threw my own power at it, carving a hole just big enough for me to scramble through.

The Belorian shrieked as it charged after me and I pushed my power into the wall, hardening it, strengthening and turning the dirt to rock as fast as I could.

I fell through the hole into the corridor on the far side just as the Belorian collided with the wall. The whole thing trembled and rocks and dirt cascaded from it to fall over me.

It wouldn't hold for long.

I pushed myself to my feet and raced on, ignoring the keen sting of pain in my arm as my blood continued to run down my skin.

The dirt wall exploded behind me as the Belorian smashed through it with a roar of rage and I screamed again as I made it to the foot of the stairs.

The doctor was just rounding the corner at the top of the first flight and her eyes widened in surprise and fear as she looked back down at me.

You're right to feel fear, bitch.

I threw my hands up and vines shot from my palms, wrapping around her ankle with an iron hold.

She screamed in panic as she reached for the vine, but I didn't give her the chance to sever it before yanking it back like a lasso.

The doctor shrieked as she flew over my head and I twisted to watch as the Belorian burst around the corner to the stairwell. The beast leapt up, catching her between its sharp jaws with a snarl of glee. It landed heavily, almost crushing me and I leapt aside, rolling away from the stairs and into the corridor.

I scrambled to my feet as the doctor's screams chased me and I turned and ran on, setting my gaze on the Medical unit at the far end of the corridor.

The meal wouldn't distract the creature for long and I needed to get as far away from it as Faely possible.

I ran down the corridor with my pulse thundering in my ears and my limbs trembling with panic.

The doors to Medical were getting closer with each step… I was making progress, but as a savage roar shook the walls surrounding me, I knew it wouldn't be nearly enough.

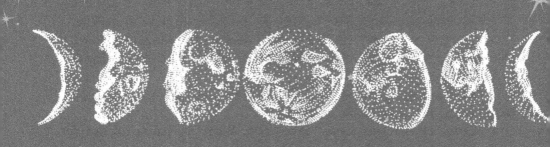

CAIN

COMMANDING OFFICER

CHAPTER FORTY TWO

I shot down the stairs with the full power of my Order fuelling my limbs. If Twelve was hurt, I'd make sure Sixty Nine and One followed her into a swift grave. I didn't know what the fuck was going on tonight, but I knew when there was foul play at hand. I could taste it in the air. And I'd sensed it around those two the second I'd walked into that closet.

I rounded into the corridor where the Psych Unit was and my heart stuttered at the sight before me. The Belorian was ripping and tearing at a mass of vines on the ground and an inmate within them crawled along, casting more and more as she tried to get past it in her tunnel. *Twelve*. The fact that she was using magic confirmed my suspicions about her having the cuff key. And though I wanted to be mad, fucking raging, all I felt was terror at the thought of her dying here.

"Has anyone got eyes on the bio-weapon?" Warden Pike's voice sounded over the radio and the Belorian's had twisted upright as it heard the noise.

I bared my fangs, preparing myself for a fight. I raised my hands, casting a pair of huge fireballs and sending them wheeling in two opposite walls. The flash fires sent the beast into a frenzy and it abandoned Twelve, crashing into one wall then the next as it chased the heat sources. The fire fizzled out and I sent two more balls toward the far end of the corridor in a blaze of red and gold.

My muscles coiled as the beast turned and raced after them and I sped forward, pulling Twelve out of the nest of vines.

"Go!" I shoved her towards the stairs as she stared up at me in surprise.

"You can't stay here," she said in alarm, looking like she actually gave a shit about me. Which would have been heart-warming if my heart was capable of feeling temperatures above zero.

"Don't go soft on me, inmate." I shoved her again and she snarled, her Wolf peering out from within her eyes. "*Go*."

"No one tells me what to do," she hissed. "What are you staying here for anyway?"

I growled, pointing at the beast's collar while it scratched at the walls, my fire tumbling down around it. "The collar's malfunctioning, I've gotta jumpstart it to get the signal reconnected."

She nodded, her jaw set. "It'll be quicker if we do it together."

The Belorian shrieked, turning back towards us and I gave up fighting her as she turned to face it at my side.

"I'm gonna get behind it," I told her, lifting a hand and sending a blinding wall of fire flaring in front of us. I shot through it on one side, making the fire bend around me as I passed through the blaze.

I raced around behind the Belorian and leapt up onto the monstrous creature, catching hold of its neck and smashing my fist against the collar. If brute force didn't do it, then I was pretty much fucked. Because I was no technician. And even if I had been, I didn't like my chances of playing with wires while the Belorian sat for me like a good dog.

My fist impacted with a solid air shield around it and I slammed to the ground, losing my footing and stumbling to my knees as pain spiked through my hand. *What the fuck?*

The beast sucked in a breath as it turned towards me and I rolled fast as it lunged for me with serrated teeth. My back hit the wall and I sent two huge flames tumbling away from me, but it didn't go after them. In half a heartbeat, I realised my knuckles had split on the shield and blood coated my fingers, the scent calling it to me. *Shit!*

I fled with my Vampire speed, panting as I reached the far wall. I'd been using my gifts to toss inmates back into their cells for the past hour and I was growing tired. If I couldn't fix that collar soon, we were fucked.

A shout of defiance caught my ear and I spotted Twelve swinging over the wall of flames on a vine. Her feet connected with the Belorian's skull, sending it stumbling backwards as it let out a roar of pain. She hung for another second, landing another solid kick to the collar before crashing to the ground beside the beast. The light stayed red and I cursed under my breath. I didn't know why the hell she wanted to help, but in that moment, I was sure as fuck grateful that she did.

The beast swung around, slashing at her with its spiny tail. One cut from those suckers and she was screwed.

I raced forward, throwing fireballs at its head to blind it, the impact making the creature back up, but its tail continued to whip about wildly. Twelve cast a spear of wood in her hand, lunging forward and ramming it into the Belorian's belly. Ichor spewed and the monster crashed back into the far wall. She tossed the spear and cast a net of vines instead, wrapping them around every one of its limbs to immobilise it for a fraction of a second. I didn't waste a single moment of the opportunity. I leapt over Twelve, using the extra strength of my gifts to propel myself higher than normal and throw another fist into the beast's collar, but this time I surrounded my hand in white hot flames. My knuckles collided with the shield and I felt it snap beneath my blow so my fist impacted directly with the metal collar. I crashed to the floor, turning fast to see if I'd fixed it as heavy breaths fell from my lungs.

The light was no longer red but green and victory tore through my chest. I snatched my radio from my hip, bringing it to my mouth and calling the Warden. "The collar's on, ma'am. I repeat, the collar is on. Take it home."

The collar blinked and the Belorian wailed, snapping the vines holding it down as it shook its head from the signal channelling into its brain. Sometimes I pitied the poor bastard for the miserable life it led inside this prison. It was nothing but a weapon given flesh. But it felt pain too. And that was just fucked up.

The monster wheeled towards the wall of flames and I dispersed them as it ran, standing back as it rushed past us in the direction of the stairs. Relief made my shoulders drop as it headed in the direction of its quarters. This nightmare was finally fucking over.

"Mason," Twelve gasped.

I turned to her, suddenly woozy and my throat tightened as I dropped my gaze to the sharp spine sticking out of my stomach. I yanked it free with a grunt of pain and blood gushed out of the wound.

In the haze of adrenaline, I hadn't felt the pain. But now it slammed into me all at once. The poison flooded my limbs and my head spun as I dropped to the ground. The spine had sliced in deep. The poison was rushing into me faster than should have been possible. I felt it wrapping around my power like cold fingers, cutting me off from my magic. The Belorian's poison was a brutal concoction of pain and destruction. It would eat away at my power then bite into my organs and rot them until I was nothing but blood and bones. With my life in the hands of an inmate who hated me, I was pretty sure I was a goner. But as Twelve dropped over me and her mouth sounded out my name, I figured there were worse ways to go.

ROSALIE

PRISONER #12

CHAPTER FORTY THREE

The Belorian shrieked as it raced away from us and the sudden calm in the aftermath of its attack froze me.

The distant sound of alarms and screams came to me from the upper levels but right here, there was nothing but me and Cain.

A groan of pain left him as he clutched the wound on his stomach and he coughed as his eyes rolled back and he fell towards unconsciousness, blood spilling between his fingers.

"No," I gasped, leaning over him where he lay on the floor. "Mason!"

His gaze slid in and out of focus as he looked up at me and he raised his bloody hand to cup my cheek. For once all the hardness and rage had left him entirely and as he looked at me, I felt like I was looking upon the real Mason Cain. The version of him which he kept guarded so tightly that I doubted he even knew it existed.

"You're going to be okay," I swore, a tear slipping down my cheek as I ripped the tattered remains of his shirt open and pressed my hands to the bloody wound which punctured his flesh.

He growled, clenching his teeth against the pain and I leaned down to press my forehead to his.

Healing magic slid from my hands and into his body, seeking out the damage and working to fix it.

I frowned in concentration as my power sped through his veins, hunting down the poison as fast as it could spread.

My Aunt Bianca had forced me to learn everything there was to know about healing magic and though I'd cursed her at the time for inflicting such difficult lessons on me, I had to admit how useful the knowledge was. When you lived my kind of life, injuries, assassination attempts and even poisoning were a regular occurrence, and you had to be able to deal with them at speed and under pressure.

Though I wasn't sure if I'd ever been tested this deeply before.

Cain's hand slid from my cheek into my hair as he drew me closer, his breath coming raggedly as I worked to heal his injuries and fought a battle against the poison in his flesh.

With a surge of triumph, I felt the moment that my magic consumed the last drops of poison and I released a shaky laugh as my magic reserves ran low. Another few minutes and I'd have been tapped out. And I wouldn't have been able to do a damn thing to help him.

Cain's breathing evened out as the worst of his injuries healed over and my heart thumped to a steady beat for the first time in what felt like hours.

I blew out a long breath as his grey eyes found mine and my fingertips roamed over the hard muscles of his stomach, seeking more wounds but finding none.

"You saved my life." Cain frowned, his voice rough as he stared deep into my eyes, seeking out my soul as if he was searching for answers.

"Just paying you back," I murmured. We both knew where I'd be right about now if he hadn't shown up.

"Is everything an exchange with you?" he growled.

"Not everything," I breathed.

His grip in my hair tightened as he dragged me closer, his mouth seeking mine as a soft moan escaped me.

My hands shifted over his body as he pressed his tongue between my lips and I drowned in the feeling of his kiss.

My gut twisted sharply at the thought of what had nearly happened to him and I shuddered as our passion deepened, his hands sliding down my body, tracing the curve of my ass before encircling my waist.

"Doesn't it feel good to be on the same team for once?" I breathed between kisses, bathing in the heat of his desire as my body arched against his.

Cain growled, pulling back for a moment as he looked at me through narrowed eyes. "You talk about playing on teams like everything is just some big game to you."

"Maybe it is," I teased, leaning forward to kiss him again.

He growled as he kissed me harder, his fingers twisting in my hair as he tightened his grip.

I moaned against his mouth as his teeth caught my bottom lip and he bit down hard.

A gasp escaped me as my magic was immobilised and my limbs lost power beneath the effects of his venom.

Cain growled darkly as he sucked my lip harder, draining what little magic I had left as his hands slid to encompass my wrists.

With a flash of his Vampire speed, he locked my cuffs again, cutting off my access to my magic and I gasped as he flipped me beneath him, pinning me to the ground with his hips.

He sucked the last drop of magic from my blood before releasing my lip from his teeth and rearing up over me.

"Did you think you were the only one who can play your games?" he growled, a line of my blood running down his chin.

"Mason, I-"

"*Don't.*"

He shot to his feet using his Vampire speed, dragging me up into his arms and flipping me around so that my back was pressed to his front.

He leaned close to me, his fangs dragging across my neck as he growled in warning. "I might want to fuck you, Twelve. But that doesn't mean I'm stupid enough to get fucked *by* you."

"I don't understand what you-"

"Are you going to tell me what you were doing down here while every other fucker in the place was running as far from the Belorian as possible?"

My heart leapt at the accusation and I wriggled against the tight hold he kept on my wrists.

"Mason, I swear, I don't know what-"

"Don't lie to me!" he roared, whirling me around and throwing me back against the wall.

His eyes blazed with fury and my pulse spiked with real fear at the promise of violence simmering in them.

"Okay," I breathed.

"Tell me why your cuffs were switched off and what you were doing down there!" He pointed at the corridor which led back to the Psych Unit and I shook my head.

"I won't lie. But I can't give you the truth," I whispered.

Cain's face contorted in rage and he sped forward, hoisting me off of my feet and throwing me over his shoulder. The world blurred as he raced downstairs and when it righted again, we were standing before the huge red door which led into the isolation unit.

My eyes widened as he made quick work of unlocking the door and within another moment we were inside and he was pulling one of the cell doors open.

"Mason, *please*," I begged as he ripped me back off of his shoulder and threw me down on the hard bed inside the cell.

"Let's see what your pretty words and filthy promises buy you in here, Princess," he snarled.

I leapt forward, catching his hand in mine as I fell from the hard bed onto my knees before him. "Don't do this," I begged. Fucking *begged,* like a dog. But I didn't care. The pain and rage in his eyes was tearing me apart and the idea of being locked up in this tiny cell was enough to make me break.

"Maybe a month in the hole will make you reconsider lying to my face," he growled, everything in him completely void of emotion.

"Please," I choked on a sob. I was breaking right in front of him, showing him the cracks in my mask. But I couldn't be locked in the dark. Not again. Not after all these years. I'd broken free of that cage and worked tirelessly to break the chains my papà had placed on my soul too. I wouldn't go back to that feeling. I couldn't.

"You once warned me not to make an enemy of you, Rosalie Oscura," Cain growled. "But you really shouldn't have been so cocky. You're not the one who holds the power here. *I* am. And you can bat your eyelashes, flick your hair, lay on the crocodile tears and even spread your thighs for me as many times as you like. But I'm not the kind of beast you can tame. And it's time you learned your lesson."

He ripped his hand out of my grip and shot from the room so fast that I fell forward, crashing onto my forearms as horror spilled through me.

My head snapped up at the sound of the heavy door slamming shut and I screamed as I launched myself at it.

"Cain!" I roared, throwing my weight against the thick metal as darkness engulfed me. "Cain!"

There was no reply, but I kept banging my fist against the door all the same, sure he could hear me.

"Please don't do this to me!" A sob tore from my throat as tears rolled down my cheeks.

Silence was my only answer and eventually I backed up, wrapping my arms around myself as my back hit the cold wall at the rear of my tiny cell.

Pain, fear and the worst of my worst memories surfaced beneath my skin as my papà's voice whispered to me in the dark.

Didn't I tell you, Rosalie? You're good for nothing and no one. You came into this world unwanted and you'll go out of it that way too. You should stop trying to fight fate. Because the world doesn't care that you exist any more than I do…

I pressed my palms down over my ears as I fought to block him out, but his poisonous words found me in the darkness like they always had.

All of my plans had gone to shit.

All of the promises I'd made meant nothing.

I was trapped alone in the dark.

And maybe that was where I deserved to be.

ALSO BY
CAROLINE PECKHAM
&
SUSANNE VALENTI

Brutal Boys of Everlake Prep

(Complete Reverse Harem Bully Romance Contemporary Series)

Kings of Quarantine

Kings of Lockdown

Kings of Anarchy

Queen of Quarantine

**

Dead Men Walking

(Reverse Harem Dark Romance Contemporary Series)

The Death Club

Society of Psychos

**

The Harlequin Crew

(Reverse Harem Mafia Romance Contemporary Series)

Sinners Playground

Dead Man's Isle

Carnival Hill

Paradise Lagoon

Harlequinn Crew Novellas

Devil's Pass

**

Dark Empire

(Dark Mafia Contemporary Standalones)

Beautiful Carnage

Beautiful Savage

**

The Ruthless Boys of the Zodiac

(Reverse Harem Paranormal Romance Series - Set in the world of Solaria)

Dark Fae

Savage Fae

Vicious Fae

Broken Fae

Warrior Fae

Zodiac Academy

(M/F Bully Romance Series- Set in the world of Solaria, five years after Dark Fae)

The Awakening

Ruthless Fae

The Reckoning

Shadow Princess

Cursed Fates

Fated Thrones

Heartless Sky

Sorrow and Starlight

The Awakening - As told by the Boys

Zodiac Academy Novellas

Origins of an Academy Bully

The Big A.S.S. Party

Darkmore Penitentiary

(Reverse Harem Paranormal Romance Series - Set in the world of Solaria,
ten years after Dark Fae)

Caged Wolf

Alpha Wolf

Feral Wolf

**

The Age of Vampires

(Complete M/F Paranormal Romance/Dystopian Series)

Eternal Reign

Eternal Shade

Eternal Curse

Eternal Vow

Eternal Night

Eternal Love

**

Cage of Lies

(M/F Dystopian Series)

Rebel Rising

**

Tainted Earth

(M/F Dystopian Series)

Afflicted

Altered

Adapted

Advanced

**

The Vampire Games

(Complete M/F Paranormal Romance Trilogy)

V Games

V Games: Fresh From The Grave

V Games: Dead Before Dawn

*

The Vampire Games: Season Two

(Complete M/F Paranormal Romance Trilogy)

Wolf Games

Wolf Games: Island of Shade

Wolf Games: Severed Fates

*

The Vampire Games: Season Three

Hunter Trials

*

The Vampire Games Novellas

A Game of Vampires

**

The Rise of Issac

(Complete YA Fantasy Series)

Creeping Shadow

Bleeding Snow

Turning Tide

Weeping Sky

Failing Light